Return from Wrath

RETURN FROM WRATH

A Novel

Bob Perry

Return From Wrath

www.bobp.biz

Thanks to Misty Curtis and Nancy Ireland for their input and insights. They helped with editing this story and so much more.

PART I

CHAPTER 1

"Let go of me!" Raquel screamed frantically, as her drunken stepfather grabbed her roughly around the waist.

The nineteen-year-old Raquel flayed her arms defensively, scratching Juan Esperanza's cheek. He angrily muttered profanities and viciously struck her with the back of his hand, causing her to stumble to the dirt floor. Raquel desperately grasped for a weapon, before he could assault her again. Her hand landed on an iron skillet, which she swung wildly. The blow made a sickening thump, quickly followed by a thud, as her stepfather collapsed limply to the ground with blood gushing from his nose. The frightened girl hastily threw some things into a sack and ran out the door into the uncertain night.

Life had once seemed hopeful and happy for Raquel, but that had been a long time ago, and years before the economic depression of the 1930s gripped the land. Her mother worked as a housemaid for the Remington family, who owned large tracts of land in central California. As a young girl, Raquel and her mother lived in an upstairs room at a big house near Fresno. Raquel remembered how the carpet felt on her bare feet when she was a little girl. She had played outside on soft green grass under the shade of towering palm trees, and she thought her comfortable life was normal for the daughter of a housemaid.

Raquel had been too young to know the scandal her birth had caused. Her mother had been banished by her family for unrepentantly having Jake Remington's child out of wedlock. The Remingtons tolerated the affair and Raquel's presence in their home for a time, but when Jake met a woman from a powerful family near San Francisco, the mother and child were unceremoniously dismissed from the house. Raquel's mother thought he had loved them. Her mother was sent to work for a family near Visalia, but that did not work out well for them.

With no family ties other than her daughter, Raquel's mother retreated to one of the squatters' camps to work as a laborer in the fields. There were few other options for a woman in her circumstance. As a skinny, awkward teenager, Raquel loathed the smells and noise of the chaotic camps. She cringed at the hungry cries from starving children and the hopeless stares from parents powerless to provide for them. More than the desperate poverty, she hated the gossiping whispers about her mother. Raquel compensated by working hard. She continued school when they first came to Visalia, but after moving between camps to follow the harvest, Raquel left school forever to pick strawberries near Tulare. After that, the fields became her education, and the lessons were hard.

The Great Depression gripped the nation, but Raquel could tell little difference in her dire condition. She learned to accept the harsh realities. Her pleas to return to the life she had known at the Remington house caused her mother to weep bitterly, and she loved her mother too much to cause her any pain. Raquel's mother was a soft-spoken woman with smooth bronzed skin and thick dark hair. Juan Esperanza offered her a house near Tipton, California, away from the bleak migrant camps in the area. The house turned out to be a two-room shack with a dirt floor. Raquel's mother could scrub the house, but her oft-drunk husband had a dark and mean soul that was impossible to clean. Her mother put up with his abuse, his drinking, and the beatings, however, to keep a roof over their heads.

Raquel worked in the fields to get away from her stepfather, and she often slept outdoors during warm weather to avoid his drunken rants. The slightly built girl had felt the sting of his belt many times. Raquel could take the beatings, but she could not endure what was happening to her mother, whose sweet and nurturing smile had been replaced by a bruised face and sad eyes. Her mother's sudden illness and death had been crushing to Raquel.

Her stepfather's continual mistreatment made Raquel shy and uncertain, even as she shed the gawkiness of her teenage years and blossomed into an attractive young woman. Raquel had a smirking but reserved smile that was rarely seen after her mother's death. Her light-brown skin and dark hair contrasted with her grayish-blue eyes. Raquel always liked her colorful eyes as a child, but now they seemed like a curse and a reminder of her mother's spoiled reputation, which Juan Esperanza often brought up during his mean-spirited tirades. The introverted Raquel had a hard enough time dealing with suddenly attentive men, but when her drunken stepfather tried to force a kiss, she had to leave.

Raquel ran from the rickety house with her few belongings in a cloth sack not knowing if her unconscious stepfather was dead or alive. She also did not care.

CHAPTER 2

Raquel walked aimlessly through the night and for most of the next day. The second night found her in front of a camp where workers were herded onto trucks to work the cotton fields south of Bakersfield. The exhausted Raquel slept at the gate of the camp. It was not her first time to sleep outside, and she doubted it would be her last. The next morning she climbed aboard a truck heading to the fields, hoping to earn enough for a meal. She did not make eye contact and desperately hoped no one would recognize her. The law had not come after her, and she assumed her stepfather had survived the blow to his face.

The rhythm of the laboring truck lulled Raquel into unconscious thoughts of nothingness. She listened to the rattling engine and tires whining on the pavement, but it did not seem real. She ignored the mixture of English and Spanish chatter coming from the twenty or so workers riding in the back of the truck. Some, like Raquel, spoke more English than Spanish. The workers crowded onto the floor of the bouncing truck. More trucks filled with Filipinos and Okies would come competing for the day's work. By sunset, the trucks would be filled with cotton, and the workers would be herded onto other vehicles for trips back to their pitiful camps scattered across the San Joaquin Valley.

Raquel's cheek and eye throbbed dully as a result of the savage blow from the back of her stepfather's hand. She tried to shift her face away from the others to hide the swollen puffiness around her right eye. She wanted no sympathy and knew she would get none from the hardened field workers.

A haggard-looking man sitting a few seats away from her shouted a profanity about her mother.

The laughter from those in the truck made the bruise above her eye more painful, as she frowned awkwardly. It would be her only defense against the slurs. The more compassionate workers and the women were sometimes more polite in indicating her illegitimacy. She had heard worse insults about her mother. At first, Raquel tried to fight back verbally, but no one cared about a young woman's feelings. She was a remnant of something they hated—the white landowners. Her mother's relationship with Jake Remington resulting in her birth made the others despise her. Raquel would endure, she had endured.

"Don't pay 'em no mind," one of the riders interjected. "They're jealous of your blue eyes. Come to the camps sometime—a girl like you don't need to work so hard."

The others laughed, and Raquel sat silently, pretending their insults did not hurt.

"Send her to the Okie camp!" another shouted, causing more laughter. "They'll think she's a squaw!"

An older woman in her early thirties looked at Raquel stoically. Raquel thought she sensed some sympathy, but the woman remained silent.

"What's in the bag?" the man asked, as he grabbed the ragged sack sitting at her feet.

The man had dark eyes and weathered features. He appeared to be in his late twenties, but looked lean and hardened. Raquel tried to keep him from taking her bag, but in the quick struggle he grabbed it, causing a worn dress, some undergarments, and a cheap necklace that belonged to her mother, to spill onto the dirty floor of the truck. The man quickly snatched the undergarments and held them up mockingly. The others laughed as Raquel struggled to retrieve her meager possessions. The contents of the bag represented all of her belongings. She fought back tears of despair as the others taunted mercilessly.

"Goin' on vacation, niño bastardo?" the man asked.

Raquel did not reply as she self-consciously stuffed things back into her bag. She had fled her stepfather's abuse, and prayed he would not find her.

"Your daddy know you've left?" the man mocked.

Raquel did not answer, but was terrified to think the man knew her stepfather and might betray her location.

"You know him?" Raquel finally asked.

"Juan Esperanza?" the man replied suspiciously. "A little. I know he owes people some money back in Tipton."

"He's my stepfather, not my father," Raquel muttered, as if that declaration made her past life with him more bearable.

Raquel hated the idea that she was associated with a man like Juan Experanza. After her mother had passed, Raquel had gone to the Remington house to find Jake Remington, her real father, to see if he could help her. Raquel had hoped he would take care of her, but she had been run off like a stray dog, without getting to see him. Jake Remington cared more about his future than the responsibilities of his past. Raquel learned she had no father and no options.

"Come on, pretty," the man said in a more conciliatory tone as he handed her the garment he had been waving in amusement. "I didn't mean nothing."

The man bullied his way into the seat next to her. He leaned uncomfortably close, and she could smell tequila on his breath from the night before—a nauseating reminder of her drunken stepfather.

"You not talkin' to me?" the man continued.

Raquel did not reply.

"What happened to your eye?" the man questioned.

Raquel unconsciously reached up to hide the bruised eye and said, "I fell."

"Looks like you fell into someone's fist," the man jeered.

"I just fell," Raquel claimed.

"I've heard about you," the man grinned, showing several teeth missing from his yellowed smile.

Raquel's cheeks flushed with anger and embarrassment causing her bruised eye to throb.

"Don't want to talk?" the man asked. "Bet if I was one of those rich white fellas, you would—just like your mother."

"Please, mister," Raquel pleaded. "I just want to work."

That was a lie. Raquel hated picking cotton. She could tolerate oranges and apricots, but picking cotton was the worst of the harvesting work. Cotton picking meant hours of hard, painful labor, bending over and pulling colorless cotton from the prickly bolls. Besides, she could not eat cotton. She was hungry and would labor in the fields all day for a chance to eat that night.

"A girl like you shouldn't have to work," the man said, "at least not in the fields."

Raquel did not respond.

"I'm Carlos," the man continued, as he reached out his hand.

Raquel resisted for a moment before shaking his rough, calloused hand.

"I could be a good friend for you," the man claimed.

By this time, the others in the truck had resumed their chatter. The woman sitting across from Raquel looked judgmentally at her with a clenched jaw, but she did not speak to the girl.

"I don't need a friend," Raquel replied.

"Everyone needs a friend," Carlos smiled wickedly. "I gotta friend. A good friend…a friend that's always looking for new girls…especially pretty girls."

Raquel understood the man's insinuation. The idea made her queasy, and the man's crude offer underscored her desperation.

"We're here," Raquel nervously replied, as the shaky truck bounced onto a dirt road surrounded by miles of brown and white cotton fields.

Before the truck came to a complete stop, Raquel leaped out and tumbled on the rough ground, ripping a hole in her already patched dress. Other trucks were at the site, but no one seemed to notice her clumsy exit. As she scrambled to collect her bag and shake off the dust, she felt a firm hand grasp her shoulder.

"Where ya' going?" Carlos teased, as he held her arm firmly in his grasp.

Raquel watched the truck come to a complete stop twenty steps away. The woman sitting across from her stared an instant before walking away. Other trucks filled with Mexican, Filipino, and Okie workers unloaded close to her. One young Mexican man stopped to help, before Carlos threatened and bullied him. The young man could not afford a confrontation, which might cost him the chance to work for the day, so he did not interfere further.

"You're hurting me," Raquel pleaded, as she struggled to break the man's grip.

"Don't be difficult," Carlos replied. "You work with me today—and I'll introduce you to my friend later."

"Let go of her!" a firm voice with a lazy drawl shouted from behind Raquel.

As she looked over her shoulder, two white men trotted toward her. Raquel did not want trouble with the foremen before the day even started, but she was thankful for the intervention.

"Mind your own business, Okie!" Carlos shouted back.

Raquel took a second look at the approaching young men, and she was relieved they were not foremen for the field. A foreman would have sent her away hungry if it was even suspected she would disrupt work. Workers were plentiful in the fields of the San Joaquin Valley in 1933, but work was scarce. These two young men did not look like the Okies that had started migrating to the fertile fields of California from the central plains of Kansas, Texas, Arkansas, and Oklahoma. Most Okies looked dirty, desperate, and almost always skinny. These boys were clean and looked well-fed.

The Mexican workers hated the Okies, because they could. They despised the white landowners, the white shopkeepers, the white townspeople, and especially the white foremen of the fields, but that loathing would have to remain secret and silent—pushed deep inside. There were no such restraints against the rage they felt toward the Okies, who had come west, pushed like the swarming locust from the great drought and famine of the American plains. Even the white people resented the unwanted appearance of the Midwestern refugees into California. They were banned from some communities, but still they came. The Mexicans could not show their frustration with the other whites, but they could hate Okies without consequence.

"I said get your hands off that girl!" the shorter of the two men demanded.

"Don't cause trouble," the taller man implored.

"Better listen to him," Carlos threatened.

"What's going on here?" a man screamed from the head of the trucks. "Get in line!"

Carlos let go of Raquel's arm at the appearance of the foreman walking from the front of the row of trucks.

"We're not done," Carlos said in a whisper to the young men.

"Get in line!" the foreman repeated.

The foreman walked grimly toward the group. He was a man of nearly forty and exuded a no-nonsense demeanor.

"Do we have a problem here?" the foreman asked, while staring at Raquel.

Carlos looked away, trying to distance himself from the confrontation while blending in with the other workers.

"No problem, sir," the taller stranger replied.

The foreman looked at the two young men for a second and said, "You two the Butler boys?"

"Yes, sir," the shorter young man replied.

"Your pa says you're workers," the foreman said, while studying the cowering Raquel.

"Yes, sir," the man affirmed.

"Your pa's a good man," the foreman said to the boys. "Don't disappoint him." The man looked at Raquel and asked, "This girl causing any problems?"

"No, sir," the young man answered. "We were just…we were just asking her some questions."

"You ever picked cotton before?" the foreman asked.

"No," the young man replied.

"How 'bout you?" the foreman asked, looking at Raquel.

Raquel nodded while avoiding eye contact with him.

"You work with these two today," the foreman instructed her. "Don't get behind or I'll run the lot of you off…I don't care who your daddy is."

"Yes, sir," both boys answered.

"And you," the foreman continued, pointing at Carlos. "Get across the road and get to work."

Carlos immediately followed the instructions and walked away, looking only at the dirt in front of him.

The foreman looked at Raquel again before giving a slight nod to the taller young man and saying, "The bags are in the truck—get to work."

CHAPTER 3

"I'm Maylon," the shorter man introduced. "This is my brother, Chili."

Maylon was a stocky young man in his twenties with tanned skin and dark hair. Although the sandy-haired Chili was younger, he was taller and more muscular. It was the brothers' relaxed demeanor Raquel noticed first. She had spent much of her life with migrant workers, including Okies, and they had always had a desperate, edgy disposition. The brothers did not look much alike, but they shared an unmistakable confidence that set them apart from the other field workers.

"I'm Raquel," the girl shyly nodded.

"Guess we're working together," the older Maylon smiled.

"Yeah," Raquel replied quietly.

"You ever pick cotton?" Chili asked.

Chili Butler had a slow, soft manner of speaking that seemed comforting to Raquel. He did not say much, but his presence exuded self-assurance, and his voice had a commanding sound to it.

"Yeah," Raquel nodded.

She had picked cotton the season before, but that harvest had seemed to last forever. Raquel sensed that she had considerably more experience than the two young men that would be her partners. If they were slow, it would cost her money, but she was still grateful to be working with them and away from Carlos.

"You don't talk much," Maylon grinned.

"No," Raquel said.

The two young men glanced at each other and smiled at the girl's blunt reply.

After an awkward silence, Raquel said, "We need to work before the foreman returns."

"Chili," Maylon ordered. "Grab those bags, and let's get to work before the foreman tells Pa."

Chili Butler strolled to the back of one of the trucks and grabbed several bags.

"Just one each," Raquel instructed, as she reached around Chili to take three of the long bags.

For the next two hours, Raquel hitched up her worn, patched dress and attacked the cotton bolls. At first she carefully and gingerly picked at the bolls, but as her fingers stung from the continual picking of the plant's rough fruit, she became less careful. When her bag was almost half-full, she stretched her back, closed her eyes for a second, and enjoyed the bright sun that was now high in the sky. Raquel could see the brothers twenty yards ahead of her. She was impressed by their energy and was surprised they had been able to work so quickly. As she watched them, Chili stopped to take off his hat and wipe the sweat from his forehead. Raquel looked too long, as the handsome young man turned to see her watching him.

Chili smiled and said, "Ya' want a drink? I gotta canteen up here."

Raquel nodded timidly and walked toward the boys.

Maylon had stopped his picking for the moment and said, "I guess we're taking to this work pretty good."

Raquel again nodded, as she took the canteen from Chili's hand. She drank the cool, fresh water and tried not to gulp it down in front of the two brothers.

"Thank you," she said, as she handed the canteen back to Chili.

As Chili offered the canteen to his brother, Raquel enjoyed the peace and serenity of the field and the kindness of her two co-workers for a second. The tranquility did not last long when she looked at the nearly full bags the brothers had been dragging.

"Oh no!" she sighed, as she looked at the bags filled with cotton bolls and some stems.

"What?" a concerned Chili asked.

"You're doing it wrong!" a panicked Raquel exclaimed, as she looked around to see if the foreman had seen them.

"Doin' what wrong?" Maylon asked.

"You're supposed to pull the cotton out of the boll and put in the bag," the girl explained. "You've picked the whole boll. They'll run us off for sure."

"Naw," Maylon consoled in an easy tone. "It was a simple mistake. I wondered how we were getting so far ahead of you."

Raquel scanned the fields again and was relieved that the foreman was across the road on the other side of the field.

"You pull the cotton out," Raquel explained again, as she quickly showed the boys the proper way.

"That'll slow things down," Chili offered.

"Of course it will," Raquel scolded. "But that's how it's done."

Raquel looked over the fields again before saying to the boys, "Go work on my bag and I'll clean up yours."

Maylon and Chili felt guilty for causing the girl extra work, but they quickly obeyed. Raquel dumped the contents of one bag on the ground and feverishly began pulling the cotton from the picked bolls. The two brothers working together caught up to her in about thirty minutes, and she still had half the first bag on the ground.

"Go on," Chili said. "I'll help Raquel."

The older brother did not argue and continued on his row.

"I'm sorry," Chili apologized. "I guess we messed things up real good."

"It was stupid," an angry Raquel replied. "You'll get me fired from this field if we don't get this cleaned up."

"I'll take responsibility," Chili said. "It was my fault."

"Like they'll take the Mexican girl's side over the white boy's," Raquel said.

"We'll fix it," Chili tried to assure, as he dropped to his knees to pull at the scattered bolls of cotton.

Raquel was angry at herself for talking so harshly to Chili. He had tried to help. She should have paid more attention, she thought to herself. After another thirty minutes, the first bag was done with only a stack of stems and bolls to show the mistake.

As Raquel poured the second bag on the ground and started pulling the cotton, Chili said, "Take this bag. I've got this one."

Raquel looked at Chili's hands. They were already cut and red from the sharp bolls.

"It'll be quicker if we do it together," she replied.

Chili nodded and smiled, as he began working on the pile of cotton. Raquel's back was already aching, but she felt good inside for the first time in a long time. On another day she would have let Chili fix his own mess, but his smile of appreciation made her feel decent for helping another person. After another hour, Raquel and Chili stood upright to try to stretch some of the stiffness from their aching backs.

"We're not too far behind, are we?" an anxious Chili asked.

Raquel surveyed the field and saw Maylon about fifty yards in front of them. The other workers had made varying levels of progress, but her group was definitely behind.

"Not too bad," Raquel answered.

"How 'bout some lunch?" Chili offered.

Raquel had not thought of eating while in the fields. That's one of the things she hated about picking cotton. When harvesting fruit or beans she could sneak a bite to eat, but picking cotton meant a long, hard day with nothing for her hungry stomach.

"I don't have lunch," she said.

"I've got plenty," Chili assured.

"Where?" Raquel asked, as she saw nothing but his canteen tied to his waist.

"In the car," Chili replied.

"You have a car?" Raquel said.

Chili nodded. Raquel had never known of anyone driving a car to the fields. Her people had always arrived in the back of a truck, but she guessed these Okies were different. Before Chili could explain more, Maylon came walking toward them dragging his long bag.

"One bag done," Maylon bragged.

"We're trying to catch up," Chili said. "Grab our lunches and bring 'em back, will you?"

"Sure," Maylon smiled.

Maylon walked back toward the dirt road where the vehicles were parked, while Chili and Raquel continued working through the second bag of cotton. In twenty minutes, Maylon returned carrying two brown bags.

"Let's eat," Chili suggested, as Raquel continued working on the cotton.

"I'm not hungry," Raquel replied.

Maylon handed one bag to Chili and coaxed, "There's plenty."

"I'm fine," Raquel said, as she continued working.

Chili stepped next to the girl to say, "Ma always packs too much. Take this sandwich."

Chili handed Raquel a sandwich wrapped in wax paper. Raquel hesitated for a moment before taking the sandwich.

Raquel timidly unwrapped the sandwich and whispered, "Thank you."

She tried to pace herself, but hunger caused Raquel to take two ravenous bites out of the sandwich until she nearly choked. The boys smiled at each other, and Maylon handed her the canteen of water. The boys were polite and did not make her feel self-conscious about hastily devouring her first meal in days.

The trio enjoyed their lunch silently until Maylon asked, "How is it?"

"Good," Raquel replied, as she wiped her mouth with her sleeve.

The sandwich was made from fresh homemade bread, with a thick slice of smoked ham, and a tomato. She had not eaten in two days, and the sandwich was delicious. Raquel had been enjoying her lunch so much that she did not notice that Chili had finished his apple.

"Did I take your sandwich?" Raquel asked. "I thought you had another."

"Don't worry," Chili smiled. "I'm a big boy and had a big breakfast this morning."

"In the camps?" Raquel inquired.

Chili looked at Maylon, whose mouth was full of a bite of his sandwich, before saying, "We don't live in the camps. We got a house in Maricopa."

A puzzled Raquel looked at the two young men while taking another bite of her sandwich.

"What?" Chili asked.

"Nothing," Raquel claimed.

"That look doesn't say 'nothing,'" Chili said.

Raquel thought for a moment before saying, "I thought all the Okies lived in the camps…or on the road."

Chili looked at his brother, before Maylon said, "We ain't no Okies."

"I'm sorry," Raquel apologized in a timid voice.

Chili laughed, "Maylon's a little sensitive. He was born in Oklahoma, and our parents are from there, but Maylon says we're not Okies."

"We're not," Maylon said. "We've been here long enough to be Californians."

"It don't matter what people say," Chili said.

"It matters to me," Maylon said. "Our pa came here twenty years ago to pump oil in the Sunset West field near Taft. These sharecroppers came with the drought. I'm no cropper."

"Why are you picking cotton, if you're so worried about what people think?" Raquel asked, as she finished the last of her sandwich.

"Pa was a farmer before he started workin' for the oil company," Maylon explained. "He thinks we need to learn to work."

"We got a little land back in Oklahoma," Chili explained. "Pa hopes to go back after he retires and wants us to farm it."

"I ain't a farmer," Maylon said shaking his head.

"You ain't anything, yet," Chili said.

"I'll get on with the oil company when things pick up," Maylon shrugged. "Maybe go to town and run a business."

"Big dreams, big brother," Chili smiled.

"Wait and see," Maylon responded.

Raquel jumped up as the two brothers traded verbal spars, and she began quickly working on her bag of cotton.

"You boys taking a vacation?" the foreman shouted from behind them.

Raquel had seen the foreman walking quickly toward them but did not have time to warn the two brothers.

"Takin' a lunch break," Maylon smiled.

"I warned you two," the foreman charged, as he stepped close to Maylon. "You slack off and you're gone."

"We've been workin' on this cotton," Maylon replied.

"You're twenty percent behind the laziest Mexican I got on the crew," the foreman said.

"We got messed up on how to pick and got behind," Chili explained.

"Stupid's no better excuse than lazy!" the foreman said sternly. "Now git, so I can put some people that want to work out here."

"That's not fair," Maylon protested. "We're doin' our best."

"You're best ain't much, and it ain't my problem," the foreman said as he looked around.

"Not your problem?" Maylon said in a more serious tone. "You can take your bags and I'd like to show you what to do with 'em. Let's get our pay and get out of here Chili."

The foreman huffed and said, "I'm not payin' for a couple of lazy Okies doin' half day's work."

"You owe us," Maylon said.

"I owe you nothin' but a kick in the pants!" the foreman shouted. "Now, git!"

Maylon stared meanly at the foreman as the man looked back toward the road. Before he could take a swing, Chili stepped to his brother's side to keep his temper in check.

The foreman shouted to a ragged-looking man wearing even more ragged overalls, "Ya wanna take this row?"

The man did not hesitate and ran with two younger boys toward the group.

"You'd replace us just like that?" Maylon fumed.

"You ain't hungry enough, kid," the foreman replied. "I could've told you that at the first of the day. These Okies will stand in the hot sun for hours to make fifty cents. Go home and tell your dad it didn't work out."

"Let's get out of here!" Maylon defiantly stated to his brother as he stomped away from the foreman.

Chili hesitated for a moment, as the man the foreman had waved over ran up. He had a thin jaw line and a hungry look to his eyes. Two skinny boys, not more than twelve years old, followed closely.

"Get to work and don't slack up on me," the foreman ordered. "I just had to fire these loafers, and I won't think twice about sending you home hungry, too. You're already fifty yards behind on this row, so get to it."

The farmer and his sons did not reply but eagerly attacked the cotton in front of them. Chili shrugged and walked slowly toward the car. He knew his father would be angry they lost the job, but he felt bad thinking that he and Maylon had taken work away from folks that really needed it.

"You too," the foreman said from behind Chili.

Chili turned around, thinking the foreman was talking to him, when he realized the man was firing Raquel from her work.

"Now wait a minute," Chili said. "It ain't her fault. She was working, but she had to clean up a mess that me and my brother made."

"Please, mister," Raquel pleaded. "I'll work hard…you won't have no trouble out of me."

"You're already trouble," the foreman stated firmly. "You already started a ruckus before the day even started with my Mexican workers, and now you've loafed with these two."

"That's not fair!" Chili shouted, as he ran up to the foreman.

"I told you to get out of here!" the foreman responded.

"Please," Raquel said in a soft voice, although she knew her pleas would not change the foreman's mind.

"Look at these Okies work," the foreman stated, as he looked at the man and his two boys working feverishly on the cotton.

"You need to pay her," Chili interrupted.

"This is America," the foreman smiled. "You don't get paid when you get fired. Now get out of here, both of you."

Chili leaned forward as if he might hit the foreman, but Raquel put down her bag and took Chili by the arm to walk away. Chili resisted for an instant before walking with her and toward his brother Maylon.

"I'd like to punch that guy in the head!" Chili fumed when he was out of earshot.

"You don't want to do that," Raquel said in an angry tone.

"Why not?" Chili asked. "I'm bigger than him."

"You'd get arrested at best or beat at worst," she explained.

"I've been in fights before," Chili assured.

Raquel continued walking for a few steps before saying, "Look at them."

Chili did not know what she was talking about for a second, and then he noticed about twenty or so men loitering around the trucks.

"They all want to work," Raquel explained. "They all need to work. They wouldn't have sympathy for you if the foreman and his men started in on you. That's just one less Okie they'd have to compete with."

Chili studied the men standing by the trucks and determined Raquel was right. The men looked haggard, hungry, and desperate. The young man once again felt guilty for taking work that he did not need.

"It still ain't fair what happened to you," Chili said.

"It happens," Raquel replied, as she began talking in a less angry tone. "The foremen look for an excuse to fire workers halfway through the day and know there's always a replacement. They don't pay us, and they'll pay the others for half a day. They get a full day of harvesting at half the price. The foremen will pocket the extra. Besides, they get to set an example to the other workers to stay in line."

"I'm sorry we got you fired," Chili said.

"I got to eat," Raquel smiled. "That's something."

"But it got us fired," Chili replied.

"It was a good sandwich," Raquel smiled.

"Should've stayed away from the gringos," Carlos shouted, as he helped another man throw a full bag of cotton into a dusty truck.

"Keep walking," Raquel whispered to Chili.

"You ignoring me?" Carlos chided, as he stepped quickly to block Raquel's path.

"We don't want no trouble," Chili said, as he stopped to face the Mexican man.

"Should've minded your own business then," Carlos sneered. "Should've stayed away from this bastardo."

Raquel surprised Chili by stepping between the two men and pushing Carlos firmly in the chest.

"Hit me!" she challenged.

"You're crazy!" Carlos shouted back.

"Hit me, and the foreman will send you away, too!" Raquel shouted.

Carlos grabbed the girl violently by the arm, nearly causing Raquel to lose her balance. The angry man's nostrils flared, as he frantically searched the fields to see if a foreman had seen him.

Before Chili could intervene, Carlos released the girl and said, "You're not worth it."

Carlos muttered some profanities in Spanish about Raquel before turning to Chili to add, "I'll be seeing you. Count on it."

Chili tried to confront the threatening man, but Raquel stopped him and pleaded, "Let it be."

Carlos glanced over his shoulder and seemed to challenge Chili to fight him, but he continued to walk away.

"I should've punched him," Chili fumed when Carlos was out of earshot.

"He's not worth it," Raquel replied.

Raquel walked away and located the bag holding her things. She looked around the miles of desolate cotton fields and contemplated the feasibility of walking. It would be too far she decided, so she would have to wait out the day and ride back with the workers.

"Need a ride?" Chili asked.

Raquel's instincts would have been to refuse the offer, but the thoughts of another confrontation with Carlos, caused her to quickly say, "Yes."

"Good," Chili smiled.

Raquel followed Chili as they approached a 1932 Ford sedan that looked nearly new.

"This is your car?" Raquel quizzed.

"Pa's," Chili said.

Maylon leaned over the steering wheel anxious to go. Chili opened the door and let Raquel slide into the back seat.

"Where to?" Maylon asked. "We got all afternoon, now."

Raquel hesitated, her mind frantically tried to think of an answer. She would not return home—she had made that decision the night before. She had hoped to find a place in one of the government camps, but now she realized how it would look for her to be dropped off at the gates of the government's sanitary camps by two white men in the middle of the afternoon. The squatters' camps were her other option. Raquel cringed to think about the sight of starving children with the clothes literally fraying off their dirty little bodies and the blank expression of absolute terror on the faces of their desperate parents at the real prospects of starvation. Life in the squatters' camps was harsh and unforgiving. Hardly any of the unfortunate families herded there had been spared the sorrow of losing a child to malnutrition. Raquel had escaped the camps before and feared having to return to them.

Before she had to answer, Chili said, "She's coming home with us."

"Huh?" Maylon grunted.

"She's eating supper at our house," Chili smiled.

"I don't want to be a bother," Raquel timidly said.

"Nonsense," Chili said. "We cost you a day of work. Ma'll be happy to have company."

Maylon gleamed at his brother with a dubious look of uncertainty about this statement before smiling and saying, "You're a genius."

"I'm always tellin' you I'm the smart one," Chili grinned.

"Pa'll be more…pleasant if we got company," Maylon said.

With a big smile, Chili turned around and said, "Will you help us out by having supper?"

Raquel nodded and returned Chili's warm smile.

CHAPTER 4

As the Ford sedan rolled down the highway, Raquel settled into the back seat, and she could easily have drifted into an afternoon nap. Raquel had only ridden in bumpy worn-out work trucks in the past, and she was not used to the smooth comfort of the passenger car. The two brothers bantered in the front seat, and Raquel was content to listen. She learned Maylon was a year older than his taller brother. Maylon was quick-tempered, opinionated, and edgy compared to his more easygoing brother.

Raquel found the brothers refreshing. Most people she knew clung to the bottom of the economic rope the hard times had brought. These boys talked in a relaxed tone and enjoyed a sunny afternoon. Chili teased Maylon about his girl, Orpha. Maylon was informally engaged to the girl and planned to marry her as soon as they could afford a place. Raquel listened carefully for any mention of Chili's girl, but heard nothing.

The Butler family lived in Maricopa in the southwestern corner of California's San Joaquin Valley. Maricopa was a peaceful town with several stores, a restaurant, and three churches. The rowdy oil town of Taft was nearby in the middle of the Midway-Sunset oil field. The stark and barren slopes of the Temblor Range, separating the valley from the coast, could be seen in the distance.

Maylon parked the car in front of a large, two-story house on the edge of the small town of Maricopa. The freshly painted home had a neat and ordered appearance. Even the small garage next to the house looked like a palace compared to the shack where Raquel had lived.

"Ma!" Maylon yelled, as they entered the house.

The Butler house smelled of apple pie, and the front room was immaculately neat.

"Ma!" Maylon shouted again.

"You don't have to yell," a woman said, as she stepped from the rear of the house.

The middle-aged woman moved quickly and with purpose. She wore a large apron over her neat, blue dress. Her brown hair was pulled back in a tight bun.

"What are you doing home so early?" the woman asked.

Maylon looked at his brother and said, "We finished."

The woman looked suspiciously at her two boys and sighed, "Oh."

Raquel stood awkwardly on the front porch behind Chili, thinking the woman intended to add a scolding to the sigh. Instead the mother looked around her sons to see the young woman standing outside.

"Do we have company?" she asked rhetorically.

Raquel stood silently, as Maylon and Chili glanced at each other.

"I invited Raquel to supper," Chili confessed.

"Raquel?" the woman said. "A Mexican name?"

Raquel nodded.

"Please come in," the woman said in a tone of forced civility.

Raquel nervously stepped into the front room.

"I'm Mrs. Butler," the woman politely introduced, "but you can call me Naomi. Welcome."

Raquel uncomfortably stood a few steps inside the room as Mrs. Butler said, "Let me take your bag."

Naomi Butler took the dirty bag and held it away from her white apron while huffing, "I'll put this in the back. Have a seat, Raquel, and I'll be back. Boys, you better get cleaned up."

Her sons obeyed without questioning their mother and left Raquel alone in the front room. She tried to sit on the front edge of the sofa to avoid soiling it with her dirty dress. Naomi Butler soon reentered the room and studied the young woman carefully with a slight scowl on her face. Raquel had seen the same look many times—at stores, in town, and from anyone who thought the Mexicans in Kern County were good only for the fields.

"I thought I knew all of my boys' friends," Mrs. Butler stated.

Raquel shifted nervously, as Mrs. Butler continued to study the girl sitting in front of her.

"What happened to your eye?" Mrs. Butler asked.

Raquel instinctively moved her hand to her face in a belated attempt to cover the bruise.

"I fell," Raquel lied.

Naomi Butler squinted as she examined the young woman carefully.

"You had some chores?" Chili said, as he came back into the room.

Naomi Butler was momentarily surprised by Chili's question, but then she said, "Yes. I need you and Maylon to go to the market for me in Taft. I want to fix chicken tonight and need some things."

"Both of us?" Chili asked.

"Yes," Mrs. Butler said, while still looking at Raquel. "You can both go and then pick up your father at the bus station. The list is on the table."

Chili shrugged. In a few minutes, he and Maylon drove off in the car.

"How did you meet my boys?" Mrs. Butler quizzed.

"We met in the fields this morning," Raquel confessed.

"I see," the disapproving mother replied. "And why are my boys home so early on a work day?"

Raquel would have liked to have lied, but Mrs. Butler's air of stern authority caused her to admit, "We picked the bolls of cotton instead of pulling the cotton from the bolls. We got behind, and they sent us home."

Mrs. Butler sighed disapprovingly, "Chili invited you?"

Raquel nodded.

"He's always finding a stray," she muttered.

Raquel frowned helplessly.

"I'm guessing you knew how to pick cotton?" Mrs. Butler asked.

"Yes, ma'am," Raquel said timidly.

Mrs. Butler continued to study the young girl before she said in a more hospitable tone, "I'm not being a very good hostess. The boys will be gone for a while, and you look like you've had a day of it. I'll draw you a bath and we'll clean your clothes before supper."

"I don't want to cause trouble," Raquel replied.

Mrs. Butler forced a smile, "No trouble, dear. You'll feel better after we get you cleaned up and into some fresh clothes."

Mrs. Butler left, but in a few minutes she guided Raquel to a warm bath with soft towels. Raquel was used to sharing an outhouse with the neighbors, so Naomi Butler's bathroom seemed luxurious. The smooth porcelain bathtub and warm water felt like an oasis from her despair of the day. She soaked for a few seconds before dipping her head and her whole body into the almost hot water. She held her breath for as long as she could before gasping for air. Raquel felt clean and right for the first time in days. She knew the euphoria of a fresh bath would be temporary, but for the moment she felt refreshed and renewed. In about a half an hour, Mrs. Butler knocked on the door and entered.

"I brought you some things to wear while I launder your clothes," Mrs. Butler explained. "They're some of my old clothes—not too fashionable, but they'll fit—somewhat."

Raquel nodded in appreciation and the older woman exited the room. The clothes Mrs. Butler left were worn, but they were soft to her skin. The dress draped over her shoulder a little much, but it was clean and felt good to her. Raquel struggled with the back buttons, when Mrs. Butler knocked again.

"Are you decent?" Mrs. Butler asked.

Raquel cringed at the question, but replied, "Yes, but I'm having trouble with the back."

"Let me see," Mrs. Butler offered as she looked at dress. "I guess I'm a little bigger than I thought, or you're a lot skinnier."

Mrs. Butler stepped behind the girl to fasten the buttons and gasped, "Who did this to you?"

Raquel groaned, "Huh?"

"Your back!" Mrs. Butler exclaimed. "There are marks all over."

Raquel did not have a full-length mirror and had not seen her back, but she soon deduced that Mrs. Butler had observed the remnants of past beatings at the hands of her stepfather.

"It's nothing," Raquel tried to explain.

"Nothing!" Mrs. Butler fumed. "I'd like to get my hands on—"

"It's really okay," Raquel said. "It's not that bad."

"When did this happen?" the skeptical Mrs. Butler asked. "These marks are fresh—just like that bruise on your eye."

"I don't remember," Raquel replied meekly.

"Come in here," Mrs. Butler coaxed.

Mrs. Butler led Raquel into a bedroom and motioned for her to lie face down on the soft mattress. The older woman gingerly peeled back the dress to examine the girl's back.

"I don't see any bleeding," Mrs. Butler said. "Let's put some ointment on it anyway."

In a moment, Mrs. Butler returned with a small jar of cream. She gently rubbed the girl's back and caressed the still visible scars and bruises. It had been many months since anyone had shown her the slightest kindness, and Raquel began crying softly.

"Does it hurt?" Mrs. Butler asked.

Raquel shook her head. She had become so accustomed to a sore back that she rarely noticed.

"Do you want to talk about it?" Mrs. Butler offered.

Again, Raquel shook her head.

After a few moments, Raquel sat up to straighten herself, and said, "I'll leave as soon as my clothes are dry. I'll be gone before your boys get back."

Naomi Butler blushed with embarrassment at her earlier rudeness, and said, "You're my guest…Chili's guest. Besides, you're skin and bone. I want you to stay for dinner. Will you?"

Raquel nodded and wiped her moist eyes.

"Good," Mrs. Butler smiled, "because I wouldn't have taken no for an answer. The boys will be back later and I'm going to start supper."

"I can help," Raquel offered.

"You're a guest," Mrs. Butler said. "I've got your clothes and your bag hanging out to dry. Lie down in the bed and rest for a while. You look tired."

"Thank you," Raquel whispered.

CHAPTER 5

Raquel nervously curled up in the bed, but tried desperately to stay awake in the strange house. She looked forward to a good meal as she listened to Mrs. Butler working rhythmically in the kitchen. She appreciated Mrs. Butler's hospitality, but she felt like the woman's kindness came from a sense of charitable obligation. The bed was soft and fresh, however, and Raquel felt clean for the first time in weeks. In a short time she drifted into a deep sleep.

In the timelessness of sleep, Raquel did not know how long she had napped when the squeaky front door creaked open. The muffled voices of Maylon and Chili Butler caused her eyes to open as the slanting shadows of the late afternoon draped across the room. As she attempted to determine the time, she heard a third more commanding voice from the front room. Raquel assumed it was Mr. Butler. She believed it must be close to six o'clock and an hour until dark. The aroma of fried chicken and baked bread reminded Raquel of the promised supper. The thought of finding a place to spend the night after dark put a frown on her face, but she was rested and would soon be fed. She could survive another night outside, Raquel reasoned.

Now fully awake, a self-conscious Raquel felt guilty for not helping with dinner, and she wished she could slip away. Her chance to escape had passed, however, as she heard steps pattering up the stairs.

The soft steps were followed by light knocking and the voice of Naomi Butler whispering, "Are you awake?"

"Yes, ma'am," Raquel answered.

The door opened and Mrs. Butler asked, "Are you hungry?"

Raquel nodded.

"Supper's ready," Mrs. Butler informed.

Raquel followed Mrs. Butler downstairs. As she looked down, she saw Maylon and Chili already sitting at the table. At the head of the table, a thin, wiry man with rugged features sat with an impatient frown on his face.

When Mrs. Butler reached the bottom of the stairs, she whispered urgently, "Boys!"

Without further explanation, Maylon and Chili stood to acknowledge Raquel's entrance. Mr. Butler continued to sit, but after a grimacing nod of encouragement from his wife, he also stood, making a point to push the wooden chair noisily away from the table with the back of his legs.

"Raquel, this is my husband, Eli," Mrs. Butler introduced. "We're glad to have you with us tonight."

After a stern look from his wife, Mr. Butler nodded and muttered, "Good to meet you."

"Maylon, say grace," Mrs. Butler ordered.

After Maylon's prayer, the family began their supper with the unmistakable uneasiness of having a stranger at their table. Mrs. Butler tried to kindle a conversation while steering away from any questions about Raquel's past or the boys' work. The dialogue was clumsy, and the sound of clanking utensils on the plates nearly drowned out the few words the family exchanged. Raquel sensed the family would have been more animated, if she were not eating with them. Mr. Butler occasionally glanced at her, but he seemed content to enjoy his wife's fried chicken for the moment.

Raquel tended to be shy, but felt obligated to say, "Thank you for supper."

The Butlers looked at each other for a second before Mrs. Butler said, "It's nothing special, but I'm glad you could eat with us tonight."

"It's a little better than the sandwich we had at noon," Chili smiled.

His smile quickly faded, as he realized that his comment was a reminder of the failed work in the field.

Mrs. Butler quickly noted, "We always keep a few chickens in the coop in the back. We usually have our chicken dinner on Sundays, but I was in the mood tonight."

She glanced at Mr. Butler, who was content to pick the last of his chicken off the bone without adding to the conversation.

"I don't know why we don't have chicken every night," Maylon added.

"Back home, we always saved the chicken dinner for Sundays, and it seemed to make the day more special," Mrs. Butler said. "You'd get tired having it every night."

"Where is home?" Raquel asked, trying to engage in the conversation.

The family did not respond for a second until Mr. Butler said, "Outside of Sayre…in the short-grass country."

"Oklahoma?" Raquel asked.

"Western Oklahoma," Mr. Butler nodded.

"Maylon told me you're in the oil business," Raquel said.

Mr. Butler grunted a laugh and said, "I guess you could say that. I'm a pumper for Sunset Oil."

"What's a pumper?" Raquel asked.

"I keep the wells pumping," Mr. Butler explained. "I make sure the gears are greased and the oil's flowing. I worked for the Deep Rock Company back home, but I got talked into coming here when they discovered the field near Taft. It was a good move. The company had this house, and the bottom fell out back home."

"But you still call it home?" Raquel asked.

"Habit, I guess," Mr. Butler smiled. "Don't guess we'll be going back anytime soon, but we still got family there."

"I thought all the Okies were in California?" Raquel asked, before remembering how much Maylon had been insulted earlier in the day.

The Butlers looked at each other for a moment, before Mr. Butler said, "Okies come from everywhere—Kansas, Arkansas, Texas—yeah and Oklahoma, but mostly they were the croppers and the folks that don't have no land of their own. I hear it's bone dry back home, and I guess they got no choice but come where there's water and crops. They're just working people…like your people, I guess, but folks around here don't have much use for 'em.

There's still plenty of people back home making it fine, but you don't hear nothing about them."

As if to change the subject, Mr. Butler asked, "How was cotton picking?"

A quiet tenseness fell over the room as both boys remained uncomfortably silent.

"Well," Mr. Butler said in a sterner tone. "I pulled some strings to get you boys some work. How did it go?"

Maylon looked at his brother and then confessed, "Not good."

"Not good?" Mr. Butler responded.

"We—we got messed up a little, and they sent us home early," Maylon explained.

"You got fired!" Mr. Butler roared. "I sent you boys there to learn to work. I picked cotton every summer since I was ten!"

"They didn't tell us exactly what to do, and we messed up," Maylon said.

Mr. Butler looked as if he would explode, when Raquel said, "They had to work with me today. I—I think I'm probably the reason."

Naomi Butler looked suspiciously at the young woman, knowing she had fabricated the story.

"What were they thinking putting you with a Mexican girl?" Mr. Butler roared.

"Eli!" Mrs. Butler scolded.

"I'm sorry," Mr. Butler stated. "I don't mean no offense to you or your people. I'm just upset. My boys need to learn the value of a dollar, and they're not going to learn it doing chores for their mom. I've got a good job, but you boys need to make it on your own."

"Times are hard," Maylon defended.

"I know times are hard," Mr. Butler replied. "All the more reason you need to grit your teeth. Nobody's goin' to give you anything in this life, son. You're wanting to get serious with your girl, Maylon, and you can't even hold a job for a day!"

"I *am* serious about Orpha," Maylon claimed.

"Looking google-eyed at some young woman won't cut it," Mr. Butler preached. "You can't expect a girl or her parents to take you seriously until you can support yourself."

"I know," Maylon replied. "You're right. I'll look for something else tomorrow."

"You gotta have determination, son," Mr. Butler reinforced. "How 'bout you, Chili? What did you think of your cotton picking?"

"Not much," Chili said bluntly. "My fingers still sting, and my back's sore."

"Back home, I'd still been picking until dark," Mr. Butler claimed.

Chili looked at his empty plate and did not respond to his father's scolding. Maylon took the opportunity to get up from the table and make a move to the front door.

"And where are you headed?" Mr. Butler asked.

"I'm going to Orpha's," Maylon said.

"It's a long walk to Taft," Mr. Butler observed.

Maylon shifted nervously, "I thought I'd borrow the car, if that's okay."

Mr. Butler fumed for a second before saying, "Put your own gas in, and don't be too late."

"Yes, sir."

"And be careful in Taft," Mr. Butler warned. "It's a tough town filled with roughnecks and worse."

"Yes, sir," Maylon repeated, as he took the opportunity to exit the house.

Mr. Butler shook his head as his older son left, "I'm going to the porch for a smoke."

Mr. Butler followed Maylon out the front door.

"I'm going to clear the table," Mrs. Butler stated, as she piled dishes on her arm, before leaving Chili and Raquel in the room alone to stare awkwardly at each other.

"Sorry to have caused trouble," Raquel finally said.

Chili laughed insincerely, "You didn't—a pretty typical evening at the Butler house. Pa thinks we're a little soft is all. It was actually a pretty short lecture by his standards. He'll usually go most of the evening talking about how things were back home and how lucky…and lazy we've gotten."

"He seems to really care about you," Raquel said. "He's probably just worried about you."

"Pa worries," Chili agreed. "But mostly he gripes."

"I was wondering," Raquel asked. "Why do they call you Chili?"

Chili chuckled, "My given name is Charles or Charlie. When Maylon was little, he'd try to say Charlie, but it come out Chili, I'm told. The name stuck."

"I think you look more like a Chili than a Charles," Raquel smiled.

"Me too," Chili said.

Mrs. Butler came in from the kitchen and said, "Chili, I need you to go check on the chickens."

"Tonight?" Chili protested.

"I had to go out there and wring the chicken myself tonight, and I want to make sure every thing's secure, so git," she ordered.

Mrs. Butler watched her son saunter lazily out the door before sitting next to Raquel.

"Do you have somewhere to stay tonight?" Mrs. Butler asked in a low whisper.

Raquel instinctively nodded her head, although she did not know where she would stay or how to get there. She had planned to find a place at one of the work camps, but it was already dark, and she imagined she would be sleeping in the open tonight. The warm afternoon would be replaced by a cool evening, but with a full stomach, Raquel knew she could manage.

"Where?" Mrs. Butler bluntly asked.

Raquel's eyes shifted nervously at the question.

"I didn't think so," Mrs. Butler said.

"How did you know?" Raquel asked.

"Call it a woman's intuition," Mrs. Butler answered. "Besides, I looked through your bag when I was washing your things. It doesn't look like you planned to go home tonight. From the looks of your back, I can't say I blame you."

Raquel looked down at her feet, embarrassed to be caught in a lie and ashamed that a woman like Mrs. Butler was able to so quickly determine the worthlessness of her life.

"You're staying with us tonight," Mrs. Butler stated. "Don't argue, because I won't take no for an answer."

"I—I," Raquel stuttered.

"No argument," Mrs. Butler interrupted firmly. "You can take the room upstairs. I'll make a cot for Chili in Maylon's room."

Raquel started to apologize for the inconvenience, but a stern stare from Mrs. Butler caused her to nod obediently.

"Now, let's get your things from the line," Mrs. Butler ordered. "I've cleaned everything and they should be dry by now."

In a few minutes, Mrs. Butler had Raquel's clothes organized in a spare drawer in the upstairs room. She showed Raquel to the washroom and gave her instructions about towels before leaving the girl alone in the warm room with a soft bed. Raquel's nervousness about staying in the strange place with people she barely knew was soon replaced by overwhelming fatigue and sleepiness. She slipped on a clean gown and settled into the fresh sheets. She heard voices a couple of times and imagined that Mr. Butler was questioning his wife about their new upstairs guest, but the voices soon muffled into unintelligible background noise and Raquel fell into a deep and peaceful sleep.

CHAPTER 6

One night turned into months of Raquel staying in the Butlers' upstairs room. Mrs. Butler told her husband the girl was doing housework and some cooking in exchange for room and board. In reality, Mrs. Butler had to teach Raquel most of the jobs, and she took care of her young guest more than Raquel earned her stay. Raquel had not lived in a house with a wood floor in years. Raquel had worked in the fields for years, and her mother always cooked their simple fare on an open fire. She was happy, however, to learn the new domestic tasks.

Mrs. Butler and her family were an oddity to Raquel in her first months there. Eli Butler constantly and harshly preached the value of hard work to his two boys, but he liked for them to rely on him for their economic security. Although Eli had the voice and demeanor to be the tyrannical dictator of the household, it was obvious to Raquel that Naomi Butler was the real boss of her husband.

Raquel spent most of her days with Naomi, whose character seemed to be a patchwork of contradictions. Naomi appeared prim and proper, which encouraged Raquel to call her Mrs. Butler, but she insisted that the girl address her as Naomi. Although more quiet and subtle than her husband, Naomi was much more stubborn than her louder spouse.

If Raquel described Naomi in one word, the word would have been "proud." Naomi kept her house in immaculate condition. Her husband's work clothes, which were often stained with grease and oil, were always spotless and pressed for the next morning's work. Naomi was especially proud of her boys. Although Naomi had been kind and hospitable, Raquel sensed she guarded against her guest getting too close to her two sons. Naomi did not have a particularly pleasant or inviting personality. She appeared cold and formal but seemed determined to display her tolerance and compassion. Raquel could not complain of her treatment in the Butler house; it had been her happiest time since her mother's death. Raquel sensed, however, that Naomi cared for her as an obligation to her own charity—the kind of compassion one would extend to an orphaned pet.

Naomi would have never spoken of the differences in their classes, but Raquel believed her light brown skin and bluish eyes made her presence in the Butler house more acceptable. Naomi was pompous about having a husband employed by an oil company instead of working in the fields. Raquel had gone into town with Naomi enough to see the older woman's pride when suggesting the young Mexican girl was a live-in housekeeper. She often talked fondly of growing up in Oklahoma, but she harbored an unspoken disdain for the migrant workers flocking to California. Naomi liked having a housemaid, which distinguished her from the farm workers and sharecroppers living in dirty tents and harvesting the fields of the San Joaquin Valley. Raquel did not mind. She had food to eat, a clean bed to sleep in, and Naomi did not beat her. For that, Raquel could easily endure a little arrogance.

CHAPTER 7

Raquel saw a change in Naomi Butler the day the telegram arrived. The normally reserved and aloof Naomi became as giddy as a schoolgirl.

"We're having company!" Naomi exclaimed. "We have so much to do!"

"Who's coming?" Raquel asked.

"Beulah Belvedere, of the Beckham County Belvederes," Naomi stated emphatically. "The telegram says she's coming for a visit in a few days. We have so much to do."

"Yes, ma'am," Raquel said.

"Beulah's my cousin, and we were best friends in grammar school," Naomi explained. "She lived at the farm down the way. She married Arnold Belvedere, and he was quite a catch. The Belvederes owned a quarter-section of grassland in Beckham County, and the general store in Sayre. Beulah's a sweet woman, but so judgmental. The Belvedere's own a store, so they're used to the best, but we'll make sure this house is spotless. I'm so excited to see folks from back home."

Raquel smiled patiently at Naomi's new found enthusiasm.

"We'll need to fix you a cot in the garage," Naomi explained. "I'll need the upstairs room for the company."

"That'll be fine," Raquel assured.

"I wish we had time to paint, but we'll just give the room a good cleaning," Naomi ordered.

For the next two days, Naomi worked feverishly to get every detail of the house in order. Raquel had become more accustomed to doing housework, and Naomi felt more comfortable giving the girl a steady stream of orders. Naomi did not know the exact arrival date for the Belvederes, but she kept the house ready anyway. Eli Butler seemed much less excited to have the Belvederes invade his home, but he did not interfere with his wife's detailed preparations.

Maylon and Chili kept busy doing odd jobs around town. They had not been able to find any permanent work, but their father had enough contacts to find them sporadic jobs. Maylon spent most of his evenings in Taft seeing his girl. Chili was home most nights, but Naomi always invented ways to keep her son and her new housemaid separated.

Raquel cleared out a corner of the garage and prepared to move any day to make room for Naomi's guest. The garage would be drafty, but it was easily cleaned and had an old wood stove in the corner that still worked. The quarters were not as cozy as the upstairs room, but Raquel knew she could make a fine place for herself in the garage.

"I'm sorry about Mom," Chili said one afternoon when he had come in from work early, and found Raquel cleaning out the garage.

"I didn't see you there," Raquel said.

"I'm sorry Mom's making you move out here," Chili restated.

"It's fine," Raquel smiled. "She's got important company coming in, and I don't mind. This cot will suit me fine."

"Important company?" Chili grinned. "Beulah Belvedere?"

"Your mother says—" Raquel replied.

"I know," Chili interrupted. "Ma goes on and on about the Belvederes but—" Chili stepped closer to Raquel and began talking in a softer, hushed voice. "I remember them from when I was a little kid. Beulah Belvedere is more self-absorbed and filled with even more self-importance than my mother."

"That's not a nice thing to say about your mother," Raquel protested.

Chili looked at her for a second before grinning, "You can't tell me you haven't noticed Ma has a streak of vanity that'd make a strutting cock blush."

"Your mother's been very good to me," Raquel answered.

"She's a good mother," Chili smiled. "A genuinely great person, but—she has a tendency to make pretty ordinary stuff seem pretty pompous."

Raquel tried to maintain an even demeanor, but Chili had made her smile by stating the very things she had noticed about Naomi Butler.

"Maybe a little," Raquel admitted with a smirk.

"You don't have to take it," Chili said.

"Take what?" Raquel asked.

"The way she treats you," Chili fumed. "Bossing you around. Taking you to town to show off that she has a helper at the house."

"I don't mind," Raquel quickly replied. "She's been good to me and—I'm getting good meals and—this place is safe. Your mother's peculiar about some things, but she cares."

"She likes you," Chili said. "Don't be afraid to stand up to Ma…she won't run you off. You're as close to a daughter as she's ever had, and she kind of likes it."

"I do stand up for myself," Raquel defended, although she was not sure she believed this statement herself.

Chili studied the girl for a moment and said, "I believe you can stand up for yourself—just don't be too surprised if Mother acts a little strange around Beulah Belvedere. She'll be bossing you around and making us all crazy trying to impress Beulah."

"Thank you," Raquel said. "But I really don't mind."

Chili looked over his shoulder and out the garage door to make sure his mother had not seen him come into the Raquel's new room before saying, "I'll see you around."

Raquel watched the tall young man walk slowly back to the house. She stepped back into the garage and continued making it a place to stay for a few nights.

After a week, the Belvederes had not shown up and the Butler house returned to its normal regiment of cleaning and domestic chores. Naomi checked the front door several times a day the first few days, but even that new habit faded when it became apparent her guests' arrival was not imminent.

On one sunny afternoon, Naomi Butler got tired of waiting and said to Raquel, "Let's walk to town and do some shopping."

Raquel had been scrubbing the linoleum floors in the kitchen and welcomed the break. Besides room and board, Naomi Butler had also bought the young woman a couple of new dresses. Raquel quickly changed and found an impatient Naomi waiting when she returned. The two women walked quickly and purposefully toward the center of town. Maricopa was a small, quaint town at the crossroads of two highways. Taft, to the east, was a bigger town with more stores, but it was also a more rowdy oil town.

Bakersfield was an even larger city, a little less than an hour's drive from Maricopa by car or a bus line that ran there. On the first day of getting the house ready for the visitors, Naomi had made Maylon drive her to Bakersfield to shop. Maricopa's business district was within walking distance of the Butler house, however, and had a grocery store, a post office, a general store, and even a dress store to meet most of Naomi Butler's needs.

Downtown Maricopa was not busy on this weekday, but there were several cars and trucks in town, mainly around the post office. A particularly battered-looking car with a similarly beat-up trunk tied to the roof was parked in front of the post office. The dusty car had steam rising from the hood, and a man looking at it, as if praying for his dilapidated vehicle.

Raquel heard Naomi whisper something about, "Okies," as they walked down the street. Like everyone else in town, Naomi tried to give the old car a wide berth. The Okies were notorious for giving the citizens a hard-luck story about needing a tank of gas, a meal, or just a handout. For everyone else, these near-vagrant people were a nuisance, but for Naomi Butler, they represented something that was an embarrassment—a bad reflection on her.

Raquel did not pay attention when Naomi Butler first slowed her walk, but she was now looking carefully at the old car with Oklahoma license plates.

"That's a Beckham County tag," Naomi whispered, although she and Raquel were walking alone and away from anyone who could have possibly heard their conversation.

The usually dusty and often rattling license plates from Oklahoma, Arkansas, Kansas, and even Texas, were a common sight in almost any town in the San Joaquin Valley. Most of the vehicles did not need such identification, because the cars and trucks were battered to a shoddy-looking state by the time they made the long trip across half the continent on Route 66. The Oklahoma license plates had county identifiers, however, and people from that state would study them, like a gypsy reading palms, to see from what part of the state the stragglers came.

Naomi crossed the street and cautiously approached the destitute-looking car trying to get a glimpse of the family. A haggard woman sat defeated on the sideboard of the car, as a man in dirty trousers looked at the open hood. Raquel nearly ran into Naomi when she stopped suddenly.

"Beulah?" Naomi called out in a voice soft enough to call no undue attention.

The woman sitting on the sideboard looked up and squinted into the sun.

"Come on, Raquel," Naomi ordered, as she began walking toward the woman.

The pathetic woman looked like a trapped animal as Naomi approached. It was hard for Raquel to believe the woman could be anywhere close to Naomi's age, but as the woman tried to straighten her tattered and patched dress, Raquel could deduce it was the family Naomi had been waiting for the past weeks.

"Hello, Naomi," the woman greeted in a proper and reserved tone of voice, as she stood upright and pulled her shoulders back to pitch her head high.

"What are you doing here, Beulah?" Naomi asked, as she now walked quicker.

"We ran into some trouble," Beulah understated.

Naomi stopped to look at the man leaning over the steaming hood. A thin man with gaunt features rose up with a puzzled and hopeless look on his face.

"Arnold?" Naomi asked rhetorically.

"Hello, Naomi," Arnold Belvedere replied.

Naomi looked at the couple for an awkward second before saying in a tearful voice, "Come here."

Naomi stepped hurriedly to the automobile and hugged Beulah tightly, as Raquel watched several steps away.

"I've been expecting you for a week," Naomi cried.

"It was a hard trip," Beulah explained.

Beulah Belvedere had been embarrassed to be found slouching on the sideboard of a broken-down car, but she quickly regained her composure and demonstrated the type of smugness Chili had predicted.

"Looks like it," Naomi observed.

"The trip across the desert was just brutal," Beulah said. "I've got these old traveling clothes on, because everything else is filled with dust."

"We'll get everything clean when we get you home," Naomi smiled. "Raquel, grab a bag, and let's get these good people to the house."

Raquel looked at the old car piled high with bags and wondered where she could start.

"This is my housemaid, Raquel," Naomi said. "She's quite handy and will get your things cleaned up in no time."

Beulah Belvedere looked suspiciously at the young woman, but she reached into the back of the car and handed Raquel a tattered suitcase.

"Run on," Naomi instructed Raquel. "We'll be to the house directly. Arnold, you don't know a wrench from a screwdriver. Come on up to the house, and I'll have Eli come take a look after he gets home from work."

Arnold Belvedere did not argue and nodded, "I'd be obliged."

As Raquel wrestled two suitcases, Naomi and her two guests exchanged small talk. Beulah made several excuses about their broken down car and appearance, as Mr. Belvedere listened silently, only occasionally smiling and nodding his confirmation. By the time the Butler house was in view, the shiny Ford was parked in front, indicating Eli and the boys were home. When Chili saw the group approaching, and Raquel carrying two bags, he trotted out to help, while glaring at his mother.

"Is that your oldest?" Beulah asked.

"No," Naomi smiled. "This is Chili…you know, Charles."

"Oh my," Beulah replied. "The baby—and he's near grown."

"He's taller than his brother, Maylon," Naomi noted. "The boys have been such a blessing around the house."

As Chili approached, Naomi called, "Come here, Chili, and meet my friend Beulah."

"Hello," Chili brusquely replied, as he walked by the two women. "I need to help Raquel."

Chili trotted to Raquel who was trailing by nearly twenty feet.

"Such a handsome boy," Beulah stated. "The girl—they aren't involved, are they?"

"Oh no," Naomi replied. "She's just my live-in maid."

"You are blessed," Beulah said, as she looked back at Chili taking the bags from Raquel.

Naomi tried to motion Chili to put the bags down, but he was determined to help.

"Let's get you inside," Naomi suggested. "I'll have Eli and the boys to get your car running."

The two women went inside the house. Eli, Maylon, and Arnold Belvedere quickly left to see if the old car could be easily repaired. Raquel hurriedly retrieved her few things from the upstairs bedroom and retreated to the garage cot she had prepared the week before. Naomi informed Raquel supper would be served at seven that evening, as if Raquel would be preparing the entire meal. Raquel knew better. Naomi was an excellent and particular cook. She liked giving the impression that she could afford a live-in maid, but she would never trust Raquel to be completely responsible for the meal. Raquel did not mind. She was glad to get away from the competitive chatter between the two women and spend a few moments in the peaceful corner of the garage.

"I'm sorry," Chili whispered, which momentarily startled Raquel.

"I didn't hear you come in," Raquel said. "Why are you sorry?"

"My mother," Chili informed. "I can't believe they loaded you down with those bags without lifting a finger to help."

"I don't mind," Raquel assured. "Your mother's been very kind to me. I'm grateful to do her errands to help pay my way."

"Old windbag," Chili fumed.

"Your mother?" Raquel asked.

Chili was surprised by the question, but he smiled, "That'd be a good description for her too. I'm talking about Beulah Belvedere. I can barely remember her from when I was a kid, but I recall even then, I thought she was a blowhard."

"Your mother seems very happy to see her friend," Raquel said.

"Yeah," Chili said. "Two peas in a pod."

Chili did not say anything for a moment, before saying, "Would you like to—I was thinking that maybe one night we could slip off to Taft for an evening. They have a picture show there and—it might be fun."

"Slip off?" Raquel asked with a sly grin.

Chili blushed and said, "I didn't mean slip off—I just thought it might be more relaxing if Ma didn't worry about where we had gotten to."

Raquel smiled at the bashful Chili and said, "I guess if we both happened to be in Taft on the same night and did go see a show, it wouldn't be slipping off, and—I don't guess it would hurt much if your mother didn't know—if we're not slipping off."

"That's what I meant," Chili assured.

"I'll see you at supper, Chili," Raquel said.

"Yeah," he replied.

As Chili left, Raquel watched him. He looked back at her a couple of times while leaving the garage, but he kept walking. Chili seemed content that his invitation had not been turned down flat, and he did not want to jeopardize that accomplishment by saying anything further. Chili walked down the street, with a little bounce in his step, to help Maylon and his father with the Belvederes' car. Raquel did not know what to make of Chili, but she reclined back in her cot for a few moments and pondered the possibilities.

CHAPTER 8

Naomi cooked her Sunday-best meal on the Thursday evening when her visiting friends, the Belvederes, arrived. Although she had boasted to Beulah that she could afford a live-in cook, Naomi was in charge in her kitchen, and Raquel was only an assistant to the process. Beulah Belvedere was not easily relegated to a subordinate in the kitchen and offered ample advice on how to season the feast.

"Where did you find the girl?" Beulah bluntly asked Naomi, while Raquel worked quietly rolling pie crust.

"Raquel?" Naomi responded. "She was working in the fields with the boys."

Naomi immediately regretted this revelation, as Beulah raised her eyebrow in interest.

"Eli likes to send the boys out to work with the harvesters," Naomi explained. "He thinks it does them some good to get their hands dirty. Anyway, they met Raquel there, and I had plenty of work for her to do here."

"What is she?" Beulah inquired, while carefully examining the young woman as if Raquel was not there.

"What?" a confused Naomi asked.

In a matter of fact tone, Beulah replied, "She doesn't look Mexican, but she doesn't look Filipino either. She's light skinned, but not white—maybe Indian or a half-breed?"

Naomi Butler could be pompous at times, but Raquel could see her employer's embarrassment at the calloused question.

"She's Mexican," Naomi stammered. "If you're so interested, why don't you ask her?"

"Can she speak that much English?" Beulah whispered to Naomi.

"I speak English," Raquel replied in a shaky tone of voice, "and some Spanish."

"Oh,'" the condescending Beulah shrugged.

"I was born in California," Raquel confirmed, "and my mother was born here as well. My grandmother, God rest her soul, was also born here, but she did speak Spanish and had to learn English."

Beulah seemed oblivious to Raquel's pointed answer and replied, "So, do you speak Mexican?"

"Spanish," Raquel nodded.

Naomi interrupted the inquisition to say, "Raquel, would you be a dear and go find the men? I'll put your pies in the oven for you. By the time they get back and cleaned up, it will be time for supper."

Raquel glared at Beulah Belvedere, but in a calm tone said, "Yes, ma'am."

Raquel folded her apron neatly and walked out the front door without making eye contact with Mrs. Belvedere.

After Raquel walked out the door, Beulah said, "She has a little bit of an attitude."

"Not generally," Naomi stated.

"You have to be careful with these people," Beulah warned. "It doesn't take much for them to forget their place."

"Beulah!" Naomi scolded.

"You saw how she spoke to me," Beulah defended. "These people are taking jobs away from hardworking white people, and don't think she won't rob you blind if you don't watch out."

"Raquel's not like that," Naomi stated. "She's had a hard life I think, but she's a good worker. Besides, I've left change around the house several times, and I've never missed a nickel."

"You're too trusting," Beulah said. "I'm just trying to warn you about how these people are. Aren't you worried about your boys?"

"What?" Naomi gasped.

Beulah looked at Naomi as if shocked at her naivety and said, "You have this pretty young girl in your home and around your two boys. Don't you worry that something—might happen? It wouldn't be a first for Eli's family."

"Raquel works and that's it," Naomi assured. "Maylon's already engaged, and Chili—well, Chili's not found the right girl yet."

Beulah shook her head and said, "Your boys aren't the concern, Naomi. This girl would see either one of them as a step up in life, and don't think she hasn't thought about it. I'm just saying I'd be very careful and keep an eye out."

"You don't have to worry about my boys," Naomi huffed. "I keep a close eye on them."

CHAPTER 9

Raquel was glad to be out of the house and away from Beulah Belvedere for a few minutes. She did not know how much time the Belvederes planned to spend at the Butlers' house, but she believed it would be too long. As she approached the small business district in Maricopa, Raquel saw Maylon, Chili, and Mr. Belvedere watching Eli Butler leaning over the dusty car.

Eli Butler slowly rose up from under the hood grunting, "Give it a crank."

Arnold Belvedere quickly followed the instructions and climbed into the automobile. The old car made a whining, clanking sound, but the car did not start.

"Give me a second," Eli Butler instructed, as he again stuck his head under the hood. "Maylon, hand me that half-inch wrench."

Mr. Butler twisted something and then used the wrench as a hammer to gently tap on one of the engine parts.

"Try it again," Mr. Butler said.

Arnold turned the starter and the car whined again until it coughed to life. A few uneven screeches from the engine, and the car idled roughly.

"Your fuel pump's about shot," Eli Butler explained.

"Will it run?" Arnold Belvedere asked.

"Maybe," Eli replied. "For a while. Give it a good tap if it don't start, and that might get the fuel flowing."

"Thanks," Mr. Belvedere said.

"Supper's about ready," Raquel interrupted. "Mrs. Butler said to come to the house and get cleaned up."

Mr. Butler had rarely talked to Raquel, since he worked late many evenings, but he smiled and said, "I don't want to keep Mrs. Butler waiting. Thanks, Raquel."

"I think if a couple of ya' could ride on the sideboard, we can get everyone home," Mr. Belvedere offered. "The back seat's pretty full up."

"I'd just as soon walk," Chili offered. "It ain't that far."

"I can walk too," Maylon said.

"I don't mind walking back," Raquel replied. "I could use the exercise."

Maylon looked at his brother for a second and grinned, "I'll ride on up then."

The three men climbed into the clattering car. Mr. Belvedere ground the gears, and the vehicle slowly moved down the street and toward the Butler home.

"Thought you might want a break from Beulah Belvedere," Chili smiled.

"Thanks," Raquel said. "I spent enough time with Mrs. Belvedere this afternoon. That old garage looks inviting."

"We better head to the house," Chili suggested. "Unfortunately, I don't think they'll start without us."

When Chili and Raquel walked into the house, the rest of the group had already gathered at the table.

"There you are," Naomi said, as she watched Raquel following Chili. "We're about to eat."

Beulah Belvedere gave Naomi a disapproving look, but she refrained from saying anything.

"What do you need me to do?" Raquel asked.

Naomi looked at Beulah and said, "Nothing dear. I've got everything on the table. Sit down and eat."

Raquel was surprised at the invitation and said in a soft whisper to Naomi, "I had planned to eat in the garage. I don't want to be an interruption."

"Nonsense," Naomi replied. "I've got plenty of room, and the garage is no place to eat a meal like this."

Raquel reluctantly agreed and took a seat next to Maylon and across the table from Chili. After the blessing, the food was passed around and glowing compliments were made about the quantity and quality of the meal.

It did not take long for the conversation to move to friends and family back home, when Naomi asked, "How's old Mrs. Goodnight doing?"

Beulah looked at her husband to encourage him to speak and Arnold sighed, "Mrs. Goodnight passed away last winter."

"Oh my," Naomi said. "I hadn't heard. Was it sudden?"

"She had been ill," Arnold Belvedere replied.

"What else have I missed out on?" Naomi asked.

"Things—things are always changing," Arnold said.

"Not for the better," Beulah added. "You wouldn't recognize the old places, Naomi. What the bankers haven't taken, the drought has. Mrs. Goodnight's farm went to auction, and there weren't but three buyers."

"At least there were some buyers," Naomi reasoned.

"Only three!" Beulah reiterated. "The two bankers and—that rascal cousin of Eli's, Beau Lobaugh."

"Beau's back in Beckham County?" Eli asked. "Thought he was still in the army—an officer or something."

"Or something is right," Beulah frowned.

"Who's Beau Lobaugh?" Maylon asked.

Beulah did not give Naomi a chance to answer as she squawked, "Beau Lobaugh is the biggest rogue and scalawag to ever come out of Kiowa County."

"He's not that bad," Naomi defended. "He's just always been a little high strung."

"High strung and a relative of yours?" Chili teased.

"Beau's your father's cousin," Naomi explained. "He's a few years younger. He was an adventuresome child, not a scalawag."

"Your mother's being too discrete," Beulah redirected. "Beau Lobaugh came back from the war and didn't give the devil about what any decent people thought."

"He came back a hero," Eli stated factually. "That's more than I can say for your side of the family."

"He was in the war in Europe?" a now-interested Maylon asked.

Beulah nodded, "He was a captain or colonel or some such rank. Married that Kiowa squaw woman from over near Saddle Mountain—disgraced his family."

"Beulah!" Naomi interrupted. "That will be quite enough."

"It's no secret," Beulah stated. "It was a public scandal."

"The boy sowed some wild oats," Eli admitted. "But we all grow up some."

"Ancient history that doesn't need to be relived," Naomi added.

"Well," Beulah continued. "He's moved to Beckham County and seems to be the only person besides the banks with money."

"How'd he make his money?" Chili asked.

Beulah studied the disapproving Naomi to gauge how much family history she could reveal before she said, "No one rightly knows, but I wouldn't be surprised if there was some mischief involved. He came back from the army and did God knows what, before buying the place south of Sayre. I'll have to admit he's more than a fair farmer. He knows how to find land with water and has drilled wells to irrigate some of his land."

"Beau was always high-spirited, but no one ever questioned his smarts," Eli said. "I heard he fixed up the old farm near Hobart and made a place out of it before his wife died."

Beulah looked like she would have liked to have said more, but instead said, "I can't say he isn't shrewd, but I wouldn't have called that squaw woman his wife."

Eli Butler looked like he might explode at Beulah's continued insults, but instead he muttered something under his breath, while Naomi implored him with a stern look to not say more.

"That's enough about the family's skeletons," Naomi said. "What else is happening? We only get the sketchiest information from people passing through."

"The Ropers lost their place, and the Buchanan's farm was auctioned too," Arnold Belvedere replied, before his wife had a chance to say more.

"The Buchanans don't have the place by the river any longer?" Naomi clarified.

Beulah shook her head, "It's been tough on a lot of folks. My nephew Frankie tried to buy it. Frankie's the handsomest and most polite young man you've ever seen. He's turned every young woman's head in the county."

"Isn't he one of those bankers you were complaining about?" Eli asked.

Beulah scowled at Eli and stated, "He's one of the good ones."

Naomi looked to her boys and added, "Beulah didn't bother telling that Frank's the son of my cousin on my mother's side."

"Slipped my mind," Beulah said with a frown. "He is from your mother's side and they are respectable. I'll vouch for that, and Frankie would've been a fine neighbor."

"He didn't buy it?" Naomi asked.

Beulah shook her head and replied, "That Beau Lobaugh bought the whole section of land next to your old home place. He's doing that tractor farming and claimin' every good piece of land in that part of the county."

"Beau's a tractor farmer," Naomi gasped.

"Big farmers are about all that's left," lamented Beulah. "If things don't change, every decent farmer left will be workin' for the likes of Beau Lobaugh."

Arnold Belvedere looked at Eli and added, "You picked a good time to get out, Eli. Things are hard back home."

"We see the folks coming through," Eli replied.

"It's not just the sharecroppers and riffraff leaving now," Beulah authoritatively informed. "Good people are getting caught up in this depression. The sharecroppers didn't have nothing to begin with, so it wasn't anything for them to pick up and move on. Most of them are malcontents and socialists anyway."

"That's enough, Beulah," Arnold Belvedere interrupted. "These folks don't want to hear about our troubles."

"Your troubles?" Eli Butler asked. "You still have the store don't you, Arnold?"

Arnold Belvedere did not reply immediately. If the Butlers had bothered to ask Raquel, she could have told them. She had seen all the signs before. The broken-down vehicle that should not have been taken across the desert, the torn and ragged hands that were not used to hard work, and the look of desperation that wrinkled the forehead in that unmistakable way. Raquel had noticed immediately, but Naomi Butler did not want to see. She wanted to spend time with her old rival and friend—to pretend things were like they had been. Raquel had observed this from the entire Butler family. They did not want to deal with hard realities and the bitter economics of the times.

"We lost the store," Arnold Belvedere finally confessed. "The land too—all of it."

"All of it," Naomi gasped.

The proud and pretentious Beulah Belvedere listened to her husband's confession in silence. She had been living the lie for the past few hours, and it had somehow been a tonic of temporary relief. Being caught up in the old rivalries with Naomi had made her forget her brutal realities for a few hours, but that temporary distraction was now over.

"We lost everything," Arnold clarified.

"Arnold was always too kind-hearted in giving credit," Beulah contended. "When the sharecroppers couldn't pay, they took the store down with it."

"It wasn't anyone's fault," Arnold said. "It's just bad times. We had mortgaged the land to try to make it until things turned up, but they never did."

The Butlers did not know how to respond, so Arnold Belvedere reluctantly said, "We're not here on vacation like Beulah might have indicated in her message. We're looking for work. We've been working the fields for gas money the last week trying to get here. Our son's already over at a place close to Santa Maria, but I thought—"

"What is it, Arnold?" Eli coaxed.

"I thought that you've done so well in these oil fields that maybe you'd know of some work I could do," Arnold said. "I just need to get a new start."

Eli Butler's pained expression could have answered the question, but he said, "Do you have any experience or mechanical skills?"

"I think you know the answer to that, Eli," Arnold said.

"Thing is," Eli continued, "times are tough in the oil field too. Seems like there's two men for every job and plenty of young bucks willing to cut corners and take chances out there. I've held on because I'm a good mechanic, but—the company's cut back my hours."

"What!" Naomi gasped.

"That's why I'm home early," Eli explained. "Don't worry; they're not laying me off or anything. There's just not enough work to go around. We'll be tightening our belts a little too."

"While you're tightening your belts, good people like us are hurting!" Beulah Belvedere exploded.

"Beulah, that'll be enough," Arnold Belvedere admonished.

"It's not enough!" Beulah shouted. "I'm living out of a beat-up old car while they have a live-in maid! Fire this Mexican girl and I'll be your maid! I know that you would love seeing me clean your dishes and mop your floors!"

An awkward silence followed Beulah's outburst, until Naomi said, "I'm so sorry, Beulah. I'm—I probably deserve that. You're welcome to stay as long as you need to as my guest. I've—I've been putting on a little bit of a show. Raquel's just living here and helping me with some chores for room and board. We don't have much, but what I have is yours."

"We won't be a burden," Arnold Belvedere assured. "We really did just want to see some old friends."

"You'd never be a burden," Naomi assured.

After a hesitation, Beulah said in a contrite tone, "I'm sorry, Naomi—for my outburst. I know you're my good friend, and it was—great medicine for me to talk about old times. It's been difficult for us."

"Of course it has," Naomi consoled. "Boys, get the Belvederes' things upstairs. They had a long, hard day, and things will be much better with some rest. You get a good night's sleep, Beulah, and things will look better in the morning."

"Thank you," Beulah replied.

The earlier energy of talking about old times and places evaporated with the stark realities of the Belvederes' situation. Naomi worked feverishly to get the Belvederes settled into the comfortable bed upstairs. A tired Raquel slipped out to her cot in the garage, wondering how long she could expect to enjoy the comfort and safety of the Butler home.

CHAPTER 10

The garage had a pungent, musty odor that was only slightly diminished by the kerosene lamp sitting on a crate by the cot in the back corner. Raquel did not mind the accommodations. The cot was firm and fresh. Raquel slipped on her night gown and prepared to nestle under the cotton sheet and wool blanket. Autumn in the San Joaquin Valley meant warm, usually comfortable days, but chilly nights. Raquel said her evening prayer when a creaking sound startled her from the dark corner at the other end of the garage.

"Are you still up?" Naomi Butler asked from the darkness.

"Yes, ma'am," Raquel replied, as she sat on the edge of the cot.

Naomi walked closer and surveyed the sparse décor, before saying, "Looks like you've made yourself at home."

"Yes, ma'am."

Naomi patted the end of the cot, before taking a seat next to Raquel.

"I wanted to apologize," Naomi stated.

Raquel shook her head instinctively, "There's no need. I'll be fine out here. The cot's comfortable, and the blanket will be warm."

"That's not what I mean," Naomi said.

Raquel listened silently, as Naomi continued, "I'm sorry about Beulah—she said some things and—it made me realize I may have said or acted in a way that's—let's just say less than hospitable."

"I can't complain," Raquel assured.

Naomi looked at the young woman a second before saying, "No, you wouldn't complain. I just wanted you to know that I've talked to Beulah and asked her to be more—sensitive."

"She had a hard day," Raquel said.

"Yes," Naomi agreed. "I think she's had a hard time of it. I—I don't think I made things much better for her. It's easier to judge people you don't know and assume they've not made good decisions, or they're lazier than should be, but to think that the Belvederes could fall so low—times are hard."

"Yes, ma'am," Raquel agreed.

"I didn't want you to take things too personal," Naomi said. "I wanted you to know that no matter what, you're welcome here."

Raquel nodded, "Thank you."

Naomi looked at the young woman as she rose from the cot and asked, "Do you have any family, dear?"

"What do you mean?" Raquel asked, nervously.

"You had to have come from somewhere," Naomi reasoned. "I know you told me that your mother has passed, but do you have anywhere to go—I mean besides your old home?"

"My mother had a brother that lived close to Los Angeles, I think," Raquel said. "But I've never met him."

"Do you have an address or anything?" Naomi asked. "Someone might be worried about you."

Raquel looked sadly at the older woman, whose features looked almost menacing in the soft glow of the kerosene lamp and said, "My mother didn't get along with her family. I have no one—no one that would want to see me."

"I see," Naomi whispered. "You're welcomed here."

"Yes, ma'am," Raquel whispered back.

Naomi would have liked to have said something more encouraging, but the day had left her tired, as she patted Raquel's shoulder and left her to her small corner of the garage. Raquel would have cried two years earlier, but now she was grateful for a place to sleep for the night. She wondered when she would be on her own in one of the squatters' camps, or on the streets, but she hoped that she could stay with the Butlers at least through the winter.

As Raquel pulled down the wool blanket to her cot, she heard a faint knock in the otherwise quiet garage.

"Who's there?" she asked.

"It's me," answered Chili.

Raquel quickly grabbed the blanket to cover herself before saying, "What do you want?"

Chili walked into the soft light and said, "I saw Ma come out here. Is everything all right?"

"Yes."

Chili stepped closer before thinking his presence might be making the girl uncomfortable.

"I just wanted to make sure you were okay," Chili said.

"I'm fine."

"My mother's a good person," Chili explained. "It's just—she's peculiar about her ways sometimes."

"She assured me that I could stay," Raquel informed.

"Oh," Chili said. "That's—that's good. I wasn't really worried about that. I was more worried that you might leave."

"No," Raquel said, shaking her head. "I'm fine, and I like it here."

"Even with Beulah Belvedere in the house?" Chili quizzed.

"She doesn't bother me," Raquel replied. "She can't make me feel worse about myself."

Chili studied Raquel for a second and said, "I'll leave you be—I was just worried. I'm glad you're staying."

Chili nodded politely and turned to walk toward the door when Raquel said, "Thanks Chili. Thanks for checking on me."

Chili stopped and smiled shyly, "It was nothing."

He took a couple of steps toward the door before stopping to say, "Besides, I still owe you a picture show."

"Yes," Raquel smiled. "I look forward to it."

Chili lingered for a second, as if he would say more, before leaving Raquel alone in the empty garage. Raquel thought about differences between the Butler family and her heartless stepfather. The Butler family had their oddities, but they cared. Raquel drifted to sleep in the cool evening wondering if she would ever learn to care again.

CHAPTER 11

Raquel spent the next two weeks in the garage. She quickly adapted to her more humble accommodations, but she had not adjusted as well to Beulah Belvedere's biting tongue. Beulah continually made sharp comments about the people she saw as causing her hardships, including the Mexican field workers. Naomi was a gracious host to her friend, but Raquel sensed that even her hospitality was being tested. The garage was not as comfortable as the house, but it was a welcomed hideaway from Beulah Belvedere.

Eli Butler still had his job as a pumper in the oil fields near Taft, but had been cut to half-days. He spent his afternoons looking for odd jobs and helping his two sons find occasional work. Thanksgiving was a week away, when Beulah Belvedere announced they would be leaving. The Belvederes heard about work near Santa Maria and decided to try the fruit harvest in that area. Naomi Butler said all the typical, gracious things a host would say about a friend departing, but everyone, including Naomi, was grateful to have Beulah Belvedere away, at least for a while.

Naomi fixed sandwiches for Belvederes' trip. They left mid-morning to drive over the mountains toward the coast. Raquel had made the trip many times and suspected that if she had not found a place with the Butlers, she too would probably be in the citrus groves picking fruit. Naomi cleaned the upstairs room and instructed Raquel to move back into the house. Raquel assured her that the garage cot would be fine, but Naomi insisted. Raquel had forgotten how soft the upstairs bed was and how much warmer the house could be. As Raquel lay in the bed her first night, she unexplainably felt a little sorry for the disagreeable Mrs. Belvedere. Raquel had been to the work camps before. The government camps for white workers were better than the squatters' camps where many Mexican families found themselves segregated from prosperity, but the Belvederes would most likely be living in a drafty tent and crowded with a multitude of others clinging to frayed remnants of hope. Naomi did not understand the hardships of the depression, and Raquel believed Mrs. Belvedere would soon learn the realities the hard way.

Thanksgiving was an unexpected blessing to Raquel. In the past, Thanksgiving Day had meant an unpaid day from the fields and possibly a charitable meal from someone eager to help those less fortunate. At the Butler home, Raquel learned Thanksgiving was special. Naomi decorated the front room, and the boys told stories of family memories. Raquel helped Naomi cook a feast that made her other delicious meals seem like snacks. The holiday featured plenty of food, lots of good talk, and a warm house to spend the holidays in. With the Belvederes gone, the family was in an even more festive state of mind.

This Thanksgiving was also the first time for Raquel to meet Maylon's fiancé, Orpha Kelly. Orpha was a loud and lively girl that contrasted with the calmer Maylon's serious personality. She had wavy auburn hair and a freckled, pale complexion. She was slightly shorter and shapelier than Raquel, and had a personality that made her immediately likable. Her father was a roustabout in the oil fields of Taft. Eli knew of the family, but did not seem to know much about them. From Orpha's bubbly and energetic personality, Raquel deduced that her family was less inhibited and less affluent than the Butlers. Orpha was about as down-to-earth as Beulah Belvedere had been pretentious. Maylon's girl seemed genuinely amazed at the size and finery of the Butler house, which caused Raquel to believe she was used to much less.

On the Saturday after Thanksgiving, Maylon wanted to go to Taft to see Orpha. With the days getting shorter, Naomi insisted Maylon take Chili along. Naomi claimed it would be safer if the two of them were together at night, but Raquel suspected that Naomi did not like the idea of Maylon being unsupervised and alone with the spirited Orpha. Chili did not miss the opportunity and suggested that Raquel ride with them, as if it were Naomi's idea. Naomi hesitated at first, but she always found it hard to disagree with her younger son.

The Ford automobile left the small town of Maricopa and headed north for the short drive to Taft. Raquel sat in the back and enjoyed the banter of the two brothers from the front seat. The car sped down the smooth paved road, as Raquel looked at the stark brown landscape passing by them. Maricopa was at the very edge of the San Joaquin Valley's fertile farmland. The road toward Taft started up the Temblor Range, which was a line of low mountains and hill country separating the San Joaquin Valley from California's coastal plain. The countryside between Maricopa and Taft was desert scrub brush and would have had no value or inhabitants except for the huge oil field under the desolate land.

The larger town of Taft had more energy than the sleepy Maricopa—a combination of prosperity and vice. Oil derricks littered the hillside around the town, while orange and blue flames danced in the sky from the surplus gas being burned from the field. In town, flashing neon signs for lunch counters, pool halls, and one-room apartments contrasted with carefully painted signs for various oil companies headquartered in the town. The stench of petroleum and rotten eggs permeated the town, depending on the direction of the wind. The locals said it was the smell of money, because the entire town's economy depended on pumping the black crude from the vast deposits below ground.

Maylon turned onto a pothole-filled gravel street a few blocks from the center of town and pulled in front of a poorly painted shotgun house at the end of the street. Orpha bounced out of the shabby house before the car came to a complete stop. Chili vacated his spot in the front seat for Orpha and joined Raquel in the back seat.

"How's everybody?" Orpha cheerfully greeted, before leaning over to give Maylon a kiss on the cheek.

"Ready to see the town," Maylon smiled.

"This town?" Orpha replied with a raised eyebrow. "There's not much to see."

"There is compared to Maricopa," Chili said.

"Maybe," Orpha admitted. "Most people think Taft's a good place to be from. All the oil execs live over in Bakersfield anyway. Maybe we'll be there someday, Maylon."

"Maybe," Maylon grinned.

"How're you doing, Rachel?" Orpha asked.

"Raquel," corrected Raquel.

"I'm so sorry," Orpha apologized.

"It's okay," Raquel said. "I'm doing fine."

"Good," Orpha smiled before asking Maylon. "What's the plan?"

"Thought we'd catch a movie and then maybe a burger," Maylon replied.

"That new Charlie Chaplin movie has a matinee," Orpha said. "We can make it if you step on it."

"That won't be a problem," Chili chimed from the back seat. "The one thing my brother can do is drive fast."

Maylon did not reply, but proved his brother right by flooring the accelerator and scattering rocks from the gravel road. The sudden speed and quick turn caused Raquel to slide into Chili awkwardly.

"Hey, you two," Orpha teased. "I'm the one engaged!"

Chili blushed and Raquel moved back to her side of the seat. In a few moments, Maylon found parking close to the Fox Theater in the downtown area of Taft. The theater was half-full for the afternoon matinee, with a combination of fidgety kids and tired adults looking for a couple of hours of escape from the dreariness of life. Raquel had only seen two other motion pictures, and this was her first comedy. Charlie Chaplin's antics as a bored production worker caused her to laugh so hard that she snorted loud enough for Chili to hear. Maylon and Orpha did not seem to notice her laughter or the movie, as they sat in the corner of the back row in a wrestling embrace.

By the time the movie ended, it was nearly dark. Orpha suggested a diner next to a building advertising one-room apartments. As they sat at the counter, Raquel watched the fat man sitting behind the cash register study her carefully. The others in the group did not notice, but Raquel had seen the look before. The man was trying to determine if she were Mexican or not. Her dark hair, brown skin, and quiet demeanor were a clear invitation to leave, but since she was with the others, the man did not bother her.

The four walked down the street looking in shop windows, while Orpha laid out her dreams for the fine house she would have someday. Raquel was content to listen to the talkative Orpha, and to have Chili walk by her side.

As the group passed a darkened door of a pool hall, Raquel heard an accented voice say, "If it ain't the 'la hija de una puta' walking the streets."

Raquel did not respond, but she recognized the voice of Carlos, who walked in front of her blocking the way.

"Leave her alone," Chili demanded.

"If it ain't the dopey Okie," Carlos leered in a curt accent. "Don't think that I don't remember you. You and me got unfinished business."

"Look," Maylon interjected. "We didn't come for trouble."

"Then walk away," Carlos challenged. "I've got some business with this one, though."

Carlos reached to grab Raquel by the arm, but Chili stopped him.

"You don't want to do this here," Orpha interrupted.

"Huh?" Carlos sneered.

"Look around," Orpha instructed. "There's got to be a hundred roughnecks within shouting distance that are drunk enough to find entertainment in beating on a wetback like you."

Carlos's nostrils flared at the insult, but looking around, he knew the girl was right.

"You better watch your woman's mouth," Carlos threatened, before retreating into the safety and darkness of the pool hall.

"Let's get out of here," Maylon suggested.

The group followed him and hurried back to the car.

Once inside the car, Orpha asked, "What did he call you?"

Raquel hesitated before saying, "It wasn't nice."

"I could tell that!" Orpha said.

Raquel thought for a moment and then said, "It's about my mother. He called my mother…something bad."

"Oh," Orpha replied. "How'd he know your mother?"

"He didn't," Raquel said. "It's…It's just my mother worked in a house and things happened."

"We better start thinking about getting home," Chili interrupted. "Ma will have the sheriff out if we're too late."

"You're right," Maylon agreed, as he put the car in gear and headed toward Orpha's house.

In a few minutes, Maylon pulled up in front of the dark house and got out to walk Orpha to the door.

Orpha leaned into the back seat and said to Raquel, "It was good to see you again. Maybe you can come to town sometime and we can do something. I work at the drugstore during the week. It don't pay much, but I get makeup samples."

"Thank you," Raquel replied.

Orpha looked at Chili and then back to Raquel before taking Maylon's arm.

"She didn't mean nothing," Chili said from the back seat of the car.

"What?" Raquel said.

"About your mother," Chili clarified. "She didn't mean anything by asking about your mother."

"Oh, I know," Raquel replied.

"Orpha's just…talkative," Chili explained.

"I like her," Raquel said. "She's always got something clever to say, and she's down-to-earth."

Chili leaned across Raquel to look out the rear window and said, "Looks like Maylon's liking her a lot, too."

Raquel looked out the window to see Maylon and Orpha embracing in the dark corner of the porch.

Chili leaned back and said, "We may be here awhile."

Raquel did not reply, as they sat nervously in the back seat.

"They're getting married in February," Chili explained.

"So soon," Raquel said.

Chili looked out the window again and grinned, "Maybe not soon enough."

"I just didn't know Maylon was getting married so soon," Raquel blushed.

"Pa got him a job as a roughneck starting next week," Chili said. "Maylon turned twenty-three last month. He'll look for an apartment here in Taft, I suspect."

"Does your mother know?"

Chili smiled, "About his engagement, yes. About a wedding after the first of the year, yes." Chili looked out the window again and added, "About Maylon making out on the front porch of Orpha's house, no."

"What about you?" Raquel asked.

"What about me?" Chili said, as he looked at Raquel.

Raquel shifted nervously in her seat and asked, "You're what—twenty?"

Chili shook his head, "No, I'm twenty-two—I just look younger. Maylon's actually adopted, so we're only eight months apart."

"I didn't know that," Raquel blushed.

Chili shrugged, "Don't matter. He's my big brother and always will be."

"What kind of work do you want to do?" Raquel asked. "I know you do odd jobs, but why aren't you out trying to make your way?"

"You sound like my mother," Chili frowned. "I don't know. I guess I haven't figured things out yet. I thought about going to Los Angeles, but I don't know. I know I don't want to get stuck in these oil fields."

"Looks like honest work," Raquel said. "Your father's done well."

Chili nodded his head and said, "Dad's done well, but if you'll look at these oil field worker's hands, you'll see a lot of digits missing."

Raquel looked confused, so Chili added, "Fingers missing."

"Oh," nodded Raquel. "You still need to find something you want to do."

Chili smiled and said, "I haven't figured that out yet."

"Maybe you should start," Raquel suggested.

"Maybe so," Chili smiled. "But how about you?"

"What do you mean?" Raquel replied.

"You're a girl of tremendous mystery."

"How?"

"You show up in the fields," Chili said. "You have this Carlos guy that seems to have a special interest in you. You've been at our house for months, and I don't really know anything about you. You've never once left to see home or family."

"I'm busy," Raquel said, shifting nervously in her seat.

Chili watched her for a second and said, "I know your mother died. I know you have a strained relationship with your father."

"Stepfather," Raquel frowned and quickly corrected.

"I didn't know," Chili said.

"I really don't want to talk about it," Raquel said. "I won't go back."

"Okay."

Raquel looked out the window at the couple still on the porch and asked, "Do you think they'll be happy?"

Chili shrugged, "I guess. Orpha's fun-loving enough to put up with a prude like Maylon."

"I think Maylon's nice," Raquel said.

"Maylon's great," Chili agreed. "But he's—he's not that personable. He's the oldest. Ma and Pa have always expected more out of him."

Raquel had observed a quiet seriousness to Maylon and had also noticed the contrast between his personality and Orpha's.

"I'm glad you're staying with us," Chili said.

"I'm glad too," Raquel smiled.

"It's been good for Ma," Chili clarified.

"She doesn't need my help," Raquel confessed.

"It's been good for Ma to have a girl around," Chili said. "I know Ma's pretty high and mighty acting, but she likes having you around."

"Your mother's been very kind to me."

"I like having you around, too," Chili clumsily stated.

Raquel did not know how to respond, so she just stared out the front window of the car.

"I shouldn't have said that," Chili sighed.

"No," Raquel quickly responded. "I like that you like me...being around."

"Really," grinned Chili.

Raquel nodded her head and smiled.

Chili leaned over as if he had something to whisper, when Maylon opened the door.

Maylon looked at the two in the back seat for a second before saying, "Did I interrupt something?"

"No," Raquel replied with a blush of embarrassment.

"Did we interrupt you?" Chili chided.

"No," Maylon sheepishly replied. "Ready to head home?"

"Yeah," Chili grinned.

Maylon waited for a second before saying to his brother, "Are you riding in the back?"

Chili shifted for a moment before saying, "I guess not."

Maylon looked through the rearview mirror at Raquel and smirked. Chili moved to the front seat, and the three made the short drive back to Maricopa.

CHAPTER 12

Through the short winter months, Raquel made frequent trips with the boys to Taft to see Orpha. Maylon's fiancé spoke her mind, and often unintentionally asked uneasy questions, but Raquel liked Orpha's honest affability. Orpha was unassuming and did not take herself too seriously. She helped Raquel fix her frizzled hair with a cut that was easy to keep and flattering. Orpha also introduced Raquel to the magic of makeup, and Raquel looked forward to the trips to see her new friend.

Eli Butler found a job for Maylon as a roughneck in the oil fields near Taft. Maylon seemed excited to have a steady job, although the work was hard and dangerous. Chili was less thrilled when Eli announced that he had also found his younger son work in the fields. Times were hard, but Maylon was satisfied he would now be able to marry Orpha. As the wedding approached, the car rides to Taft became more frequent.

There was another reason Raquel liked traveling to Taft. She and Chili had become comfortable in the back seat of the Ford sedan the past weeks, as they waited for Maylon to say good-bye to Orpha. Raquel looked forward to the drive back to Maricopa when Chili would put his arm around her and snuggle her gently, while a grinning Maylon would drive alone in the front seat.

It was three days before the wedding, when Raquel nuzzled against Chili's chest with his arm draped around her. Raquel's eyes were partially closed as she enjoyed the warmth and safety of having Chili near her. She did not know what to think at first as Chili's arm stiffened, and he gently pulled it from around her shoulder to his side. As the car slowed down, Raquel opened her eyes to see the headlights illuminating a glaring Naomi Butler standing on the front porch watching them.

"Hi, Ma," Maylon greeted, as he eased out from behind the wheel. "Didn't think you'd be up."

Naomi Butler did not speak, as she watched her younger son Chili try to slip out of the back seat. Raquel sat alone in the car for a brief moment, until she too got out of the car. Naomi did not speak, but there was no need. Raquel could sense the disapproval, both in Naomi's solemn stare and the tense quietness from Maylon and Chili.

"Raquel," Naomi finally said coldly. "Could you go to your room? I need to have a word with my boys."

Raquel nodded and quickly stepped by Naomi. She was relieved her employer did not say more, but had a sick feeling in the pit of her stomach about Naomi's disapproving look. Raquel hated the fact that she might have gotten Chili into trouble with his mother, but she also felt unsettled by how Naomi might react to her. Raquel went upstairs and put her back against the closed door. She tried to muffle the tears and sobbing, while listening to the conversation downstairs.

All she could hear at first were muffled whispers. The soft voices eventually evolved into occasional animated words that she could almost understand. Raquel heard enough to know Maylon had been dismissed from the conversation and Chili was now taking the full brunt of Naomi's criticism. The specific words were unintelligible, but Raquel had no difficulty interpreting the gist of the exchange. After a while, Raquel prepared for bed and collapsed into the soft pillow. Raquel was sick at causing the conflict between Naomi and her sons, but she also lamented the feeling that she was not acceptable to the Butler family. Raquel doubted she was good enough for any family, as her tormented mind searched for some meaning or purpose to her life.

Raquel convinced herself that she must leave, but the same daunting problem perplexed her—she had nowhere else to go that would provide the same safety and comfort as the Butler's home. She knew she could not stay, however, and as tears moistened her pillow Raquel put a plan together. She had two dollars and could catch the eight o'clock bus to Bakersfield for twenty cents. The asparagus harvest would begin in a few weeks and strawberries a few weeks after that. She had heard there were shelters and charities in Bakersfield, and it was close to all the fields in the southern San Joaquin Valley. She would not be a problem for the Butlers, and could not endure being thrown out by them. Sleep did not come easily for her even after the house became quiet.

CHAPTER 13

A sunny but chilly morning greeted Raquel as she slipped silently out of the house. She faced an unknown and unsure future. It was just after dawn, and Raquel was relieved that Naomi had not yet started cooking breakfast. Raquel walked quickly down the street with her small bag of belongings. She stood in front of the bus station to try to soak up the warmth of the first early morning rays of sunshine, and to block the cold morning breeze. She had wanted to leave a note to apologize to Mrs. Butler and say good-bye, but Raquel did not want to chance having to confront the woman face-to-face.

The bus arrived on schedule and departed Maricopa half-full, with only two stops on the ninety-minute ride to Bakersfield. Raquel sat in a seat by herself and watched the dry countryside pass by her bus window. She felt numb. She held no grand illusions that things would be better in Bakersfield, but Maricopa was behind her. She would not be able to see Maylon get married but was confident she would not be missed. More than anything, she would lament leaving Chili. Raquel had grown close to him and believed Chili felt the same, but she would not put him in conflict with his mother.

The bus rolled down the highway, as Raquel calculated how long she could make her meager savings last. She heard honking from behind the bus, but did not think much about it until the bus started to slow down. As the honking became closer, Raquel looked out the window to see the Butler's Ford screaming down the highway with headlights flashing. The agitated bus driver stopped the bus, and Raquel's heart beat faster. Chili had come for her. She did not know how they would make it, but at the moment she did not care.

The annoyed bus driver slammed the door behind her. The engine roared, as the driver hustled to get back on schedule.

Raquel's exhilaration vanished as she peered through the glare of the windshield. The door on the driver's side of the Butler's car slowly opened, and Naomi Butler stepped out from behind the wheel with a scowl on her face. Raquel wanted back on the bus, but it was already rolling down the road.

"Where are you going?" Naomi asked.

Raquel looked at her feet and then said, "I thought I would try to find some work in Bakersfield."

"Why?"

Raquel had not expected the question and thought how to politely answer when she said, "I didn't want to cause your family…I didn't want to cause you any trouble."

"I don't understand," frowned Naomi.

"The argument last night," Raquel said, with a puzzled expression. "I know how unhappy you were with me."

Naomi studied the young woman for a moment and said, "You've got to be careful about what you think you know."

"Yes, ma'am," Raquel said meekly.

Naomi Butler looked around the vacant countryside trying to determine what to say next, while Raquel's heart beat nervously under the woman's scrutiny.

"You don't have to call me ma'am, Raquel," Naomi finally said. "I'm sorry you overheard my fight with Chili, but I'm confused. Why did you leave?"

"Chili," Raquel confessed.

"Yes."

"You saw us together," Raquel continued. "You saw us in the car."

"Yes," Naomi nodded.

"You were angry at Chili, for being with a girl like me," Raquel surmised.

"What kind of girl?" Naomi questioned.

"A girl like me with no future," Raquel explained. "A girl with no family and no prospects."

Naomi stared at Raquel for a moment before saying, "Is that what you think of me…that I care about your family or where you come from?"

"Everyone does," Raquel replied.

Naomi stepped close to put her arm around Raquel's shoulder to say, "I wasn't angry at Chili because of you. Chili quit his job in the oil fields yesterday. I love my son, but his irresponsibility is taking him nowhere fast. Eli came home nearly sick he was so angry and disappointed. I don't mind that Chili likes you, dear."

"Chili likes me?" Raquel asked.

"I've known that since the first day," Naomi said. "I know you know it too."

"I thought…I thought you would be angry," Raquel said.

"With you, no," Naomi assured. "I'm no blueblood. Maylon's part Indian."

"Maylon and Chili are part Indian?" Raquel clarified.

Naomi did not respond immediately, knowing she had said more than she intended.

Finally Naomi confessed, "Maylon is. He's adopted. Eli and I took him when he was a baby. His mother died when he was born. It's been so long that I don't ever think about it anymore…I don't know why that came out now."

"You don't mind me being with your son?" asked Raquel.

Naomi shook her head, "I may seem grouchy—probably a little too high and mighty for my own good, but I know goodness when I see it—and I see it in you."

Raquel smiled for the first time that morning, as Naomi said, "Maybe you're what Chili needs to grow up—seems to have Maylon on the straight and narrow to have found a good California girl."

Raquel's smile broadened as she wiped tears from her eyes, as Naomi squeezed her shoulder tightly.

"How did you find me?" Raquel asked.

"You've been up at dawn to help me in the kitchen every morning since you came," Naomi explained. "When you didn't show up this morning I went to your room to see if you were ill. After I saw you had left the house, I walked to town. I watched you get on the bus, but couldn't catch it in town. The boys and Eli weren't dressed yet, so I got the car keys. I nearly didn't get the blasted thing in gear, but once I got rolling, I caught up."

"I didn't know you could drive," Raquel said.

"I didn't either until this morning," Naomi said slyly. "I guess a woman can do a lot of things when she has to."

"Thank you for coming for me," Raquel said. "I'm sorry I…ran off."

"Let's get home," Naomi smiled. "We need to get breakfast and get your things back in your room."

CHAPTER 14

Maylon and Orpha were married in the front room of the Butler home in a simple wedding performed by a preacher Eli knew. The couple drove to Visalia for a two-night honeymoon near the great redwood forest, before returning to rent a one-room apartment in Taft. Orpha beamed with giddiness when Naomi and Raquel visited the apartment the first time. Naomi could not keep from making comments about the cramped size and the fact that the place did not have hot water, but Orpha seemed proud of her new home.

Eli Butler pulled some strings and got Chili his job back. Eli and Chili rode together most days, and Naomi closely monitored her son. The likable Chili tolerated the oil fields and kept on his mother's good side, but he still was searching for what he wanted to do with his life. Chili and Maylon had often talked about trying their luck in Los Angeles, but after the wedding, Maylon seemed content in Taft with his life and with Orpha.

Late spring approached, and the activity in the small crossroads town of Maricopa increased, as hundreds of migrant workers struggled to find jobs in the fields, planting and harvesting. The weather was in that perfect time between being warm and hot. Naomi and Raquel were home alone with the screen door open when a timid knock interrupted Raquel's mopping of the kitchen floor.

"Would you get that?" Naomi shouted from upstairs, where she was making the beds.

As Raquel approached, she saw two men standing in front of the screen door. The men were dressed in shabby clothes that had dozens of sloppily sewn patches on them. The taller man had a raggedy beard, and the young man did not look as if he were yet shaving.

"Sorry to disturb ya' ma'am," the taller man greeted.

Raquel braced herself against the screen door to keep it closed, as the men stood on the other side, a few steps from the door.

The tall man made eye contact with the shy Raquel, and tilted his head slightly when he asked, "You wouldn't have any chores for us to do, would you? We missed out on the trucks this morning and could sure use some work."

"I don't know," Raquel stammered.

"How 'bout some food?" the man asked. "We could sure use a meal."

Before Raquel could answer, Naomi walked down the stairs and asked, "Who is it?"

"Some men," Raquel answered.

Naomi stepped in front of Raquel and said forcefully, "What do you want?"

"Good mornin' ma'am," the taller man greeted. "My name is Hank Tilley, and we's seeing if'n you could spare a meal or had some work for us."

"There's work in the fields," Naomi stated. "I've got chores of my own to do."

"I'd be glad and grateful to help," the man offered.

"Where are you from?" Naomi pointedly asked.

"From?" the man replied.

"You can't tell me, can you?" Naomi charged. "My bet is you ride the rails for free and live off the naïve generosity of hardworking people. I also suspect you're given to liquor and vice."

"Now, ma'am," the man replied. "I won't lie. We get from place to place on the extra space on the trains, and I have been known to tip a few brews back when I can find 'em, but they don't interfere with work."

"When you can find them," Naomi fumed. "I can smell you from here and it smells like you've been bathing in whiskey."

"Now, ma'am, that ain't exactly a Christian attitude," the man argued. "We're just a couple of fellows down on their luck. This depression's hard on a man. It'd kill my dear momma to know I's out having to ask for a handout. I'm sure a fine Christian woman like yourself could see a way to help those needing a hand up."

"A hand up!" Naomi preached. "All you want out of life is a hand out! You're able-bodied enough. You need to clean yourself up and dry out. The good book says 'If you won't work, you won't eat.'"

"Ma'am, we're willing to work," the man said. "I can bust wood, sweep this porch."

The younger man was getting antsy and shifted nervously on the step of the porch as if he wanted to leave. The older man, however, stood his ground and seemed determined to shame Naomi into giving him something.

"I don't have any extra work," Naomi stated firmly. "I've taken this girl in to support and she does all my extra work."

"Maybe you could spare a nickel or a dime so's we could get a bite in town," the man begged.

"I won't give you a penny," Naomi charged. "You'd most likely spend it on liquor and that'd take you no nearer to finding a job than you have now. I have a husband and two boys that get up every morning to work hard for what we have. I clean their clothes and make sure they're rested and ready to make something out of themselves. I would suggest you do the same thing!"

Naomi slammed the wood door on the man and retreated to the kitchen to make sure the backdoor was secured as well. Raquel stood speechless at Naomi's stubborn unwillingness to help the men. Naomi unapologetically sent the men on their way without even a small reward for their panhandling.

"That's what's wrong with this country," Naomi vented. "We have too many vagrants and hobos harassing the hardworking folks. You don't help these people by giving them something for nothing."

"He offered to work," Raquel noted.

"Ha!" Naomi replied. "That man was a shameless grifter—and that boy with him is just learning his bad habits. I bet that man hits up every town with a bus stop seein' who he can dupe. If you give one of these hobos a meal, pretty soon you'll have an army of these lazy misfits at your door taking advantage of your kindness."

Raquel had learned that it was pointless to argue with Naomi. Her employer was not a particularly heartless woman, but she was very opinionated and did not change her mind often. Raquel had learned that it was better to let her vent, than try to change her mind.

"I've got work to do upstairs," Naomi moaned. "Don't answer the door if they come back."

Raquel nodded and watched Naomi march back up the stairs, as if the interruption had somehow put her hopelessly behind. Raquel went quietly back to the kitchen and made two sandwiches. She slipped out the door to find the two men a few houses down the street, and she gave them their lunch.

CHAPTER 15

When spring arrived, Beulah and Arnold Belvedere returned from the coastal plains after working in the orange orchards for the winter. Raquel moved back to the garage. The nights were getting warmer, and she was happy to be separated from the overbearing Beulah Belvedere. Raquel did what she could to stay away from the opinionated visitor, but Naomi insisted she eat supper with the family.

"The Belvederes will only be here a couple of days," Naomi explained, "and I want you there."

Raquel did not look forward to hearing Beulah Belvedere rant against the world, but was relieved the visitors were only planning to stay a short while. Naomi had bought Raquel a fancy new dress and asked her to wear it for dinner that night. Raquel loved the dress and was happy to oblige. Raquel could tell a difference in Beulah Belvedere the moment she entered the room. The woman who previously stayed with the Butlers hinted that she had an inflated sense of self-importance, but that Beulah Belvedere had been down on her luck enough to keep some of her arrogance hidden behind the transparent humility of her circumstances. Raquel did not know the cause, but could tell by Beulah's posture and manner that something had changed.

"We're heading home," Beulah proudly stated, as the group sat down for supper.

"Home?" Naomi quizzed.

Beulah nodded in a slow, determined way and explained, "My nephew, Frankie, has bought the old hardware store. He's running the bank for his father in Sayre, and they picked up the old store for pennies on the dollar. He's got so many things in the works right now that he doesn't have time to fiddle with the hardware store. He wired us last week and asked if Arnold would be interested in managing the store."

"Congratulations, Arnold," Eli smiled.

"Thanks," Arnold replied. "After a few months of picking oranges, getting back in a store sounds good."

Beulah was somewhat perturbed at Mr. Belvedere's revelation that he had been engaged in manual labor the past months as she said, "We were really just helping manage some of the work at the orchard. I did enjoy the oranges, but it's not work with a future."

"Somebody's got to do it," the more humble Arnold noted.

"True," conceded Beulah, "but I'm glad to see you back in the store again. You'll be a great blessing to Frankie."

"Frankie's blessed without us," Arnold quipped. "Your sister married well, and the Suttons always seem to land on their feet."

Beulah frowned at her husband and said, "Frankie's from good stock all right, but it will be good to be home."

"I'm envious," Naomi sighed. "I miss home, too."

"You'll have to come visit," Beulah said. "We're moving back into a big house in town. It needs some work, but it'll be fit in no time."

"Where exactly is home?" Orpha innocently asked, as she munched on some of Naomi's green beans.

Beulah looked at the brash young woman for a moment before announcing, "Sayre—Sayre, Oklahoma, in the western part of the state."

"What's it like?" Orpha asked.

Beulah did not respond immediately, so Naomi answered, "It's home to us, honey. Sayre's a small town by the North Fork of the Red River—the country's wide open and great land for grain, cotton, and cattle—at least when the rains come."

"It used to be a great place to raise a family, before the banks and the tractor farmers took over," Beulah fussed.

"It's still a great place for family," Naomi defended. Turning to talk to Orpha, Naomi said, "We only came out west for the oil job. We still have a quarter-section of land outside of town."

"You own a farm?" Orpha smiled.

"A small one," Naomi affirmed.

"You'd better be careful about that," fumed Beulah. "Beau Lobaugh'll take the run of it if you're not careful. I wouldn't be a bit surprised if he's running cattle on it now, knowing him."

"So what if he is?" Naomi replied. "It's not like we're using it now."

"I know you don't think much of him," Eli interrupted, "but Beau's family."

"Some family," Beulah murmured.

"Speaking of family, how do you like my new addition?" Naomi smiled.

Beulah did not understand the question, but Arnold said, "Welcome to the family, Orpha."

"Thank you," Orpha blushed.

"Yes, dear," Beulah added. "It's so nice to have you join us for dinner."

"I've heard a lot about you," Orpha said with a slight smirk, which almost caused Raquel to giggle.

Raquel had warned Orpha about the brazen and presumptuous Mrs. Belvedere, and Beulah had not disappointed in her boastful behavior.

"That's nice," Beulah smiled, "but we've heard almost nothing about you."

Orpha finished chewing her food and replied, "There's not much to tell. I've lived near Taft all my life. My daddy works as a roustabout. Me and Maylon have a place in Taft, and I work at the drugstore in town."

"You work?" Beulah asked.

Orpha nodded.

"A married woman working outside the home?" Beulah repeated.

"It's not great money," Orpha replied, "but it gives me something to do, and I get a discount on all kinds of things. I'm learning to help girls fix their hair and hope to be a hair dresser someday."

"You're not ready to start a family?" Beulah asked.

"Sure," Orpha sweetly smiled. "We're working on that."

Maylon blushed noticeably at the frank reply from his wife, when Orpha continued, "That's the great thing about hairdressing. You can do it right in the kitchen. All you need is a sink, some clippers, and some imagination. Look what I did for Raquel."

Raquel now squirmed as all eyes focused on her. She had been content to listen in silence and let Beulah Belvedere's scrutiny concentrate on Maylon's wife. Raquel straightened her new dress and tried hard not to touch her hair that curled cutely on her shoulder.

"Yes, it's quite a transformation from the ragamuffin girl we met last time through," Beulah said pointedly.

"Beulah!" Naomi scolded, while the others listened uncomfortably.

"What?" Beulah said, while tilting her head. "I was giving the girl a compliment."

"You were being rude," Naomi stated flatly.

"These people shouldn't be so touchy," Beulah replied. "I was just commenting on how much more stylish the girl looks now, although she does seem overdressed for a housemaid."

Chili shifted in his chair as if he would interrupt, but before he could say anything, Raquel said, "Mrs. Butler invited me to this dinner as a guest. She bought me this dress and didn't want me working in the kitchen tonight."

"That's silly," Beulah bellowed. Turning to Naomi, she said, "Why do you keep a girl, if you're going to do all the work?"

Naomi's cheeks flushed pink with anger and her nostrils flared as the normally composed woman said, emphatically, "What goes on in my house is none of your business, Beulah Belvedere. When you go back home and open up your house, you can do what you want, but when you're in my house, you will treat my guest—all of my guests, with respect."

The room was silent after Naomi's outburst. Chili took Raquel's hand to help calm her shaky nerves.

It looked like the frowning Beulah might say more, when Naomi calmly addressed the small party and said, "I'm glad everyone's here tonight. It's been such a blessing to have Orpha added to our little family. My sons have jobs. We have plenty to eat and a comfortable place to live. I'm glad to see my friends, the Belvedere's, heading home to better times. I do have an announcement that will multiply our blessings in this house. Chili has asked Raquel to marry him, and they plan to wed next month. Since Raquel doesn't have much real family, it was up to Eli and I to give our approval."

Naomi hesitated for a moment to make eye contact with Beulah Belvedere before saying, "I've grown to appreciate Raquel's fine qualities as a lady, her quiet and diligent ways, but more importantly, the positive effect she's had on my boy Chili. Raquel dear, you're like the daughter I never had—at least until Orpha came our way. I look forward to you and Chili sharing many happy years together and having you as my daughter-in-law."

Beulah Belvedere was speechless, but her gawking stare told of her disapproval.

The bubbly Orpha was the first to confirm the announcement by squealing, "I've told Maylon since the first time we met you that there was something going on between you two. I'm so excited. I've never had a sister! I knew you and Chili were seeing each other, but I had no idea. When's the date?"

Chili Butler may have had difficulty finding out what he wanted to do with his career, but he had figured out part of his future several months earlier. That summer he had proposed to Raquel and asked her to marry him. Raquel had always been afraid to test Naomi's true feelings about her, but was pleasantly surprised when Naomi gave her blessing with a smile and even a hug. Naomi did not often display even that much emotion, but Raquel was relieved to hear her future mother-in-law's bold proclamation in front of Beulah Belvedere.

"We haven't set a date officially," Raquel quietly answered, as she purposely avoided any eye contact with Beulah Belvedere.

"Next month," Naomi interrupted.

Raquel looked over at the beaming Chili and nodded sweetly.

By this time, Beulah Belvedere had regained some of her moxie, and she understood that her social situation was now clearly elevated over her friend's, as she smugly said, "Such interesting news. Congratulations, Naomi. Will it be a church wedding?"

Naomi shifted nervously as she said, "We'll have the wedding here at the house."

"How nice," Beulah replied with an artificial nicety. "Will the priest come here?"

Raquel did not comprehend the intent of the question at first, but before she could answer, Naomi said, "We'll have a preacher."

"Aren't you Catholic?" Beulah asked Raquel in a calm voice.

Raquel nodded in agreement, which caused Beulah to rear back in her seat and glare at Naomi.

Beulah looked at Raquel and asked, "Are you okay with that, dear?"

"My family won't mind," Raquel replied meekly. "I go to church with Naomi now."

"It will be beautiful," Orpha proclaimed. "I can't wait."

Orpha looked around at the tense room and said to Raquel, "Why don't we go upstairs and make some plans?"

Raquel nodded, and Orpha led her by the hand to an upstairs room, away from Beulah Belvedere.

In a whisper, Orpha asked, "How did you keep from slapping that old biddy?"

"She's Mrs. Butler's friend," Raquel explained.

"I thought Naomi was going to slap her for you," Orpha smirked. "I'm not sure she won't yet!"

Raquel smiled thinking about how good it had been to have Naomi stand up to the obstinate Beulah Belvedere. Her smile melted to a frown, however, as she remembered how Beulah had made her feel.

"Are you okay?" Orpha asked.

Raquel nodded and thought for a second before asking, "Are you happy?"

"Sure," Orpha chirped.

"I know you're happy," Raquel said. "I meant are you happy with Maylon—with being married."

"Of course," Orpha beamed. "Maylon's the sweetest thing, and he's just so good to me. I know he seems kinda quiet and moody sometimes, but that's just his way. He treats me special. I had three brothers and I've never been treated like a princess before, but that's how Maylon makes me feel."

Raquel smiled thinking of what her life might be like with Chili Butler.

"Of course, Chili's different," Orpha grinned. "He's handsome for sure. In fact, I noticed him at the social before Maylon, but Chili's younger, and Maylon just determined right away that he was going to be special to me."

"That's nice," Raquel said.

"It'll be nice for you, too," Orpha assured. "Chili's a swell guy."

Raquel smiled, but Orpha could tell something was wrong.

"What is it?" Orpha asked. "Something's the matter."

Raquel nodded, "I'm fine."

Orpha was not convinced and declared, "You can't let people like Beulah Belvedere get you down. You know what they say, 'Narrow minds and fat heads go hand in hand.'"

Raquel sniggered loud enough that she was afraid the people downstairs would hear.

Orpha quipped, "If you like that one, you'll love a chip on the shoulder means a lot of wood in the head!"

Raquel laughed loud enough that she was sure the entire house heard.

Orpha leaned over to Raquel and whispered, "I was talking about Naomi on that second one!"

Raquel put her hand over her mouth to keep from laughing louder.

"I mean, I love my mother-in-law," Orpha explained. "But even you'd have to admit she's a little full of herself."

"Not compared to Beulah Belvedere," whispered Raquel.

"That's pretty harsh coming from you," Orpha laughed. "I swear, I've ran into a hundred of these Okies and not found two that could be as irritating as Naomi and Beulah."

Raquel giggled with Orpha, but then she asked in a more serious voice, "I'm a little worried."

"About what?" Orpha asked. "I was just joshing. Naomi loves you."

"I know," Raquel said. "Naomi can be particular, but she's always been good to me since the first day. It's just—I'm just worried about fitting in. Chili and I are—different. We come from different backgrounds. I'm afraid—I'm always a little afraid that the Butlers tolerate me—that somehow Chili could do better."

"I'm one Butler woman that can say that Chili's lucky to have found you," Orpha declared. "It's not where you come from; it's where you're going. You're going to be good for Chili. I believe that. He needs someone like you to—he needs someone to take care of, someone to be responsible for."

"I want to make him happy," Raquel said.

"You will," Orpha assured.

The two girls talked about their lives and their dreams until Maylon timidly knocked on the door to tell Orpha that it was time to go. Raquel slipped outside to her cot in the garage, as Orpha and Maylon left. She did not feel like subjecting herself to more of Beulah Belvedere's smug looks of disapproval. Naomi brought her breakfast the next morning in the garage and encouraged her to take her time getting ready for the day. By the time Raquel dressed, the Belvederes were gone, and she was relieved.

CHAPTER 16

The practical Naomi did not worry about the details of Raquel's simple wedding, but focused more on giving life advice to the engaged couple. Naomi pressed Chili to make decisions about his future, and daily explained to him the new responsibilities he had promised to undertake in having a wife. Naomi seemed excited about the marriage, but always appeared hesitant to completely let go of her youngest son.

Orpha energetically took on the task of decorating the front room of the Butler home for Raquel's wedding. When Maylon and Orpha had married the previous winter, her bouquet had been the only flowers in the room. Orpha made sure the room had ribbons and flowers to welcome her new sister-in-law to the Butler family.

Maylon had done well in the oil fields, and Orpha had kept her job at the drugstore. Naomi fussed regularly about the inappropriateness of a married woman working, but Orpha was not deterred by her mother-in-law's criticism. Soon, Maylon and Orpha rented a little bungalow house in Taft. The house was small and needed repairs, but they could afford the twenty-dollar-a-month rent. Orpha proudly showed off her new home as if it were a mansion.

"If a strong wind blows, the place is likely to splinter," Naomi complained.

"It's a fine place for a young couple," Eli replied. "Orpha's happy with it. There's a lot to be said for being content."

Naomi scowled and shook her head at her husband, but did not debate the topic.

For Chili and Raquel, the options were more limited. Orpha had recommended a little cottage north of Visalia for their honeymoon. Chili took a week off work for the trip. Raquel and Chili found some time to walk among the wonders of the giant Sequoias.

Chili had not been as diligent as Maylon with work, however. Chili had not asked for permission to be gone on his week-long honeymoon, causing him to lose his job. Eli pulled some strings to get Chili more work in the oil fields around Taft, but it would be low-paying work that was dangerous and sporadic. The normally opinionated Naomi was uncharacteristically calm about the development. She offered to let Chili and Raquel live in the small upstairs bedroom. Raquel had hoped they could move into an apartment in Taft, but Chili was satisfied to take the small room.

It took a few weeks, but soon married life in the upstairs bedroom became normal. Chili would travel to Taft with his father, and Raquel would work in the house with Naomi. The relationship between the two women changed, but the evolution happened so gradually that Raquel could not consciously determine the date that Naomi started treating her as a daughter.

Being Naomi Butler's daughter-in-law came with challenges, and Raquel believed her mother-in-law's dogmatic and blunt personality would never change much. She became calloused to the regular criticism and correction that Naomi's persona regularly shared. Raquel, however, realized that Naomi's meddling comments were rooted in genuine concern for her wellbeing. Raquel had once become hardened to the physical beatings at the hands of an angry and hardhearted stepfather who took out his frustration about his life on her. Naomi cared, and Raquel appreciated the attention. Raquel learned to smile and tried to please her mother-in-law. Many times her polite smiles were motivated by thoughts of what the quirky Orpha would say about their mother-in-law's peculiarities.

Raquel did notice her mother-in-law's kinder side, which Naomi seemed determined to keep hidden in the thick veneer of practical sensibility. Naomi would take food to neighbors in need and helped those less fortunate. Naomi's charity, however, had to be on her terms and meet her definition of worthiness. She still treated any hobo or Okie that she encountered with contempt when they dared knock on her front door. Naomi would, however, help with a soup kitchen or work to mend clothes for the poor, who were in abundance in the San Joaquin Valley.

The life Raquel had grown used to at the Butler house changed abruptly on the most typical of days. On a quiet Tuesday morning, Naomi's frantic screams woke Chili and Raquel in their upstairs bedroom. They ran down the stairs to see a frenzied Naomi wearing a white nightgown—her graying hair hanging below her shoulders. Naomi's face seemed twisted and strange, but the thing Raquel noticed was that it was the first time she had ever seen her mother-in-law with her hair down.

"What is it?" Chili shouted, as his mother continued to let out hysterical cries that were unintelligible.

"Your father!" Naomi was finally able to gasp.

Chili and Raquel entered the room to see a pale Eli Butler sweating and twitching unnaturally.

"Pa!" Chili shouted.

Eli did not respond.

"Pa!" Chili yelled again to his unresponsive father.

Eli Butler looked to be in pain, but his eyes were closed as if he were asleep.

"How long has he been like this?" Chili barked.

"Since I woke up," Naomi cried. "Your father tosses and turns most nights, so I don't know."

Chili looked at his wife for some guidance about what to do, but Raquel was too stunned to give advice.

"We need a doctor!" Chili shouted, as if his unconscious father might hear his loud voice.

Chili's panic seemed to make Naomi aware of the crisis, and she said in a calmer voice, "Go get the doctor, Chili. He'll know what to do."

Chili nodded and ran upstairs to quickly put on trousers before sprinting out the door to get Dr. Combs, Maricopa's only doctor, who lived several blocks away.

"What can I do?" Raquel asked, as Naomi stood dazed by the side of the bed.

The question again caused Naomi to think, as she said, "I need to dress. Can you stay here with Mr. Butler? I need to get ready for the doctor."

Raquel nodded, although she would have preferred running down the street with Chili to find the doctor. The activity seemed to steady Naomi, as she grabbed some clothes and tried frantically to pull herself together. Raquel was left alone for a few minutes with the convulsing Eli Butler. She felt fear that she had not experienced since the death of her mother, as the gentle Eli groaned unconsciously in the now-disheveled bed. Not knowing what to do, but sensing that she needed to do something, Raquel took her father-in-law's clammy hand. The simple gesture steadied Eli in some way, and he opened his eyes for a moment to stare blankly at the ceiling.

"Mrs. Butler!" Raquel screamed.

The half-dressed Naomi ran into the room.

"His eyes opened!" Raquel exclaimed.

Naomi leaned over her husband and said, "Eli! Eli! Why won't you answer me?"

Naomi nearly collapsed in despair, as Raquel guided her to a chair.

"It'll be okay," Raquel tried to assure, as she stepped back to the unresponsive man.

It took thirty long minutes, which seemed like hours before Chili returned with the doctor. Dr. Combs checked his pulse, looked at his eyes, and attempted to get some response.

"We need to get him to the hospital in Bakersfield," Dr. Combs stated in a calm but serious tone. "Do you have a car?"

"Right outside," Chili replied.

"Good," the doctor said. "We don't need to waste time."

Chili, Raquel, and the doctor wrestled Eli Butler gently into the back seat of the Ford.

As Naomi climbed into the back seat, she looked at Raquel and cried, "Go tell Maylon!"

In seconds, the car sped toward the hospital, fifty miles away. Raquel stood alone in the silent house and plotted how best to get to Maylon. It was a short trip, but too far to walk. She hurried to the bus station hoping she would not have to wait too long for the bus. The bus had gone, but she managed to catch a ride with two oil field workers driving a truck that had her in Taft in fifteen minutes. She went to the drugstore to inform Orpha and got directions to find Maylon.

Raquel had spent most of her life in the emerald asparagus fields, the colorful citrus orchards, and even the plain brown cotton fields of the valley. The oil field looked to her like a desolate and dangerous gateway to hell. Raquel had seen the man-made forest of spindly oil derricks from a distance on her many trips to the town of Taft, but actually being among the towering metal-framed structures was like entering a different world. The clanking sound of metal was interrupted only by the shouts of men trying to get Raquel's attention, and the constant hiss of gas being burned from pipes overhead.

"Señorita!" a large man covered in black grim shouted, as Raquel walked by. "I get off at six! Are you going to be in town tonight?"

Raquel ignored the man as several other workers laughed and whistled. The taupe-colored sand was a web of dirt ruts caked in a brownish-grime of petroleum winding through the endless oil derricks. A constant scent of oil choked any fresh air from the rocky hills. Raquel yelled over the noise at a foreman to ask the location of Maylon's rig. The man shouted back and pointed. He was neither rude nor helpful. The man busily went back to his work and left Raquel to approach the towering derrick where six men wrestled machinery.

"Maylon!" Raquel screamed, when she saw him covered in a coat of oily soot and dirt.

Raquel's presence confused Maylon. He quickly turned a few valves on the piping coming from the ground and trotted toward Raquel. He said something to her, but the clanking noise drowned-out any chance of comprehension. Maylon took Raquel gently by the arm and guided her behind one of the many tin buildings scattered between the giant wood derricks, which blocked some of the chaotic noise from the rigs.

"What are you doing here?" Maylon yelled with a kind smile on his face.

"Your father!"Raquel shouted. "You need to come."

"What?" Maylon replied.

"Your father's sick," Raquel tried to explain. "They've taken him to the hospital in Bakersfield."

Maylon's pleasant smile faded, and he walked quickly to a man that looked to be the supervisor of the group. The man nodded unsympathetically, and Maylon returned to lead Raquel from the maze of equipment and confusion back to town.

When they got closer to town and the noise abated, Maylon anxiously asked, "What's happened?"

"I don't know," replied Raquel. "Your mother woke up this morning, and he was acting strange. She couldn't get him to completely wake up, so the doctor came."

"Is he in pain?" Maylon asked.

Raquel shook her head, "I don't think so, but you should come."

"Sure," a concern Maylon said. "I've got to tell Orpha."

"Orpha knows," Raquel stated. "She told me where to find you."

"Let's go," Maylon directed.

Maylon walked quickly to an old car he had bought after he moved to Taft. It was a rickety-looking contraption compared to the nice Ford automobile the Butlers owned, but Maylon could keep it running. He sped to the drugstore where Orpha worked, and in minutes the three were racing toward Bakersfield.

"Slow down!" Orpha demanded several times, but Maylon drove wildly over the graveled roads that provided the most direct route to Bakersfield.

Maylon would comply for a moment and take his foot off the accelerator to pacify his wife, but he did his best to keep up his speed. The trip to Bakersfield could take as much as an hour, but Maylon pulled in front of the hospital in almost half that time. The two women followed in his wake, and they quickly located Naomi and Chili in the hallway.

"Is he okay?" Maylon anxiously inquired.

Naomi did not look normal, as she had dressed quickly and had not spent much time on her long, dangling hair, which she usually tucked neatly in a curly bun. The normally poised and controlled Naomi had a frightened, uncertain look that Raquel had never seen.

"I don't know," Naomi shakily replied.

"He's with the doctor now," Chili explained.

"Let's go," Maylon said, as he made a step toward the double doors separating the visitors from the rooms.

Chili reached out to stop his brother and said, "We tried. The nurse said we'd only be in the way, and if we wanted to help we needed to stay here."

Maylon thought for a second before nodding his head in agreement.

"What happened?" Maylon asked.

"I don't know," Naomi said, shaking her head. "He seemed fine last night, but when I woke up this morning, your father was just numb."

"Numb?" Maylon responded.

"He didn't move, he didn't talk, he just laid there twitching," Naomi explained.

"The doctor didn't say anything?" Maylon asked.

"To get out of the way," Chili replied. "You'll know when we know."

The group stood apprehensively in the hall as nurses, doctors, and orderlies calmly went about their duties, as if nothing was happening out of the ordinary. Orpha went over and put her arm around the trembling Naomi while they waited. Maylon soon joined her and had one arm around Orpha and the other around his mother. The group waited in the hallway of the hospital for over an hour as they occasionally speculated about Eli's status.

"Mrs. Butler?" the doctor announced unemotionally, as he stepped from behind the double-swinging doors, in the early afternoon.

"That's me," Naomi responded worriedly, as she unconsciously straightened her hair.

The doctor looked up at the sound of the southern plains accent and appeared to study the family for a moment before saying, "Your husband's resting in a room now."

"Is he okay?" Naomi asked restlessly.

"Yes," the doctor responded. "He's stable for now."

"Thank goodness," Naomi sighed. "Can I see him?"

"Yes, but—" the doctor hesitated. "He's in a negative pressure ventilator and won't be able to speak."

A bewildered Naomi looked pitifully at the doctor, trying to understand her husband's condition.

"He's in an iron lung," the doctor explained. "We use them for polio patients to help them breathe."

"Eli doesn't have polio," Naomi said, shaking her head.

"No," the doctor confirmed.

"There you are," Dr. Combs greeted, as he walked down the hallway.

"Dr. Combs!" Naomi cried. "What can you tell me?"

The doctor from the hospital stepped aside to let Dr. Combs explain, "He's doing fine, Naomi, but Eli's had a stroke. He hasn't been responsive yet, and the hospital's put him on their iron lung."

"Oh my," Naomi groaned.

"He's stable now and resting," Dr. Combs said. "But—we'll know more in a day or two."

"Eli will be all right?" Naomi pleaded.

Dr. Combs sighed deeply, "We hope so. It's hard to tell how these strokes will go or how major this one is until he's responsive.

He may—he may be fine in a few weeks or—he may have some paralysis. It's not uncommon."

"I see," Naomi said, as her voice transitioned to a tone of resignation.

"We'll know more in a day or two," Dr. Combs tried to assure. "For now, there's nothing more to do. I'd go home and get some rest. The hospital will call as soon as anything changes."

Naomi nodded, and the doctors left the family to mull over the news. Naomi went in to see Eli encased by the huge machine. There were two of the breathing machines in the room, but only Eli lay silent and still in the iron lung's clutches.

"Is he in any pain?" Naomi asked the nurse.

"No," the nurse reassured with a smile. "He's resting fine."

Naomi looked over the cylinder-shaped contraption and said, "Is this safe?"

"Very safe," the nurse smiled. "I know it looks like a beast of a machine, but it helps our patients breathe better when they're incapacitated."

Naomi looked like she might touch the machine, but instead she gently caressed the cheek of her unconscious husband.

"Get well, my dear," she whispered softly. "Get well."

CHAPTER 17

The doctors told Naomi to go home, but she did not leave the hospital for three days. Naomi sent Chili and Raquel to pack her a bag, because she planned to stay until she could will Eli back to health. Chili and Raquel would have enjoyed the time alone in the big Butler house, but the house was filled with an ominous foreboding about the fate of Eli.

Raquel and Chili made their way to Bakersfield to the hospital every day. Maylon had wanted to stay with his mother, but Naomi convinced her oldest son that Eli would be happier if he stayed on the job. On the fourth day, Chili and Raquel arrived to see a more relaxed and optimistic Naomi.

"He's awake," Naomi greeted.

Chili walked by his mother and through the doors to see his father. Raquel and Naomi followed. Eli Butler lay inside the massive respirator with only his head sticking out. His eyes were open, but he had a strange contorted look to his face.

"They say they'll take him out of this thing tomorrow," Naomi said, as she tapped on the iron lung. "They said he could breathe on his own now, but they want to make sure."

"How're you doin' Pa?" Chili said softly, as he leaned toward his father.

Eli Butler tilted his head and looked at Chili with an expressionless face.

"He can't talk," Naomi explained. "At least not yet. The doctor says he'll probably get the feeling back in his face in a few days and should be able to speak then."

Eli had always been a humble and unassuming man. His actions spoke louder than his words, and the words he did speak were usually measured and brief. Today he looked frail and fatigued, but he was alert. Chili looked at his father and tried to smile bravely.

"We better let your father rest," Naomi suggested.

Chili nodded and led the group out the door and back to the waiting area of the hospital.

"What's wrong with Pa?" Chili pointedly asked.

"He's had a stroke," Naomi replied. "It's not uncommon for a person to have some paralysis—temporary paralysis on one side of the body. Your father's stroke was massive, and it'll take some time for him to get back on his feet. He'll get better."

"He looks like his face is all twisted up," Chili fumed. "Can't they do an operation or give him some medicine or do something."

"They are, dear," Naomi assured. "He's stable, and that's the main thing. Your father's a strong man. He hasn't missed this many days of work since we came to California, and he'll be back, I'm sure."

Chili nodded and looked back through the doors to where his father rested.

"Will you come home now?" Raquel asked Naomi.

"I'd have thought you two newlyweds would want an old woman like me to stay away as long as possible," Naomi replied.

Raquel blushed in embarrassment, but smiled at Naomi's comment. She took it as a good sign that her mother-in-law could see some humor in the world after the past days.

"We miss you," Raquel finally said.

"I may come home for tonight," Naomi said. "I think I need the rest."

"I could stay with him," Raquel offered.

Naomi smiled, "I would feel better if someone would."

Raquel nodded, and Chili said, "Let's get back home, and maybe we can come tonight with Maylon."

Naomi agreed and left the Bakersfield hospital for the first time in four days, while Raquel stayed with her ailing father-in-law.

Raquel, Chili, Naomi, and Maylon took turns staying with Eli the next few nights. Maylon looked exhausted after his hard day of working, but he was stubborn about taking his turn at the bedside. Eli Butler was taken off the respirator and immediately looked better. His color improved, and his eyes were sharp and focused. He was still not able to speak, which frustrated him, but he could nod responses and could even scribble short notes with his right hand, even though he was naturally left-handed.

The family sensed relief in Naomi's disposition as Eli continued to improve. By the end of the second week, Eli was able to grunt his frustration at being kept in the hospital. When the doctor scheduled his release for the next day, Naomi worked feverishly with Raquel to put the house in shape for the homecoming.

Chili drove the family Ford over to bring Eli home, but by the look on the nurse's face and the hacking cough coming from his room, Naomi knew things had changed. Eli developed severe chest pains in the night and a high fever by morning. He was taken back to the respirator, but the severe chills and shaking increased. The doctor tried a variety of medicines, but by nightfall he came to see Naomi.

"Mrs. Butler," the doctor stated stoically. "I think you better go see your husband. I'm so sorry. He's taken pneumonia. I'm afraid we've done all we can."

"What do you mean?" a shaken Naomi responded.

"Mr. Butler's not going to make it," the doctor explained.

Naomi stood speechless for a moment. Maylon was the first to push by the doctor and make it into his father's room, followed by Chili. Orpha and Raquel guided Naomi by the arm to join the two brothers. Eli was able to open his eyes, but he looked tired and weak. He looked as if he sensed he was losing the battle; he looked as if he were giving up. Naomi cried, and Eli looked like he would speak, but all he could do was cough uncontrollably.

Orpha stayed as long as she could, but eventually Eli's suffering became too much for her. Naomi, Chili, Maylon, and Raquel stayed. Eli rallied at one point and seemed to have his cough under control. Raquel could see the hope in Naomi's eyes, but when she looked back at Eli, she sensed the quiet, kind man knew the end was near. He raised his hand at one point as if to reach out for Naomi, but the massive respiration apparatus keeping Eli temporarily from death's cold hand was in the way. Eli Butler passed away a little after midnight. Raquel had seen hardships and had been with her mother when she passed away. This night was harder than Raquel could have imagined, and she left Eli's room with a strange surreal feeling of dread. The Butlers had been a family. They had become her family. Eli had been caring, diligent, and good. He had made the Butler family good, and Raquel found it difficult to reconcile that someone as good as Eli Butler could be gone.

CHAPTER 18

Chili pulled in front of the Butler home a little before dawn. Naomi was numb with fatigue and hopelessness. After two weeks of believing Eli Butler's absence from the house would be temporary, the place seemed empty and hollow without the prospect of his return.

Neighbors brought food and gave their condolences, but their thoughtfulness seemed strangely unreal as well. Raquel knew within her rational self that Eli was gone, but she caught herself forgetting and thinking he would return. All the trappings of the funeral and the compassion shown by those who did not know Eli as well as the Butler family, served as cold reminders that he was gone. The calm perseverance Naomi demonstrated during the stay in the hospital vanished during the weeks after the funeral, and she had trouble making the simplest decisions.

When the undertaker tried to make arrangements for burial, Naomi could only say, "He always wanted to be buried at home, so it doesn't matter. Do what you will."

Eli Butler was buried with a simple marker in the large cemetery in Bakersfield. The funeral director offered to take the body back to Maricopa, but Naomi could not see the point.

Maylon missed a week of work, but he was able to get his job back, although there were many more workers than jobs in Taft. Chili could not see his way back to the oil fields, and after visiting them, Raquel was more understanding. The oil fields were rough and hard like the men that work them. Maylon could adapt to the harsh environment, but Chili was not like his brother. Chili worked sporadic odd jobs and managed to find some work harvesting.

Naomi had been the undisputed master of all things domestic at the Butler home. She was not, however, included in any of the financial operations of the household. Eli earned the money, made the deposits in the bank, and paid the bills. He had managed the finances for the family from a small drop-lid desk that sat in the corner of the back room. Everyone knew the desk belonged to Eli. It was his domain.

Naomi shopped with local merchants with charge accounts that Eli would then pay. Eli never criticized and rarely questioned his wife, who had demonstrated the frugality to match the family's income. Naomi kept a little cash in the house for emergencies—usually five to ten dollars, but never more than twenty dollars. It was a couple of weeks before bills began arriving.

Raquel had noticed the ashen-look on Naomi's face when she opened the mail on the third day of the month.

"Chili," Naomi said in almost a whisper that afternoon. "Go find Maylon, and see if he can come this evening."

Chili nodded his understanding and headed to Taft in the car. Raquel stayed with her mother-in-law during the quiet afternoon. Naomi kept busy and did not give indications that anything was wrong, but Raquel sensed a tenseness and concern from her mother-in-law. Chili, Maylon, and Orpha arrived close to seven. The summer afternoons were long, and over an hour of daylight still lingered, as long shadows began forming across the Butler's front yard.

"Hey, Ma," Maylon greeted, as he hugged his mother on the front porch. "What's for supper?"

"I've got a stew," Naomi replied. "Hello, Orpha."

"Hello, Ma Butler," Orpha replied.

The family shared their meal with some small talk about Maylon's job, Orpha's customer experiences, and the difficulty many, including Chili, were having finding steady work. Raquel listened to them, but she was more interested in the quiet Naomi, who seemed distant and apart from the conversation.

"What's goin' on, Ma?" Maylon finally asked, as he finished a slice of apple pie.

Naomi at first seemed stunned by the question, but then she replied, "I wanted your opinion about some things—Chili's too. You've always had a good head on your shoulders for numbers and such, Maylon. I thought I'd have you boys go through some things with me tonight."

Maylon immediately noticed the change in his mother's countenance, and he asked, "What's wrong?"

"I don't know if anything's wrong," Naomi tried to assure. "It's just—I got the hospital bill today, and I don't know much about how to read these things."

"How much?" Maylon asked.

Naomi stepped over to a stack of papers to hand Maylon the bill and said, "Two hundred and seventy dollars."

"Two hundred and seventy dollars!" Maylon exclaimed, as he took the piece of paper.

"Yes," Naomi nodded. "It was ten dollars a day for the room and another hundred or so for the doctor and medicines."

"That's steep," Chili interjected.

Maylon looked at the bill for a moment and sighed, "That sounds like a lot."

"It's not like they were able to help much," fumed Chili.

"I telephoned today," Naomi shared. "The hospital says that's the going rate for a private room—the ventilator thing he was on was expensive too. They asked if I had insurance."

"Do you?" Maylon asked.

"I was hoping you might know," Naomi replied. "You and your father were always close."

"I don't know about any insurance," Maylon said. "Pa kept all his papers in the desk in the back. Have you looked there?"

"No," Naomi confessed. "I haven't had the heart. I thought maybe you could help me go through things tonight."

"Sure," Maylon replied. "Let's take a look, Chili."

The two boys headed back to the desk, followed by their mother. The drop-lid desk creaked open with neat stacks of papers filed in cubbyholes.

"I've got some other bills," Naomi confessed. "I didn't know what to do."

"Bring them," Maylon instructed, as he began looking over the papers.

Raquel and Orpha cleared the table and did the dishes while Naomi and the boys searched through Eli's financial affairs. The two girls made small talk and exchanged stories about the idiosyncrasies of their husbands. Orpha made Raquel giggle a couple of times, but the atmosphere in the house made it seem inappropriate, so she muffled her amusements.

"Let's see what they're up to," Orpha suggested after the better part of an hour, when they had finished cleaning the kitchen.

Raquel sensed the mood had not improved as they walked into the room.

"How's it going?" Orpha cheerfully asked.

Maylon's expression told the story, but he said, "I don't know yet."

Maylon turned to his nervous mother and asked, "Is this it? Are there any other savings accounts or insurance or anything?"

"Not that I know of," Naomi sighed.

Maylon said in a terse tone of voice, "I'm showing you owe bills for nearly three hundred and fifty dollars, and I'm only seeing forty-seven dollars in the savings account. Do you have any other money?"

"No," Naomi answered worriedly. "I usually keep a little in the house, but I've spent it all."

"There's got to be something else," Maylon reasoned.

"I had no idea the hospital bill would be so much," Naomi murmured.

"Do you know of any other accounts Pa might have kept?" Maylon asked. "Is there any place else he could have put things?"

"I know every inch of this house," Naomi declared. "There's not another dime or piece of paper I don't know about. This desk is where your father kept everything."

Maylon sighed heavily, "There's got to be something else."

"His pension," Naomi remembered. "He'll have a pension due, and I haven't seen a red-cent of that."

"The pension," Maylon said in a relieved tone. "That should help. I bet the hospital will let you set up some kind of payment. Once we know what the pension is, we can put things right."

"Thank goodness," Naomi said. "I've been worried for a week, and then this hospital bill came in. I—I didn't know what to do."

"I'll check with the company tomorrow and see what I can find out," Maylon said. "It'll be fine I'm sure."

CHAPTER 19

Two days later, a man showed up in a large black car, wearing a suit and carrying a briefcase. The man also carried a small box that fit neatly under his arm. Naomi had been expecting Mr. Williams from the Midway-Sunset Oil Company.

"Hello, Mrs. Butler," the man greeted, as he stepped onto the front porch.

"Hello, Mr. Williams," Naomi replied. "This is my daughter-in-law, Raquel."

Mr. Williams looked at Raquel carefully before saying, "Good to meet you."

"Will you come in?" Naomi asked.

Mr. Williams nodded and followed her into the house. Mr. Williams was a tall, distinguished-looking man with graying temples and a firm, authoritarian presence. He seemed pleasant, but the man did not smile or show any emotion.

"I apologize for being so long coming," Mr. Williams said, after sitting down in the front room. "My condolences for your loss. Eli was a good man and served the company well."

"Thank you," Naomi replied. "It was a shock to us."

"I'm sure it was," Mr. Williams said.

Mr. Williams sat awkwardly and silently for a few moments before Naomi asked, "I was wondering if you could tell me something about Mr. Butler's pension plan."

Mr. Williams sighed heavily and said, "Yes—yes that's part of why I came to see you."

The stoic man looked at the two women for a moment and then continued, "Eli cashed out his pension last year. I've brought the contents of his desk for you to go through and thought it might help."

"What does that mean?" Naomi asked, while shaking her head. "What do you mean he cashed out his pension?"

"Eli took the money out of his pension last year," Mr. Williams explained, "almost $3,200. I took the liberty of going through some of Mr. Butler's papers when I was packing them up. There's a deed for some property in Oklahoma."

"The home place," Naomi said. "One hundred and sixty acres and a house."

"Yes," Mr. Williams nodded. "Looks like Eli took his pension and paid the mortgage and taxes on the place. I saw a receipt from the First National Bank and Trust in Elk City—Oklahoma. It released the loan. The other papers show that he paid the back taxes. Were you planning on returning to Oklahoma?"

Naomi thought for a moment and replied, "We had talked about it, but not now. With the drought and all, there wouldn't be much point. Besides, Eli's work was here."

"Yes," Mr. Williams said. "We will miss Eli."

"So how much can I expect?" Naomi asked. "Will I get some kind of check each month?"

Mr. Williams shifted nervously and sighed, "That's what I've been trying to tell you, Mrs. Butler. There is no pension. Eli took the money out. I've brought a check for seventy-five dollars, but that's all the equity he had built back since he cashed out his pension."

"But Eli's worked for your company for nearly twenty years," Naomi protested. "He's hardly ever missed a day of work and would do anything for the company."

"We appreciate Eli's devotion," Mr. Williams conceded. "He was a good employee and a fine man. The fact is, he had a pension and took the money to pay off some land. That was his choice. I'm sure you could sell that place and set up some kind of annuity."

Naomi stared blankly at the man and said, "You know how things are, Mr. Williams. Things are hard here, but worse back home. I see the refugees come here nearly every day with little of nothing. I couldn't sell that place for pennies on the dollar, if that. You're a businessman; surely you know it."

"That's not my concern," Mr. Williams declared. "I have a responsibility to look after the company's interest. I sympathized with your loss, but this check will fulfill our obligations."

"I see," moaned Naomi.

"I am sorry for your loss," Mr. Williams restated.

Naomi nodded and looked at the floor before saying, "Is that why you took six weeks to pay your respects? Did your conscience feel that embarrassed to tell a widow that she had nothing?"

Mr. Williams jaw tightened slightly. Looking solemnly at Naomi, he said, "No. That's not the reason I've delayed."

Naomi looked up from the floor and tried to put on a brave face in front of Mr. Williams.

"I've delayed coming to try to help your family," Mr. Williams said. "Part of our deal with your husband when he came to work was to provide him housing away from Taft. This house belongs to the Midway-Sunset Oil Company. I've put off coming out here to let you stay as long as possible. We've hired a new foreman, and I've come to let you know that you'll need to get out by the end of the month. I'm sorry for the short notice, but I've tried to sit on this as long as I could."

Naomi could not speak and stared blankly at Mr. Williams. Raquel put her arm around Naomi and tried to comfort her.

"I am sorry," Mr. Williams said, as he rose to leave. "I wish you well and good day."

Naomi nodded, but she could not bring herself to speak. Mr. Williams hesitated, and then walked to the front door to leave, before stopping.

At the front door he turned to Naomi to say, "I know this news has not been good. I truly wish it could have been better. I know Eli had another son that had done some work for us in the past that didn't work out so well. If he's still looking for a job, have him come see me and I'll be sure he gets another shot."

The stunned Naomi could not reply, but she nodded dispassionately. As Mr. Williams left the two women behind, the screen door slammed shut, causing Naomi to jump slightly.

"What are we going to do?" Naomi whimpered softly.

Raquel did not have a good answer, but muttered, "I'll go look for work tomorrow."

Naomi reached out and touched Raquel's hand and moaned, "When Chili comes home, go get Maylon for me. He'll know what to do."

Raquel nodded.

Naomi looked at her young daughter-in-law and wanted to say something comforting. Raquel had always been quiet and loyal, and Naomi had proudly lived with the knowledge that she had the means to help take care of the girl. Now she did not know if she could take care of herself.

"I'm going to rest for a while," Naomi finally said.

Naomi retreated to her bedroom and left Raquel alone in the front room. Raquel had never seen her mother-in-law look so lost, so needy. The uncertainty of the next meal or a place to sleep at night was not new to Raquel, although she had grown accustomed to the comfortable life of living with the Butlers. Raquel did not worry about herself, but she did worry about Naomi's ability to survive her newfound destitution.

CHAPTER 20

"They can't do that!" Chili shouted. "This is our house!"

"The man said the house belongs to the company," Raquel tried to explain to her husband while Naomi listened silently.

"We can get a lawyer," Chili stated defiantly. "You can't just turn people out into the streets."

"I've seen the papers," Naomi stoically stated. "Mr. Williams is right. This house was part of Eli's job, and he's not with us anymore. Besides, I can't pay the bills I have now—much less rent. A lawyer can't help with that."

Raquel moved over to put her arm around Naomi, who sobbed into a lace handkerchief. Chili curbed his indignation and moved to the other side of his mother.

"Maylon will be here soon," Naomi said. "He was going to talk to some people. He'll know what to do."

Maylon and Orpha showed up a little before seven. Maylon's body language foretold that he had no good or encouraging news.

"Pa paid off the place in Oklahoma," Maylon informed, "but he cashed in his pension to do it."

"We can't move back there," Chili protested. "It's hard enough finding work here. I've seen the people in the fields from there. It's worse."

"We'll get things figured out," Maylon said. "It'll just take time."

"Can you get things figured out before the end of the month?" Chili said sarcastically.

"It won't help to fuss," Naomi interrupted. "We've got to take a look at what we've got to work with—we'll make a list of our options."

"That's a good idea," Maylon confirmed.

Chili did not reply, but he nodded his approval.

"What do we have to work with?" Maylon asked.

Naomi shook her head, "I owe about four hundred dollars and don't have any money. I talked to the hospital, and they said I could pay ten dollars a month, but I don't know where that will come from."

The room was silent until Raquel said, "We'll have to move, right?"

Naomi nodded.

"This is a big house," Raquel observed. "You won't be able to find anything with this much space, and if Chili and I move out, you won't need so much room. You could sell some of the furniture."

"Yes," Naomi agreed. "I won't get much for it, but you're right Raquel, I have to get rid of some things. I'll start sorting things out tomorrow."

Maylon looked at his brother and said, "Mr. Williams said he would help get you a job roughnecking."

Chili sighed, "I'll look into it."

"You've got to take it," Raquel said. "It's a steady job, Chili. I know you don't like the oil field, but it would be some good money, and we could get our own place."

"I said I'd look into it," Chili replied tersely. "We're not leaving Ma like this though. We'll find a place, and she can move in with us. No need paying two rents."

"Of course," Raquel smiled. "But if you take the job in Taft, seems like it would make sense to move there."

"Taft?" Chili sneered.

"She's right," Naomi said. "We could find a place in Taft, and if you find work there, we won't need the car. I bet we could get a good price for the car."

"Sell the car!" Chili protested.

"It'd about pay our debts," Naomi said. "We could start fresh."

"I could find work," Raquel offered.

"Doin' what?" Chili said.

"I don't know," Raquel confessed, "but I could do something."

"We're looking for another girl at the drugstore," Orpha said. "You'd be good there, and it's within walking distance."

"We don't know where we'll be living," Chili said.

Orpha looked at Maylon before saying, "If you haven't found a place by the end of the month, you can move in with us. It's not much, but there's a back bedroom, and we could make a place in the front for Naomi. You'd save a month's rent, and then you could get a place on your own."

"I can't impose on you like that," Naomi tried to protest.

"It's not an imposition," Maylon smiled. "We got room. Chili and me can walk to work, and I got my old car. We can manage for a month or two."

Naomi looked at Chili, and he shrugged, "I guess."

Raquel was more enthusiastic in saying, "Thank you Orpha. We'll get some money saved and find a place on our own real soon."

Orpha smiled. "Things are going to be fine."

CHAPTER 21

Naomi did not get much money for the furniture she had to sell, but she did get a decent price for the Ford, which allowed her to pay most of the bills. Naomi, Chili, and Raquel temporarily moved into Maylon and Orpha's small house. In a few weeks, everyone seemed to be adjusting to the cramped living quarters. Mr. Williams was good to his word, and Chili once again had a job working as a roughneck on a crew in the oil fields. Although Taft and Maricopa were only a few miles apart, the two places were so different that it was hard for the Butlers to believe they were living in the same part of the country.

Maricopa was a small, sleepy town, where neighbors were nosey enough to know what was going on, but polite enough to mind their own business. Taft's population included several thousand more people, and the whole town had a chaotic, frenzied atmosphere. The oil field men worked hard for their money, and there were plenty of distractions to help them spend their wages. Maricopa did not have a single store that sold beer, while Taft had a half-dozen establishments dedicated to getting men drunk. The town had several pool halls which doubled as places to gamble, where men would risk a month's pay for a chance to make some easy money. There were even a couple of buildings, just outside the jurisdiction of the town's police department, which offered temporary companionship for the single men—and some of the married men. Taft was a working town with many more men than women. Family men generally lived in places outside of town—the bosses and owners lived in the more prosperous Bakersfield about forty miles away.

Raquel labored each evening trying to clean and press Chili's work clothes. She knew her husband did not like working around petroleum. Chili did not like the noise, confusion, or smell of the oil field, but work was hard to come by, and he was making the best of it. He hated Taft, but that was where the work was. Raquel looked forward to finding a place of their own, but she knew it would be hard to move from their new home without a car. She did not mind. Raquel had lived in worse places. The camps were more dangerous for a girl like her, and living with her stepfather had been even worse.

Raquel and Naomi were home alone most afternoons, but they busily worked on keeping the small house neat. Naomi was a proud woman now cast in a humble place, and Raquel wondered how her mother-in-law would handle her lowly circumstances. Naomi attacked the new challenge by putting on a brave veneer of cheerfulness and hard work. Naomi had bossed and directed Raquel's work in the past, but now she became a partner in the labors, and rarely asked her daughter-in-law to do anything. Naomi seemed determined to make sure everyone knew she could and would work through the present difficulties.

"Raquel!" Orpha shouted, as she returned from work on a Thursday afternoon.

"What?" Raquel asked the excited young woman.

"We're finally going to hire a girl to work in the drugstore," Orpha explained. "I've told them all about you, and Mr. Franklin said he'd see you tomorrow. The pay's not great, but the hours aren't bad, and you get discounts on things."

"Thank you, Orpha," smiled Raquel.

Raquel had wanted to work for several weeks, but there were not too many opportunities for women in Taft. She had decided to go back to the fields to harvest, but that work was not steady and would mean traveling further up the valley. Raquel kept a tin can under her bed with money she had saved from Chili's pay. The can had four dollars and seventeen cents, and she looked forward to adding to the amount so that she and Chili could finally have a place of their own.

"We'll go first thing tomorrow morning," Orpha said. "Is Naomi here?"

"She's in the backyard," Raquel replied.

"I'll go tell her that she'll be on her own during the days," Orpha smiled.

Raquel watched Orpha skip out to the backyard and smiled at her sister-in-law's energy. Raquel felt relieved. She looked forward to making a little money, but she also looked forward to giving Naomi some space during the day. Raquel liked and appreciated her mother-in-law, but she believed the time had come when they both would enjoy some time away from each other.

Maylon made it home and looked tired after a hard day's work. He smiled, however, when Orpha came into the front room to hug him. Raquel had gotten used to the house getting crowded in the evenings. The men would come home dirty from work. They would get cleaned up and the women would start working on their clothes. Chili came home a few minutes after Maylon. He was covered in brown and black grit, but his left arm was conspicuously wrapped in a crimson bandage.

"Your arm," Raquel gasped. "What happened?"

The grim-looking Chili looked down at the bandaged arm and said, "The pipe rigging came loose. I barely got out of the way, but the arm got cut pretty bad."

"You gotta keep alert," Maylon said.

"I did," Chili fumed. "The blasted foreman didn't check the rigging. I guess he figured a couple of workers were cheaper than wasting fifteen minutes."

"Oh my," Naomi cried out, as she entered the room. "What's happened?"

"Chili cut his arm," Maylon explained.

"I nearly lost it," Chili complained. "If you killed a mule in the oil field, they'd have to buy a new one. If they kill a man, they just hire another."

"Let me see it," Naomi demanded.

Chili reached out his arm, and Naomi gingerly unwrapped it to reveal a deep, jagged cut on his forearm almost three inches long.

Naomi was unfazed, "Get some water, Raquel. We need to clean this real good, or it might get infected."

Chili winced when his mother used soap and water on his wound, but he muffled his scream when she poured alcohol on it. Naomi had nursed Eli's cuts and injuries for nearly thirty years. She knew it was better to cause a little pain when the wound was fresh than to wait for it to fester.

"It'll be better in a day or two," Naomi said, as she bandaged and wrapped the arm.

Naomi noticed Raquel watching carefully. "Body parts are always aching in the oil field," Naomi explained.

"I'd like to ache that foreman's head," Chili said angrily. "When I complained, he said there were men living on a cracker a day that would love to have my job."

"You can't talk like that to a foreman," Maylon scolded.

"The man's probably right," Naomi sighed. "Labor's more abundant than work these days."

"Oil field trash is all we are!" Chili exploded.

"Don't you say that!" Naomi chided. "We're not oil field trash. You're father was one of those foremen for twenty years. He never lost a man and made a good living for his family."

"Pa ain't around anymore," Chili sighed. "The oil company don't care about anything, but making a few dollars more. I ought to talk to some of those union boys always trying to rile up the pickers. They'd have a heyday in the oil patch."

Maylon rose up and said forcefully, "Don't you ever say that again! There ain't no place in the oil field for no union. The work's hard, and you got to be careful, but the pay's good. People around here even hear you say the word *union*, they'd most likely bust your head. Pa'd bust your behind if he was still with us."

"Both of you quit fighting," Naomi ordered. "We got enough problems without fussing among ourselves."

"Raquel," Orpha interrupted the tense conversation. "Why don't you tell Chili your news?"

It took Raquel a second to think of what Orpha was talking about, but then she said with a subtle smile, "I'm going to see about a job tomorrow—at the drugstore. Orpha thinks I might have a chance."

"It's a cinch," proclaimed Orpha.

Chili looked at his brother, before taking a deep breath to say, "That's great. That will help us save for a place of our own. That'll make Maylon happy."

"I never said I wanted you to leave," Maylon replied.

"I know," Chili admitted. "It's just a little tight around here, and I think we could all use some space."

Maylon nodded and said, "Let me know if you have problems at work. I've been at it awhile and kinda know how things work. I know there are plenty of knuckleheads out there, but watch yourself and you'll be okay."

"Thanks," Chili nodded. "I just had a bad day today."

CHAPTER 22

Raquel woke early the next morning to cook breakfast for Chili and Maylon. As soon as the men left for work, she started getting ready for her day. Orpha loaned her a pretty blue dress and helped fix her hair with a ribbon. On final inspection, Orpha said the old shoes Raquel wore would not do. She took off her new shoes and, with a little paper in the toe, made them fit.

"You look like a store girl now," Orpha grinned. "Pretty as a peach."

Raquel looked herself over and sighed, "Thanks, Orpha."

"Are you nervous?" Orpha asked, as she tucked and straightened the last details of Raquel's wardrobe.

"A little," Raquel confessed.

"Don't be," Orpha smiled. "You'll be perfect."

The two women left the house on a sunny and warm morning to walk the three blocks to the store. Raquel felt happy and fortunate for Orpha's help. Orpha helped her to believe in herself, and she imagined how much fun it was going to be walking to work each morning with her friend and sister-in-law. Raquel calculated how much money she could put in savings, and she guessed she and Chili could afford a place of their own in a couple of months. She thought how wonderful it was going to be to have an apartment she could call her own, and she believed Chili would be more relaxed and happy in a place of their own.

Raquel's buoyant mood and optimism vanished the second she stepped into the drugstore to meet Orpha's boss. Orpha left Raquel with the store owner and sensed something was out of place, though she could not exactly determine the cause. Raquel knew. She had been with the Butlers so long that she had nearly forgotten, but she had seen the look before. The store manager was polite and asked a few questions about her experience and education. Raquel knew she had none, but she also knew that it did not matter as soon as the man saw her.

"I'm sorry," he said. "If I needed someone to clean or sweep, I'm sure you would be dependable. I'm looking for someone to work the counter. I would have thought Orpha would have told you."

Raquel wanted to say something, but knowing it would be pointless, she just listened quietly.

"I can't have a Mexican girl out front," the man continued. "What would that say to my customers about my business? I don't have any work for you right now."

"I understand," Raquel whispered. "I'm sorry I took up your time."

Raquel did not understand, but she was accustomed to the prejudice. She wanted to scream out. She wanted to have a chance, but she knew that would do no good, except to embarrass and make things difficult for Orpha. Raquel could not look Orpha in the eye, as she slid silently out the door and tried to disappear into the sunny morning. She felt as if the whole world was staring at her, yet she felt so exceedingly alone. Raquel walked quickly away from the drugstore with feelings of humiliation and despair. She would not be working, and she would not be moving out of Orpha's small house any time soon.

Few people were on the streets of Taft at this time of day, but Raquel did not make eye contact with anyone. She wandered the side streets for nearly an hour before deciding to go home. Naomi looked at her with a raised eyebrow when she returned. Naomi could see the disappointment, but did not say anything at first. Raquel appreciated that. She did not want to explain or complain. She had learned early in her life that things were what they were. Raquel tried to avoid Naomi altogether, but in the small house it was impossible.

"Back so soon?" Naomi cheerfully greeted, as she folded sheets that came fresh from the clothes line.

"Yes," Raquel answered.

Naomi had her back to Raquel, but she could sense the disappointment in the girl's tone.

Turning to face her daughter-in-law, Naomi asked, "Are you all right, dear?"

Raquel nodded and kicked off the shoes Orpha had loaned her.

"You don't look alright," Naomi said. "I'm guessing you didn't get the job."

"No," Raquel confessed.

Naomi knew there was more to the story than the simple answer she received, but believed she would not understand the feelings behind Raquel's defeated tone.

"Life's full of disappointments," Naomi tried to comfort.

"I know," sighed Raquel.

"You want to talk about it?" Naomi asked.

Raquel did not answer for a moment and then took a breath to say, "They didn't want someone like me."

Naomi felt a crush of guilt as she remembered her first impressions of Raquel. She stepped toward her daughter-in-law and hugged her shoulder gently.

"People can be foolish," Naomi fumed, "but I'm glad."

"Why?" Raquel asked. "I thought you would have wanted Chili and me to start making it on our own."

"That's Chili's responsibility," Naomi preached. "I'm glad, because I'll have you here with me. I'll have to confess, I wasn't looking forward to spending all my afternoons alone."

Raquel smiled sweetly and felt some comfort in Naomi's attempt to make her feel better. Naomi wanted to do more, but she could not relate to the indignity of being labeled undesirable. She did the only thing she could; she helped Raquel keep her mind occupied by working with her in the small house for the rest of the morning.

"I can't believe it!" Orpha bellowed, when she stormed home for a quick lunch. "They didn't even give you a chance!"

"It's okay," Raquel said. "I wasn't what they were looking for."

Orpha looked at her with a frown and revealed, "He said, 'I can't hire a Mexican, Orpha. You should've known that.' I thought they wanted someone who would do a good job. I can't believe he would say that to me. It's not like you even look Mexican."

"I have your sandwich ready," Naomi said, in an attempt to get the feisty Orpha to stop talking about the failed interview.

"I have half a mind to quit myself," huffed Orpha. "It'd serve 'em right. I'm the only one there that has a clue where the inventory is in that place."

"You can't do that," Raquel said. "It might not have been the best job for me anyway. I'm shy, and I think they wanted someone with more personality."

Orpha knew that even with Maylon's job, she needed to work to pay for their place and help support the family.

Orpha sighed heavily, "But you looked so beautiful this morning, and I could just see us working together."

Raquel nodded, as Orpha stepped to her and gave her a hug.

"It'll be fine," Raquel assured. "Chili and me are already saving some money up living here and I'll find something else to do. We'll move out before too much longer."

"Don't you worry about that," Orpha smiled. "We're family and family sticks together—especially when you have to work with a fat-headed boss."

"He was just a little fat-headed," Raquel grinned.

Orpha stared at Raquel for a moment and said, "That's about the meanest thing I've ever heard you say—I kinda like it."

CHAPTER 23

Raquel did not fret long about her disappointment in missing out on the job at the drugstore. She went back to work at the house to help the family where she could. Her ability to get the grease out of Chili and Maylon's clothes was not missed by others in the oil field, and she started taking in laundry during the day to make money. Even with the extra work, it seemed painfully slow saving for an apartment.

Maylon and Orpha's small home left little privacy, and Naomi's snoring from the front room sometimes kept the whole house awake for hours until she would turn over. Still the family settled into their new routine, and Naomi was starting to get back some of the bossiness that had been missing since the passing of her husband.

Naomi and Raquel spent their days keeping house and doing laundry. Orpha arrived home later in the afternoon, and the three women would work together on their simple supper. Maylon would come home from work tired, but in a generally good mood. Chili, however, was less reliable. He rarely came home in a pleasant demeanor, and he usually arrived later than Maylon. As the weeks went on and the summer days started to get shorter, Chili would sometimes come home after dark. In time, this too became normal, and Raquel went to bed alone many nights while Chili would sneak home later in the night.

One night, Raquel was resting alone in her bed when a noise from outside startled her. She could not determine the source, but the unnatural noise frightened her at first. Raquel was barely able to contain a scream when the bedroom window opened from the outside.

"It's me," Chili whispered, as he climbed in through the bedroom window.

Raquel stared at her husband who was crawling across the floor when she said, "What are you doing?"

"I didn't want to wake Ma," Chili explained.

Raquel reached over and turned on a small lamp by the bed to see a dirty Chili standing at the foot of the bed. Chili's late nights had raised the ire of his mother the past weeks, but this was the first time he had used the bedroom window to get past her.

"You better whisper softer then," Raquel scolded in a hushed voice. "What are you doing out so late?"

"Don't be mad," Chili grinned, as he reached over to kiss his wife.

Raquel instinctively pulled away. Chili was still grimy from the oil field, but that was not the reason. The smell of alcohol reminded Raquel of her stepfather.

"You've been drinking!" Raquel whispered flatly.

"Not drinking," Chili replied, "celebrating."

Chili reached into his pocket and let ninety-two one dollar bills rain down on the bed next to Raquel.

"Where did you get this?" Raquel asked, as she raked the money close to her.

"Let's just say I had a little luck tonight," Chili boasted.

"This is enough for us to have our own place!" Raquel smiled.

"Almost," Chili replied, as he began picking the money back up.

"We need to put this with our savings," Raquel said.

"Naw," Chili shrugged. "You keep the savings. I'm going to invest this and make us a little nest egg so we can not only get our own place, but get out of this town—maybe Los Angeles."

"What kind of investment?" Raquel asked warily.

"Don't worry your pretty little head," Chili smiled.

"Are you gambling?" Raquel asked pointedly.

"I'm not gambling," Chili said. "I'm playing cards at a place downtown."

"Gambling," Raquel groaned. "Do you know what that would do to your mother if she found out?"

"That's why she don't need to know," Chili grumbled. "Card playing's not gambling. Roulette—dice, that's gambling. Cards are about knowing what you're doing."

Raquel did not look convinced.

Chili held up his wad of cash and proclaimed, "And I know what I'm doing."

"That's nearly a month's pay," Raquel protested. "Let's get a place of our own."

Chili reached down to touch his wife's cheek and said, "We will. By the end of the month I promise. You won't have to do the laundry for this oil field trash, and I may even hire someone to do things for you."

"I don't need that," blushed Raquel. "I just want a place of our own and for you to be happy."

"I am," Chili smiled. "And I'll be happier when I can take care of you properly."

Raquel did not tell Naomi of Chili's windfall, and it turned out to be a good thing. Chili snuck back in through the bedroom window a few nights later in a foul and temperamental mood. He had been drinking again and managed to lose all of the ninety-two dollars that had been his. Raquel did not scold him, but Chili could see the disappointment in his wife's eyes.

Autumn came, and the days started getting shorter as the first wet days of the rainy season began. Maylon and Chili's work clothes were now sometimes muddy in addition to being grimy. Chili had been coming home earlier, and Raquel prayed that he had learned his lesson about gambling. She was more relieved that Chili had come home without the stench of alcohol on his breath. She still had the money they had saved from Chili's pay, and she still believed they could move out on their own soon. The family was settling into a schedule, and it looked like a more positive routine for Chili.

The door slamming mid-afternoon marked an end to the new optimism the family had achieved. Chili walked angrily and defiantly into the front room, while Raquel and Naomi stared at him.

"Come back here!" Maylon shouted, as he entered the front door before the women could speak.

"What!" an exasperated Chili shouted back.

"What's going on?" Naomi demanded, as Raquel and Orpha moved closer to their agitated husbands.

"I'll tell you what's going on," Maylon huffed. "Chili's got us both fired!"

"What?" Naomi gasped.

Maylon stared angrily at his brother and then said, "Chili flew off the handle this afternoon—"

"The pipe nearly took my head off!" Chili defended.

"It didn't!" Maylon replied. "If you'd keep your eyes open and your mouth closed, things would be fine."

"I could have been killed," Chili explained.

"Are you okay?" a concerned Raquel asked.

Chili nodded.

"We're not okay!" Maylon tersely responded. "We have no jobs. No job means no money."

"I told you the accident wasn't my fault," Chili sighed. "The guy didn't secure the pipe, and it could have killed all of us."

"You didn't have to scream that you were going to start a union to the foreman," Maylon scolded. "I told you to keep your mouth shut."

"They fired you?" Naomi asked.

"Both of us," Maylon clarified. "I've been there over a year, and my boss had to let me go once word got out that my brother might be a union organizer."

"That's why we need a union!" Chili said.

The small table by the front door crashed as Maylon tackled his taller brother and tried to push his face into the wood floor.

"Stop it!" Naomi screamed.

Maylon let go of his brother and shouted, "Are you happy now! You won't have to worry about the union ever because we're both black-balled now!"

"I'm sorry," Chili said, as he picked himself up.

"You're sorry!" mocked Maylon. "I've got forty dollars to my name, and the rent's due the end of this week. I won't be able to find a job for twenty miles around and you're sorry!"

"Raquel and I will move out," Chili said.

Raquel moved closer to Chili and grabbed his arm, while a frustrated Maylon stared silently at the floor.

"Maylon," Orpha pleaded.

Orpha did not have to say more, as Maylon said, "It's getting cold out, and I can't have my brother out on the streets."

The previous flurry of shouting was now contrasted by silence, as the entire household seemed to ponder their dire reality.

"We can make it," Orpha finally proclaimed boldly. "I'm due a raise, and we have enough for the rent. We can tighten our belts a little more."

"I'm making some money doing laundry," Raquel added. "Chili and I have almost thirty dollars saved."

Maylon nodded his head, and Chili shuffled his feet.

"I guess we have a couple of weeks to get things straightened out," Maylon conceded. "I still don't know what we're going to do. Orpha don't make enough each month for the rent on this place, much less food. We can't afford to pick up and move with her working, though. I guess something will turn up."

"I'll make it up to you, Maylon," Chili said with a determined look in his eye. "I know I should've kept my mouth shut and just took it. I know that's what you'd done. I don't know how, but I'll make it up to you."

"You don't have to make up anything to me," Maylon said. "You're my brother."

Naomi stepped up to grab both of her sons by the arm and said, "It will be fine. We're Butlers, and things will work out."

"I know," Maylon said, "but I still don't know what I'll do for work."

"We could go work the fields," Chili suggested.

"I don't mind picking cotton, but the season's all but over," Maylon noted. "There won't be much need for field work until spring. It's nearly the first of November, and we'll need to pay some rent and eat between then and now."

"The Belvedere's went to the coast last winter," Naomi remembered. "They worked in the orange groves near Santa Maria."

"Oranges are harvested nearly year round," Raquel added.

"That sounds promising," Maylon conceded, "but we'll have to find a place, and it'll cost some money to move."

"I can't move," Orpha said. "I got my job. Besides—I got family here. They ain't much, but they'll help out when they can."

"We wouldn't have to move," Chili said. "It's only two and a half—three hours at the most."

"It's warmer on the other side of the Temblors," Raquel added. "You could camp out for a few days and come home every week or so."

"I like camping," Maylon pleasantly said. "What do you think, Chili?"

Chili smiled, "I'd like picking oranges better than cotton."

"We've got a couple of weeks to work things out," Maylon said.

"I can pick too," Raquel offered.

Chili smiled at the offer and said, "Thanks dear, but you can make more doing laundry for the oil trash right here."

"See," Naomi said. "Things are starting to look better already."

CHAPTER 24

Maylon and Chili decided to try their luck over the mountains in the orchards near Santa Maria the first week of November. In the meantime, they had two weeks to get ready. Maylon had enough money saved to pay the rent through the first of the year. Orpha and Raquel worked during the two weeks leading up to the brother's trip. Maylon had been right. Work in Taft was almost impossible after the word got out that the boys had been fired by the oil company. Maylon drove his old car back to Maricopa to find a few odd jobs to do. Maylon also had a friend from his old hometown that let him use his garage and tools to get his old car closer to road-worthy condition.

Chili kept busy in Taft doing odd jobs. He left in the mornings and brought back some money every couple of days. He was vague about the kind of jobs he could find, but he seemed happy for the moment, and Raquel was pleased. The idea of going to Santa Maria to pick oranges appealed to Chili, and Raquel knew he was glad not to have to work in the oil fields.

Raquel's arms were wet to her shoulders from doing laundry when she heard the knock on the door late in the afternoon.

"I'll get it," Naomi offered.

Raquel continued her labors until she heard a voice speaking in broken English and more Spanish. She dried herself and stepped to the front door to see Naomi talking to a young Mexican boy at the door.

"Senorita Butler," the boy said anxiously.

"I'm Mrs. Butler," Naomi repeated, as she had obviously been trying to communicate with the boy.

When the boy saw Raquel, he looked past Naomi and said, "Senorita Butler?"

"I'm Mrs. Butler," Raquel confirmed.

"Chili's wife?" the boy clarified.

Raquel nodded and spoke to the boy in Spanish. The boy replied quickly, and Raquel listened. She did not speak Spanish often, even before coming to the Butlers, but she could make out what the boy was telling her.

"I've got to go run an errand," Raquel told Naomi.

"What's going on?" Naomi asked, unable to understand more than an occasional syllable from the boy.

"Nothing," Raquel lied. "I'll be back soon."

Raquel did not give Naomi a chance to question her further, as she bolted out of the house, followed by the Mexican boy. The boy continued to give her details, but she had already figured out the emergency by the time she stood in front of the Eight Ball Pool Hall. The words "Eight Ball" were hand painted over a neon sign saying "Pool Hall." The store front had been painted green at one time, but the color was now a faded memory, as large flakes of paint clung to the bare wood siding.

Raquel stepped into the dark room that smelled of stale beer, tobacco, and body odor. A fat white man sat on a stool by the front door and studied her carefully.

"Chili Butler's woman?" the fat man asked, as he puffed on his cigarette.

Raquel nodded, "His wife."

"You better get him home before he gets hurt," the man instructed, as he nodded at a door at the back of the pool hall. "I run a respectable place here. You need to remind your husband about that."

Raquel followed the Mexican boy to the back door that opened up into a smaller room with a naked electric light bulb swinging from the ceiling.

Raquel shrieked when she saw a man punch Chili in the stomach, which caused him to crumble to the ground. Raquel ran to his aid, and it was obvious that Chili had already taken more than one punch.

"If it ain't the la hija de una puta," the familiar voice of Carlos taunted.

Carlos spoke English with a thick accent. He smiled evilly at Raquel, and she remembered his insults from her work in the cotton fields.

Carlos looked around and taunted, "This don't look like your kind of place. I'd thought you'd been more on the edge of town."

Raquel ignored the man's insult and whispered to the drunken Chili, "Are you okay?"

Carlos pushed her aside and kicked Chili in the ribs, causing him to groan loudly.

"Leave him alone!" Raquel shouted. "You'll hurt him!"

Carlos grabbed Raquel by the arm and said, "I've already hurt him. I'm going to hurt him real bad if he don't get me my money."

When Raquel tried to break the man's grip, Carlos slung her across the room and caused her to stumble to the dirty floor.

"I warned you, gringo," Carlos mocked, as he bent over the wounded Chili. "You can't come into a place like this and gamble with money you don't have."

"I'll get your money," Chili groaned.

"How?" Carlos shouted. "You don't got no job! You don't got no money!" Grinning wickedly, Carlos added, "Maybe your woman can work it out. She already owes me."

"I owe you nothing!" Raquel screamed from the floor, as she looked up at the man.

"Juan Esperanza left a lot of people hanging when he died," Carlos sneered. "He always hinted that you were his collateral."

"He's dead?" Raquel muttered.

Raquel had not seen or heard from Juan Esperanza since moving in with the Butlers. She often had nightmares about the vile man since she had run away, and she lived with the uneasy feeling that her stepfather would someday show up to try to take her away.

"How?" Raquel asked.

"I don't know," Carlos sneered. "Probably drunk himself to death."

Raquel looked nervously at Carlos, but felt a sense of relief to know she had not killed him that night. Carlos walked over to her, grabbed her by the arm, and roughly stood her up. Chili tried to protest, as Raquel struggled to get away. The door busted open, and the fat man from the front stepped into the room.

The fat man barked, "You can't manhandle a white woman like that, Carlos. Get your hands off her."

"She ain't white!" Carlos informed. "She's as Mexican as me."

"Oh," the man said, as he looked closer at the defenseless girl. "It don't matter. I won't have you abusing a woman of any kind in my establishment. Looks like you've taken your pound of flesh from this fellow. I don't have no problem if a welcher don't pay his debts, but I don't need the cops down here. Let the girl take him home, and you can finish your business outside of my place—or stay out of my back room altogether."

Carlos did not argue with the man, but bent down to whisper to Chili, "Once again, I have to tell you that this ain't over."

Carlos signaled the two other men to follow him, but he stopped to look at Raquel and said, "I'll be seeing you, too."

After the fat man poured a bucket of water on Chili's head, he was able to stand and walk away with Raquel's help. The two did not speak on the short walk home. Raquel did not want to ask questions, and Chili did not have the energy for explanations.

"Wait here," Raquel instructed, as she snuck into the small house to get a bowl and a rag to try to clean Chili's swollen face.

Raquel sighed as she could tell that she would not be able to cover the bruises and small cuts.

"What's going on?" Naomi asked, as she looked out the back screen door.

Raquel did not know how to answer, but Chili confessed, "I've messed up, Ma. I've messed up good this time."

"What's happened to your face?" a concerned Naomi asked, as she walked closer.

"He got in a fight," Raquel tried to explain without getting into the details.

Chili looked at his young wife and smiled before saying, "I've been at the pool hall, Ma."

Naomi did not immediately understand, so he said, "I've been gambling. I won some, but then I lost some too."

"Chili!" Naomi scolded.

"That's not all, Ma," Chili continued. "I've been drinkin' pretty good too."

Naomi did not respond but looked blankly at her son.

"I—I don't know what's been going on in my mind," Chili tried to explain. "It seems that I've messed everything up—for you, for Maylon."

Looking at Raquel, Chili said, "I especially hadn't done much to take care of you."

Naomi sighed heavily and said, "Chili, when are you going to grow up?"

"I don't know, Ma," Chili frowned, "but I think I better start."

Chili looked at Raquel and said, "I'm so sorry. I'm sorry that you had to see me like that today. I'm sorry for a lot of things."

"But you'll stop this foolishness," Naomi said.

Chili nodded, "I promise. When Maylon gets home, I'm going to try to make things right with him. I've wasted my money, took advantage of his good nature, and cost him his job. I'm going to see if he'll still take me with him to Santa Maria to pick oranges. I can make it up to everyone, I swear I can."

"Don't swear," Naomi implored. "But I think having a talk with Maylon could do you some good. I think a change of scenery will do you both some good."

"Thanks, Ma," Chili said. "I think I'll go in now and try to get some rest before Maylon makes it home."

Chili went inside the house and Naomi asked Raquel, "How long have you known?"

Raquel did not answer at first, but then said, "A couple of months."

Naomi looked over the neighborhood and turned her face to the sun to try to glean some of the late afternoon warmth.

"How long have you known?" Raquel finally asked.

Naomi looked at her daughter-in-law and sighed, "Longer than that, I'm afraid."

CHAPTER 25

Maylon wanted to go looking for Carlos, but Chili talked him out of that. Maylon scolded his brother's lack of judgment, and the brothers had a long talk, punctuated by some shouting and some forgiveness. Maylon could never stay mad at his younger brother long, and the two agreed they would get an early start tomorrow for Santa Maria. Raquel again offered to go with them, but they convinced her Naomi needed her at the house.

Chili seemed determined to confess his past weaknesses and turn his life around. Raquel was happy about that prospect. Chili, however, did not have the courage to tell his wife that he had taken the money she had so diligently been saving in her tin can. She found that out when she put the few cents she had earned doing laundry into the can the next day.

The boys left before dawn, planning to see what work they could find for the week, before trying to make it back home by Saturday night. If the work was there, they would make arrangements to spend more of their winter nearer the coast.

Maylon and Chili had been gone two days, when Raquel was startled by a mid-afternoon knock on the door. Naomi had been napping in the back of the house, so Raquel straightened her dress and stepped to the front door. She opened the door a few inches before recognizing Carlos standing on the porch. Before she could slam it shut, he forcefully pushed the door open.

"Nice place," Carlos said.

"Get out," Raquel pleaded.

"What?" Carlos asked. "You're not glad to see me?"

"No!" Raquel said.

"Who is it?" Naomi asked, as she stepped from the bedroom.

Carlos cursed in Spanish before saying in English, "Go away old woman. This don't concern you."

Raquel was surprised when Naomi obeyed and returned to the bedroom.

"Get out!" Raquel demanded.

"Unh-uh," Carlos muttered. "I'm not leaving 'til I get my money—or something else."

"I don't have any money," Raquel said nervously.

Carlos moved uncomfortably close saying, "I guess it'll be something else."

He grabbed Raquel by the arm and pulled her close to him. Before she could scream in protest, a pistol shot roared through the small house. The next sound Raquel heard was the metallic clicking of a pistol being cocked.

"You're going to leave this instant!" Naomi barked, as she pointed the pistol at the man's head.

Carlos sneered and looked like he might test Naomi, before letting go of Raquel and stepping slowly toward the door.

"You heard me, git!" Naomi shouted.

Carlos continued moving toward the door, as he stared coldly at Naomi and then Raquel.

"Tell Chili I'm coming for him!" Carlos angrily threatened, as he stared at Raquel. "Next time I'll get what's owed me one way or another."

Carlos then looked at Naomi meanly and threatened, "You better keep that pistol close, old woman. I'll remember you, too."

"Don't threaten me, you piece of trash!" Naomi barked harshly. "I'm telling the law that you came in here threatening two decent women—one of 'em a widow of an oil field worker. They're more likely to string you up than lock you up."

Carlos glared at Naomi, but he did not challenge her. He knew she was right. He took one last look at Raquel before slipping out the door. Raquel quickly locked the door and looked out the window to see Carlos trotting away from the house. Raquel looked back at her mother-in-law to see Naomi shaking and holding the pistol at her side. Raquel stepped to the stunned woman and gently took the pistol from her.

"Where did you learn to shoot?" Raquel asked.

"Huh?" the shaken Naomi stammered. "My daddy taught me. I hadn't touched a gun in years. This pistol belonged to Eli."

"You scared Carlos away," Raquel said.

Naomi nodded her head and said, "Yes. I guess I did. Are you okay?"

"Yes," Raquel confirmed.

"Was that the man that beat up Chili?" Naomi asked.

"One of them," Raquel said.

"Chili owes him money?" Naomi said.

"I think so," Raquel answered.

"My Chili," Naomi sighed. "So smart in some ways and so dumb in others. What has he gotten himself into?"

"He's working in the orange orchards now," Raquel tried to assure. "He'll send for us soon, and we can get away from the past."

Naomi looked at Raquel and said, "The past isn't that easy to get away from."

Naomi glanced down at the floor and said, "I've put a hole in Orpha's floor. Maybe Maylon can fix it."

"Better the floor than the roof," Raquel said.

Naomi laughed half-heartedly, "I think you're right."

Raquel walked closer to Naomi and looked at the small hole in the floor when Naomi asked, "What did that man mean when he said he'd get his money or something else?"

Raquel hesitated in answering and Naomi said, "I'm old, but not stupid. He meant that he would—do something to you?"

"Carlos is a bad man," Raquel said. "I knew him from working in the cotton fields before Chili. He—he thinks I'm bad, too."

Naomi looked at her embarrassed daughter-in-law and said, "How could he think such a thing."

Raquel did not answer so Naomi put her arm around the girl and said, "I've never asked much about your past. I believed that was your own business. I've seen the marks on your back and know things must have been difficult."

Raquel nodded and said, "My mother kept house for a rich family in the valley. My real father doesn't have anything to do with me. He sent my mother and me away. It was humiliating to my mother when she was let go and things got bad for her. My stepfather was a drunk and—a beast. He's dead now, and I'm glad. Carlos knew him. Men like Carlos and my stepfather hate everyone. It fills them up and makes them want to make everyone as dirty as they are."

Naomi did not respond, but stepping to Raquel, she gently hugged her.

"Do we need to get the police?" Raquel asked.

"I don't know how much help the police would be in this town," Naomi sighed. "Chili's been branded a union man, and now he's got gambling debts. I think Carlos will stay clear of my pistol. The boys will be back in a few days, but I think we're ready for a new start somewhere away from here."

CHAPTER 26

The house had been thick with humidity, as a steady rain turned the dirt-covered front yard into a muddy mess. Raquel went to bed later than usual after she helped Orpha clean her shoes and stockings from the mud. The sheets were sticky and damp, but the quiet house and the occasional patter of rain helped her sleep soundly. The knock on the door startled her in the early morning dawn. Her first thought was that Carlos was back. She quickly pulled on a robe, and could see Naomi standing in the front room holding her pistol. The second knock on the door woke Orpha.

"What's going on?" a sleepy Orpha asked.

"I don't know," Naomi whispered.

"What are you doing with a gun?" Orpha asked.

"Being careful," Naomi explained. "Raquel, you stay back. I'll check to see who it is."

Naomi cautiously peered out the window and immediately put her pistol to her side, before putting it under the cushion of the chair.

"It's the police," a confused Naomi said.

Naomi pulled her robe tightly around her and opened the door to say, "Good morning officer. Can I help you?"

"Good morning," the man politely greeted. "Is this the Butler home?"

"Yes," Naomi confirmed. "Yes it is."

"Are you Mrs. Butler?" the officer inquired.

Naomi replied, "One of them. My two daughters-in-law live here as well."

The officer stepped inside the dark house and looked around at the humble furnishings before saying, "Mrs. Butler, I have some bad news."

"What?" Naomi stammered.

The officer ignored her and continued, "There was an accident on 166 this morning. I'm afraid your boys were in one of the cars."

"Accident?" Naomi said faintly.

"They both were killed," the officer finally revealed.

Naomi collapsed into the chair, as Raquel and Orpha ran to assist her.

"There must be some mistake," Orpha said in a stunned tone of voice. "Maylon's coming back Saturday."

"I'm sorry," the officer said. "We made positive identification."

"It can't be," cried Raquel. "There must be some mistake."

"Again, I'm sorry," the officer repeated. "I know this is a shock, but there's no mistake."

The three women now all cried in disbelief, and it was Naomi who was the first able to compose herself enough to ask, "What happened? Where?"

"They must have run into fog," the officer explained. "They veered over the center line and hit a truck."

The three women listened in silent shock.

"They didn't suffer," the officer tried to console. "They were killed immediately. I'm sorry to have to be the one to bring the news, but I was first on the scene. Is there anything I can do?"

"Where are they?" Naomi asked.

"The bodies are at Sam Witherow's place on Asher Street," the officer explained. "He'll take good care of them. Since you're residents, you should be able to bury them at Westside."

"Thank you," Naomi said in a tone of grim resignation.

The officer nodded and left the three grieving women to their sorrows.

"It's over," Naomi moaned in a pathetic wail of disbelief. "I've lost everything."

Raquel spent most of the next few days attempting to console Naomi while trying to make sense of the loss herself. The always practical Orpha had to take charge in making the arrangements. Naomi had wanted to move the boys to the cemetery in Bakersfield, but the kindly Mr. Witherow convinced her that a burial at the public cemetery in town would be more economical. Orpha made the decision, and the two brothers were laid to rest side by side in a simple service attended by the three women, some friends from Maricopa, and a few of Eli Butler's co-workers from the oil field.

Raquel, who had cried often with Naomi, was especially heartbroken when Orpha finally broke down in her bedroom and wept for most of the first night after the funeral. Naomi was silent and had a haunting glassy-eyed look to her. Orpha was the first of the women who appeared to regain her countenance, and after a few days she went back to work. Raquel also got back to the business of cleaning clothes, although her heart was not in it, and the piles of laundry only reminded her of the husband she had lost.

A few weeks later, Thanksgiving came with another day of crying and bitter memories for the women. Orpha spent a few hours with her family, but Raquel watched Naomi stare blankly at the wall for much of the day. Christmas was even worse, as Orpha worked extra long hours in the depressingly short days of winter. By mid January, the days were getting longer and the nights less cool, but gloom and despair still hung heavily over the small house.

As May approached, Orpha returned home one evening with an anxious and defeated appearance, as she sat heavily in the chair in the front room.

"I don't know what we're going to do," Orpha lamented. "I'm at my wit's end. I've used up all the money Maylon had saved. Even with the money Raquel brings in, I don't see how we can pay the rent on the house another month and buy groceries. I think we're going to have to find a cheaper place."

"The oil company didn't have any pension money for Maylon?" Raquel asked.

Orpha shook her head and replied, "They said he didn't work long enough."

"I'm going home," Naomi announced strangely.

"Home?" Orpha asked with a suspicious raised eyebrow.

"This place has held nothing but misery to me, and I'm going home," Naomi explained. "I've got a hundred and sixty acres and a house Eli bought with his pension back in Beckham County. I'm going home. I'll grow turnips to eat before I endure another month in this place."

"You have a hundred and sixty acres and a house?" Orpha said. "And you've been living in this dump?"

"I have a place near Sayre, Oklahoma, bought and paid for, and I'm going home," Naomi announced defiantly.

Orpha looked at Raquel and smiled strangely before saying, "I'm with you. I'd rather grow turnips than spend my life in that drugstore."

"I'll go where you go, Naomi," Raquel confirmed.

Naomi looked oddly at the girls and smiled, before saying, "Yes, I'm going home. I don't know how, but I'm going home."

For the next few days the three women eagerly made their plans. The car had been destroyed in the accident, and Naomi was the only one who had ever even driven a car. First class rail tickets would cost nearly forty dollars, and even coach tickets were twenty-nine dollars. The only option was a three-day bus ride that would cost fifteen dollars one way. By selling what few belonging they had, the women would have enough for the trip and about fifty dollars to start their new lives.

The last night in the small house felt empty and desolate as all the furniture was gone except for a small rug that hid the bullet hole in the floor from Naomi's pistol shot. All their possessions were packed in six small bags, and they planned to sleep on the floor until the bus left the next morning. Raquel and Orpha had dutifully gone about the task of moving, but Naomi had been sullen and quiet the last two days.

"I want you to know how much I love you girls," Naomi said in a quiet but serious tone. "You've been more precious than any real daughters could have possibly been. You loved my boys, and that makes you a part of me forever."

Naomi looked at her two daughters-in-law and continued, "Orpha, you're the most spirited and likeable girl I've ever known. I hope you know how much Maylon adored you."

"I know," Orpha whispered.

"Raquel," Naomi said. "My Chili loved you too, and I appreciate how you were helping him become the man I know he could have been."

Naomi stopped and fought back her tears before saying, "My sons meant the world to me, and now you both are all that remains. I have no other sons, and I'm too old to have that blessing ever again. I want you girls to go back to your families. You're both still so young and pretty. I want you to meet nice boys and have a full life. I want you to have families and have some of the joy that once was mine. I truly want you to be happy, but I don't think the prospects are good where I go. I'm going home to die, but I want you to live. I don't have the heart to see you marry—although I want that for both of you."

"We won't leave you," Orpha cried.

"I want to be with you, too," Raquel affirmed.

"You don't understand," Naomi sniffled. "You won't be leaving me, because I'm leaving you. Return to your families. May God love and be kind to you, as you have loved my dead sons and been kind to me. God willing, you'll find a home, a good husband, and healthy children."

Naomi stepped to each girl and gently kissed their cheeks and handed them an envelope and said, "I cashed in your bus tickets. Here's the money we've raised. Go back to your families and live well. I'm leaving you tonight because I'm afraid I won't be able to say good-bye tomorrow. I've thought this through, and I've made up my mind. I don't know if our paths will meet again, but I truly, truly want you both to get on with your lives. Forget about me, but know that I love you."

The girls cried and pledged that they would go with her; Naomi picked up her two bags and said, "Good-bye, my dears."

Naomi did not give the girls a chance to argue, as she marched out the door to leave them in the empty house. Although she could hear them crying from the porch, Naomi fought the urge to turn around, and walked slowly to the bus stop to wait for the next bus out of town. Summer was not far away, but the night air was still cool. Wispy patches of the Tule fog danced among the street lights, adding to the deep sadness Naomi felt. She was leaving everything behind, but knew the girls would be the better for it.

The bus station was closed, and no one was around to disturb her solitude. Neon lights from some of the late-night establishments glistened off the damp pavement, as Naomi settled into a hard bench and pulled her coat tight to wait for the bus that was scheduled to arrive in about an hour. Naomi stared into the desolate night when she heard the faint patter of footsteps. She looked up to see Raquel walking quickly toward her.

"I told you I'm going alone," Naomi said, as Raquel approached. "I can't help you and I can only imagine more tragedy if you stay with me. Be a good girl like Orpha and go back to your family."

Raquel put her bag by Naomi, took a seat, and said, "You are my family—you're my only family. I won't go back from where I came. Where you go—I go. Where you stay—I stay. If that means we both die in your home, I want to be buried there with you. I am your family, Naomi. I have nowhere else to go."

Naomi looked at the girl that had been sitting by her and sobbed, "That's about the longest speech I've ever heard you give, but I still think you should at least stay with Orpha."

"Orpha has family," Raquel said. "You're my family."

Naomi turned back to look straight ahead and did not say more, but a voice from behind them said, "I'm your family, too."

Orpha walked up behind the bench and put her arms around Naomi and Raquel.

Naomi turned around to look at Orpha before saying, "At least you've had the good sense to leave your bags behind."

Orpha smiled and said, "I may be opinionated, but I know when you're right. Moving back with my parents for a time will be best, but I couldn't let you leave like this. I couldn't let either of you go without telling you that you'll always be a part of me and a part of my family. Raquel, you're the sister I never had. I am going to miss you, and the laughs we've had."

"I'll never forget you, Orpha," Raquel replied. "I will never smile without thinking of you."

Orpha stepped around the bench and knelt down in front of Naomi to say, "You're a part of me more than you know. I believe things are going to be good for you, and I wish I could go with you, but my place is here—for right now. I need to stay. I can't go with you."

The three women continued their tearful farewell until the bus screeched to a halt in front of the bench.

As Raquel followed Naomi onto the bus, Orpha said, "Take care of our mom, Raquel. Godspeed until we meet again."

The door shut and Raquel looked out the window to see Orpha standing alone, sobbing, as the bus pulled away from Taft, California, and the life Raquel had known.

PART II

CHAPTER 27

Maricopa was the first town on the bus route coming out of Taft. Raquel looked over to watch Naomi as they passed through their old hometown. Naomi sat silently with a slight frown on her face and her eyes looking straight ahead, as if afraid of seeing ghostly memories from a happier past that seemed so long ago now. Raquel looked out the window and could see the former Butler house down the block. A shiny new car was parked out front, and it looked as if the house had been freshly painted.

Raquel had fond memories of Maricopa. It was where she had found refuge with a family that was as caring as her own family had been cruel. Maricopa had been where she had fallen in love with Chili. Maricopa had some fond memories, but she was glad to have it behind her. She did not know what an uncertain future might hold, but she hoped Naomi's home might be a place for her to start again.

Naomi looked solemn as she stared blankly at the passing landscape. Raquel worried about her mother-in-law. Naomi had never been deprived. Raquel could teach her how to survive, but she knew Naomi would have to be willing to adapt. Raquel hoped things would be better in Oklahoma, but she did not have great optimism. She had worked in the fields with the Okies and knew they were a hard-luck lot. Naomi believed, however, that home would have some hope. Belief was a powerful force, and Raquel needed something in which to believe. For now, she would put her faith in the despondent woman in the bus seat next to her.

The bus stopped in Bakersfield to let off a few people and take some more passengers. As the bus traveled east, the lush green fields of Bakersfield faded to the brown, arid Mojave Desert. Barstow was the first stop past Bakersfield. Raquel and Naomi took their bags and stepped out into the hot dry desert air. It was mid-morning, and many of the passengers took the break to have a late breakfast. Raquel and Naomi munched on apples that Naomi had packed, and enjoyed stretching their legs.

Barstow was a smaller town than Bakersfield, but it had an energy that made it seem larger. The town sat at the intersection of two railroads, but more importantly two highways—U.S. 466 and U.S. 66. One road led northeast toward Las Vegas and Boulder City. The place had been an intersection of hope for thousands who had flocked to the desert to build the great dam there. Route 66 headed east and cut through the great Southwest and Midwest of the United States to Chicago. The route trekked through Arizona, New Mexico, Texas, Oklahoma, Missouri, and Illinois. Raquel and Naomi would make half the trip on the great "Mother Road" to their new home.

At Barstow, travelers from Southern California, including the great city of Los Angeles, intersected with those coming from the San Joaquin Valley as far north as San Francisco. The bus riders were an eclectic mix of peddlers, farmers, and others traveling across the great western United States. After an hour, Naomi and Raquel prepared to board their bus heading east on Route 66 and ever closer to Naomi's home.

"Is this seat taken?" a short, unshaven man with a snarling smile asked.

"No," Raquel instinctively answered.

The man, who wore a worn, old suit sat down in the seat immediately in front of Raquel and Naomi. He had a slouching posture and an uneven smile showing his yellowed teeth. The man nervously scanned the other passengers.

His manner had already made Raquel uneasy when he said, "You're a pretty little thing."

Raquel smiled uncomfortably, and now dreaded the next leg of the bumpy bus ride that promised to be filled with unpleasant and unwanted conversation.

The bus filled with passengers, and Raquel was feeling trapped, when the man asked, "What's your name, sweetie?"

Naomi was about to interrupt the man's dialogue when a deep voice from the aisle said, "Excuse me. I think you're in my seat."

"Are you talking to me?" the short man sneered.

The man with the deep, comforting voice smiled pleasantly and said, "Yes. I had asked this young lady to hold my seat, but she's being too polite to tell you to leave."

The man with the pleasing smile talked calmly but forcefully to the shorter man. He wore a white linen suit that was wrinkled from the trip, but his neatly combed hair, and trimmed thin mustache conveyed a sense of confidence and prosperity.

"This is a public bus," the short man declared. "I don't see no name on this seat. I can sit where I want."

The short man turned back around to talk to Raquel when the man with the deep voice said, "Listen friend. This is going to be a long trip. These women don't want a bum like you bothering them all afternoon. You're in my seat. Leave or I'll complain to the driver. They don't like trouble, and he'll put you off this bus if I fuss."

"He'll put you off with me," the short man reasoned.

"Maybe," the man with the deep voice replied, "but you won't be bothering these fine ladies either way, and if you and I get off this bus together, we'll figure some things out before the next bus arrives."

The short man looked over the tall man with the deep voice and said something under his breath.

"Listen, fella," the man with the deep voice said with a smile. "There's a seat right up front. Take it, and we'll all get along fine."

The short man looked down while he contemplated his choices. The man with the deep voice winked at Raquel before focusing his glare back on the short man.

"I'm sorry," the short man grunted.

As he gruffly left, the short man clumsily bumped into the taller man before losing his balance and nearly falling into the women behind him. The taller man straightened him up, and the shorter man moved to the seat toward the front of the bus.

"Thank you," Naomi said in a whisper, when the man was down the aisle. "I don't think that man would have left Raquel alone the whole trip."

"Raquel," the man smiled. "What a beautiful name."

Raquel blushed at the man's compliment, as he continued, "My name is Jack—Jack Fisk."

"Good to meet you, Mr. Fisk," Naomi said.

"Please, just call me Jack," he said. "All my friends do, and it looks like we'll get to know each other quite well on our long ride today."

Jack Fisk looked around the nearly full bus and asked, "Could I take this seat?"

"Of course," Naomi smiled.

"Thank you," Raquel said. "I wasn't looking forward to talking to that man all afternoon."

"I'm guessing you both have a long ride today?" Mr. Fisk quizzed. "How far are you going?"

"We're heading to Sayre, Oklahoma," Naomi shared.

"Sayre?" Mr. Fisk asked. "I've traveled this route from Chicago to Los Angeles many times, but I don't remember stopping in Sayre."

"It's a small town," Naomi explained. "Most folks traveling through stop in Elk City down the road."

"A long trip," Mr. Fisk sighed. "I suppose you'll be stopping somewhere for the night?"

"We're planning on making it to Flagstaff tonight," Naomi explained. "We'll try to get an early start tomorrow morning."

"What takes you fine sisters to Oklahoma?" Mr. Fisk asked.

"Oh, Mr. Fisk!" Naomi giggled. "We're not sisters, of course."

Jack Fisk smiled slyly and said, "I'm mistaken."

"I'm Mrs. Butler's daughter-in-law," Raquel explained.

"Oh," Mr. Fisk sighed. "Two women traveling alone? Your husbands must be worried sick?"

Raquel and Naomi became awkwardly quiet as the pleasant Mr. Fisk smiled graciously before noticing their silence and saying, "Have I said something I shouldn't have?"

"No," Naomi finally said. "It's just—we've recently lost my son—Raquel's husband—in an automobile accident."

Mr. Fisk gasped faintly and removed his hat before saying, "I'm so sorry. I must be the biggest clod on the planet with my insensitive curiosity."

"You couldn't have known," Naomi said.

"Still, I feel terrible," Mr. Fisk stated. "You two unfortunate ladies must allow me to buy you supper this evening when we reach Flagstaff. I insist."

"There's no reason to insist," Naomi assured. "We would love to dine with you tonight. Wouldn't we, Raquel?"

"Yes," Raquel smiled. "It's nice to have someone so familiar with the road."

"If you'll indulge me one more question, I'm curious as to your destination," Mr. Fisk said. "What takes you to Sayre?"

"I have a ranch there," Naomi boasted. "One hundred and sixty acres."

"A real live rancher," gleamed Mr. Fisk. "How interesting."

"I've been away for a few years," Naomi explained with a glimmer of her old swagger and boastfulness. "My husband was in the oil business in California, until recently."

"Again, I never cease to be amazed at the interesting people you meet on the bus," Mr. Fisk said. "The train's an okay way to travel, but it seems so impersonal, and it can't drop you on the street like the bus."

"This is my first bus ride," Naomi stated. "Our other trips have been by car."

"I'm guessing your husband was not able to drive you this trip," Mr. Fisk observed.

Naomi shuffled her feet and then said, "I'm sorry that I've put you in another awkward situation, Mr. Fisk. I too, am recently widowed. That's why we're leaving California, and heading back to the ranch."

"I'm horrified at my callousness," Mr. Fisk stated. "Please forgive me."

"No reason to ask forgiveness," Naomi said. "You're just being good company, and with some of the riffraff on the roads these days, we are honored to have you accompany us."

"The pleasure is mine," Jack Fisk replied.

As the bus bounced through the deserts of western California, Jack Fisk engaged Raquel and Naomi in conversation. Raquel enjoyed his kind comments and congenial manner toward her. He had a way of making her feel important, and she found him quite charming. What really impressed Raquel, however, was Mr. Fisk's affect on Naomi. She had lost some of the self-assurance that had defined her when she lost Eli. She had turned even more sullen and quiet since the passing of her two boys. Mr. Fisk seemed like a tonic for Naomi, as she cheerfully engaged him in conversation and exaggerated her station in life and the optimism of returning to the home place. Raquel did not mind the embellishments, and she enjoyed seeing flashbacks of the Naomi she had known when she first came to the Butler house.

By noon, the landscape had turned browner, rockier, and hotter. A little after lunch, the bus reached Needles, California. The wind felt like a furnace, but the passengers were glad to be off the bus for a short time. Mr. Fisk encouraged his new friends to eat light, and he promised them a big meal in Flagstaff, Arizona, where he said the temperature would be cooler and the restaurants better. Naomi looked at Raquel and took advantage of Mr. Fisk's suggestion, claiming that they had planned only on snacking on fresh fruit on the trip through the desert.

Arizona looked much like western California, except the landscape became more rugged and hilly after the bus crossed the Colorado River. The bus was stifling hot. Raquel, who was more accustomed to working in the heat, managed to keep comfortable with her fan and an open window. Raquel frowned slightly when she thought of how Orpha would have scolded her for letting the wind blow through her hair. Jack Fisk did not seem to mind her unruly hair, and made several nice compliments about Raquel's complexion and bluish eyes. Naomi, however, did not fare as well in the heat. She was more red-faced and perspired heavily, although she continually tried to tidy herself up with her handkerchief. The bus made a short stop at Kingman, Arizona. During the stop, Naomi hurried to the lady's room to try to freshen herself with a damp rag.

Jack Fisk had been right. As the afternoon sun moved behind the bus to the west, and as they rose in altitude, the bus and the temperature became more bearable. By the time the bus made its last stop for the evening in Flagstaff, the air felt cool and fresh. Flagstaff was the biggest town they had seen since Bakersfield. It featured several nicely signed hotels close to the highway. The town was at a crossroads on the east-west Route 66, the magnificent Grand Canyon to the north, and the desert metropolis of Phoenix to the south. To Raquel, the cool fresh air of Flagstaff and the prospect of a hearty meal, made her think the place was a small piece of paradise.

CHAPTER 28

"Let me get those," Jack Fisk offered, as Raquel exited the bus followed by Naomi.

Raquel scanned the passengers and watched the short man that had bothered her earlier in the trip disappear around the corner of the bus station. Raquel handed Naomi's bag to Mr. Fisk and then helped her mother-in-law down the steps of the bus.

"It feels like you have an icebox hidden in here," Mr. Fisk smiled.

Naomi blushed at Mr. Fisk's teasing and replied, "I'm so sorry, but I thought it would be easier to manage one bag instead of two."

"Not a problem," Mr. Fisk assured. "I tell you what, there's a great little place right down the street where we can have a fine supper. Let me take these bags to the Aldridge Hotel, and I'll have them checked so we don't have to tote them around town."

Naomi glanced at Raquel nervously, "Mr. Fisk, we don't have reservations at the hotel."

Raquel felt sorry for her mother-in-law. All afternoon, Naomi had been putting on a show for the amiable Mr. Fisk about a comfortable life that did not exist for her any longer. The two women had carefully planned their budget for the trip, which included an overnight stay in the bus station at Flagstaff.

"That's okay," Mr. Fisk smiled. "The manager's a friend of mine, and he'll be happy to check these bags until we finish supper."

"That would be convenient," Naomi conceded. "Thank you again, Mr. Fisk."

"Tell you what," Mr. Fisk said authoritatively. "You ladies freshen up, and we'll meet at the Grand Café in half an hour. Supper's on me tonight, and you'll not believe the coconut cream pie they make there. It's a little piece of heaven."

With a slight grunt, Mr. Fisk hoisted the bags and walked away from the two women, toward the Aldridge Hotel. The sun was hanging low in the western sky, and the refreshing cool air of the high plains was starting to feel a little chilly.

"I don't know about you," Naomi said, "but I'm starved."

Raquel nodded and then said, "Do you think we should have given our bags to a stranger?"

Naomi appeared surprised by the question, but after a brief pause said, "Mr. Fisk isn't a stranger. We spent the entire day with him. Don't be so suspicious, Raquel. You can tell a lot about a man in an afternoon. I'm a good judge of character."

After trying to convince herself with her explanation, Naomi said, "Why don't you peek around the corner all the same."

Raquel did not hesitate, as she walked swiftly to the corner to spy on Mr. Fisk. As he had described, the tall Aldridge Hotel captured the last rays of the setting sun on its upper floors. Raquel quickly identified the tall Jack Fisk in his white linen suit wrestling the two bags toward the hotel. Another figure captured her attention as well. The short man she had encountered earlier stood outside the hotel facing her. Although she tried to turn away, she was sure the man had spotted her. She peeked over her shoulder to see Mr. Fisk enter the hotel. The short man looked at her a moment, and then turned to walk away. Satisfied that her bags and Mr. Fisk were safely in the hotel lobby, Raquel returned to a somewhat anxious mother-in-law.

"Well?" Naomi quizzed.

"He took the bags to the hotel," Raquel confirmed.

Naomi, who looked embarrassed for doubting Mr. Fisk, said, "It was silly to think otherwise."

"I also saw the short man from the bus," Raquel said.

Naomi shook her head, "We definitely owe Mr. Fisk our gratitude for rescuing us from that ordeal today."

Raquel nodded as she looked back toward the corner.

Naomi looked at her daughter-in-law and said sincerely, "You shouldn't be surprised."

"Surprised?" Raquel said.

"You're an attractive young woman," Naomi said. "For reasons I don't completely understand, you seem ignorant of the fact. You will have men approach you often and persistently. You will, unfortunately, grow out of that stage of life. I'm living proof of that. But while you're still young and have your beauty, we'll have to be careful to take full advantage."

The doe-eyed Raquel watched and listened to her mother-in-law's lecture, as Naomi continued, "The trick for you is to find the right kind of man—a man of substance—and a man of means. A man like Mr. Fisk with an affable character and some prospects—a businessman or professional of some kind would provide for you well."

Raquel smiled at Naomi's blunt, but well-intentioned advice and said, "Let's take care of one thing at a time. Let's get cleaned up and enjoy our meal. I'm famished."

Naomi agreed and the two women took a few minutes to freshen up before walking to the Grand Café. Raquel could almost hear Naomi's silent sighs when Jack Fisk was waiting for them at the entrance.

"Are you ready to eat?" Jack Fisk cordially greeted.

"It smells scrumptious," Naomi nodded.

"You won't be disappointed," Mr. Fisk assured. "How about you, Raquel? I find riding the road gives me a tremendous appetite."

"I'm hungry," Raquel confirmed.

Jack Fisk led the ladies into the restaurant and even ordered for them after asking some questions about their individual tastes. He ordered both women a large steak with baked potato. It was a much more expensive meal than they would have ordered for themselves, and it had been months since they had tasted a cut of meat as fine as the one served by the Grand Café. Mr. Fisk added to the pleasant evening by entertaining the two women with his engaging conversation.

It was dark outside, when Mr. Fisk said, "Oh, no."

"What's the matter?" Naomi asked.

"That was stupid of me," Jack Fisk sighed, as he feverishly patted his coat and trouser pockets. "I seem to have left my wallet."

"Oh, dear," Naomi gasped.

Jack Fisk was unfazed as he seemed to remember something and said, "I laid down in the room for just a minute when I checked into the hotel this afternoon. Undoubtedly, I left it in the room."

Naomi looked nervously at Raquel, as Mr. Fisk said, "I'm going to order the both of you coconut cream pie for dessert while I run to the room and fetch my wallet."

"That's not necessary," Naomi said.

"I insist," Mr. Fisk smiled. "It won't take long."

"But you'll miss your dessert," Naomi suggested, "and after you've talked about it all afternoon."

Jack Fisk quickly replied, "I'll go ahead and order mine and have it when I return. I'll only be gone a minute."

Before Naomi could offer to pay, Jack Fisk rose with a slight bow and headed to the man behind the cash register in front of the restaurant. The man nodded to the two women, and Jack Fisk tipped his hat before heading toward the hotel. In a few minutes, the waitress brought three large pieces of pie to the table. Raquel nibbled at hers, but Mr. Fisk had not exaggerated about the sweetness of the tasty dessert. The women finished their dessert and had several cups of coffee while Mr. Fisk's pie stared at them from his empty seat.

"Will there be anything else?" the waitress asked, as she put the ticket on the table.

"We're waiting for our friend," Naomi replied.

"No hurry, but here's the check," the waitress smiled.

Naomi timidly peeked at the ticket on the table and moaned softly to herself.

"Expensive?" Raquel asked.

Naomi nodded, "Seven dollars and forty-two cents."

That amount would have been close to the weekly grocery budget for the family back in Taft.

"Where do you think Mr. Fisk is?" Raquel asked.

"He'll be here in a minute," Naomi confidently and hopefully declared. "He must have gotten delayed."

Raquel nodded and looked at the piece of pie sitting in front of the empty seat.

"Can we do anything else for you?" the man from behind the cash register asked.

"We're just waiting on Mr. Fisk," Naomi replied. "He went to his hotel room, but he'll return directly."

The man looked around the emptying café and said, "The guy that ate with you earlier?"

Naomi nodded.

"Listen ma'am," the man said. "He left over an hour ago. Told me to have a good night when he left. I appreciate the business, but you've tied up this table most of the night. This isn't your house, it's a restaurant. I don't make money unless people are in these seats eating. The waitress don't make money unless she turns these tables. I need you ladies to pay up."

"Of course," Naomi nervously fidgeted. "Let me see what I have here. Raquel, what do you have in your purse?"

"Sixty-four cents," Raquel answered, as she looked quickly through her coin purse.

Naomi swallowed nervously, "Mr. Fisk said he would be right back."

"Listen, sister," the man said in a stern tone. "I don't know what kind of game you're trying to play, but it's time for you to pay up and leave."

The man picked up the ticket and looked at it before saying, "You owe seven dollars and forty two cents. You have the money don't you?"

Naomi sighed heavily and answered, "We were expecting Mr. Fisk to pay. I only have three dollars with me now. The rest of my money is at the hotel."

The man stared at Naomi and then at Raquel before sighing and saying, "Here's what we're going to do. You're going to go to the hotel, and this one's going to stay here. If you skip out like your buddy, I'll have this pretty thing locked up by the cops before I close."

"There's no reason to be rude," protested Naomi. "I'll go get your seven dollars and forty two cents and be right back."

The man held out his hand and said, "Give me the three dollars you have and bring me the rest."

"I'll be back in a minute, Raquel," stammered Naomi.

Raquel nodded, and Naomi hurried toward the door.

"And don't forget the tip, you deadbeat!" the man shouted, as Naomi left Raquel alone.

The man looked over Raquel, "I hope for your sake that she comes back."

CHAPTER 29

The restaurant was nearly empty when Naomi returned. She did not have to say a word for Raquel to know something was terribly wrong.

"Well?" the man said. "Did you bring my money?"

"We've been robbed," whimpered Naomi.

"A likely story," the man stated sarcastically. "I'm calling the cops."

"Yes," Naomi said. "Please, we need to find my bag immediately."

"I'm not calling the cops to find your imaginary bag and money," the man huffed. "I'm having you two thrown in jail!"

"But all my money was in that bag," Naomi pleaded.

"You people are all alike," the man scolded. "You're all going to California without enough in your pocket to buy a sandwich. I might have let you go with just a sandwich, but you ate my best—and most expensive piece of meat."

"We're not going to California," Naomi announced.

"You got that right," the man growled. "You're headed to jail."

"Sir," Raquel interrupted. "You've got to believe that we did not plan this, but we're victims."

"Tell it to the cops," the man insisted.

"Will the police give you the money we owe you?" Raquel asked.

The man thought for a moment and stared skeptically at the two women.

"They will not," Raquel said. "I'm sorry to have eaten your food, but surely there is a better option than putting two innocent women in jail."

"If you're innocent," the man huffed.

"We are, sir," Raquel said. "I—I have done a fair amount of cleaning, and I can make this place spotless."

"It'd take you four days to make four dollars scrubbing floors," the man scoffed.

"I'll help," Naomi said.

"Okay, two days," the man replied.

Raquel looked at the man and said, "Sir, I will make this place spotless by morning, and we can sell back our bus tickets to pay our bill."

"Raquel!" Naomi protested. "How will we get home?"

"You won't get there any quicker in jail," the man stated.

"So you are agreeable to me working and then getting you the money tomorrow?" Raquel asked.

The man thought for a moment and then said, "I get out of here by eleven. Get to work, but I'll hold those bus tickets until morning."

Raquel nodded, as she searched for her ticket to hand to the man.

Naomi fidgeted and then said, "My ticket's in my bag."

The man sighed angrily, but Raquel said, "The one ticket should pay the bill in the morning."

The man clutched Raquel's ticket and nodded his approval of the plan.

"Could I ask one favor?" Raquel continued.

"You're pressing your luck," the man said.

"Please let my mother-in-law contact the police," Raquel requested. "That's our best hope of paying our bill anyway. We've been taken advantage of, and I am sure the police will not be sympathetic to a man who would victimize two women traveling alone."

The man did not agree immediately.

"I work hard, and I work fast," Raquel pleaded. "You have my ticket, and I'll be here. My mother-in-law will not be as much help as me."

The man nodded reluctantly and said to Naomi, "Okay. Go see if you can get my money."

He then turned to Raquel and commanded, "The mop and rags are in the back."

CHAPTER 30

Raquel attacked the café with a rag, a bucket, and a mop. She started in the back room and worked her way through the kitchen, as the staff started to shut down for the evening. By the time she made it to the dining room, all of the customers but one had left. There was no sign of Naomi, but Raquel hoped she was making some progress with the police. The man behind the cash register watched her carefully as he waited for the last customer to settle up his bill. Raquel was under a table scrubbing the floor, when she heard the bell ding indicating someone was entering the restaurant. She looked up, but was disappointed to see a customer leaving and Naomi still missing.

The man stepped to the door, and Raquel heard the heavy cadence of his steps as he walked up behind her while she was kneeling on the floor. The man did not say anything, but gently touched her shoulder to encourage her to stand.

"You've done enough," the tired man said. "The customers are all gone."

"I'm almost done," Raquel nervously said. "I'll hurry."

"I said you've done enough," the man repeated.

"I don't know where my mother-in-law is," Raquel pleaded.

The man looked out the window of the locked restaurant and said, "She must still be at the station."

"I'm so sorry about tonight," Raquel said, as she fought back tears.

The man looked around the empty restaurant and said, "You're a good worker. If you need a job, I'll put you to work."

"We're headed to Oklahoma," Raquel explained.

"I didn't think anyone went *to* Oklahoma," the man said. "I thought that was a one way trip west."

"My mother-in-law has a place there," Raquel said softly.

"Do you have a room in town?" the man asked.

Raquel shook her head.

The man shuffled his feet nervously and said, "I got a room with a cot in the back. It's not much, but you and your mother-in-law can stay the night if you want."

Raquel did not reply.

"It gets cold here at night, even in the summers," the man explained. "You don't want to be on the streets. Go find your mother-in-law and take the room. One of you can have the cot, and the other can make a pallet. You've got this place spotless."

"You would do that?" Raquel asked. "I thought you wanted to send us to jail?"

"I overreacted," the man said. "You get pretty hardhearted working in a place like this. If you're not tough, you'll give all your profits away. Here take this."

The man handed Raquel back her bus ticket.

"Don't you need this?" Raquel said. "In case the police can't find Mr. Fisk?"

"The cops won't find Mr. Fisk," the man said. "I've seen his kind before. They don't think about nothing but themselves. What kind of heel would stick a good kid like you with the bill? Take the ticket—you've done enough."

Raquel took the bus ticket and said, "Thank you—thank you Mr.—I'm sorry, I don't even know your name."

"Al Benton," the man introduced.

"Thank you, Mr. Benton," Raquel smiled.

"Go find that other woman," Mr. Benton instructed. "I'll be here another thirty minutes shutting down, if you want that room in the back."

"Thank you," Raquel said. "Thank you very much."

After getting directions from Mr. Benton, Raquel raced toward the police station to find Naomi. She stopped in the Aldridge Hotel on the chance that maybe something had happened to Mr. Fisk, but the night clerk had not heard of the man and did not know of any bags stored there. Raquel quickly walked toward the police station. Her heart sank when she saw Naomi sitting pathetically on a bench in front of the station.

"Naomi," Raquel whispered to get the older woman's attention.

Mr. Benton had been right. The night air was cool and promised to be cold by morning. Naomi sat on the bench and seemed to be in a trance as she was slow to respond to Raquel.

"Naomi," Raquel repeated in a louder tone.

Naomi did not look at Raquel, but said, "I've ruined us."

"Of course you haven't," Raquel replied. "I've been worried about you."

"I've been talking to the police, for what good that did," Naomi explained. "They sent someone to the hotel, but no one had heard of Mr. Fisk. I've been such a fool."

"Don't say that," Raquel tried to comfort.

"The police think I've been swindled," Naomi confessed. "They said there are several men—they call them grifters—that work these bus routes, looking for stupid women to take advantage of. I guess they found one today."

"Will they get our money back?" Raquel asked.

Naomi finally looked up at Raquel and cried, "They don't think so. I told them my story, and they said Mr. Fisk sounded like a grifter they had heard of. They said he worked with another shorter man. I told them about the short man on the bus, and they thought they were probably working together. Two passengers on that bus had their pockets picked. In fact, they said the short man was the brains of the operation. They said Mr. Fisk asked all those nice questions just to see how gullible I would be. The police said they didn't think his name was even Fisk. I guess the jokes on them, though."

"Why?" asked Raquel.

"With all my bragging about a ranch and a husband in the oil business, Mr. Fisk probably thought we were worth wasting an afternoon on. He'll be surprised when he finds out how little are in those bags."

"But that's all we have," Raquel said.

"I know," Naomi cried, as she buried her head in Raquel's shoulder. "I've lost everything by being a foolish old woman."

Raquel let Naomi cry for a moment and then said, "Look what I've got."

Raquel reached into her pocket and handed Naomi the bus ticket.

"How did you get it?" Naomi asked. "That despicable man was no better than that scoundrel Mr. Fisk!"

"Mr. Benton gave me back the ticket," Raquel said.

"Who's Mr. Benton?" Naomi asked.

"The man from the restaurant," Raquel explained. "After I worked so hard cleaning, he gave me back the ticket. And—I've got some good news."

"What?" Naomi said.

"I've got a place for us to stay," Raquel said.

"Where?" Naomi asked.

"Mr. Benton has a room in the back, and he said we could stay there for the night," Raquel smiled. "It's getting cold and late. He'll only be there a few more minutes, so we need to hurry."

Naomi looked suspiciously at Raquel, but then she got off the bench and began walking. In a few minutes, they were back in front of the Grand Café. Mr. Benton was still there, as he had promised. He showed Raquel the back room and showed her where some old sheets could be found. Naomi watched the man closely and suspiciously, without saying much to him.

"Hope you ladies get some rest," Mr. Benton said, as he prepared to leave for the night.

"Thank you," Naomi finally said.

Mr. Benton nodded and said, "My wife'll be back in the morning."

CHAPTER 31

An exhausted Raquel quickly fell asleep on the floor of the back room at the Grand Café, while Naomi snored away on the cot. She awoke to the clatter of dishes and the sound of bacon sizzling.

"It's morning," Raquel whispered, as she gently tapped Naomi.

Naomi appeared disoriented and confused, but quickly gained her bearings and said, "We better dress."

Raquel nodded, and the two women quickly prepared for their day.

They were startled by a tap on the door, and a woman's voice asking, "Ya'll hungry?"

The door creaked open and a middle-aged woman in a brown dress and gray hair pulled into a bun stepped in to say stoically, "My husband said to give you breakfast."

"Thank you," Naomi nodded. "Thank you for letting us stay the night."

"Al didn't ask me," the woman replied bluntly. "Which one of you is Raquel?"

"Me," Raquel replied.

Mrs. Benton examined the young woman before her and said, "You did a bang up job on this place last night. I've been coming in mornings for eight years having to scrub the mess from the night before. I feel like I've had the morning off."

"Thank you," Raquel replied.

"I guess you two had a day of it yesterday," Mrs. Benton said.

"Yes," Raquel agreed. "We were swindled."

"It happens," Mrs. Benton said. "There's too many characters on the road these days if you ask me. I've got eggs and bacon if you're hungry."

"Thank you," Raquel nodded.

Raquel and Naomi followed Mrs. Benton into the dining room where several customers were already seated. Two waitresses scurried to fill coffee cups and take orders. Mrs. Benton brought Raquel and Naomi a plate of eggs and bacon when they were seated.

After Mrs. Benton left, Raquel asked, "What are we going to do?"

"I don't know," Naomi replied. "I'll go back to the police to see if they found anything, but I don't know what good that will do."

"Mr. Benton said I could work here," Raquel said.

Naomi looked around and said, "Mr. Benton was kind last night, but we can't live in that back room, and I'm afraid it would take a couple of weeks to make enough for another bus ticket."

"What if we cash in the ticket and get two tickets as far as we can go?" Raquel suggested.

"Maybe," Naomi said. "I don't know exactly how far we could get. Besides, we'd still have no money and be stranded somewhere else eventually."

"I guess we're stranded no matter what," Raquel frowned.

"Maybe the police will have our money and my ticket," Naomi said.

Raquel nodded, although she knew there was little chance of that happening.

"Where are ya' going?" a man asked, sitting in the booth behind Naomi.

Naomi looked at the man without answering him.

"Oklahoma," Raquel said, as Naomi looked at her.

"Oklahoma," the man frowned. "I can't help you there. I'm headed to Santa Fe. That'd get you part way."

Raquel looked at Naomi, but she could tell the older woman was reluctant to hitchhike.

"When are you leaving?" Raquel finally asked.

"I'm on the road as soon as I eat breakfast," the man said. "I'm John Cook, by the way."

John Cook was a large, barrel-chested man who wore a neatly starched, red-plaid flannel shirt and looked like he had not shaved in several days.

"I drive a rig," John Cook said. "I make the run between Phoenix and Santa Fe a couple of times a month. The company don't like me picking up hikers, but the company can't get mad about something they don't know."

"Could you give me a minute to check on something at the police station?" Raquel asked.

John Cook looked at the two women, "You ain't in no trouble with the law, are you?"

Naomi turned around and said, "Do we look like criminals?"

John Cook blushed slightly, "No ma'am."

"Mr. Cook, we were robbed last night," Raquel explained. "We thought the police might have recovered our property and a bus ticket to take us home."

"Good luck with that," John Cook said sarcastically.

"Could you give us a minute to check with the police and cash in our bus ticket?" Raquel asked sweetly.

John Cook looked like he would say no, but nodded and said, "Don't dillydally. I'm on a schedule and can't wait. I'll eat my breakfast slow and grab a cup of coffee. If you're back by then, I'll give you a ride to New Mexico."

"Thank you," Raquel said. "Let's go, Naomi."

Naomi stared at the truck driver as she slid out of the booth and followed Raquel out the door.

"I don't like this," Naomi complained, once they were outside.

"It's a ride, and it won't cost a thing," Raquel said.

"I bet Mr. John Cook wouldn't be so all fired up to give us a ride if you weren't young and attractive," Naomi huffed.

"He seemed nice," Raquel said.

"You've got a lot to learn about men pretending to be nice," Naomi coached.

"I don't see that we've got a lot of options," Raquel said. "Unless the police have our money and your ticket, we're stuck between here and your home. We can cash in this ticket for enough to live on for a couple of days and maybe catch another ride tomorrow."

"I still don't like it," Naomi said.

Naomi went to see the police while Raquel walked quickly to the bus station to cash in their one ticket. Raquel came back in fifteen minutes with eight dollars and a few pennies. Naomi was slumped on the bench in front of the police station where Raquel had found her the night before. Raquel could tell the police had no good news for them.

"We don't have anything but the clothes on our backs," Naomi moaned. "Why would that scoundrel take our clothes? Looks like he'd of at least had the decency to just rob us and leave us some dignity."

Raquel did not have the time or energy to listen to Naomi complain, so she said, "Let's hurry. Maybe we can still catch that ride."

Naomi lethargically complied and followed Raquel back toward the café.

"Mr. Cook!" Raquel shouted, as she spotted the man walking out the restaurant.

"You about lost your ride," John Cook said, without breaking stride.

"So we can still ride with you?" Raquel asked, as Naomi tagged behind.

John Cook nodded, "If we don't waste more time."

Raquel stopped to look at a big truck pulling a trailer that had red lettering that said Phoenix Citrus.

"Here she is," John proudly announced, as he opened the passenger door to the cab of the truck.

Naomi pushed her way past Raquel, to the disgruntled frown of John Cook to take the middle seat. Raquel had to gently push Naomi up into the cab. John cranked the engine. With a bellow and a pop, the big machine coughed to life.

"She don't like these cold mornings," John explained. "It's a good thirty degrees hotter in the valley."

"Thanks again for the ride," Raquel said.

"No problem," John said. "This old road gets pretty lonely. I like having the company."

"You haul citrus?" Raquel asked.

John nodded and said, "Mainly oranges. I got a stop in Albuquerque and then finish in Santa Fe."

The truck lurched forward, which caused Naomi to nearly fall into Mr. Cook. She quickly regained her balance, and soon the truck was rolling down Route 66 and into a bright morning sun.

"I hate this trip east," John Cook complained. "You drive all morning with the sun in your eyes on the way out and all afternoon back into the sun getting home."

Raquel had worried about awkward conversation with a stranger, but the chatty truck driver made sure that would not be an issue with his nearly constant talking. He tried to flirt with Raquel even though Naomi glared angrily at him when he made even the most innocent comment. Mostly, he talked about how lonely driving a truck could be, while telling them about the landmarks and local history of eastern Arizona. Raquel did not mind his stories or even his awkward compliments aimed at her. The only distraction was his habit of looking at the passengers as he talked, which caused Naomi to yelp several times for him to keep his eyes on the road.

"I know a great diner in Gallup," John announced, as the trio crossed the border into New Mexico. "Best burger this side of Texas. Grilled onions and only ten cents."

"That would be fine," Naomi said, pleased to have an affordable meal for the day.

Gallup was a town situated in a dry valley of scrub brush, overlooking mountains to the north that still had a few reminants of snow on some of the higher peaks. John Cook drove slowly past a railroad car that had been converted into a small diner. He parked his rig about a half block away and stumbled out of the cab on his bowed legs.

Folger's Diner was located on the edge of town. The highway in Arizona, had been a combination of rough pavement and gravel, but the road into Gallup, New Mexico, had been smoother. The dust had caused Naomi to wheeze, sneeze, and cough for much of the morning, but had not interfered with the truck driver's one-sided conversation. The Phoenix Citris Company truck had provided a bumpy, dusty ride compared to the passenger bus the day before. By the time John brought the truck to a complete stop, the Butler women needed a break.

Route 66 was the personification of western America in many ways. A combination of cross-country travelers and local residents using the road—an eclectic group of travelers and vehicles from coupes, sedans, and various types of trucks. Traffic whizzed by going both directions, as Raquel helped Naomi out of the truck's cab. Raquel fought back a smirking smile at the sight of her mother-in-law. Naomi took great pride in her appearance. She had worn a nice dress and shoes for the bus ride home. Her hair was always tidy, and Naomi took great care to check her complexion regularly. The truck ride had changed all of that. Naomi's dress was a wrinkled mess, and her cheeks were flushed pink from the warm ride. Her usually tame hair had frizzed into a clump on the side of her head. Raquel knew her mother-in-law would have screeched in shame if she could see herself now.

"Thank goodness we're stopped," Naomi huffed in a whisper. "I'm not sure which hurts more, my derriere or my ears from Mr. Cook's incessant talking."

"Let's get cleaned up," Raquel suggested. "I'm hungry."

Naomi nodded and the two women found the ladies room at the side of the diner. The restroom was small and dingy, but it had running water. Raquel felt somewhat refreshed, as she stepped back into the bright sunshine while waiting for Naomi to try to pull herself together. John Cook stood at the door of the diner and waved for Raquel to join him.

"I'm waiting for Naomi," Raquel smiled, as she held her ground.

John frowned and nodded before walking into the small diner to make his order. Raquel stayed outside, content for the moment to not answer prying questions from the talkative truck driver.

As Raquel waited, she noticed a jalopy-looking truck with a mattress tied over the hood, and a collection of personal items hung on every available space, which gave the vehicle the appearance of a rolling junkyard. Steam bellowed out of the radiator, and two men stood over the old truck as if trying to nurse it back to health with prayer and faith. Raquel counted nine people milling around the beat-up truck. The two men at the hood looked to be brothers in their late twenties. The grandfather headed to the diner, followed by two skinny girls in overalls. The mother fanned an older woman resting in the back of the truck, and a pregnant woman accompanied by her husband fanned as well.

"Look at that rabble," Naomi said, as she joined Raquel.

"Must be a family," Raquel said.

"Let's go inside," Naomi suggested.

Raquel nodded and followed Naomi past the truck and the family, who were obviouly not going into the diner.

When Naomi reached the back of the vehicle, she stopped suddenly and whispered, "Oh, my."

Raquel watched her until Naomi said, "Those plates are from Oklahoma."

Naomi hesitated a moment and then asked the woman fanning the old woman, "You coming from Oklahoma?"

"Yes, ma'am," the woman drawled.

"Where from?" Naomi asked.

"Sequoyah County," the woman answered. "Had a place near Sallisaw."

"Are you heading home?" Naomi asked.

The plump woman from the back of the truck had a twisted look of angst to her face as she answered, "Don't rightly know where home is. We're headed to California. The men folk have a flyer saying they need eight hundred pickers for the orchards. For now, this truck and our tent is home, but I hear fine stories about California. Where you from?"

Naomi looked into the crowded back of the truck and said, "I'm heading home to Sayre, Oklahoma, in Beckham County out west."

The woman frowned and said, "We drove through Sayre on the way out. Hope things are better there than in the Cookson Hills."

"I've got a place there," Naomi assured.

"Good luck to you," the woman said. "We sure left plenty of it back there."

"Good luck to you, too," Naomi said, as she stepped away from the family.

As the women headed into the diner, the grandfather and the two skinny girls headed out carrying a half loaf of bread and two sticks of hard candy. The man stoically nodded to them, and the two girls happily and eagerly licked their candy. Naomi stopped at the door of the diner and watched the family load up and drive west toward California.

"They've got a long, hard trip," Raquel said. "I've seen folks like that plenty of times in the fields. They may need eight hundred pickers, but there'll be two thousand show up for those jobs."

"They don't know what they're getting into," Naomi agreed. "Still, they have each other. Maybe that's enough. I'd sure trade places with that woman to be heading west with both of my sons with me."

"I know," Raquel whispered.

Raquel and Naomi found John Cook sitting at a booth with his food in front of him. The two women took their seats and ordered a hamburger to share. John Cook continued his steady talk about his life and his philosophy. The tasty hamburger filled their stomachs, but the family outside reminded them of all they had lost. For the first time all day, Raquel was grateful to have the talkative truck driver provide all the conversation.

CHAPTER 32

"I got to get on the road," John Cook announced, as he stood up to pay his ticket. "I've got a schedule to keep."

"Of course," Naomi replied. "Let me finish my coffee, and we'll be ready."

Naomi enjoyed her last swallow of coffee when the door bell of the diner rang, indicating another customer was either coming or going. Raquel was the first to glance at the newcomer, and Naomi could tell something was wrong.

"You!" Raquel charged angrily at the sight of Jack Fisk standing in front of the door.

Jack Fisk still wore his white linen suit, and beamed with his infectious, likable smile.

"Hello, again," Jack Fisk replied, after a slight hesitation.

"You took our things!" Raquel barked, as she stepped up to the man.

Jack Fisk carefully scanned the dining room before saying, "I've been looking everywhere for you."

Raquel did not look convinced, but Naomi finally squirmed out of the booth and scolded, "Mr. Fisk you have greatly inconvenienced us. Do you have our bags?"

"At the bus station," Jack Fisk replied.

A doubtful Raquel said, "Show us."

"Surely you won't begrudge a hungry traveler a sandwich first?" Jack smiled.

"Show us now!" Raquel firmly demanded.

"Ladies, I really need to get rolling," a nervous John Cook announced. "I've got a schedule to keep."

Raquel kept her eyes fixed on Mr. Fisk but said, "Thank you so much for the ride, Mr. Cook, but Mr. Fisk has some business that we need to attend to, so we won't be riding with you to Albuquerque."

Mr. Cook looked over Mr. Fisk and replied, "Suit yourself."

After Mr. Cook exited the diner, Jack Fisk asked, "Sure you want to give up your ride? Mr. Cook looked like an amiable character."

"Where's our money?" Raquel demanded.

Mr. Fisk looked around the diner and could tell the conversation was beginning to draw unwanted attention.

"Let's talk this over outside," Mr. Fisk suggested.

Raquel nodded, and the two women followed him to the dusty parking area adjacent to the highway.

"I know there must be some explanation," Naomi said. "Do you have our money?"

Mr. Fisk smiled pleasantly and said, "There is an explanation, Mrs. Butler, and I am so sorry for inconveniencing you. I left to get my wallet that evening and ran into a little trouble."

"What kind of trouble?" Raquel asked.

"I ran into an old aquaintance," Mr. Fisk explained, "that claimed I owed him money. He took your bags as collateral, I'm afraid."

"Oh, my," Naomi moaned. "You informed the police?"

Raquel looked at her hopeful mother-in-law and said, "He didn't go to the police."

"You're quite right," Mr. Fisk admitted. "I've been trying to get the bags back and returned to you."

"You said you *had* our things," Raquel said.

Mr. Fisk did not respond after being caught in his lie.

"What did you really do with our money?" Raquel asked pointedly. "Tell us the truth this time."

Mr. Fisk fidgeted for a moment, before saying in a less superficial tone of voice, "Okay, I took your things."

"What!" Naomi exclaimed.

"He robbed us," Raquel clarified.

"Not exactly robbed," Mr. Fisk defended. "No one got hurt. I wouldn't hit or take advantage of a woman by force."

"You did worse," Raquel scolded. "You left us stranded with nothing but a bus ticket and resturant tab!"

"Well," Mr. Fisk sighed. "It's what I do—It's how I make my living."

"How could you?" Naomi shrieked.

"How could I?" Mr. Fisk responded. "You're one to talk. You convinced me that you were a woman of some means—a husband in the oil business, a ranch back in Oklahoma. I barely got thirty bucks out of that scam and had to split it with a partner to boot."

"The short man from the bus?" Raquel said.

Mr. Fisk nodded.

"That was all the money we had in the world to get home!" Raquel said.

"Where are our things?" Naomi asked. "My clothes and other items?"

Mr. Fisk swallowed hard, "Back in Flagstaff. I traded the bags to a couple of hobos for a bottle—of whiskey."

"You drank up our property!" shouted Raquel.

"Keep it down," Mr. Fisk said. "Listen. I've ran into some bad luck. I'm as broke as you are right now."

"I've got a good mind to go to the police," Raquel said.

Mr. Fisk took a step away from the women and said, "I don't think that'll do you much good."

"And why not?" Raquel questioned. "I don't imagine the law would think highly of a swindler taking advantage of two defenseless women."

Mr. Fisk was now walking quicker, as he said, "Any beef you have with me happened in Arizona—not New Mexico. I think you'll find the local law is very clear about their jurisdiction, particularly this close to the border."

As Mr. Fisk now began running away, Raquel shouted, "We'll see about that!"

"He's getting away!" Naomi said.

"Stay here," Raquel implored, as she began running after him.

Mr. Fisk now sprinted away from the diner and toward town. Raquel did her best to keep pace, but wearing shoes and a dress, she was barely able to keep Mr. Fisk in sight. As she got further into town, she saw the police station and the bus station near it. Raquel watched Mr. Fisk mingle with the other passengers at the bus station and decided to try the police.

"Please help me," Raquel panted, as she stumbled into the police station.

A young officer sat at a desk in the empty station and said, "Settle down. What's happened?"

Raquel tried to catch her breath as she said, "Jack Fisk stole my luggage the other night! He's at the bus station now!"

"Wait a minute," the young officer stumbled. "Tell me exactly what happened, when, and where."

"Last night," Raquel explained. "We had supper with Mr. Fisk. He stuck us with the bill and took our bags, including some money and a bus ticket."

"Here in town?" the officer asked.

"No!" Raquel replied, angrily. "We were in Flagstaff last night."

"That's Arizona," the officer explained.

"Could you at least check and see if he has any of our things?" Raquel asked, in as calm of a voice as she could manage.

The young officer looked at her a moment and said, "I guess it couldn't hurt to check things out, but if this man hasn't done anything in New Mexico, I don't know if we can help."

"Please hurry," Raquel implored.

The officer gathered his gear and followed an anxious Raquel outside. Raquel walked with more urgency than the officer and she nearly stepped in front of a departing bus.

"Watch yourself," the office scolded.

Raquel looked into the bus to see a gloating Jack Fisk waving at her as the bus accelerated down the highway.

"There he is!" Raquel shouted, as she pointed frantically at the bus.

"Who?" the officer asked.

"Jack Fisk!" Raquel replied. "He's on that bus. Stop him!"

The officer looked at the bus getting smaller as it sped down the highway and said, "It won't do no good."

"What!" Raquel exclaimed. "I saw him."

The officer looked around the busy bus station and replied, "That bus is headed west. It's not more than twenty miles to the border. I can't find a car and possibly catch it before it crosses over. Even if I did, I don't have any evidence or way to identify the man."

"I saw him!" declared Raquel. "I can identify him!"

"Listen," the policeman said, as he studied Raquel. "The buses bring people in and out of here every day. I can't go hassling the bus company and stopping buses because some girl says something happened in Arizona."

"You mean some Mexican girl," Raquel hotly replied.

"I didn't say that," the officer replied defensively. "It's a jurisdiction issue. I have an obligation to protect the citizens of this city, and as far as I can tell, that doesn't include you. I'm sorry you've been wronged, but there's nothing else I can do for you today."

Raquel wanted to say more, but she nodded as the officer walked casually back to the station. She then walked to the ticket window and asked the destination of the bus that just left.

"Winslow, Arizona, is the first stop," the ticket woman replied. "That bus route will terminate in Needles, California, tonight."

"Thank you," Raquel sighed, as she began the long walk back to find Naomi.

CHAPTER 33

"If that's not a pickle!" Naomi fumed, when Raquel told her the story about Jack Fisk catching the bus west into Arizona. "I guess decent women can get no satisfaction from the law in New Mexico!"

"Do you think we should go after him?" Raquel asked. "We might have enough for one ticket to Winslow or even back to Needles."

Naomi thought for a moment and then said, "No dear. That's taking us the wrong direction, and we would have to split up. I don't think we'll ever get anything out of Mr. Fisk but more frustration."

"You're right," Raquel sighed. "I know it."

"We found a ride to here alright," Naomi suggested. "Surely Mr. Cook is not the only honest man on the road. Perhaps we can hitchhike our way home."

"I don't think we have many other options," Raquel admitted.

With a sly smile, Naomi said, "We have one thing going for us."

"What's that?"

"You," Naomi chirped. "I'm betting there's not many drivers out there wanting a grumpy old woman like me riding along, but you—you're young and eye-catching. I think we'll be able to find a ride by the end of the day. Oh, we'll be careful, that's for sure, but we'll make it. We've got to get some things, though. We can't make it cross country with nothing but the clothes on our backs."

Raquel nodded in agreement and the two women walked back toward town to find a five and dime store to purchase their supplies. In less than an hour, they both had a cloth bag filled with a change of clothing and other supplies for their trip. The two women returned to the diner to nurse a cup of coffee through the afternoon, waiting to find their next ride.

As the afternoon turned to evening, the earlier optimism about catching a ride vanished. Most of the travelers were heading east, and Raquel was too shy to ask many for a ride. After the cashier explained that they would need to buy supper or leave, the dejected women stepped into the dusk without a ride or a place to stay.

"What are we going to do?" Naomi said, as they walked toward town.

"We'll find a place to rest and try again tomorrow," Raquel said. "We'll be fine."

Raquel did not know how much of that statement she believed, but she did know they needed to find some place for the night.

"How much do you think a hotel room would cost in this place?" Naomi asked hopefully.

"More than we have," Raquel replied.

The thought of sleeping outside caused Naomi to pull her arms around herself to brace against cooling air from the nearby mountains.

"We need to find a bench or someplace off the ground," Raquel said. "Put on the extra dress and stockings you bought earlier."

"Over my clothes?" Naomi asked.

Raquel nodded. She had spent many nights away from home before she came to live with the Butlers. She knew very well that the desert nights could feel cold and last forever, if the chill got to you.

"What a mess I've gotten us into," Naomi complained. "We'd be better off back in Taft or even Flagstaff."

"We're closer to your home," Raquel tried to encourage.

It had been a cloudless, warm afternoon, but the light north breeze brought a cool evening, and even with the extra clothes, Raquel could hear Naomi shivering. She went to a church building to knock on the door, as Naomi protested. There was no answer and no shelter to be found as the evening turned into a dark, moonless night.

"Let's keep walking," Raquel suggested. "It will help us keep warm."

Raquel knew they could not walk all night any more than they could walk to Naomi's home, but the night stroll kept her mind off the cold breeze. Raquel was looking for any abandoned building or house that might provide some relief. She even considered going to the police to see if they could be locked up for vagrancy, although she was convinced Naomi would not submit herself to such an indignity. A faint glow and smoke across the tracks caught Raquel's attention, and she nudged a shivering Naomi toward the promising flame.

The two women walked across the railroad tracks and toward the light, a few hundred yards away, in a small ravine. Raquel knew where they were headed, but she did not have the energy to agrue with Naomi about their straggling into a squatters' camp for the night. As they approached the light, they could hear the muffled banter from a group of twenty or so people living in a shanty village close to the railroad.

"It's a hobo camp," Naomi protested, as Raquel kept walking.

"They have a fire, and you're cold," Raquel said.

The conversation hushed as the two women stepped into the camp. A fire simmered in a metal barrel in front of a ragtag tent stained the color of the ground, with rotting canvas and frayed flaps held together with rusty baling wire. Several shaky wood shacks and dugouts surrounded the camp, with flickering fires creating dancing shadows in the night, which made the structures look eerie and hopeless. A small house made of fruit crates and burlap sat in the center of the destitute community, with an old man looking tired and disinterested at their arrival.

"What do we have here?" a male voice from the small group around the tent exclaimed.

"Entertainment!" another voice shouted, as others laughed.

"They're dressed a little fancy for our party," the male voice replied.

"We don't want trouble," Raquel said. "We just wanted to warm by your fire for a few minutes."

"For free!" one of the men shouted.

"We don't have any money," Raquel said, as she slowly approached, unsure of the consequences of her decision to come to this place.

"A pretty little thing like you don't need any money," the man jeered. "Come here and I'll keep you warm."

"Leave her alone!" Naomi screeched.

"Or what?" the man threatened.

Raquel stopped a few yards away from the warm fire, as Naomi clutched to her arm.

"I said we didn't want trouble," Raquel restated. "We just want to warm by the fire."

"I know you," a man from one of the tents several yards away said.

"Know who?" the man who had been mocking the women said.

A tall man in shabbily patched clothes stood up, followed by a shorter, younger man.

"Yeah," the man said. "I've seen you somewhere."

"I don't think so," Naomi said defensively.

The man stepped closer to them in the dark firelight and said, "No, I've definitely seen you somewhere—California maybe?"

"We're from California," Raquel admitted. "Taft—and Maricopa."

"Maricopa!" the man said, as he came into full view.

"You," Naomi sighed.

The man smiled and said, "You recognized me now."

Naomi nodded.

The man talked to the rest of the group and said, "I came to this woman's house looking for some chores to do. I was looking for a meal, I was. What I got was a lecture. Yes, I remember you!"

Naomi did not reply, but she clearly recalled the man who had come to her house to bum a meal.

"You're a long way from home, lady," the man sneered. "A long way from home."

"Stay back," Naomi threatened, causing the man and the rest of the group to laugh loudly.

"This lady's quite a one for lectures," the man continued. "I remember you. She said, 'I wasn't looking for a hand-up, but a hand out.'"

The group booed and hissed at this statement, while Naomi shuffled her feet uncomfortablly.

"I remember you well," the man continued. "Quoted the good book to me."

The men laughed and slowly moved to surround the two women.

The man talked louder now and quoted, "She said that a man that, 'won't work don't deserve to eat!'"

"Sir," Naomi tried to explain. "I'm sorry you felt insulted, but please leave us alone."

The man leaned close to Naomi and said in a softer tone, "Looks like things have turned around a little since Maricopa. Looks like I'm the one that can lecture now."

"Leave her alone," Raquel stated forcefully, while pulling Naomi behind her.

The tall man straightened up and said to the group, "I remember this pretty one, too!"

"Tell us more," one of the other men coaxed.

"Please leave us alone," Raquel pleaded in a timid voice. "We just wanted to warm ourselves by the fire."

"I remember this pretty little thing well!" the tall man shouted loudly. "She looked as kindly at me and my friend then, as she looks nervous now. After the old woman sent us away with a lecture and a hungry belly, this one found us down the street and gave us a lunch, but that's not all!"

The forceful and loud proclamation of the man caused the others to quiet down and listen as he said, "She was nice to me and my friend that day. She had a smile and showed some kindness that I'll not soon forget."

Raquel sighed in relief, as the man said to her, "My fire is your fire."

He then stood up and said to his group, "And don't any of you ruffians disrespect these women or you'll be answering to me."

Raquel looked at the tall man and whispered, "Thank you."

CHAPTER 34

"I'm Hank," the tall man wearing shabby clothing and a week's worth of beard introduced. "My partner here is Harry. Come to our fire."

The younger man nodded nervously, as Hank led them to a patched tent with a fire in front. The ragged camp had about twenty dwellings, including worn tents and lean-to shacks made with various highway signs, fruit boxes, and cardboard. The group at this shanty-town consisted of down-on-their-luck men and a few women. The people looked dirty, tired, and hopeless at first impression, but there was something about their manufactured independence that gave them an unusual sense of dignity. They had a built-in mistrust of well-dressed people that had any signs of prosperity. They studied the two women carefully before returning to their own discussions and conversations, while basically ignoring the new visitors that followed Hank and Harry to the tent.

Hank offered a rickety stool to Naomi and unceremoniously plopped onto the hard ground. Harry, who was younger and quieter, sat down with a little more grace.

Hank patted the ground and said to Raquel, "Sorry, we only have the one chair, but you might as well make yourself at home close to the fire."

Raquel nodded and found a spot close to Naomi, near the small fire that had more embers than flame.

"I've seen a lot of folks traveling on the rails, but I've never been more surprised to see a couple of ladies like you here," Hank said, while he threw a small piece of wood on the fire.

Naomi sat silently, and Raquel nodded politely.

"I could give you a lecture about mercy and hospitality," Hank scolded Naomi. "The good book talks about such things."

"I'm sorry," Naomi said softly.

Hank looked like he might say more, but instead he poked at the fire with a stick.

"Thank you for letting us sit by your fire," Raquel said.

Hank grinned, "Shucks, ma'am. It's only a fire. It'll warm up a dozen as easy as it warms up one."

"Still, I thank you," Raquel said quietly.

Hank leaned back on his side after the fire flamed a little higher and asked in a serious tone, "Wanna tell your story?"

"Excuse me?" Raquel replied.

"Your story," Hank said. "Everyone on the road has a story. Take Harry and me. I had a nice little life once. It might not have been up to your standards, but I had me a job and a little woman."

"What happened?" Raquel asked.

Hank looked into the dark sky, as if searching for an answer, and said, "A lot of bad luck—I guess a lot of bad luck I helped make. I took to the drink a little more than my woman could appreciate. She weren't no fine lady like yourself and we weren't church-married as such, but she was a woman with some standards. I lost my job to the depression and what not. Things got a little tough—then things got bad. My woman blamed me somehow. Maybe she should've. Her mother—a meaner woman you've never met—poisoned her against me. Reminds me of your traveling buddy some."

Raquel glanced at Naomi, but her mother-in-law stared blankly into the fire ignoring the insult.

"Anyway," Hank continued. "Work was hard to find, and I fairly well wore out my welcome in town. My woman ended up runnin' off with some preacher man. I took off for Lubbock to work in the stockyards. Bad work it is, and my only comfort come from the drink. I ran into some trouble in Lubbock and been on the road since. Hadn't been home in so long I can hardly remember."

"Where's home?" Raquel asked.

"Higgins, Texas, ma'am," Hank replied. "A little speck of a town so close to the border you could say it was in the armpit of the Oklahoma panhandle. Nothing going on in or out of town but the railroad. One day I piled into the back of an empty freight car, and I've been riding the rails since."

"Will you ever go back?" Raquel asked, as the fire warmed her cheeks.

Hank shook his head and said, "Naw. The town's too small, and everyone there knows me a bit too much. There's not much I miss—a desolate place with nothing but scrub brush and a few head of cattle. Looks pretty much like New Mexico and Arizona put together."

"There is a little diner there, though," Hank smiled. "A place called 'West of the Line.' My ma used to run the place. The best chicken fried steak ever put on this earth. When I get hungry sometimes, it seems all I can do is think about that piece of chicken fry. I'll tell you one thing, if you ever find yourselves close to Higgins, you'd better stop in and try it. That's the only time I get sick for home when the hungries get me—of course, I could say I get homesick an awful lot these days."

Hank stretched out his long legs and said, "I should've asked already, but you women eat today?"

Raquel nodded and said, "We had a nice lunch."

"That's probably a good thing," Hank grinned. "We don't have much but mutton stew, and it's been ripe for about two days now. Hunger's a powerful sauce though, and we've been eatin' good off it for a week now."

"Your friend don't talk much," Raquel observed, as she nodded toward the younger man.

Harry looked to be in his early twenties and had a smooth face except for a patch of whiskers on the tip of his chin.

Hank laughed and said, "No, Harry don't talk much. Say hello to the ladies, Harry."

Harry shifted nervously and stuttered, "He—Hel—Hello."

The embarrassed Harry looked away and Hank said, "He can talk better than that, but Harry gets real nervous around strangers. Ain't that right, Harry?"

Harry nodded and smiled shyly.

"I ran into Harry about a year ago," Hank explained. "He'd come from a farm somewhere back in Iowa. We paired up in Idaho a couple of summers ago, and he was not much more than a skeleton. We've been buddies since, and there's not a better person to listen than old Harry. I take care of Harry, and he takes care of me."

Raquel smiled at the young man who grinned at the compliment.

"You've heard our story," Hank said, as he stirred the fire again. "But I get the feeling you're avoiding yours."

"We're traveling east," Raquel explained. "We've had some bad luck the past couple of days."

"You must have had a genuine disaster to end up here," Hank said. "Last time I saw you two, you were living high on the hog. Ain't that right, old woman."

Raquel interrupted and said, "I've been rude. We should have introduced ourselves. I'm Raquel Butler and this is my mother-in-law Naomi Butler."

"Mother-in-law," Hank said. "That must mean you're married?"

"Was married," Raquel said. "My husband passed away a few months ago. Naomi's lost her husband, too—and another son—just recently."

Hank removed his tattered hat, and Harry followed suit, as Hank said, "I'm truly sorry ma'am. I've been having fun with you, but I didn't know you'd had such a loss."

"I've lost everything," Naomi said, as she continued to stare into the fire. "I've tried to bring my daughter home, but now that's gone badly, and I'm afraid I've ruined everything forever."

Hank laughed pleasantly and nodded at Harry before saying, "I tell Harry here all the time that things are rarely as good or as bad as they seem. Look around."

Naomi lifted her head from staring at the fire and looked at the routine activities of the camp.

"Each and every one of these folks got a story," Hank explained. "None of 'ems too lucky, you can imagine. But I've learnt a few things in my years on the road, and people are tough when they have to be. They can survive more than they ever thought they could. You got to just learn how."

"Nothing I've lost can be replaced," Naomi scoffed. "My sons, my husband, my money. All I wanted to do was to get home, and now that seems a million miles away."

"Where's home?" Hank asked.

"Sayre, Oklahoma," Naomi said.

"I know where Sayre is, and it ain't no million miles away," Hank reasoned. "How is it you two fine ladies started out on a trip like this without money or a ticket?"

Naomi fought back tears of regret, so Raquel answered, "We ran out of money after our men passed on. Naomi has a place back home, and I'm meaning to get her there. We sold what little we had left and had enough for a bus ticket and some cash for expenses. We ran into a man on the first day that stole our money and one of our bus tickets. We cashed in the ticket we had left and plan to hitchhike our way east."

"We were swindled," Naomi complained.

"Sounds like it," replied Hank.

"A man approached us on the bus," Raquel said. "He was a very pleasant fellow that entertained us most of the day. He invited us to lunch and even offered to put our bags up at his hotel while we ate. He stole the bags and stuck us with the meal."

"The old swoon-and-swipe," Hank said factually.

"Huh?" Raquel replied, as Naomi tilted her head to listen.

"You develop a relationship, build some trust," Hank explained. "Sometimes you use something that's a perceived threat to build that trust."

"He had a partner," Raquel confirmed.

"Could've been Lucky Luke," Hank said, as he thought.

"Coulda been Smilin' Jack," Harry added, with much less stutter than before.

"His name was Jack Fisk," Raquel stated.

Hank looked at Harry for a moment and his face twisted angrily before saying, "Harry's right, it was Smiling Jack."

"The man's name was Jack Fisk," Raquel said.

Hank explained, "You never use your real name when pulling a con. Jack Fisk is one of Smilin' Jack's aliases. Who knows what his real name is."

"Can you help us get our money back?" Naomi asked.

Hank looked at Harry again and the young man smirked, as Hank said, "Smilin' Jack's a slick one. Your money's gone. Smilin' Jack could charm the rattle off a rattle snake, but the man's got no scruples."

"Are you a con man, too?" Naomi pointedly asked.

"A con man?" Hank replied. "Not exactly and not nearly as skilled as Smilin' Jack. I'd never target a widow woman—especially one with no money, that's for sure."

"I had money—at least some before Mr. Fisk—or whatever his name is took it," Naomi complained.

"Smilin' Jack moves fast and often," Hank said. "You'll never catch up to him."

"That's what the police told us," Raquel confirmed. "We've got less than a dollar between us. That's why we came to your fire."

Hank shook his head and said, "It ain't fair how hot it gets in the day and how cold it feels at night, but don't you worry, I'll show you some things to get you back home."

"I'm not going to lower myself to be a swindler," Naomi defiantly stated.

"You'll be surprised what you'll do when you're up against it enough—or hungry enough," Hank assured. "You ladies have a place to sleep tonight?"

Naomi looked at Raquel nervously, unsure how vulnerable she needed to seem to Hank.

Raquel said, "No, Hank. We thought we would get warm and then try to find a bench close to the bus depot."

"The bus," scoffed Hank. "That's a sure way to get the coppers running you in for vagrancy. Stay here in camp. I'll fix you up with some California blankets and you'll be safe for the night."

"California blankets?" Raquel asked.

"Newspapers," Hank explained. "They'll keep you warmer than you think, just don't roll too close to the fire. You'll see. Things will look brighter tomorrow. I'll personally see about getting you some accomodations to get you home."

CHAPTER 35

Raquel woke up on the cold ground. The night had been long and unsure. She and Naomi had made a bed of old newspapers by the fire in the hobo camp. She tried not to make noise in the soft dawn light, as she examined her surroundings. Raquel could tell Naomi was still sleeping by the woman's rhythmic snoring. She also sensed someone moving behind her. As she slowly rolled over, she saw Hank and Harry stoking the morning fire.

"The old woman can saw logs," Hank said when he saw Raquel awake.

Raquel sat up to feel the cool of the early morning.

"Better try some of this fire," Hank offered. "It'll be a hot day for sure in a few hours, but there's nothing like the morning fire to get you going."

Raquel brushed and dusted her dress as well as she could, and took the invitation to join the two men at the fire.

"I'm betting you two haven't spent much time sleeping under a bedroom of stars," Hank said.

Raquel looked at Naomi who rustled in her bed of newspapers and appeared to be waking, as her snoring changed to a morning cough.

"More than you'd think," Raquel said. "I've spent nights close to the fields to work the next day plenty of times.

"Back in Cali," Hank nodded to Harry. "That's a place to winter for sure. How about your traveling partner?"

"I think Naomi's more comfortable in a bed," Raquel said.

Hank chuckled, "Ain't we all. I don't think I've touched a bed that was more than a cot in more than six months. I got myself put in the coop a couple of winters ago—jail time that is—in Winslow. It was a right nice place to be locked up."

"What did you do?" asked Raquel.

"Slept in the city park and made a nuisance of myself until they gave me a jolt in the boogle," Hank said. "Took me two weeks to get there."

"You wanted to go to jail?" Raquel frowned.

"Sure," Hank boasted. "No better place for a cold winter than jail. Fresh cots, grub, and sometimes interesting stories to boot. That was before I hooked up with Harry here. Harry's too young to make it well in jail, so we've been keeping to the warm areas this year. That's what brought us to your part of Cali back in the winter."

Naomi groaned miserably, as she struggled to untangle herself from the wads of paper. Her hair was a tousled mess, while her cheeks looked sunken and tired.

"Sleep well?" Hank greeted.

"Not at all," Naomi complained.

Hank laughed, "You either slept some or there was a grizzly bear in camp last night."

"What are you talking about?" Naomi asked, as she staggered to the small fire.

"Your snoring was enough to keep half the camp awake," Hank said.

"I don't snore," Naomi defended.

Hank looked at Harry and then Raquel before saying, "My mistake."

People milled around several small fires around the camp. The place had an almost surreal appearance with the nighttime glow of campfires, but in the morning light, the two women could tell the place was dire and desperate.

"Harry, take the girl down to Blinky's and see if you can scratch up some breakfast for our guests," Hank ordered.

Harry nodded and started off, when Hank said, "Take some clean cans—and the girl."

Harry nodded again and grabbed several tin cans that had been rinsed for use. Raquel followed the young man, although Naomi nodded as subtly as she could for her to stay.

"Time for you and me to have a talk," Hank said to Naomi.

Naomi huffed, "I don't see we have much to talk about Mr.—What is your given name? I'm not comfortable calling you Hank. It's too familiar."

Hank shook his head, "Tilley. Hank Tilley."

"I don't see we have much to discuss, Mr. Tilley," Naomi concluded.

"You're a hard one," Hank said. "I could see that the first time you turned us away, but you better listen and listen good. I've been thinking about your story from last night, and you're in a bad way out here on your own."

"That's not news," Naomi shrugged.

"You're going to have to make some changes—in your attitude, if you're going to think about getting that girl home," Hank said sternly. "I'll have to confess, there's a part of me that'd like to see you in your place, and I thought about that some last night, but I've decided to help you."

"Help me?" Naomi replied, in a tone that bordered on scoffing.

"Help the both of you," Hank impatiently said. "What you're doing now's the first thing that's gotta stop."

"Stop what?" Naomi asked.

"Your attitude," Hank said. "This is a good jungle you stumbled into last night, but you can't count on being so lucky every time. There's some mean people out there. People that's been down on their luck so long it's made 'em hard. People that'd like nothing better than to put an uppity shanty queen like yourself in her place. You gotta realize you're not in your fine home dictating terms to these people anymore. You're in our world, and I'm trying to help."

Naomi took the scolding silently, but nodded that she understood.

"I'm tellin' ya' this, cause my mother was a good, hardworking woman," Hank said. "I got captured by the alcohol, and it still beats me most of the time, but I know right from wrong. Not everyone you meet in this world has that kind of compassion."

"Is that why you take care of the boy?" Naomi asked.

"Harry don't need much takin' care of," Hank said. "I found him wandering the rails a few years ago, and he looked about as pathetic as you do now. Family had left him—don't really know why, but he had no one. I took him in and taught him some tricks, that's for sure, but he's pulled me out of a face-down drunk more than a few times, and he's got my back. That means a lot out here. You're lucky I've got the boy to look out for, or I'd most likely be drunk right now, and then where'd you be?"

"I've got Raquel," Naomi said.

"That you do," Hank smiled, "but you don't seem to understand that she's taking care of you now."

"That's ridiculous," Naomi fussed.

"I'm not going to argue with you," Hank fumed, "but when you think about it, you'll know I'm right. That girl don't need to be out here on the road. I've determined to help you, but you've got to listen for once."

Naomi scowled uncomfortably, "I'm listening."

"First off," Hank began, "you got to stay far away from Smilin' Jack."

"Mr. Fisk stole our money," Naomi protested.

"Sounds just like him," Hank admitted. "He may look like a saint, but he's a mean one—and quite a womanizer. I'm surprised he left your girl be, but if he's running with Ned Farrell like you said—"

"The short man," Naomi interrupted.

Hank nodded, "He's a smart one, and he can make Smilin' Jack stay in line for a while. Like I said, you've got to stay clear of Smilin' Jack, cause he'll likely come after the girl, if he has the chance."

"Raquel's a sensible girl," Naomi said.

"I've seen that," Hank agreed. "But Smilin' Jack could coax a nun out of her knickers, if he wanted—trouble is, if can't, he's been known to be—more violent when he don't get his way."

"Oh, my," Naomi sighed.

"My point," Hank said. "Stay clear of him. Next you gotta be more careful where you wander through at night. You were lucky to find this jungle, but not all these camps are this way. Be suspicious of everyone—especially if they're too nice or too mean. I can get you home, but you're going to have to do some things to get there."

"What kind of things?" Naomi asked.

"Mostly legal and mostly moral," Hank assured, "but they'll test your scruples a bit I'm guessing. The best way east is not hitchhikin' but riding the rails. Hitchhikin's dangerous, especially with a pretty girl like you're traveling with. You're just as likely to be hit in the head and left behind, traveling with a pretty girl like that. Riding the rails is your best bet—at least until you're closer to home."

"We don't have money for a train ticket," Naomi said.

Hank shook his head, "You don't need no ticket to ride the rails, you just got to be smart."

"Isn't that like stealing?" questioned Naomi.

"Those are some of those scruples you'll have to swallow," Hank said. "It ain't like stealing. The train company's runnin' those trains empty or full—not costing them a cent. Only thing is, they don't always see things that way. That's why you gotta be smart and careful. The Atchison, Topeka and Santa Fe runs through here. We call it 'All Tramps Sent Free.' It's a fairly easy line to catch. Places like Gallup are good and bad for riding the rail. The camps are nice and friendly, but the trains don't stop here so much, so you've got to pick your spot to catch a ride. In the big cities like Albuquerque, the trains come and go all the time so there's more chances, but the people get meaner."

"In the camps or in the train yards?" Naomi asked.

"Both," Hank said. "Be careful. Eventually you'll have to ditch the Santa Fe and grab a ride on the Rock Island. That's a problem, cause the Rock Island don't like anything riding for free. Don't matter none, cause there's always a way on, but you'll have to work for it, and heaven help you if you get caught."

"Jail?"

"A beating," Hank answered grimly. "Let's have a look at your supplies."

"Excuse me," Naomi protested.

"We gotta take a look at what you've got to work with," Hank said, as he grabbed Naomi's tote.

Naomi did not protest, but looked nervously as the scruffy tramp rummaged through her bag.

"There's not much to use here," Hank sighed. "We'll have to go shopping today."

"We don't have a dollar between us," Naomi huffed.

Hank smiled slyly, "You can do a lot of shopping without a dime."

"You mean stealing?" Naomi said.

Hank shook his head, "Depends on your definition, but we got to get you some things, if you're going to get home."

"Like what?"

Hank looked through the few items and replied, "These toiletries of yours aren't worth much, but they won't slow you down. I don't see any trousers—I don't see much clothes at all."

"I don't wear trousers," Naomi stated. "We put on all our clothes last night when it got cold."

"You won't have to worry much more about cold nights this time of the season," Hank said. "You'll have to learn to wear trousers, though. It won't take no effort, and you'll find'em a bit better for traveling anyway. The trousers will be good for the girl as well. It'll help plenty if we can get her looking more like a boy. Lookin' pretty like she does'll be a distraction we don't need. We gotta get you looking a little more desperate for our purposes."

"That shouldn't be hard," Naomi lamented.

"Don't fret," Hank said. "I'll take you as far as Texas, and you'll be practically home by then. Here, add these things to your bag."

Hank handed Naomi a bottle of whiskey and a kitchen knife.

"I don't drink," Naomi said.

"It ain't for drinking," Hank explained. "You get any cut or scrape, you pour some of that on it quick. Infections kill nearly as many as falling off trains does out here."

"I know that," Naomi said. "I've doctored my husband's scrapes and cuts for years in the oil field. What do I need the knife for?"

"That's the best tool in your bag now," Hank coached. "You can cut up an apple, use it to cook. It's just a kitchen knife I found, but I put a good edge on it, and it'll cut through a squirrel if you're hungry enough."

Naomi made a face at the unpleasant suggestion, but Hank continued, "Squirrel tastes mighty good if you hadn't eaten in a couple of days. Keep that knife handy, it's for protection too. There's some real characters out here if you ain't careful."

Naomi frowned and asked, "Why are you doing this? You've made it obvious that you don't think much of me. Why all the help?"

Hank looked over the woman and could tell he finally had her attention when he said, "Life's hard out here, but I manage. You spend your day living off the charity of others and—well—swallowing about all of your pride. Maybe a fellow has to give back sometimes."

"Like you're doing with Harry?" observed Naomi.

"I don't know about that," Hank said. "I don't want to see that girl having to make it out here. She's got too much life left in her to be out here. Speaking of which, here comes Harry and the girl now."

CHAPTER 36

Raquel walked toward the fire where Hank had been tutoring Naomi. Harry followed Raquel and both carried cans of food.

"What did ya' find?" Hank greeted.

"Some kind of egg hash," Raquel answered. "It don't look like much, but I tried some and it's tasty enough."

"Blinky's resourceful," Hank said. "He can take a little of everything and with a little salt and maybe some pepper, make it edible. Blinky found a little farm not far from here, and he's been harvesting eggs the past weeks."

"Stealing," Naomi huffed.

"The chickens don't mind," Hank reasoned. "He only takes a few each night so the farmer don't get wise. A man's got to eat, and this hash keeps us from begging one meal a day and bothering respectable folks like yourself."

Naomi did not respond.

Raquel carefully studied the tension between her mother-in-law and Hank before saying, "Breakfast tastes good anyway, Naomi. Maybe we can do something for Blinky someday. What have you two been doing while we've been gone?"

Hank waited for Naomi to say, "Mr. Tilley has been helping me—plan our way back. He's telling me we need to get some things for the trip."

Raquel looked at her cup of food and said, "Hope it don't take more than fifty cents or we're out of luck."

"Don't you worry about that none," Hank smiled. "Harry and me will go shopping here in a minute. It won't take much. Your shoes'll be the hard part. You need some more sensible shoes, and shoes are hard to come by. Let me finish my hash and we'll be gone."

"What will we do?" Naomi asked.

"Stay here and clean up a little," Hank said. "No one will bother you in the camp."

Naomi looked around the dirty campsite and sighed heavily. When Hank finished his breakfast, Harry followed him into town and left the women behind.

"How do they expect us to clean this place?" Naomi fumed, once they had left.

"We can't hurt it any," Raquel smiled.

For the rest of the morning, Raquel, with some help from Naomi, did her best to tidy up the space around the patched tent. She stacked some wood neatly by the fire. After a couple of hours, Naomi flopped down on a soft patch of ground and moaned miserably.

"What have I got you into," Naomi groaned.

Raquel sat down close to her and smiled, "An adventure?"

Naomi shook her head, "I've taken you to the wilderness with not a resource in sight."

"We got each other," Raquel said. "I've seen hard times before."

"I should've found some other way," Naomi sighed.

Raquel looked up at the blue sky above and reasoned, "Sometimes life doesn't give us many options. We're going to make it fine. In a few days, we'll be back at your place. I've always done the work for the landowners. I'm kinda looking forward to working for myself."

Naomi smiled, "I can't wait to see the old place. I'm sure it needs some work, but it'll be home for us. I just can't believe I've put my fate in the hands of that hobo, Mr. Tilley. They've been gone all morning and for all we know, they skipped town and left us here."

"If they did, we've inherited a nice tent for the night," Raquel teased. "They'll be back."

"I can't believe I'm saying this, but I hope so," Naomi fumed. "Mr. Tilley gave me some advice today on how to get home and—he gave me a little hope. I needed some."

"Hope keeps us going," Raquel smiled. "If you don't have hope, what do you have?"

"Mr. Tilley says he's going to put me in trousers," Naomi said.

Raquel fought back the urge to smirk at the proper Naomi, but instead she just nodded.

Naomi continued, "He says you need to dress more like a boy out here. Says it'll be safer."

"That sounds sensible," shrugged Raquel. "You'll have a hard time chasing down a train in your dress and heels."

"That's another thing," Naomi said. "I just don't feel right about stealing a ride on the train."

Raquel thought for a moment, "I don't see where we'll be hurting anybody—the train's going to roll with or without us on it. I think Hank's right. It'll be our best way home. We'll be hurting the train company a whole lot less than Mr. Fisk hurt us."

"Mr. Tilley said we need to stay clear of that fellow," Naomi shared.

Raquel nodded. A rustling sound from the tall grass startled Raquel before she could continue the conversation. In a few seconds, Harry sprinted out of the weeds with Hank stumbling close behind."

"Is—is—is—they's a coming?" Harry stuttered.

Hank looked back over his shoulder and motioned for the group to be quiet.

He watched and listened for a moment before saying, "No one's coming down here."

"What have you done?" Naomi whispered.

"Getting supplies," Hank said. "You don't have to whisper. The police don't ever bother comin' down here unless there's been mischief."

"Has there been?" Naomi quizzed.

"Not much," Hank replied, as he tossed Naomi a bundle of clothes and a pair of boots.

"Where did you get these?" Naomi asked.

"You ask a lot of questions for a charity case," Hank said. "We've been glomming the grapevine most of the morning. I knew the boots would be hard to come by. That's why we had to dash for it. Sorry about you little missy. We couldn't find a spare pair of boots, but your shoes'll do fine for catching a ride."

"I hate to ask," Naomi tiredly sighed, "but what's 'glomming the grapevine' even mean?"

Hank looked at his partner and said, "It's kinda like shopping on a clothesline. We look around for clothes that might fit—and might not be missed too much, and we borrow them."

Naomi shook her head and said, "You were right—I didn't want to know."

"I almost forgot the big news!" Hank excitedly added, while the women listened.

"There's a hobo special coming through town tonight," Hank said.

"In English?" Naomi sighed.

"A train of empty boxcars," Hank said. "There ain't many empties travel east. The bulls don't pay much attention to a hobo special. This is a small town, and most trains pull right through town without slowing down, but this one's supposed to slow down."

"Why?" Raquel asked. "If it's pulling empty cars and there's nothing to load here, why would the train slow down."

Hank smiled slyly, "This one's smart. There's a lot of ways to slow down a train that don't want to. Grease the track, put a log on the rail, or coax some farm animal in front of the locomotive. I was tellin' some fellows about having some green riders, and they're going to help us. The train will have to slow down, and then it'll take some time getting its speed up. We'll hop it and be in Albuquerque tonight. Now, let's try on those new duds."

CHAPTER 37

Raquel covered her mouth to muffle her laughter when Naomi came out of the tent wearing the clothes Hank had brought. The proper and refined Naomi wore a pair of trousers cinched at the waist with a piece of rope, and a plaid, flannel shirt that was many sizes too big. The oversized outfit was complemented by a pair of dusty boots.

"Good," Hank said, as he stood up to walk toward Naomi. "It fits."

"This is ridiculous," Naomi seethed. "I can't wear this."

"Why not?" Hank asked. "They're clean."

"They don't fit," Naomi explained. "The sleeves are too long, and the trouser legs are dragging the ground!"

Hank pulled out a large pocket knife, and without asking, began cutting the trouser legs at the ankle.

Naomi yelped, but Hank casually said, "Be still or you'll cause me to cut your leg."

Raquel glanced at Harry and could tell he was getting as much entertainment as she from the bickering encounter and wardrobe alteration.

"Don't touch the sleeves!" Naomi ordered, once Hank had finished cutting the legs off the pants. "I'll roll them up!"

Naomi's commanding tone of voice, even when faced with wearing the humbling garb, added to the absurdity of the scene.

Raquel decided to rescue her mother-in-law by making a few tugs on her clothes and saying, "It's not that bad. They're comfortable, aren't they?"

Naomi pulled herself away and said, "Easy for you to say. Your clothes fit. I've never worn trousers before, but these don't feel right."

"It was easier to find clothes for the girl," Hank stated factually. "We found some clothes from a twelve-year-old boy for her to wear, but for you, we had to look for—"

Hank stopped speaking suddenly.

"Look for what?" Naomi demanded.

Hank cleared his throat nervously, "We had to find something with a little more—caboose in the seat."

The blunt appraisal of her physique left Naomi speechless. Raquel now bit gently on her knuckle to suppress her laughter at Naomi's look of bewilderment at the unintentional insult.

"The clothes will work fine," Hank said, in an attempt at tactfulness. "Besides, you'll only need these for a day or two, and then you can get back into your skirts."

"What do you mean?" Naomi asked, trying her best to maintain an even tone of dignity.

"We got a train tonight," Hank said. "I told you, there's a freight train rolling through tonight. Blinky's got it set up to herd some borrowed goats from the farmer down the way onto the tracks. He'll get the train to slow down as it rolls past town, and we'll jump it."

"Did you hear that?" Naomi smiled, as she turned to Raquel. "We're going home!"

Hank spent the rest of the afternoon giving the two women a tutorial on how to catch a ride on the Atchison, Topeka, and Santa Fe railroad. Raquel noted a remarkable transformation in Hank Tilley from their first meeting. The scruffy-looking man, who had begged for food with his hat in his hand, now spoke authoritatively and with purpose when teaching the women the tricks of his trade.

The plan seemed simple enough. They would go to the edge of town and wait in a ditch for the train. If things went well, Blinky would signal the train about the hazardous goats on the tracks. Hank did not think the train would come to a complete stop, but he claimed that would be good. If the train did not stop there was less chance that a bull, the railroad's own police, would check things out. Hank would go first to get the door open and hop on board. Naomi and Raquel would follow. Harry, the fastest runner, would catch the train before it regained its speed. The moon was nearly full, and Hank said there would be plenty of light. He did not know the exact schedule of the train, but he said they would not need to get to the tracks until just before dark.

Twilight faded to the moon glow of a cool New Mexico night as they huddled in the ditch about fifteen steps from the steel rails. About a dozen other people waited close by to catch a free ride east. Raquel found herself instinctively whispering, although Hank had explained there was no need.

"When's the train coming?" Naomi barked, after waiting in the dark nearly two hours.

"Be patient," Hank said. "This ain't no passenger train where you can go to the station and check the status. Freight trains run on their own schedule."

Before Naomi could complain more, the mournful sound of a distant train whistle interrupted her.

"I hear it!" Raquel said.

"That's it," Hank smiled, as he patted Harry on the back. "It'll be a few minutes, so get ready. Remember, run with the train as much as toward it. You'll get killed if you fall under the wheels. I'll grab you and pull you in. Okay?"

Naomi and Raquel nodded nervously. After waiting in the moonlit night, they could hear shouts coming from the direction of the train. They could soon determine it was Blinky warning the engineer about the livestock on the tracks. His ploy worked, as the next sound was the screeching of metal-on-metal from the brakes and the release of steam, as the hulking train tried to lose momentum.

By the time the train approached their hiding place, another belch of steam and the sound of steel wheels spinning, indicated the locomotive was determined to regain its speed.

The next minute was a blur of activity, as Hank shouted, "Now!"

Hank Tilley was not a young man, but he had surprising bounce in his long legs as he ran with almost a skipping gait toward the train and a car with the door slightly ajar in the middle of the line of boxcars. Several other people made a dash toward the now accelerating train, including Raquel and Naomi. Raquel gave Naomi a gentle push to get her moving, but the older woman delayed just an instant as she dropped her small tote of belongings. When Raquel got her moving again, she looked up to see Hank kneeling inside the train car with his hand extended. Harry had sprinted past the two women and effortlessly leaped into the car with minimal help from Hank.

The train, which had been moving at a walking pace, had now accelerated to a slow trot. Raquel threw her tote sack into the freight car and reached for Hank's hand. He easily lifted her into the car.

"Hurry!" Hank shouted, as Raquel maneuvered herself to her knees to look out the open door.

Naomi was laboring, but still making good progress toward Hank's outstretched hand. Five feet from the door, Naomi bobbled and ran awkwardly for a few steps, before falling to the ground a few feet from the dangerous steel wheels.

"Get up!" yelled Hank, as Naomi was the last person left who had not found a place on the train.

Naomi obeyed and took a few steps parallel to the tracks. The train was now moving faster, but only at a trot's speed.

"Hurry, Naomi!" Raquel implored.

Raquel could tell that Naomi had a few seconds of opportunity to make the train as it began to speed up and Naomi was becoming winded.

"You can make it!" Raquel encouraged.

Naomi stumbled again and fell hard onto the rocky ballast of crushed stone.

"Naomi!" Raquel screamed.

Without hesitation, Raquel leaped from the moving train and fell awkwardly onto the rough ground. She rolled slightly, but recovered herself in almost one motion and ran toward Naomi, who was still on the ground about thirty yards away. Behind her, she could hear Hank shouting at Harry who had also exited the train. By the time she got to Naomi, the train had accelerated to a fast run. Naomi sat by the speeding train and panted heavily.

"Are you okay?" Raquel urgently asked, as she bent down to examine Naomi.

Naomi could not catch her breath to answer, but nodded affirmatively.

A scrape on her elbow and a torn hole in the knee of her pants seemed to be the extent of her injury.

"Ah—ah—are you—you—okay?" Harry stammered, as he ran up to the women.

"Fine," Naomi gasped.

Raquel looked at the train and could barely see Hank leaning out the door of the freight car in the moonlight. As the caboose of the train passed, Raquel watched Hank leap from the train into a grassy slope nearly two hundred yards away.

"Are you sure you're okay?" Raquel asked, as Naomi tried to stand up and check herself for damage.

With Harry and Raquel's help, she stood up and said, "I feel a little beat up, but I don't think anything's broken."

Raquel looked at the scrape on Naomi's arm and then looked at the deeper cut on the knee.

"This looks bad," Raquel sighed, as she tried to get a better look at the bleeding knee in the light of the moon.

Naomi dug through her bag and handed Raquel the bottle of whiskey Hank had given her.

Raquel looked strangely at her teetotaling mother-in-law, when Naomi explained, "Pour some on the knee to disinfect it."

Raquel nodded and struggled to open the bottle. From behind her she could hear the muffled cursing from Hank Tilley as he approached. Raquel poured a small amount of the alcohol on the wound, and Naomi grimaced in pain.

Hank Tilley was now closer and cursing angrily at the women. He continued cursing for the remaining fifty yards as he walked steadily toward them.

"You don't ever jump from a moving train!" he shouted at Harry, as he grabbed the young man roughly by the collar before pushing him away.

After more profanities, he looked at Raquel and shouted, "He knows better, but you started this when you jumped. What were you thinking?"

"Naomi fell," Raquel explained.

Hank mumbled several more expletives before sarcastically scolding Naomi by saying, "You can walk home as far as I'm concerned! That train was barely moving. All you had to do was get the lead out, and we'd be riding comfortably on the train that's halfway to Albuquerque by now!"

"I'm sorry," Naomi whimpered.

Hank muttered some more vulgarities before looking at the bottle Raquel held in her hand.

"Give me that!" he demanded, as he grabbed the bottle and quickly took a drink.

Hank swore some more, took a quick look at the cut on Naomi's leg and said, "I won't have good liquor wasted on an antique zook!"

Hank took one more swig from the bottle before marching off and leaving the small group by the side of the tracks.

"What's a zook?" an angry Naomi asked Harry.

"Yo—you don't wanta know," he stuttered.

"Will he be okay?" Raquel asked, as she watched Hank vanish into the dark shadows of the night.

Harry shook his head and said, "Don't know."

CHAPTER 38

Raquel and Harry braced Naomi, as she limped between them. Harry did not talk, as he led them back toward the camp. When they returned to the ratty tent where they had stayed the previous night, two shabbily-dressed strangers roasted a small animal over a fire. Without saying a word, Harry steered the women clear of the old tent and instead walked toward Blinky's campsite. Life in the hobo camp was communal, and Harry understood he had no more claim to the old battered tent than the two men that now occupied it. He also knew he did not want a fight without Hank around to help.

"Maybe we can find a cheap place in town for tonight," Naomi suggested.

Raquel tiredly said, "The few cents we had left are in our sacks headed east. I left them on the train without thinking."

"It was my fault," Naomi replied. "You should have just left me here."

Raquel smiled, "I don't know the way home, without you."

As the trio approached the fire in front of a small shack built with scraps of wood and some old highway signs, Blinky stood up to take a defensive posture before saying, "Oh, it's you."

"Can—can we—share yo—your fire?" Harry asked.

"Sure," Blinky replied.

Blinky was an older man with a grizzled gray beard and a noticeable lumber to his walk. His eyes shifted and blinked rapidly, which gave him his descriptive name. He had the nicest place in the hobo camp and was as close as there was to a permanent resident. He was friendly and likely to share what he had, but he also seemed guarded and suspicious of strangers like Naomi and Raquel.

"Hurt your leg?" Blinky asked, as Harry and Raquel helped her sit by the small fire.

Naomi nodded and grunted as she tried to stretch the wounded leg.

"I saw you take a spill trying to catch that train," Blinky said.

"I'm clumsy, I guess," Naomi sighed, as she tried to be pleasant to the man who allowed her to share his fire.

"Ha!" Blinky grunted. "Too old more like it."

Naomi grimaced in a pathetic acceptance of the man's observation.

"Hank should've known better," Blinky said. "I hadn't caught a rolling train in five years myself, and I used to be about as clever a hobo as you'd ever find on the rails."

"I think Mr. Tilley wishes the train had rolled over me," Naomi said.

"Naw," Blinky said, shaking his head. "Hank's an okay guy. Let me take a look at that leg."

Naomi sat motionless, as the old tramp grabbed her ankle to extend the leg, and rolled the cuff of the trouser up to the knee.

"You cut it good, you did," Blinky observed. "Harry, fetch my bag and a bottle from the house, will you."

Harry nodded and quickly disappeared into the ramshackle hut Blinky called a house. In a moment, Harry returned carrying a jug of liquor and a small canvas bag.

"You better have a snort of this," Blinky said, as he handed the jug to Naomi.

"I don't drink," Naomi defiantly replied.

"It ain't for your amusement," Blinky retorted. "You've got a deep cut and I'm aiming to stitch it up for you."

"You will not," Naomi protested.

"You'll wind up getting it infected or gangrene," Blinky factually stated. "I've stitched up hundreds of these things. It'll leave a scar so small on your knee that you'll think it's a beauty mark."

"I should go to the hospital then," Naomi said.

Blinky laughed, "Not in this town—not likely. They'd take a stranger like you out to the edge of town and dump you there."

"Let him fix your leg, Naomi," Raquel said. "It's late, and he's right. We're as much likely to get run out of town as to find help at this hour."

Harry pulled up his shirt to show a small scar on the side of his stomach and said, "I got it awhile back and—and—and Blinky fixed it good. I—I seen cuts like that get bad."

Naomi's silence indicated that she would consent to Blinky's offer to help.

"Take a swig of this," Blinky said, as he handed her the jug. "It'll help."

Naomi hesitated and then took a drink as she gagged and coughed on the harsh brew. Blinky took the jug back and quickly poured a generous amount on Naomi's wound. Naomi let out a muffled scream at the stinging pain, and Raquel took her hand.

"Take another drink," Blinky ordered. "A big one this time. It'll help. Now this will sting just a might, but look away and it'll be over in a minute."

Naomi swallowed another mouthful from the jug and looked up into the clear, starry night, as Blinky quickly made five stitches with a needle and thread. She winced with each stitch, but did not make any noise.

"There," Blinky smiled, "that wasn't too bad."

Naomi, who still had a grimace on her face looked at the leg and said, "No, it wasn't too bad. Where'd you learn to do that?"

"You learn a lot of things on these rails," Blinky smiled. "I learned to fix people up in the war in Europe, though."

"You were a soldier?" Naomi asked.

Blinky nodded, "I worked on an ambulance. This cut of yours would have been a scratch there, but I learned 'bout infections and such, anyway."

"Thank you," Naomi said softly, as she slid down her pant leg.

"Better let the air get to that tonight," Blinky said, as he stopped her and rolled the pant leg back up above the cut.

"You've been so kind to us," Raquel said. "Thank you."

"Ain't nothing to be nice," Blinky smiled. "Don't cost a thing, generally."

"But there seems to be so little of it," Raquel replied.

Blinky thought for a moment and said, "You got a point. Don't know why that is. I guess people get busy and their frustrations get in the way of being nice."

"Like Mr. Tilley," Naomi said.

"That's not fair, Naomi," Raquel scolded. "Mr. Tilley has treated us well."

"He didn't talk so nice to me tonight," Naomi said.

"Hank's a good fellow," Blinky added. "He just lost his temper."

"I'll say," Naomi fumed.

Raquel interrupted Naomi's complaining to ask, "What is Mr. Tilley doing out here? He seems like a smart man that could have a job if he wanted."

Blinky leaned back and looked into the sky, as if searching for some hidden wisdom and said, "There's a lot of fellows out here and I guess about as many reasons why they're on the road. Most think us hobos are just bums that are lazy and won't work. I guess there's some of that for sure."

Blinky smiled slyly and continued, "I guess I might be in that crowd. Some are running from the law. Some take to the drink a little too much—I might be in that crowd, too sometimes. Some are just plain crazy, and some don't have no family to call their own like old Harry here. Some are just plain out of options."

"What kind of man is Mr. Tilley?" Raquel asked.

Blinky thought for a moment and replied, "Some of all, I suppose. Hank told me one time that he had a nice little life once. He took a little too much to the drink, and then jobs got hard to come by. Things happened, and he took to the bottle."

Blinky looked at his small audience for a moment before adding, "I heard Hank got in a bar fight out in west Texas—a man ended up dead. Don't know the reasons, and if'n Hank was drunk enough, he probably didn't either. Most likely manslaughter, but

Hank didn't stay around to find out. He left town and the state. To this day, Hank will not ride the rails through Texas."

"That's still no excuse for him to curse at me like he did," Naomi fretted.

Blinky smiled and said, "Hank was mad. You only get mad if'n you care, and there are some out here that say a person shouldn't care, but Hank ain't got that hardhearted, yet. That's why he takes care of this boy—that's why he helped you. You know what set Hank off?"

Naomi sighed, "I fell and missed the train, and he had to jump."

Blinky shook his head, "That ain't it. I was watching. You had a shot at running that train down, even as slow as you waddle. You quit. You quit, and that's what set Hank off."

Naomi looked away but did not defend herself.

"When you live out here like we do," Blinky explained, "you get surrounded by people that have quit—it engulfs you like stink on a pig. They's quit on life most times. Hank saw a chance to get you home, and that probably made him feel a little like a man again. Hank was mad about having to jump off a train he'd already caught, but he was probably more mad about losing his temper. Hank did all he knew to do so he took the bottle and forgot his troubles for tonight. We'll find him tomorrow. He'll be sleeping off his pain then."

"I told you not to blame Mr. Tilley," Raquel said. "If we have any misery on this trip, it's because of Mr. Fisk."

Suddenly, Blinky looked seriously at the two women and asked, "Smilin' Jack?"

Naomi answered, "That's what Mr. Tilley called him. We met a Jack Fisk on the bus and he stole our money. Do you know him?"

"Heard of him," Blinky nodded. "Hank's had some history with him back in Texas."

"Mr. Tilley told us to stay clear of him," Naomi sighed.

"Good advice," Blinky said. "He's shifty—and mean. Hear he's runnin' with Ned Farrell these days. Shiftiest grifter this side of Texas."

"I don't expect we'll see Mr. Fisk again," Naomi shrugged.

Blinky shook his head and smiled, "You never know who you'll see again on the rails."

Naomi said, "Thank you for your help, Mr.—"

"Just Blinky," the man smiled.

"Thank you, Blinky," Naomi said.

"No need," grinned Blinky. "Sorry I don't have no grub for you tonight."

"That's okay," Naomi grimaced. "Mr. Tilley thinks I need to lose some of my caboose, anyway."

The group laughed at Naomi's candor, and a little after midnight, Naomi and Raquel nested near Blinky's fire for the night.

CHAPTER 39

Raquel and Naomi spent the next two nights at Blinky's fire before Hank Tilley stumbled back into the camp about noon with a black-eye and bruised face. He was drunk, but able to walk, as Harry ran to help him.

"What happened to you?" Blinky said, without getting up from the stump where he was perched.

Hank garbled some words that were incoherent.

"Mr. Tilley!" Naomi shrieked at the site of the beaten man.

She took a step toward Hank, but he put out his hand and shouted, "You!"

Naomi stopped, as Hank slurred, "You caused all this when you fell by the train—"

Hank looked around in his stupor and said, "No! You started this when you stumbled into camp."

"I'm so sorry," Naomi cried.

"You should be!" Hank proclaimed, as he stumbled to his knees and nearly brought Harry down to the ground with him.

In a calm voice, Blinky said, "Get 'em inside, and I'll grab my bag to fix 'em up."

Naomi stood helplessly, not knowing how to react, when Raquel said, "I'll help Mr. Tilley. Naomi, go find some clean water."

Naomi nodded obediently, as Raquel and Harry moved Hank into a cot inside Blinky's shack. In a few minutes, Naomi returned with a pail of water. Raquel took it inside, and Naomi waited outside with Harry.

When Raquel returned, Naomi asked, "How is he?"

"Drunk," Raquel stated. "Beat up some, but mostly drunk."

In a moment, Blinky came out, and Naomi asked, "Is he going to be okay? What happened to him?"

"He'll be fine," Blinky assured. "He went into town drunk and got into a fight."

"Is that why he's so beat up?" Naomi asked.

"I'm betting Hank did okay in a fight," Blinky surmised. "Even drunk, he can usually hold his own. This beating came from a cop's billy club. I told you, this town ain't so kind to hobos—especially one causing any trouble. Some towns, they'll throw ya' in jail, and you'll get a shower and a meal. You get on the wrong side of some cops and you get a knuckle-sandwich and a ride out of town. Hank's been stumbling back here for most of a day, but he'll be fine with some rest."

"What can I do?" Naomi asked.

Blinky scratched his balding head and said, "Stay close to the door and offer 'em some water from time to time. Don't let him have a sniff of my drink or he'll be off again. He needs to sleep mostly."

Blinky looked at Raquel and motioned, "Come with me."

"Where are you taking her?" Naomi demanded.

"Into town," Blinky answered. "We're going to find some grub."

"You're going to leave me here with him?" Naomi sighed.

"No," Blinky smiled. "I'm leaving Harry here to chaperone."

Blinky nudged Raquel's arm and said, "Let's go, girly."

Raquel followed the old tramp and headed up a slight embankment toward town. They made their way through thick, tall grass and soon found themselves close to a neighborhood of modest, but neat, bungalow houses.

"That old woman's slowing you down," Blinky stated.

Raquel did not respond.

"You'd do fine out here without her," Blinky said. "She's got an attitude and still thinks she's something she ain't. You got the humility it takes to survive the road—ain't so confident about the woman. A pretty girl like you could make out in a lot a ways without her slowing you down."

"I'm not a pretty girl," Raquel curtly replied. "I'm a plain, old boy. Remember?"

Raquel showed off her raggedy trousers and cap.

Blinky laughed, "That was a good trick Hank pulled, trying to make you look like a boy. It'll save you some frustrations on the road, but you ain't completely fooling everyone."

Blinky stopped Raquel to pull out her shirttail, and he adjusted her cap to cover more of her face.

"There," he said, once he was satisfied. "You look a little more boyish now."

Raquel frowned, but she continued to follow the old man.

"Naomi's not slowing me down," Raquel finally declared.

"Bull," Blinky replied. "If she'd got herself on that train, you'd be halfway home now."

"There is no home without Naomi," Raquel said.

Blinky stopped and asked, "What do you mean?"

"I don't have a home or a family without Naomi," Raquel replied. "She took me in when I had nowhere else to go. The place we're headed is her home, not mine. I've seen squatters' camps that would make your little jungle look like a government camp."

"Don't you have no family or nothing?" Blinky asked.

Raquel shook her head.

"You didn't come from nothing," Blinky prodded.

"I have nothing to go back to," Raquel said. "Naomi took me in and let me be her family. I won't abandon her now."

Blinky nodded his head in satisfaction, "Loyalty's an admirable trait—maybe out here more than in the regular world. Everybody needs someone."

Blinky stopped at a house in the middle of the street that needed a coat of paint and a fence mended.

"Here we are," Blinky said, as he studied the house.

"Here we are, where?" Raquel asked.

"Our meal's here," Blinky replied.

"Do you know these people?"

"Of course not."

"Why this place?"

Blinky looked at the inquisitive girl and said, "You're one for questions all the sudden."

"I'm curious why we stopped here," Raquel said.

"Getting a meal's a good skill to learn," Blinky nodded. "Never go to the house closest to the tracks. They get hounded all the time by punks and road kids that don't know what they're doing. Never go to the nicest house on the block. They look like they could afford to share, but I've never found much generosity there. This house is perfect. Needs a little work, and is right in the middle of the block. Now all I need you to do is stand behind me and look hungry."

"That'll be easy," Raquel said. "I'm starving."

Blinky smiled, "Try to look a little sad and pathetic, too."

Raquel nodded and followed a few feet behind Blinky. He knocked on the door and there was a shuffle of noise inside the house. The motion stopped, and Raquel thought the occupant probably decided to see if the two tramps would go away. Blinky looked back to assure Raquel that they needed to hold their ground. In a few moments, the door opened. A woman wearing an apron and in her early thirties peered from behind the door.

"Good afternoon, ma'am," Blinky greeted politely.

"Hello," the woman muttered suspiciously.

"I was walking down the street and noticed the house could use a little care," Blinky observed. "Some paint maybe, or if you have some tools and some screws, I could fix that fence."

"I gotta husband," the woman said.

"I suspect he's at work, ma'am?" Blinky asked.

"Yes," the woman admitted.

"I bet he's a busy man, and I'm sure he wouldn't mind seeing some of these outside chores done," Blinky said.

"We don't got no extra money for handyman work," the woman frowned.

"I wouldn't need no money or nothing," Blinky replied. "You see, the truth is, me and this boy are travelin' west to work the fields. Our old car broke down outside of town, and it's taken about all our cash to get repairs. Thing is, we hadn't ate in about two days now. I'd never ask for a handout, but if you could spare a sandwich or an apple—especially for the boy, I'd appreciate it."

The woman stared silently at Blinky and Raquel but did not commit immediately. Blinky patiently stood his ground and forced the woman to tell him no.

After the wait, the woman said, "Come to the back, and I got some sandwiches and an apple for you."

"You're a fine Christian lady," Blinky smiled. "Could you write down this address so I can send you a payment when we reach our destination?"

"Just come to the back," sighed the woman. "I got plenty today."

The woman disappeared inside, and Blinky smiled as he led Raquel to the back of the house. The woman handed them a sandwich and an apple each.

"Thank you so much," Blinky beamed. "The boy here needs to eat, but I'd like to get started on that painting or fence work if you'd show me the way to the tools."

"That won't be necessary," the woman said. "Enjoy your sandwich, and have a nice day."

"Thank you, ma'am," Blinky smiled. "You're a fine lady."

"Tha—," Raquel started to say in her regular voice before she remembered her disguise.

"Thank you," Raquel repeated in a deep tone.

"His voice is cracking," Blinky explained without hesitation.

The woman looked suspiciously at the two as an embarrassed Raquel stared at her shoes.

"Just leave the plate on the step," the woman finally said.

Blinky nodded, and the woman disappeared into her humble house. Blinky and Raquel quickly devoured their sandwich and took the apples with them as they hurriedly walked around the corner to the next block.

"That's how it's done," Blinky boasted.

"You lied to her," Raquel said.

"Oh, no, lied?" Blinky said with a sneer. "Not really."

"Not really?" Raquel huffed. "We're not broke down on the road. We're not headed to California, and I'm not a boy."

"Details," Blinky said. "I told her what she needed to hear to do the right thing, and she feels like she's a better person for being benevolent."

"I know you weren't going to do no work," Raquel fumed. "How'd you know she wouldn't send us on our way?"

"Preparation," Blinky said. "I know that a house in the middle of the street don't get hit up for a handout as much as one on the corner. The place was nice but needed some repair, so my offer to help seemed genuine. I also picked a house that looked like it was in a little distress. There was no way she's going to have the paint or supplies to do the work. Rather than admit she's nearly as poor as I am, she shared a little food and felt good about it."

Raquel looked at Blinky, but did not pass judgment, as she took a bite of her apple and felt the hunger pain fade for the first time in two days. Blinky picked out three more houses, all at least a block away, and collected several more sandwiches and apples. He did run into one problem when the woman of the house shared that her husband was a mechanic. Blinky got the food and made a quick retreat back to the tracks before the woman could help any further. By dark, they returned to Blinky's shack and shared the spoils of their afternoon's work. Raquel had known hunger, but had forgotten how the feeling could dominate one's thoughts. For Naomi, hunger was yet another new experience that she was learning.

Raquel could tell that Naomi wanted to ask questions about how they got the food, but the older woman ate her meal in silence. Raquel fell asleep in front of the fire, a little before midnight, with a full stomach for the first time in days. Blinky had taught her how to beg and scavenge for food, but as Naomi enjoyed her meal, Raquel did not have the heart to share that some of it had been retrieved from the scraps left in the trash bin behind a restaurant in town.

CHAPTER 40

Blinky and Raquel spent the next day panhandling in town with poorer results. They had come close to attracting the attention of the police, and Blinky decided to return to the camp by the middle of the afternoon. They learned later that some vagrants had stolen some groceries, and there was an uneasy feeling that the police would come investigate. Several new men had gathered around the old tent where Hank and Harry had camped, and Raquel had done her best to stay clear of the rough-looking men.

After dark, Raquel put a couple of small sticks on the fire and prepared to sleep under the clear skies with a full stomach after enjoying a stew Blinky had made from their day of scavenging. Harry had made his own small fire a few yards away, and Blinky shared his small hut with the recovering Hank. As Raquel looked toward the patched tent where Hank and Harry had once stayed, she saw the shadows of three men walking toward Blinky's fire.

"How goes it?" one of the men asked, as the other two fanned out on each side of the hut.

Raquel looked around and soon decided the hard and desperate-looking men were talking to her. In the moonlight she could see a dull gaze to their listless faces, as if they were protecting themselves against any hint of compassion. Their affable greeting masked a cunning cruelty nurtured by survival instincts from months of destitution.

"Fine," she muttered, trying to disguise her normally soft voice.

"Dinner smelled good down here tonight," the man said, in a tone of artificial civility.

"Yes," Raquel replied. "Sorry we don't have any left."

"We's ate," the man said, as he moved closer.

Raquel could smell alcohol on the man's breath from several feet away. Blinky heard the voices and stepped out of his shack.

"What are you boys doin' out so late?" Blinky asked.

"Nothing," the man to the left said. "Thought we'd investigate the camp a little before turning in for the night."

"You boys ain't from around here, are you?" Blinky said.

"Naw," the man in the center replied. "We come in from Arizona—a couple of nights ago."

"You up in that tent?" Blinky asked.

"Yeah," the man replied.

Blinky looked suspiciously at the men, "You boys have anything to do with that robbery in town today?"

"You ask a lot of questions," the man stiffly replied.

"Well, I'm about as close to a permanent resident as this place has got," Blinky explained. "This is a good camp, and we don't like no trouble. Cops don't neither, but if the town's people feel threatened, they'll clean us out. My friend inside is proof of that. He got beat up pretty good for drinkin' and disturbin' the peace."

The man slowly stepped closer to the fire and said, "We don't want trouble. We're just seein' what the camp had to offer."

As Blinky nodded, the man suddenly lunged for Raquel and grabbed her roughly around the waist. She tried to get away and squealed, but the man held her tight, as he tossed off her cap.

"I told you!" the man shouted. "I told you this weren't no boy!"

"Let me go!" Raquel screamed, as she struggled to free herself.

"I told you that we're looking for what entertainment this town had to offer!" the man taunted.

Naomi charged the man and yelled, "Let her go!"

The man easily pushed Naomi to the ground with one hand as he wrestled with Raquel and pushed the older woman viciously with his foot, causing her to roll toward the small fire.

In a calmer voice, Blinky said, "Put that girl down."

"Or what?" the man asked.

Harry charged the man, but one of the other strangers knocked him to the ground with a board and kicked him repeatedly in the ribs.

"You want some more of that, old man!" the man shouted, as Raquel struggled and cried for help while Blinky watched helplessly. "Keep an eye on the old man!"

The man forced Raquel to the ground and said excitedly, "I told you this weren't no boy!"

The man violently tried to pin Raquel to the ground, as she scratched and clawed at him. The man slapped her fiercely, which stunned her for a second, as he meanly forced her to turn onto her stomach. He put his knee in her back and held her with the full force of his weight. A trickle of blood streamed from her lip, as she tried to catch her breath. She could see Blinky being held and Harry rolling in the grass in pain. Naomi screamed helplessly while the three men laughed at the mayhem. As Raquel struggled to escape, she heard a violent thud before feeling the pressure of the man's weight removed, as he was tossed to the side.

Hank Tilley threw the man several feet and yelled, "Leave her alone!"

The man who had kicked Harry rushed Hank, but in one motion he blocked the man's assault and landed a hard right hand on the side of his head knocking him cold. Blinky then stomped on the man's foot that had restrained him and found a stick to beat him with. The man that attacked Raquel quickly bounced to his feet and took a punch at Hank. The taller Hank dodged the attacker and quickly responded with two quick jabs before wrestling the man to the ground.

In the scuffle, the man that fought with Blinky retreated, while the man that had been punched in the head staggered away after him. The man that attacked Raquel battled with Hank. After a few frantic seconds, Hank managed to pin the man to the ground and started hitting the man repeatedly. Raquel looked at Hank from the ground and could see rage in his eyes, as he beat the man mercilessly.

"Stop, Mr. Tilley!" Naomi finally implored, while she stepped toward him and grabbed his arm to keep him from landing another blow.

Hank was wild with fury but soon came to his senses and looked at Naomi an instant, before letting the man go. He snorted heavily and stood over the other man, who wiggled in pain on the ground.

"Get out before I finish you!" Hank screamed, at the defenseless man.

An angry Raquel kicked at the man as he squirmed on the ground. To her surprise, he did not groan, but moved away from Hank. She watched him with a sigh of relief as he crawled away into the darkness.

"If I ever see you again, you'll regret it!" Hank shouted into the darkness, as the men retreated.

"Your hands," Naomi cried, as she looked at Hank's bloody fists.

"They're fine," he curtly replied.

Hank turned to Raquel and asked, "Are you hurt?"

Raquel had pulled herself to her knees and fixed her torn shirt, before softly saying, "No."

Hank still had a wild look in his eyes, as he scanned the dark edges of the camp to make sure the men had left.

"I'm fine," Raquel said, as she stood up and walked toward him. "Thank you, Mr. Tilley."

"Are you sure you're okay?" Naomi asked nervously.

"Yes," Raquel nodded, as she took Hank's hands and said, "We need to clean these up."

Hank did not reply, but Naomi said, "I'll get some clean water."

In a moment, Naomi gently wiped the dirt and mud from Hank's hands, as he slowly recovered from his rage and became calmer.

"Thank you, Mr. Tilley," Naomi said. "Once again, you've saved us. I'm so sorry I caused all of this."

Hank did not reply at first, but then said, "I'm fine. Check on the girl. Blinky can fix me up."

Naomi nodded and handed her rag to Blinky, as Raquel said, "I'm fine, really."

Hank asked Blinky, "Is the boy okay?"

Blinky said, "He's fine. He'll have some bruised ribs, but nothing got broken."

Hank looked at Naomi and said sternly, "I told you it's dangerous out here. I gave you a knife. Why didn't you use it?"

Naomi was temporarily surprised at the scolding, but then replied, "It's in my bag. I wasn't thinking. It all happened so fast."

"I gave you that knife for a reason," Hank said. "Next time, you put that blade in the stomach of the first vulture that comes after either of you like that."

Naomi nodded sheepishly.

Hank looked at Naomi and said apologetically, "I can't be mad at you. I gave you some whiskey, too, and—I guess I didn't put that to good use."

"I'm so sorry for everything," Naomi sobbed.

"Don't cry," Hank huffed. "I'm the one needs to be sorry. I shouldn't have gone off the handle like that. I shouldn't have gone on a bender. I said I'd get you home and I—got distracted."

"After all you've done, Mr. Tilley?" Naomi said. "You could never think that you would need to apologize."

"Be still and let me clean your hands," Blinky complained.

Hank nodded and said to Raquel, "Go fetch your cap, and let's try a little harder to look like a boy. I told you there are some mean characters out here, and I can only take you as far as the Texas state line."

Raquel nodded and picked her boyish hat from the ground.

Blinky looked at Hank and then said to Raquel, "If you want, I got some scissors in the house. I could trim your hair to where it looks—a little more like a boy."

"You can't cut her beautiful hair," Naomi protested.

"It's okay," Raquel said. "Orpha would have a fit if she saw how messy my hair has gotten on this trip. Short hair will be easier to keep and—I don't want any more attention like tonight."

"Short hair won't protect you from meanness," Hank said.

"I know," Raquel replied. "Go ahead and cut it off. It'll grow back."

Blinky disappeared into his shack for a moment, before returning with a large pair of shears. Raquel sat nervously and Naomi let out muffled squeals as the old man cut off chunks of her hair.

"That's not too bad," Blinky analyzed, as he took a step back to see the hair cut in the glow of the fire.

Naomi sighed heavily, but refrained from commenting.

Hank tried to be more encouraging about the hair cut by saying, "We'll still need to keep some dirt on your cheeks, but the short hair will make it easier to pass for a boy. After riding a boxcar all night, you'll be glad to be able to rinse your hair out and put it under a cap."

"You're still going to take us east?" Naomi asked.

Hank nodded.

"Even after I missed the train?" Naomi continued.

"That was my fault," Hank admitted.

"You bet it was," Blinky scolded. "You can't expect a greenhorn woman that lived her life in the kitchen to run down even a slow train."

"You got a better idea?" Hank asked.

"Of course," Blinky said slyly.

"Why didn't you say something?" Hank glared.

"You never asked," Blinky complained. "You got to get on the train standing still."

"That's a great idea," Hank mocked, "but there ain't two trains a month stop in this town, and the bulls can watch a train like it's a bank vault in a small yard like this."

"That's true," Blinky admitted, "but there's a turn-off seven miles east of town. At least twice a day, some train has to pull off to let the westbound pass."

"Seven miles?" Hank thought.

"Sure," Blinky nodded. "You hike out to that side track and wait for a train going on the farm and you'll be free riding to Albuquerque."

Hank looked at Naomi, as if to determine if she could make the trip.

"I'd leave in the morning," Blinky suggested. "Those boys will sober up by then, and they might want some payback. You find a good empty, and you might find a ride to the state line."

"I'd take Albuquerque for now," Hank said. Turning to Naomi, he asked, "How 'bout it? Can you make the hike?"

"Of course," Naomi stated. "I'd walk a hundred miles to get out of this place."

"Let's hope seven's far enough," Hank said.

CHAPTER 41

Hank, Harry, Raquel, and Naomi marched out of the camp early the next morning, heading east toward a switching station. The bright sunshine soon transformed the cool dawn to a pleasant morning. After the first mile, Hank and Raquel walked ahead of Harry and Naomi, who lagged behind.

"Get the lead out!" Hank shouted back at Harry and Naomi.

They nodded and waved, but continued their lethargic pace.

"Do we need to wait?" Raquel asked.

Hank looked back and said, "Naw. They'll catch up in time."

"Naomi's leg's bothering her," Raquel said.

Hank nodded, "Harry's got some bruised ribs, from last night, but he'll be able to keep up with the old woman."

"Naomi's not that old," Raquel defended.

Hank laughed, "She ain't that young, either."

After a few hundred yards of walking, Raquel asked, "Why are you helping us?"

Hank looked up into the blue sky before saying, "I've just let you use my fire and tried to get you on a train east. No big deal."

"It's a big deal to me," Raquel said.

Hank thought for a moment and replied, "I don't know. That spinster mother-in-law of yours reminds me of my mother some, I guess. Real particular about the rules and all."

"Naomi's set in her ways," Raquel explained. "She's always been good to me."

Hank looked at Raquel and asked, "How's the lip this morning?"

Raquel touched her swollen lip lightly and replied, "It's fine—a little sore."

Hank nodded and continued walking, as Raquel felt the back of her neck and her freshly cut hair.

"It don't look that bad," Hank tried to assure. "The short hair, I mean. Besides, it'll grow back in time."

"I could've fought him off on my own," Raquel said.

Hank looked at the girl and smiled, "I'm betting you could. I didn't see any harm in me getting a few swings in, though."

"I never saw anyone fight like that," Raquel said.

"What do ya' mean?" Hank asked.

"You moved quick, but with no wasted motion," Raquel observed. "I've seen plenty of fights before, but nothing like last night."

"I fought some when I was younger," Hank admitted.

"A prize-fighter?" Raquel asked.

Hank chuckled, "Nothing so fancy. I was always good at fightin' and drinkin'—not a good combination. I never learned to give up one or the other. That's what keeps me out of the state of Texas—but that was a long time ago."

"It seems like everything was a long time ago," Raquel lamented.

Hank looked at her and said, "You're awful young to say something like that."

"Sometimes I feel older," Raquel shrugged. "You want to go back to your home—to Texas?"

"Naw," Hank said, shaking his head. "There's nothing for me there."

"But it's your home," Raquel said.

"Home's what you make it," Hank smiled.

"And your home's the road?" Raquel asked.

Hank nodded, "Home's wherever the rails take me—except for Texas."

"Why?" Raquel asked. "You seem like a capable fellow. Why not have a job and settle down?"

"Now you're meddling," Hank laughed. "I like the road."

"I've been without a place before, and I didn't like it much," Raquel grimaced.

"To each his own," Hank said. "I like the freedom—no one telling me what to do or when. If I had a job and settled down, I'd have plenty of people tellin' me what to do."

"I guess I can see that," Raquel frowned.

"It's different for a woman," Hank said. "Your kind's more suited to settling down."

Hank looked back at the lagging Naomi and continued, "Your mother-in-law won't make it out here."

"She's tougher than you think," Raquel said.

"What's your story?" Hank asked. "What brings you to the middle of New Mexico with that old windbag?"

"I told you," Raquel said. "We're heading home."

Hank looked at the girl and said, "You avoided the question the other night, too. Everybody's got a story. You and that woman look like the odd couple out here."

"It's hard to explain," Raquel admitted.

"At the pace those two are walking, we got most of the day," Hank said.

Raquel sighed heavily, "My mother died a few years back, and it was a bad time—bad enough that I left home. I tried working the fields, but it's hard for a girl—to work and have people leave you alone."

"A pretty girl, you mean," Hank said.

"I never feel pretty," frowned Raquel.

Raquel walked a few yards before continuing, "I met these two boys, and they were different than anyone I had met before. They had a family, they were—decent. They invited me home. Naomi found out I didn't have anywhere to go and took me in. I fell in love with her younger son, and she always treated me like a daughter. I know Naomi seems a little prickly, but she cares—and you can't fake that. My husband was killed in a car wreck—crashed in the fog. My mother-in-law was all the family I had. We didn't have much reason to stay and she had a place back in Oklahoma. We had enough to make the trip, but things went badly."

"Smilin' Jack," Hank muttered.

"He took us good," Raquel said. "Now we're depending on your generosity, Mr. Tilley."

Hank walked a little further before saying, "You're a good girl, Raquel. I knew it the first time you brought us sandwiches back in Maricopa. We'll get you home. I'll see you to Clovis. I got a sense about these things, and I think you're going to make it just fine."

Hank looked back at Harry and Naomi and shouted, "If you two don't pick up the pace, the sun's going to be down before we get there!"

The two plodded on and the group made it to the switching station about three in the afternoon. The switching station featured a small shack and two parallel tracks where one train would park while the other passed. The countryside was brown, and by mid-afternoon, hot. The group found a shady place in a shallow ravine a few yards from the tracks. Hank gave them instructions to follow his lead. He explained that the train would come to a stop and the crew would make a walk around. After the rail men left, the group would find an open car to hop and wait for the train to head east. The rest of their afternoon involved waiting in the shade for the train.

Hank and Harry got bored after a couple of hours and took a short hike to explore and see if there were any dwellings or people close by, while Raquel and Naomi rested against the rough wall of the ditch.

"I miss my kitchen sink the most," Naomi lamented, as Raquel carefully looked down the vacant train line.

"Huh?" Raquel replied.

"I know it sounds strange," Naomi said. "There's so many things not to like out here. The smells, no bathrooms, and all the dirt everywhere, but I most miss being able to turn on the faucet to wash my hands."

Raquel laughed, "There's a lot of things I miss about our old home, but I don't think I would have picked the kitchen sink."

"I know it sounds ridiculous," Naomi said, "but that's what I've thought about the most."

"When we get home, we'll make sure you have a big porcelain sink," Raquel assured. "I hope you have a big stove to cook a roast in, as well."

"Amen to that!" Naomi said. "I don't think I've ever been as hungry as I have the past few days."

Raquel did not respond immediately, but then said, "I have."

"You poor dear," Naomi said. "I'm so sorry to bring you to a place like this, and last night—I don't know what we would have done without Mr. Tilley."

Raquel nodded her head, "I'm okay, and yes, Mr. Tilley has been very kind."

"It's because of you," Naomi said.

"Maybe he just wants to do the right thing," Raquel replied.

Naomi shrugged, "Maybe."

"I've been hungry before," Raquel confessed. "Hungrier than I am now. Mother went away one summer to find work. She worked far away that year. I was a young girl and never had enough to eat. The camps were terrible—not what I was used to. When you get that hungry, all you can think about is food. You determine that you'll do anything not to be hungry again. Mother came back, but that's the year I started working the fields. Even if they wouldn't pay, I knew I could eat. We were so hungry that summer. I think that is why Mother decided to marry that horrible man. She thought it would help, but I think it drove Mother to her grave."

"You poor thing," Naomi sighed, as she moved to give her daughter-in-law a gentle hug.

"I don't mean to complain," Raquel quickly said.

"You never do," Naomi replied.

"Tell me what the house is like again," Raquel said.

Naomi looked into the blue sky for a moment before smiling, "The house isn't as big as the one in Maricopa, but it has a porch that goes around three sides of the house where you can have your morning coffee to see the sunrise—and your evening tea watching the sunset. It's a white framed house with a wire fence around the yard. A big pecan tree shades the south side, and there's a mimosa tree to the west."

"Sounds great," Raquel smiled.

"I'm sure the old place needs a little work, but it's paid for," Naomi said.

A whistle in the distance indicated a train was approaching.

"Where are the men?" Naomi frantically asked, as she raised her head to look for them.

"I don't know," Raquel said, as she too searched the horizon. "I'll go find them."

Raquel walked out of the shallow ravine and still did not see the men. The train's whistle blew again, and she shielded her eyes from the afternoon sun and nervously scanned the horizon. When she did not see anyone, she walked away from the tracks, thinking that they would have surely heard the train, if they were close. After walking a few hundred yards to a high place, she saw the two men walking casually back toward the switching station. Raquel ran toward them frantically waving her arms.

"Hank!" she yelled, as the men continued to walk at a leisurely pace.

"What are you shouting for?" Hank asked.

Raquel struggled to catch her breath and said, "Train's coming."

Hank calmly looked toward the switching station, which was several hundred yards away and asked, "Where's the sun?"

Raquel was confused, but pointed west to the afternoon sun.

"Where's the train whistle coming from?" he then asked.

Raquel pointed back to the east.

"Unless you're heading back to Cali, there's no rush," Hank said. "We'll get back in time either way."

Hank led the group back to the shallow ravine where an antsy Naomi clutched her canvas tote and prepared to catch the train.

"Relax, woman," Hank said when he saw Naomi. "The train's heading west."

Naomi looked above the rim of the ravine and her shoulders dropped in disappointment.

"Will there be an eastbound train, soon?" Naomi asked.

Hank watched the approaching train and said, "Not likely. The train ain't slowing down, and besides, we need the eastbound train to park, not the westbound."

"What does that mean?" Naomi asked.

Hank took a seat to lean his back against the dirt wall of the ravine and said, "It means there's not an eastbound train coming soon or this one would pull over to make way. I'm guessing we're at least three hours from another train coming. Any eastbounder would have to be west of Gallup by now."

"Blinky said there would be a train," Naomi fretted.

"There will be," Hank said. "We just don't have a schedule for it."

Hank could tell the woman was not convinced and he added, "It's for the best. By the time the train switches, it'll probably be dark. It'll be easier for us to hop then anyway."

"How do you know that?" Naomi said. "How do you know any train will come here?"

Hank looked irritated at the question, but he reached into his bag to hand Naomi a battered map and said, "This is my Bible out here. This map's got every station, junction, and switching station in the western United States marked on it."

He pointed at the map that Naomi had unfolded and said, "Here's the line running from Needles to Clovis. At least twice a day, an eastbound and westbound train have to pass on this track. This is the place they'll switch. We don't exactly know when, but I promise you, there'll be a train parked here by morning."

"How can you be so cocked sure?" Naomi huffed.

Hank leaned back against the ground and said, "On my hike, I went by the switch, and I could tell the tracks were polished. There's been trains here regular and often or the track'd be rusted."

"Oh," Naomi sighed.

"I never seen a woman so bent on inventing things to worry about," Hank said.

"It's called being responsible," Naomi fumed.

"Well," Hank sighed, "it's making me tired. Best thing we can do is take a nap and get some rest. I walked around this whole countryside, and there don't seem to be a person living within three miles. We'll get some rest and hop the train to Albuquerque tonight. There's a soup kitchen at the mission downtown, and we'll get some grub in the morning. With any luck, I'll have you to Clovis by tomorrow night. From there, you can practically see Oklahoma."

Naomi would have liked to complain more, but Raquel interrupted to ask, "You keep saying Clovis, Mr. Tilley. Why?"

Hank looked away and said, "Clovis has a big rail yard, and it's on the border with Texas. I've told you I can't go to Texas. Once I get you to Clovis, though, I just got to make sure you get pointed toward Amarillo or you end up in San Antonio. Past Amarillo, you switch trains at Pampa. Pampa's a nice town for Texas. Once you get there, the train'll take you straight to Oklahoma—and Sayre."

"That's home," Naomi said.

"That's right," Hank replied.

Raquel shifted nervously for a second and then asked, "Mr. Tilley, why won't you go to Texas? I know you got into trouble, but you haven't said why."

Hank looked somewhat put out by the question, but then answered, "I got in some trouble a few years back. I was drinking with Smilin' Jack one night in a dive of a bar near Lubbock. Smilin' Jack had violated some poor farmer's daughter, and the man came for a piece of him. It weren't no fight of mine, but somewhere in the fray, he hit me with a pool stick. The man said the wrong thing, and next thing I know me and Smilin' Jack was whaling away at him. I's too drunk to know if it were me or Jack, but he pinned it on me and skipped town. The sheriff swore out a warrant for my arrest, so I ran. I ain't crossed the state line since."

"That's a terrible story," Naomi said.

"Yes indeed, ma'am," Hank said.

"How long ago?" Naomi asked.

Hank thought, "It was 1928 so I guess about six or seven years by now."

"What's the statute of limitations?" Naomi asked.

Hank grimaced, "I live with taking that man's life every day and forever."

"But you're not even sure if you did it," Naomi observed.

Hank replied, "I was there, I was drunk, and I could've stopped it. I knew Smilin' Jack was a scoundrel. What kind of man stands up for someone like him? No, ma'am. I got what I deserved. If I'd taken care of Smilin' Jack back then, you two ladies would be home by now."

Naomi looked at the man carefully before saying, "Mr. Tilley, a person can't be responsible for anyone but themselves. You've taken your time to be good to us, but Jack Fisk or Smiling Jack or whatever he goes by isn't your fault. I don't know what you've done in your past, but I know you live with a mountain of guilt. You've been a protector, and—as patient as you could be with me. If you ever find yourself near Sayre, Oklahoma, you always got a place at my table."

Hank smiled, "Thanks, ma'am, but it's hard to get to Oklahoma without going through Texas. One wrong step, and I'd be in jail and they don't forget about their warrants in Texas."

Raquel thought for a moment and said, "You could always go through Kansas."

Hank laughed, "If'n I ever find myself in Kansas, I might just do that."

Raquel was unsure why Naomi had changed her attitude about Hank Tilley, but she could see a transformation in the way the two talked to and treated each other going forward from that afternoon. The group waited in the ravine for the train until dark. The night was mild, and even Naomi waited patiently. A train heading east pulled to the side track just as Blinky had predicted. Hank watched the crew make a quick survey of their train before heading to the small shack for coffee and a game of cards. Hank took Naomi by the arm and led her to a boxcar toward the end of the train. He slid the door open and boosted Naomi into the car before helping Raquel.

The inside of the boxcar was dark, but Hank struck a match so they could see that the car was half empty, with crates stacked on the locomotive side. The boxcar had a stale smell of sawdust and cardboard. Hank pushed a couple of crates to the side to make a hiding nest for the four of them. Hank and Harry seemed relaxed, but Naomi and Raquel sat nervously and quietly hoping they would not be found as stowaways.

A little after midnight, the group heard the faint whine of a train's whistle in the distance. The whistle became louder, until they could feel and hear the rumble of the other train passing on the main line. After a few minutes, their train lurched ahead jerkily. The steel wheels seemed to groan underneath them, but the train slowly and surely gained momentum. The train seemed to lose some speed as it crossed the switch back onto the main line, but then blasts of steam could be heard as the train clicked along rhythmically on the steel rails.

Raquel's excitement about moving east kept her awake for a while, but soon she drifted into a peaceful slumber as the steady sounds and motion of the train rocked her to sleep like a lullaby. She awoke a little after midnight when the train started losing momentum.

"What's happening?" she groggily asked.

Hank had the door cracked open and peered into the dark night. Naomi and Harry were still asleep.

"Come see," Hank said.

Raquel stood up and tried to steady herself from the combination of motion and fatigue. She stepped cautiously toward the door and stood beside Hank.

"You'll see it in a minute," Hank said.

"What?" Raquel asked.

"Just wait," Hank grinned.

Raquel looked into the night and could barely make out the passing ground as the train continued down the tracks. There was a partial moon shining in the clear sky and she could see the iridescent blue glow of the dark horizon in the distance.

"Here it comes," Hank smiled.

As Raquel continued to look out the door, the train moved over a slight rise in front of them. Suddenly, she could see the bright lights of Albuquerque. The train was almost to the town, which looked like it sat in a shallow bowl surrounded by brown dark hills.

"I never get tired of seeing this town at night," Hank said. "It's like you're nowhere, and then you make that last rise and see the city lights."

"It's pretty," Raquel said, as she stared at the approaching city.

"Get up," Hank whispered to the sleeping Harry and Naomi.

The two got to their feet and joined Raquel and Hank at the door.

"We'll be pulling into the station in a few minutes," Hank explained. "I don't know where this train's a headin'—so—we'll need to get off and get our bearings. The bulls in these cities are likely to be meaner, so watch yourself. Before the train comes to a stop, we'll need to jump. Harry'll go first—I'll follow." Hank looked at Raquel, "You get off after me."

Raquel nodded, indicating she understood.

Hank then stepped to Naomi and pointed, "You'll need to get off last. The train should be rollin' slow by then, but I wouldn't wait until it stops completely."

Naomi nodded.

Hank took a deep breath, "If we get separated, head for the camp south of the tracks. I'll find you."

The group nervously surveyed the upcoming terminal, as Hank carefully judged the speed of the train. When it slowed to a trot, he motioned Harry to hop off into the night. The young man effortlessly slid off the car and landed gracefully on his feet. The older Hank followed and he looked back to watch Raquel stumble for the first few steps until gaining her balance. Naomi sat on the side of the car as it slowed, but was unsure about leaping to the rocky ground below.

"Jump!" Hank whispered, trying to will the woman off the train.

"She's afraid," Raquel said, as she began trotting to match the train's slowing speed.

Raquel soon gained on the train as it slowed coming into the rail yard that was eight or nine tracks wide. She instinctively stopped as the train halted just short of a switch, when she noticed two large men walking parallel to the tracks. One swung a nightstick, and the other carried a rifle. As Raquel worriedly surveyed the situation, Hank ran up behind her.

"Stay back," Hank said, as he pulled Raquel to the shadows of a fence.

Raquel complied, as Hank said in a hushed tone, "She needs to get back in the car or they'll see her."

Naomi sat in the doorway of the railcar unsure of what to do. By the time she decided to exit the train, the two rail detectives had seen her.

"Stop!" one of them shouted.

Naomi took a step, before the man angrily repeated, "Stop, I said!"

Raquel moved to help Naomi, but Hank grabbed her by the arm. She watched helplessly as the two rail detectives put their flashlights on Naomi.

"You can't help her," Hank whispered. "They won't hurt a woman. Stay here."

Raquel held her ground for a moment, as Hank clutched her arm.

When one of the men roughly pushed Naomi against the railcar, however, Raquel broke free of Hank's grip and screamed, "Don't hurt her!"

"No!" Hank urgently whispered, as Raquel ran toward the defenseless Naomi.

Hank stepped back further into the shadows, as the flashlights scanned the area and settled on the approaching Raquel.

"Don't hurt her!" Raquel repeated.

"Stay back!" one of the men demanded while the other held Naomi against the railcar.

"Run!" Naomi cried.

Her plea for her daughter-in-law to run was too late, as one of the rail detectives walked quickly toward Raquel. In one smooth motion, he swung his nightstick and caught her behind the knee, which caused her to tumble to the rocky surface of the rail yard.

"You think you can steal a ride!" the man shouted, as he swatted Raquel across the back with his stick.

Raquel let out a muffled groan, but Naomi screamed and tried to get to her. The man with the rifle, however, used it to pin her to the railcar.

"Stay put, lady," the man said to Naomi, as the other man circled Raquel who was trying to get to her knees.

The man standing over Raquel said meanly, "There ain't no such thing as a free ride, boy!"

Before Raquel could stand, the man hit her with the back of his hand, which sent her tumbling to her back.

"She's a woman!" Naomi screamed, as Raquel lay sprawled on the rocky ground.

The two men looked at each other for a second, until the man who had slapped Raquel grabbed her by the collar and stood her up. He threw her cap to the ground and looked at her raggedly cut, short hair.

He squeezed her shoulders and yelled, "It is a girl!"

"Bring her here," the man holding the rifle said, as he held Naomi back.

The man held Raquel tightly by the arm, but he guided her toward Naomi with a gentler touch than he had used earlier. The woozy Raquel stumbled, but the man led her close to Naomi. Out of the corner of her eye, Raquel could see Hank moving closer. She tried to shake her head at him inconspicuously to deter his attempted rescue. Naomi broke free and grabbed her daughter-in-law away from the man's grasp.

"Can you believe it?" one of the rail detectives said to the other. "Two dames out here after midnight."

The other man nodded and then asked in a more civil tone, "What are you ladies doing here?"

Naomi quickly replied, "We rode the train from Gallup."

The man looked at the other man and then said, "Don't you know it's against the law to steal a train ride?"

Naomi held Raquel in her arms and said, "We lost all our money, and we need to get home."

"Where's home?" the man asked.

"Oklahoma," Naomi replied.

"We didn't know that was a girl coming toward us," the man explained. "It's dangerous out here. You never know what's around the corner. Two ladies shouldn't be out like this."

The man seemed to realize something and suddenly moved his rifle in a more defensive position and asked, "You have men folk around?"

Raquel looked around nervously, but could not see Hank or Harry.

"No," Naomi declared. "My husband's passed on. This girl was married to my son, he's dead too. We're on our own."

"Ma'am, riding these rails is illegal and dangerous," the man explained.

"I didn't see any harm," Naomi said. "The train car was half empty. It couldn't have cost any more steam to have us ride along. We didn't hurt anything."

The man sighed, "That ain't the point. Jumping a train's dangerous enough, but there's characters out here. Plenty of them."

"We're careful," Naomi said.

The other man stepped forward and took Raquel by the chin and used his flashlight to examine her.

"Did I do that?" he asked, as he referred to her swollen lip.

Raquel reached up to touch her lip that was bleeding slightly and said, "Only part. It was busted already."

The man frowned and dug into his pocket and handed her a handkerchief and said, "I'm sorry. Take this."

Raquel took the handkerchief and nodded to the man.

The man with the rifle asked, "Have you two eaten today?"

Naomi looked at Raquel and shook her head, "Not today."

The man looked at his partner before saying, "I'm going to have to run you in."

"What?" Naomi protested. "That's not necessary. We haven't hurt or stolen anything, I promise."

Raquel quickly added, "Please don't arrest us, sir. We're law-abiding citizens and my mother-in-law has never seen the inside of jail, even to visit someone. Please."

The man did not respond, but Raquel continued her plea by saying, "We'll get off the property and won't cause a minute's more trouble for you. We're sorry, and we've learned our lesson, I promise."

The guard held up his hand to stop her pleading and said, "Ma'am, this is one of the toughest shantytowns in the southwest. You've told me you don't have money and haven't eaten today. I'll take you to the jail—the women's jail—and they'll get you cleaned up, get you a bed, and get you a meal. I'm not punishing you; I'm trying to help you."

Raquel looked down at her feet and tried to avoid having to look at Naomi. She knew the officer was right. There were worse places than a night in jail, but she knew Naomi would be humiliated.

"Thank you," Naomi said graciously, as Raquel lifted her eyes to see the dignified woman accept the help. "A clean bed and a meal would be helpful."

The two men led Naomi and Raquel away with their rifle lowered and the nightstick in the belt. The two women were taken to the city jail that smelled of stale bleach and clamored with chaos from the night's vice. In less than an hour, however, they had their first meal of the day, the first clean bed in a week, and the first shower since they left California.

CHAPTER 42

Naomi and Raquel were released by mid-morning after their overnight stay in the Albuquerque city jail.

"How do you feel?" Raquel asked.

Naomi looked at the traffic on the street and said, "Fine. I actually slept pretty well."

"Over here!" a whispered shout came from the nearby street corner.

Harry stood nervously on the sidewalk wearing his worn-out overalls. He waved frantically at the two women, and looked anxiously at the people passing him. As Raquel walked toward the shabbily dressed Harry, she noticed how out of place they were among the other people on the street, who wore business suits and store-bought dresses. Raquel and Naomi now looked like the rest of the transients nearer the rail tracks. The nicely dressed people avoided eye contact with the women as they walked away from the jail. Raquel knew the feeling of being an outsider. Words and actions did not speak as loud as the unmistakable way people tried to ignore them. As she glanced at Naomi, she sensed how uncomfortable her mother-in-law was with people stepping out of their way to avoid any possible contact with the lower classes of society. Raquel took Naomi by the arm, and the two unwanted women met Harry on the corner.

"Ha—Hank's a—a waitin' for us," Harry stuttered.

Raquel and Naomi nodded, anxious to get off the street to somewhere less conspicuous. Harry walked quickly with his eyes glued to the pavement, as they moved through the downtown area and closer to the tracks. As they approached the rail terminal, they were surrounded by industrial warehouse buildings that were stark and cold with the occasional sound of men and machinery moving freight from the trains to the storage areas. They weaved their way through several parked trains and a couple of slow-moving ones to the other side of the tracks. After climbing a small rise a couple of hundred yards on the other side, the group saw several acres of tents, shacks, and other dwellings. Dejected-looking men skulked over burning barrels of fire, as smoke oozed into the overcast sky. The camp in Gallup had a few dozen people; this city of refugees had hundreds, if not thousands of people milling about the brown, desolate landscape.

A steady and continuous low rumble of conversation from the people loitering about the rag-tag camp could be heard from all corners. The entire shanty-town had a nervous energy of desperation and despair. Men outnumbered the women three to one, but Raquel noticed several families trying to survive in the ramshackle of temporary buildings and open latrines.

Hank Tilley was talking with a small group of men in front of a piece of canvas hung on two poles to provide shade from the sun. When he saw the women approach, he nodded to the men and walked quickly to join Naomi, Raquel, and Harry.

"Good news," Hank smiled. "I've been talkin' to some fellas, and they say there's a train headin' out tonight that's going straight through to Amarillo. We get you on that train, and you're half way home."

"Tonight?" Naomi said.

Hank nodded, "Leaves after dark. I saw the rail cops were goin' to take you to jail last night, and I decided not to jump in. I knew you'd be in for a hot meal and a clean bed for the night. Now the jail here might be plenty nice for you ladies, but these rail bulls are mean as coyotes, and they take it personal when folks try to jump the train out of Albuquerque. Don't you worry none, though, cause I gotta plan. I'll create a ruckus with the bulls and get 'em distracted. You'll be able to slip on smooth as a peach."

Naomi shook her head nervously, "Mr. Tilley, I appreciate your kindness more than you know. I'll never forget it. But—I'm nearly fifty with a sore knee—and I'm too old to be jumping trains. I can't let you get in another fight on my account."

"Won't be no trouble," Hank said.

"No," Naomi interrupted. "I'm going to do the sensible thing—the thing I should've done back in Flagstaff, if I hadn't let my pride get in the way. I'm wiring some people from back home for the money for a bus ticket that will take us home."

"Ma'am, I can get you home," Hank protested. "I promise."

"I know you can," Naomi said.

"I'm sure of it, too," Raquel agreed.

"We're causing you way too much trouble," Naomi explained. "This will be best. I'll wire for the money, and we'll be out of your hair."

"Ain't been no trouble," Hank assured.

"You're too kind, Mr. Tilley," Naomi smiled.

Hank thought for a second before saying, "If you've made up your mind, maybe we can get you some lunch."

"We had a good meal last night," Naomi said.

"You won't be getting your bus ticket until this afternoon or even later," Hank noted. "The mission across the tracks has some fine soup, and all it'll cost is sittin' through some preaching."

Naomi looked at her daughter-in-law and nodded, "I don't know about you, Raquel, but I could use a good cup of soup."

"We've got to eat," Raquel said.

Hank Tilley seemed to be energized by the women taking his suggestion, and he said enthusiastically, "We'd better get going, cause with this mob, it's likely to get crowded."

With his long, high-stepping strides, Hank Tilley led the group through the hobo jungle and toward town. The meandering throng of people seemed to sense it was close to soup time, as many of them began to wander in the direction Hank was leading. By the time Hank got his small group to the soup kitchen, there was a line. Naomi pointed out the Western Union office they passed two blocks down the street.

As the group waited patiently in line for their soup and sermon, Naomi asked, "What will you do now, Mr. Tilley?"

Hank seemed temporarily surprised by the question, but said, "I'll stay here a day or two—maybe more. The city's got a good climate this time of year, and there's a couple of places to get soup and even a bed, if the weather turns bad. When summer gets hotter, I'll probably head north—Colorado, maybe even Wyoming."

"You do spread yourself over a considerable territory, Mr. Tilley," Naomi smiled.

"By winter, I may even make it back to Cali," Hank Tilley grinned slyly. "Might try that house back in Maricopa to see if'n the new tenant's more hospitable than last year."

"Oh, Mr. Tilley," Naomi blushed.

It took almost an hour to get in the door of the mission that was serving the soup. Raquel and Naomi were ushered into an auditorium with wood pews to listen to a fiery preacher shout about temperance, responsibility, the wrath of God, and ironically God's grace. Raquel noticed Hank and Harry sat on the edge of their seat, as if the sermon were singing from heaven, while Naomi frowned and fumed during the man's preaching. After the sermon, the audience was lined up again to walk across the alley to a long room with large kettles of soup and clanking metal cups.

A tall, fierce-looking woman stood at the head of the line supervising the activities. The woman had visible wrinkles from years of frowning, and had sharp, angular features that gave her the appearance of being inconvenienced by the herd of people there for free food.

When Naomi got her chicken noodle soup dumped in her metal cup, she muttered under her breath, "Looks like one noodle and water poured over a chicken, to me."

"Do you have a problem?" the tall woman scolded.

Naomi did not realize at first that the woman was talking to her, as Hank diplomatically said, "No problems here, ma'am. The soup's as hot as the preacher's lesson—and a fine lesson it was."

The woman did not respond to Hank's compliment, but looked at Naomi to scold, "Perhaps if you would apply yourself to some constructive labor or learn not to complain, you could afford a soup more suited to your taste."

Naomi set her jaw to say, "If I was trying to really help the poor, I'd put a little more chicken in the soup and a little less spite in the sermon."

"This is a free country," the woman said. "We help those who want help. We can't help those who are—ungrateful."

Before Naomi could retaliate to the woman's scolding, Raquel said, "We are grateful, ma'am. My mother-in-law is not feeling well today. We lost all our money on the bus a few days ago, and we've been out on the road since then. Thank you very much for the meal."

Naomi held her tongue, and the tall woman looked over the heads of Raquel and Naomi, as if they were not there. Naomi continued to stare at the woman, but Raquel nudged her through the line to a less conspicuous place to have their soup. After quickly eating their meal, the group slipped out of the door and away from the judgmental eyes of the tall woman.

"Sorry to cause a scene," Naomi apologized, once they were outside.

"No need," Hank laughed. "Old Doubting Deloris does the Lord's work with a vengeance. She don't mean nothin' by it, but she's always quick to scold those of us she sees as off the Almighty's path."

"Thank you for the soup," Raquel said. "And thank you for everything you've done for us."

"Weren't nothing," Hank shrugged.

"Mr. Tilley," Naomi said in a formal tone. "I guess this is where we part paths. I'm heading to the Western Union office and hope to have money for a bus ticket and expenses by tonight. Where can I find you to repay you for your trouble?"

"Told you," Hank protested. "Weren't no trouble."

Hank turned to Harry and said, "We better be gettin' back. I worked out a deal with some of those fellas to let us stay near that tent in case it rains. We better let these good ladies get on with their trip."

Turning to Naomi and Raquel, Hank said, "Good luck to you. I mean that."

"Good luck to you, Hank," Raquel smiled, as she stepped in to give both of the men a gentle hug.

Naomi fought back tears, as she said, "I wasn't kidding, Mr. Tilley. If you're ever near Sayre, come for a hot meal and a bed."

"Thank you, ma'am," Hank smiled, as he nudged Harry back toward the hobo camp.

After the two men had turned the corner, Naomi said, "I can't believe I'm saying this, but I think I may miss them."

"I will, too," Raquel sighed.

CHAPTER 43

Naomi still wore the poorly-fitting trousers, as she and Raquel stepped through the front door of the Western Union office. Raquel carried the small canvas tote that had Naomi's dress, what was left of their money, and the kitchen knife Hank had given them. Raquel was stuck with her trousers, plaid shirt, and short hair, since she had lost her dress on their first failed attempt at hopping a train.

"Excuse me," Naomi greeted the clerk, in a tone of voice that did not match her appearance. "I need to send a telegram."

The neatly dressed clerk looked over the two women for a second before handing Naomi a form and saying, "Write your message here, and I'll send it."

Naomi thanked him and retreated to a small stand up counter with a pen hanging on a chain.

Naomi concentrated and whispered to herself as she wrote, "To Beulah Belvedere: We've had some trouble in New Mexico. Could you please wire me twenty dollars immediately to this address? We will be in Oklahoma in a couple of days. Thank you, your friend, Naomi Butler."

Naomi handed the slip of paper to the clerk, as he studied it and asked, "Where do you want the wire sent?"

"Sayre, Oklahoma," Naomi replied.

The clerk studied a chart, counted the words, and said, "That'll be a dollar twenty-three."

"A dollar twenty-three!" Naomi exclaimed. "Why so much?"

"You've got thirty-four words going to Oklahoma," the clerk explained. "That's the price."

"Can't you do it cheaper?" Naomi asked.

"The minimum charge to Sayre, Oklahoma, is forty-three cents for ten words," the clerk replied. "Ten words is the minimum; each word is extra after that."

"I see," Naomi said. "Let me have another slip, please."

"Yes, ma'am," the clerk said.

Naomi took the slip of paper and went back to the stand-up desk to revise her message.

"How much money do we have?" Naomi whispered to Raquel.

"Thirty-five cents," Raquel answered.

Naomi shook her head and said, "We're stranded here because of eight cents. Where are we going to find eight cents?"

Raquel thought for a moment and then said, "Figure out how to write the message in ten words, and I'll find the money."

Naomi nodded, as Raquel slipped out of the Western Union office and quickly walked down the street. Eight cents seemed such a small amount, but to Raquel it felt like it would be nearly impossible to find in time. She had thought about heading to the hobo camp to find Hank. He would know what to do, although she doubted he had the spare change. Besides, she would not feel right taking Hank's money.

Raquel headed to the only place she thought she had a chance of finding the money quickly—the soup kitchen. It was later in the afternoon, and fewer people stood in line for a cup of hot soup or hotter preaching. Raquel walked past the entrance to the mission and went in through the back door to the soup kitchen. The tall woman still stood over the other workers and looked fiercely and suspiciously at the small group standing in line for soup. Raquel was sure the woman saw her, but the tall woman seemed determine to ignore the short-haired girl wearing the boy's trousers.

"Ma'am," Raquel asked timidly, as she approached the woman.

The woman did not immediately acknowledge her greeting.

"You may remember me from earlier," Raquel continued. "I was here with my mother-in-law a little over an hour ago."

The tall woman finally looked at Raquel and said, "I remember—the ungrateful woman."

"Yes, ma'am," Raquel admitted. "The thing is—we've been real down on our luck. I know you must here these kinds of stories every day."

"By the hundreds," the woman scowled.

Raquel swallowed hard, "Yes, ma'am. We aren't used to having to ask for a handout, but all I need is eight cents and we can wire for some money to help us find our way home."

"If I gave eight cents to every person passing through these doors, the mission wouldn't have enough for the soup we're able to give now," the woman explained.

"I know," Raquel said. "I hate to ask, but we're not from here and don't know anyone else that could help. I'd be willing to do anything. Wash clothes, do some sewing, clean your mission—anything. When we get home and back on our feet, we can send you a donation."

The woman did not answer, but continued to look over the few people still lining up for food.

"Please," Raquel pleaded. "I'll do anything."

"I will, too," Naomi said from behind Raquel.

Raquel turned around to see her mother-in-law standing a few feet behind her. Naomi stepped around Raquel to stand face-to-face with the tall woman.

"I'm very sorry for my behavior earlier," Naomi said. "You are doing a tremendous work here, and I know that I was not counting my blessings as I should have earlier. I can be a prideful and cynical woman, but I'm trying to get my daughter-in-law home. I've lost everything this past year—not just a house, a car, and my money. I've lost a husband and two sons. All I have left in this world are two daughters-in-law and a piece of property my husband left me. I know I don't deserve any consideration, but I also know you're here to help people. I'll do anything if you find your way to loan us eight cents. I'll scrub toilets and clean out the outbuilding if need be, but I want to get home."

The woman did not say anything, but reached into a pocket of her dress and removed a coin purse. She slowly opened it and handed Naomi a dime.

"Thank you," Naomi said softly. "Thank you so much. What can I do for you?"

The woman did not answer for a minute and then said, "I want you to be kind to someone for no reason sometime. Take this, and I hope it helps."

"Thank you," Naomi repeated.

"Thank you so much," Raquel said, as she gently took Naomi by the arm and led her toward the door.

"If you need a place to stay for the night, the YWCA down the street has some cots," the woman said. "They get crowded sometimes, but tell them Deloris sent you. It's just a few hundred yards from the bus station."

"Thank you," Raquel said.

Raquel and Naomi walked to the exit of the soup kitchen, when the tall woman stepped toward them and said, "I lost my boy this past year, too. May God be with you, and may you find some peace."

Naomi wiped a tear from her eye and stepped to the woman and said, "Bless you, and bless the work you do in this place."

The woman nodded without saying more. Naomi and Raquel walked quietly back to the Western Union office.

Naomi sent a message to Beulah Belvedere that read, "BEULAH. WIRE TWENTY DOLLARS TO THIS STATION. EMERGENCY. NAOMI."

CHAPTER 44

"How long will this take?" Naomi asked the clerk at the telegraph office.

The clerk studied the short message and answered without looking at Naomi, "I'll send the message right now. It'll be up to the sender when—or if they respond. Once they wire the money, this office can deliver the wired amount."

"So, you don't know," Naomi said.

The clerk sighed heavily, "No, ma'am. You can check back later, and I'll get a delivery confirmation once the message has been received. After that, it's a matter of getting a response. Is there an address where this office can contact you?"

"No," Naomi replied nervously. "We'll check back."

Naomi nodded to the clerk before leaving the office with Raquel.

"It's a waiting game now, I suppose," Naomi said to Raquel.

"What do you want to do with our afternoon?" Raquel asked.

Naomi frowned, "I guess we need to go to the bus terminal and check the schedule."

"It's two blocks down," Raquel offered.

"You lead the way," Naomi said. "I'm too tired to think."

Raquel fought back the urge to smirk at her grumpy and tired mother-in-law, as she gently took her arm and walked slowly toward the bus station. The roar of the bus engines and the noisy excitement of the terminal encouraged Raquel, as she realized these silver chariots of the highway could bring them home in less than a day.

Raquel studied the schedule and said to Naomi, "Looks like there's three busses that leave in the morning and one in the afternoon."

"Four o'clock," Naomi said, as she looked at the schedule to see the time for the last bus leaving Albuquerque. "It's a quarter to two now. Beulah better hurry or we're stuck here another day."

Raquel nodded and stepped up to the ticket window to ask, "How much for two tickets to Sayre, Oklahoma?"

The man looked at the two women, who still wore their trousers, and announced, "Two dollars and eighty-three cents each—cash."

Raquel ignored the man's disapproving tone and said, "Thank you."

Raquel could tell that Naomi wanted to respond to the man's rudeness, but she stepped in front of her mother-in-law and said, "Let's go."

"I'm tired of wearing these clothes, "Naomi fussed, as they moved away from the ticket window. "Let me have the bag. I'm changing."

"Here?" Raquel asked.

Naomi nodded affirmatively.

"That's a good idea, "Raquel said.

Naomi found the women's restroom and changed into her wrinkled dress. She tried to pamper her hair as best she could. In less than twenty minutes her dress and demeanor improved.

"Sorry we don't have a change of clothes for you," Naomi said.

"I'm fine," Raquel smiled pleasantly. "I'm kinda getting used to wearing pants."

Raquel had lost her belongings when the two women tried to hop their first train in Gallop.

"What now?" Raquel asked.

"We can't do much with two cents," Naomi fumed.

"We could walk around and see the town," Raquel suggested.

Naomi shook her head, "I've seen enough of Albuquerque, thank you very much. I just want to go home."

"Maybe in a few days," Raquel smiled.

"For now, let's find a place to sit," Naomi said. "My feet are killing me."

"You look tired," Raquel said, as she put her arm around Naomi's shoulder. "Let's get out of the noisy terminal. I think I saw a park down the block. Let's find a cool place in the shade and enjoy some of the afternoon."

Naomi nodded, and let Raquel guide her through the busy terminal and to a small park. Naomi grunted slightly when she plopped onto the first park bench she found.

"We'll need to find a place to stay," Raquel suggested.

"Hopefully, we'll have hotel money by the time the Western Union office closes," Naomi said.

"The woman at the mission said they had beds at the YWCA," Raquel reminded.

Naomi shook her head, "Beulah will send the money, and we'll be in our own room tonight."

"We could plan for the worst case," Raquel suggested.

"Fine," Naomi moaned. "We'll check back at the telegraph office before four, just in case the money comes in time to catch that last bus. If we don't hear anything about the wire by five o'clock, we'll find a cot at the YWCA."

"That sounds like a plan," Raquel said.

The two women sat silently on the bench for several minutes, enjoying the peacefulness of the small park.

"It's been quite a trip," Naomi finally said.

"Uh-huh," Raquel agreed. "We've seen a different part of the country than you're used to."

"That's for sure," Naomi said. "At least the company's been good."

Raquel smiled at her mother-in-law's compliment.

"You know," Naomi continued. "Eli always wanted to take a vacation cross-country to visit back home. He said it was only a two-and-a-half-day drive and good road most of the way. I always fretted about having to eat out and stay in strange hotel rooms. I guess he thought the trip would be too much trouble, and we never got around to it. Eli always kept a good car. He was a terrific mechanic. If I only had that car now, I'd head east and wouldn't stop until we pulled into the road in front of the home place."

"I'd help drive," Raquel said. "But I think I may keep these clothes. No wonder men get so much done when all they have to do is pull up their pants and put on a shirt for the day."

"Oh, Raquel," Naomi sighed. "I don't want to ever see you in anything but pretty dresses again. And your hair—I can't imagine what on earth convinced me to let that crazy old tramp cut your hair so short."

"It's not so short," Raquel smiled, as she reached up and touched her hair. "It's almost covering my ears."

Naomi made a twisted face and shook her head.

Raquel giggled at her mother-in-law's misplaced concern for her appearance after what they had been through and assured, "It'll grow back, Naomi. It's not like I'm needing to look pretty now."

"You're always pretty," Naomi said. "Inside and out. I can't believe those fools thought they could make you look like a boy."

"Those fools kept us fed and took care of us the past week," Raquel said. "And they provided me with this wardrobe."

Naomi laughed, "Oh, you."

"You want to stay here while I check on the wire?" Raquel asked.

Naomi groaned, as she struggled to stand up and said, "No, we'll stay together. Besides, I better keep this old knee limber in case we need to walk all the way home."

The two women strolled slowly to the Western Union office and arrived a half hour before four. Naomi was disappointed that the wire had not been received, but she did not seem surprised. Sending a wire meant that someone had to find Beulah. Although Sayre was not a large town, there were plenty of reasons that Beulah could not be found immediately. Naomi knew Beulah would be home before dark to start supper. She thanked the clerk, and the two women walked leisurely back to their park bench.

When Naomi returned at five o'clock, she was edgier about the missing telegram. She had convinced herself that Beulah would have been home by then. Not only did she not have the money for a hotel room, Naomi still had not gotten confirmation that the message had even been received. Raquel convinced Naomi that they needed to find a place to sleep for the night. The YWCA was five blocks away, in a less affluent part of town. Naomi waited outside as Raquel went in to see if they could stay the night. The woman at the front desk initially said they were out of room, but when Raquel mentioned the woman at the mission, the YWCA found two cots that they placed at the end of a long room close to the back exit.

Raquel felt relieved that they had found a place besides the city jail to sleep for the night. The YWCA would have little privacy, but it would be warm and safe. Naomi was becoming more agitated about not getting confirmation that Beulah Belvedere had received her message. She checked at the Western Union office at seven o'clock and again at eight. Although it was dark, Naomi insisted that they make one last attempt before the office closed at nine o'clock.

"I can't believe it," Naomi whimpered, as they left the Western Union office and heard the clerk lock the door behind them for the night.

"We'll try in the morning," Raquel encouraged.

"Where could she be?" Naomi whined.

"She's probably been out," Raquel said. "Maybe she went out of town for shopping or something."

"I just knew we would have that money today," Naomi said. "I've been such a fool. If I'd swallowed my pride when we first ran into trouble, we'd be home by now."

"We'll get there," Raquel said. "I promise. At least we have a place to stay for the night."

"Thanks to you," Naomi said.

"It's okay for someone to look after you every once and awhile," Raquel teased.

"Well," Naomi smiled. "It won't be the Ritz, but that cot at the YWCA is sounding pretty good right now."

The streets were dark as they walked through the business district and toward the YWCA. A few people lingered, but the streets were, for the most part, clear. Two blocks away from their night's destination, a pleasant voice from a dark alley caused Raquel to stop where she stood.

"Good evening, ladies," the calm voice of Jack Fisk greeted.

The women stared at the approaching man, but neither one responded to him.

The man walked closer and said, "That's no way to treat an old friend."

"You're no friend of ours," Naomi said tersely. "You stole our things and have caused us considerable inconvenience Mr. Fisk—or are you going by Smiling Jack tonight?"

Jack Fisk did not lose his composure as he said, "Smiling Jack? You obviously have me mistaken for someone. Maybe you ladies have been on the road a little too long."

"Because of you!" Naomi charged.

"We've learned a lot about you," Raquel added.

"Who's been spoiling my reputation?" Jack Fisk said, as he slowly walked closer to the women.

"You have no reputation with us," Naomi said. "We know you are a cheat and a scoundrel."

Jack Fisk did not lose his calm and agreeable demeanor, as he said, "I realize that it may seem that way, but from what I've heard, this Smiling Jack is a fairly spiteful individual. I pride myself on being pleasant as I work my way through life."

"We know that you showed us no kindness when you left us stranded in Flagstaff," Raquel charged.

"Looks like you've managed okay," Jack Fisk smiled. "Except—my word! What have you done to that beautiful hair of yours?"

Jack Fisk laughed jovially, as he now stood close enough that he was able to reach out and touch the chopped off ends of Raquel's cropped hair.

Raquel moved her head slightly to avoid the man stroking the tips of her hair, as she said, "What you've done to us is of little concern compared to the injustice you caused my friend, Mr. Hank Tilley."

The mention of Hank Tilley transformed the calm manner of Jack Fisk to a more serious and almost agitated demeanor.

"You've seen Hammerin' Hank?" he quizzed.

"This morning," Raquel stated defiantly. "He told us all about you and how you caused him trouble with the law."

Jack Fisk tried to regain his earlier charm, but his tone of voice was more rushed and harsh than it had been before.

"Hammerin' Hank's in town?" Jack Fisk clarified.

"As of this morning," Raquel said proudly, sensing that Hank Tilley was causing her tormenter some discomfort.

Jack Fisk smiled fiendishly and smirked, "I don't know which is worse, to be stupid or unlucky. Hammerin' Hank's surely had his share of both. Yeah, I knew your Mr. Tilley a few years back. It's not my fault that he can't hold his liquor."

"Mr. Tilley has endeared himself to us greatly," Naomi said. "He's told us what a snake you can be."

"Shut up, old woman!" Jack Fisk shouted loudly and angrily. "You have no idea how hard it is to pretend to be nice to a hypocritical windbag like you!"

Naomi took a step back at the sudden and violent outburst. As Raquel moved to be closer to Naomi, Jack Fisk grabbed the girl's arm roughly and jerked her back toward him.

"You're not going anywhere!" Jack Fisk declared forcefully.

"Let go of her!" Naomi screamed, as she moved to get him away from Raquel.

Jack Fisk easily and forcefully pushed Naomi to the ground, and smiling meanly said, "Get away, old woman! I don't have any use for you!"

Dragging Raquel away, he said, "I have something in mind for you, though, my little darling. I like that little boy's haircut—and your new-found loathing of me."

Raquel struggled, but the man was strong and determined, as he yanked her toward a dark alley. She cried and screamed, but the street was empty and the man muffled her mouth with his large hands. As she fought furiously to free herself, the man suddenly stopped and seemed to go rigid for an instant, before stumbling limply to his knees, and collapsing to the pavement. Raquel gasped to catch her breath for a second, and then she saw Naomi standing over the man with a bloody knife in her hand.

CHAPTER 45

"I've killed him!" Naomi shrieked, in a strange muffled cry.

Jack Fisk laid face down and did not move. A crimson puddle of blood pooled by his right shoulder.

"What have I done?" Naomi whispered softly, nearly to herself.

Raquel cautiously moved closer to look at the fallen man.

"I've killed him dead," Naomi murmured.

As Raquel bent down to check on her attacker, a man's voice from the alley yelled, "They're robbing him!"

Raquel squinted into the darkness, but could not determine how many men had witnessed the attack.

"I saw her stab him, and now they're robbing him," the man roared.

The man was forty or fifty yards away when he emerged from the dark shadows into the illumination of a street lamp. Raquel gasped when she recognized the short man they called Ned Farrell, who had been Jack Fisk's accomplice on the bus.

"They murdered him, and now they're robbing him!" the man continued to shout.

Raquel looked at Naomi and said, "We got to get out of here."

Naomi was numb and did not respond for a second, but as Raquel grabbed her firmly by the arm, she began to move. Raquel did not have a plan, except to get away from the man that was shouting accusations at them. She looked nervously to see if there were any police, but she kept walking away from the short man.

He stopped at the fallen Jack Fisk and yelled, "He's dead!"

Raquel could not think straight. The man leered at her with a mean frown. All she had wanted minutes before was the warm, safe bed waiting for her at the YWCA. Raquel believed going back to face the accuser would be trouble for Naomi. Almost unconsciously, Raquel kept Naomi walking away from the downtown area until she recognized that they were in the warehouse district close to the railroad tracks. Sirens now blared in the background adding to the urgency Raquel felt. As she crossed the tracks, Raquel could see the faint fires from the hobo camp several hundred yards away. Her only plan now was to find Hank Tilley. At worst, Raquel believed that mingling with the transient horde in the camp would be a good place to hide, until she could think straight.

The relative calm of the shanty town seemed disconcerting to Raquel, as she tried to calm her nerves. The camp chatter and the curious looks from people watching two women walk into the camp after dark did not seem real to Raquel. She walked toward the open tent where she had last seen Hank Tilley. He had talked about a train leaving tonight, and she feared he would be gone.

"There he is!" Raquel cried out, when she saw the lanky Hank standing near a barrel fire close to the tent where they had found him earlier in the day.

Raquel urged Naomi to hurry, but her mother-in-law walked as if in a trance.

"Mr. Tilley!" Raquel yelled.

Hank Tilley turned around to see the two women and smiled warmly. His pleasant grin soon vanished, as the women came closer. He could tell something was not right.

"What are you doing here?" Hank asked.

"Mr. Tilley, we're in some bad trouble!" Raquel exclaimed.

"What kind of trouble?" Hank asked calmly, but with a sense of concern. "I thought you were getting money wired this afternoon."

"The money didn't come," Raquel explained, "but that's not the trouble."

"I've killed a man," Naomi stated factually and stoically.

"What?" Hank asked warily.

Naomi did not explain, but showed Hank the bloody knife that she still held in her hand. Hank stood in silent shock, but he took the weapon from her.

"We ran into Jack Fisk," Raquel said. "He grabbed me and Naomi stabbed him in the back. He fell limp and—and we ran here."

"I stabbed him in the back," Naomi sobbed. "I didn't know what else to do. I can still feel the blade sinking into him like it would go into a piece of roast."

"Get me some coffee over here!" Hank shouted to a group of men, including his traveling companion Harry, standing by the fire. "You need to calm down, Mrs. Butler. Things will be okay. We just need to get some coffee in you."

Naomi took the tin cup filled with coffee and sipped it, as her hands shook violently.

"That must be what all the commotion is in town," Hank said, as he looked back across the tracks.

"I killed him, and now they'll come for us," Naomi said.

"Sounds like self-defense," Hank tried to comfort. "Smilin' Jack's got a record as long as the Grand Canyon is wide. The cops'll understand."

"Ned Farrell was there," Raquel said nervously. "He ran after us. He said we killed Mr. Fisk."

Hank rubbed his chin and said, "Ned saw the thing?"

Raquel nodded, "He yelled at us and said we were robbing Mr. Fisk. He shouted loud enough for everyone to hear, that we had killed him and was trying to rob him."

"Did you wait for the police?" Hank asked.

"No," Raquel frowned. "I—I couldn't think straight. I—should've stayed and let the police handle things, but we were in jail last night, and the short man seemed angry and bent on doing us in. I didn't know where else to go, Mr. Tilley, so I came here looking for you."

"We'll get it figured out," Hank said, as he grinned at the young woman. "I'm no lawyer, but you ladies are in the clear. Ain't no reason to hang around here and find out, though. We need to get you out of New Mexico—tonight."

"Can you help us, Mr. Tilley?" Raquel pleaded.

Hank Tilley said, "Consider it done. You stay here and keep pouring coffee into Mrs. Butler. I'll check around and see what I can find out."

Raquel nodded and watched Mr. Tilley disappear into the confusion of the hobo camp.

"I'm done for," Naomi said. "I might as well turn myself in. The despicable Mr. Farrell is going to lie, just to spite me."

"It'll be okay," Raquel tried to assure. "Remember, you saved me from that vile and horrible man."

Naomi nodded her head and seemed to regain some of her senses, as she said, "Yes—Yes. God knows what that evil man might have done. I—I couldn't think—No one was there to help, so I stabbed him."

"It was self-defense," Raquel said. "Mr. Tilley said so himself. I can testify to that."

Naomi frowned, "But who knows what the little man, Mr. Farrell is telling the police right now. I'm betting they're searching for us."

Naomi suddenly stood up and looked suspiciously at the many people milling about the camp.

"There's Mr. Tilley," Naomi said, as Hank stepped quickly toward them.

"We're in luck!" Hank gleamed. "The train I told you about this mornin' is leaving in a little more than an hour."

"What else did you find out?" Raquel timidly asked.

Hank frowned as he confessed, "Word around camp is that Smilin' Jack's dead. Heard some fellows gossiping about it, but they didn't say nothing about two women, so we got time to get you out of here."

"Won't the police be watching the trains?" Raquel asked, with a raised eyebrow.

"Not more than normal," Hank said. "I'm betting Ned Farrell didn't hang around for no police—no way. We're going to get you on that train headin' home, and we're doing it right now."

"Tell us what to do," Raquel said.

"Follow me," Hank motioned with his head, as he started walking toward the train tracks.

Raquel grabbed Naomi by the arm and gently forced her to move to keep up with the fast-walking man. A few yards from the rail yard, Hank stopped in the shadows to let the women catch up.

"There she is," Hank said, as he pointed toward the tracks. "The one we want is on the second set of tracks at the end."

Raquel looked through the dark night and could see the freight train preparing to make its departure.

"Curse the luck!" Hank sighed.

"What is it, Mr. Tilley?" Raquel quickly asked.

"The rail bulls are out in force tonight," Hank pointed out, as Raquel could see two or three men patrolling the rail yard close to the train heading east."

"Police?" Raquel asked.

"Naw," Hank said. "Rail police. They're thick in this yard. That's not all."

"What?" Raquel said.

"The only car you've got a good chance of catching is that hopper car near the switch house," Hank explained.

He pointed at the open car designed to carry coal, rock, and other bulk freight items. Raquel nodded to affirm that she saw it.

"It'll be empty heading east," Hank said. "You won't have a roof over your head tonight, but the weather looks okay."

"How do we catch it?" Raquel asked.

Hank pointed toward the switch house and said, "Get yourself as close to that switch as possible. I'm going to head right toward this boxcar in the open. The rail bulls'll be on me like flies on a dead squirrel. When they do, you high-tail-it up those steps and into the battle ship."

Raquel's puzzled look indicated that she did not understand.

"The battleship," Hank repeated. "The hopper car with the steel sides. It's called a battleship. Get yourself over the top as quick as you can."

Raquel repeated, "Get into the open car and don't be seen."

"You got it," Hank said. "You understand, Mrs. Butler?"

Naomi nodded once to indicate her comprehension.

"Don't you look back," Hank ordered. "Don't you make a sound until that train pulls clear of the city. It's warm enough that you should be okay in the open. Keep your head down and stay on this train until you come to Pampa, just east of Amarillo. You should be there by morning. The train'll slow down south of town at the switch near Belen, and it'll stop in Clovis and Amarillo, but you stay in that car and out of sight. Even if the rain's comin' like it did in the days of Noah, stay in that battleship. They won't search it, if you keep your head down and stay toward the locomotive end of it. You'll have to change trains in Pampa to get where you need to go, but you'll be out of New Mexico and close to home. You're on your own from there."

"You don't go to Texas," Raquel stated.

Hank smiled, "I don't go to Texas—just like you'll need to stay out of New Mexico for a while."

"What about you?" Raquel asked. "What will you do when they catch you?"

"Don't worry about me," Hank grinned. "I'm sober as a preacher and can hold my own against them until you're on that train. After that, I'll go to town and see what I can find out about Smilin' Jack."

"Mr. Tilley—Hank," Naomi said in an urgent tone. "My friend is wiring me money and should be in the Western Union office by tomorrow morning. I want you to pick it up for me. Here's my receipt."

"I don't know when I can catch up to you ma'am," Hank protested.

"The money's yours," Naomi offered. "It's the least I can do for your considerable trouble."

"Let's not worry about the Western Union tonight," Hank replied. "Let's get you on that train. You ready?"

Raquel and Naomi nodded. Hank Tilley pointed at the switch house, and the women walked cautiously toward it trying to stay in the shadows as much as possible. Once they got as close as they dared, they watched Hank Tilley walk stealthily toward a boxcar out in the open.

"Hey!" one of the railroad police shouted. "We've got one!"

Hank did not stop and headed straight for the train.

The railroad police cursed and then shouted, "Stop, you tramp! Stop, I said!"

Hank gestured defiantly at the man and kept moving. By that time, he had the attention of four of the train's security that now raced to intercept the bold man.

"Look at him," Raquel whispered. "He looks like a magnificent matador charging a raging bull."

The first railroad detective tried to tackle Hank, but he easily pushed him aside. The second took out a nightstick, but Hank deflected the blow and punched the man, knocking him to the ground clutching his nose. The third and fourth railroad bulls cautiously approached on either side of Hank to block his path. The other two men had also recovered, and they all charged him at once.

Raquel wanted to call out, but remembered her instructions, as she whispered to Naomi, "Let's go!"

With a firm tug on Naomi's arm, Raquel moved her mother-in-law out of the shadows and toward the waiting train. Raquel glanced back toward the rear of the train and could tell Hank Tilley was holding his own in the growing brawl happening in the open area of the rail yard. Raquel kept Naomi moving, but she could hear the sounds of the gathering crowd of rail workers and tramps eager to witness a good fracas. Naomi hesitated when they got to the coal car. Raquel practically lifted Naomi up to the first step, and then ungracefully pushed her posterior. Naomi grunted and groaned, but made it to the top of the ladder. Naomi muffled a scream, as she fell into the empty car and landed hard on the metal side. Raquel also tumbled in and almost landed on top of Naomi. The sky was dark, but Raquel was relieved to see that they were alone in the coal car.

"We made it," Raquel whispered.

Naomi nodded and put her head on her knees. The sounds from the fight grew, as more people joined the cheers and taunts.

Shortly after they had cleared the top of the coal car, Raquel could hear a voice shout, "He's running."

The noise and confusion faded as the sound of the mob and the loud cursing from the railroad security moved away from them.

"We're safe," Raquel whispered.

"For now," Naomi sighed.

CHAPTER 46

The dark, moonless night made it hard to see inside the hopper car. Raquel could tell the steel walls were vertical by feeling her way around in the dark. The floor was uneven and slanted toward the center. The car had an oily, dirty smell from its primary cargo of coal. The car was empty, and the train was headed to the coal country of Kentucky and West Virginia. Raquel wrestled a silent and numb Naomi to a place where her mother-in-law could lean back in the dark railcar. After a few minutes, the clamor from the fight faded away, as the two women waited anxiously in silence.

The quietness of the night was peaceful, but the women were apprehensive. They sat silently for what seemed to be an hour, except for Naomi's occasional muffled cough from the dusty hopper car. Neither woman had a watch. Time did not seem real to them. Raquel looked worriedly at her mother-in-law, who had a defeated and faraway stare as she gazed at the gloomy, empty railcar. Raquel wanted to talk to her and help her feel better, but she remembered Hank's instructions to remain quiet.

A few minutes later the stillness of the night was broken by a soft but terrifying sound. Outside the railcar, Raquel could hear the gentle crunching of gravel as footsteps approached. Raquel's eyes had adjusted to the darkness somewhat, and she glanced at Naomi to see that she too heard the danger. The noise in and of itself would have caused no concern on a normal night, but this was no ordinary evening. Raquel gasped ever so slightly, as she realized that she had been holding her breath, and she had to make herself consciously remember to breathe as the footsteps steadily approached.

Raquel's eyes widened in terror, as she noticed Naomi trying to suppress a sudden urge to cough. The footsteps had to be coming from a rail detective, Raquel believed. If they were caught and taken to jail, Raquel could only imagine what might happen. Raquel concentrated, as if to will Naomi to fight the compulsion to cough and clear her throat. The footsteps came to a crescendo immediately outside the railcar. Raquel could breathe in air but struggled to exhale. A sense of relief flooded over Raquel, as the footsteps started to slowly fade away in the distance. The reprieve from terror was short-lived, however, as Naomi could no longer contain the tickle in her throat and exuded a muffled cough.

The steps stopped, and Raquel tried to control her urge to scream in panic. The silence was cruel and tense, as Naomi was nearly in tears trying to contain another impulse to cough louder. In a few seconds, the footsteps continued, and Raquel nearly cried with joy when the steps headed away from them. A few minutes after the noise from outside the railcar disappeared, Naomi succumbed to a hacking coughing fit. She tried to suppress it by putting her head into her arms. Raquel could not resist the suspense any longer, and she climbed to the top of the car to carefully peek at the dimly lit rail yard. Satisfied they were safe, Raquel moved beside Naomi and let her cough into her shoulder.

"It'll be alright," Raquel whispered. "We're alone."

Naomi nodded. Her head was now buried in Raquel's shoulder, and she cried softly, which seemed to help restrain her coughing. In a few more minutes, Raquel heard more sounds from outside the railcar, but this time it was the busy commotion of the train pulling out of the rail yard. A loud, whining whistle blasted into the night, steam hissed, and steel wheels screeched on the rails, causing a noisy confusion. The train lurched forward, roughly tossing the women into the steel side of the car. Raquel did not mind. The train was moving and taking them away from Albuquerque.

Raquel looked up at the sky and could see the reflection of the city lights for a few minutes, but as the train gained speed, the night was dominated by the brilliant shining stars of a clear, desert night. In about half an hour, the train slowed. Raquel ignored Hank's instructions and peeked over the side of the car to get a look. She saw a sign that said "Belen, New Mexico," before she slid back to the bottom of the car.

"What is it?" Naomi lethargically asked.

"We're in Belen," Raquel said. "The train's making the switch to head east like Hank said."

Raquel smiled peacefully as she leaned against the hard steel side of the car, which caused Naomi to ask, "What are you so happy about?"

"Belen is Spanish for Bethlehem," Raquel explained. "Maybe we'll find some peace on the rest of our trip."

"I wouldn't count on it," Naomi fretted.

Raquel did not try to change her mother-in-law's mood as the train slowed and bumped as it switched to the eastward track. After a few nervous moments, the train's engine strained to pick up momentum, as it headed into the desert night.

"We should be safe now," Raquel said, while looking at the clear skies above them.

"I'm sorry," Naomi said stoically. "I'm sorry for everything, but particularly for being fussy."

"It's okay," Raquel tried to assure. "We're going to be okay now."

Naomi nodded, but did not respond. Her coughing was becoming more frequent and violent. Her eyes stared straight ahead as her gaze fixed on the blank steel side of the railcar.

"Try to sleep," Raquel suggested.

"I will," Naomi said, as she laid her head back into Raquel's shoulder.

Naomi looked around the dark, stark railcar, laughing strangely and cynically.

"What is it?" Raquel asked.

"I picked a fine time to get rid of those trousers," Naomi said. "I thought I was through traveling like this. I don't know what I've done, but I think God must be punishing me for some secret sin—maybe it's my pride."

Raquel put her arm around Naomi to comfort and warm her before saying, "I think God has more important things to do besides punish us. We've got each other, and we're going to make it."

"I'm not so sure," Naomi sighed.

"We're on a train heading east," Raquel said. "That's a start in the right direction."

"I've killed a man tonight, Raquel," Naomi stated stoically. "I've lost my husband, my sons, my money, and now—and now I guess I've lost my senses."

"Things will be okay when we cross the state line," Raquel assured.

"What then?" asked Naomi.

"We'll make it home," Raquel answered.

"Home," Naomi huffed.

"We will make it home," Raquel defiantly reaffirmed.

Naomi did not say anything, but then replied, "That's what's worrying me. That short little man—what's his name?"

"Hank called him Ned Farrell," Raquel answered.

"He was friends with that man," Naomi reasoned. "They were partners. Surely they talked. If they talked, this Ned Farrell knows all about us, including where we're going. I'm afraid this train ride, might be the last free air I breathe. I expect the police to be waiting when we finally get to our home."

"We don't know that," Raquel tried to assure. "Hank said a man like Ned Farrell would not likely to go to the police with his record of misdeeds."

Naomi fell back into a surly melancholy, as she stared blankly at the rusting steel wall of their railcar. Raquel squeezed her tighter and gently rubbed her arm.

"Let's worry about those things tomorrow," Raquel suggested. "Try to sleep. You'll feel better when the sun comes up. I'm sure."

Naomi did not respond, as she leaned silently on her daughter-in-law's shoulder. Raquel could not tell if her mother-in-law slept, as the train bumped down the tracks steadily. Raquel was exhausted and believed she would be able to sleep on the late night trip, but the madness of the day tormented her mind. Naomi had been right. The man that held their future in his hand with his lies and deceit knew they were heading to Sayre. They had been lucky to get out of Albuquerque, but Raquel did not know if the future held any hope. They were safe for tonight, however, and she tried to cling to any small blessing.

Raquel did not know how much time passed before the clicking of the steel wheels lulled her to sleep. The jerking of the braking train startled Raquel, and caused her to awaken fully alert and uneasy. She looked up at the sky that was still dark and filled with a beautiful tapestry of twinkling stars in the moonless night. As the train continued to slow, she could tell they were back in a city by the glow of the electric lights dimming the starry sky. Naomi continued to sleep, as the train screeched to a halt. Raquel almost expected to hear the sound of police diligently searching the train, but instead heard the tired sounds of the rail men doing the routine work of shuffling cars to their designated tracks.

In a few minutes, the train once again lurched ahead and accelerated down the dark tracks. As the city lights faded, Raquel gently moved away from the sleeping Naomi and positioned herself to peek over the top of the hopper car, although Hank Tilley had given her explicit instructions to keep her head down. In the darkness, Raquel struggled to see the passing countryside, but she did catch a glimpse of a sign on the westward way for Clovis, New Mexico. Raquel slid back to the bottom of the car and next to Naomi. They had made it, Raquel thought. If they were not already in Texas, they would be in a matter of minutes. She had an overwhelming sense of relief, although crossing the state line did nothing to erase the turmoil of her past few days.

As she contemplated the circumstances of their escape, Raquel felt a sadness thinking of how Hank Tilley had wanted to see them to Clovis. She had always thought it strange that Hank considered the invisible state line between New Mexico and Texas, as some impenetrable barrier. She now frowned at the irony of crossing that line herself, knowing she would now have that same feeling about ever returning to or through New Mexico.

At least we made it this far, Raquel thought. As the sleeping Naomi continued to cough in the dry, cool evening air, Raquel wondered if that would be far enough.

CHAPTER 47

Raquel awoke to a hint of dawn in the eastern sky and a foul odor of manure, as the train slowed. Naomi rested against her shoulder as they rocked down the railroad. The two women had spent the night huddled in the bumpy hopper car, and had seen half of two states looking up at the starlit sky during their intermittent sleep. Raquel gently moved Naomi to one side and peeked over the top of the railcar. She had caught the first whiff of the strong stench a few miles back, but hoped it would soon pass. Her curiosity now got the best of her, as she climbed to the top of the hopper car to look across acres of feedlots packed with cattle.

"Where are we?" Naomi groggily asked.

"Amarillo," Raquel replied, as Naomi sat in the bottom of the hopper car.

"I slept that long?" Naomi muttered.

Raquel nodded, "How do you feel?"

"Beaten up," Naomi complained. "This steel is hard."

"It didn't keep you from snoring," Raquel smiled.

"I guess," Naomi said. "What's that smell?"

"Cows," Raquel replied.

Raquel had intended to take a quick look and then keep her head down, but was captivated by the vast flatness of the west Texas countryside. The entire trip across the southwest had featured great stretches of vacant land, but most of the arid landscape had rugged hills and features to distinguish it. This land appeared as flat as a table top as far as the eye could see, devoid of any tree or vegetation taller than a bush.

"I'll be glad when we're past them," Naomi said, as Raquel rejoined her.

"Me too," Raquel said.

The train jerked to a complete stop a few minutes later and the two women huddled close to the wall of the railcar, hoping they would not be discovered. Raquel was more relaxed in the morning light than she had been the previous evening. If they were caught in Texas, they would be cursed at and probably escorted off the property, but she doubted they would be taken to jail. They were also closer to home. Hank had told them to stay in the car until a stop on the other side of Amarillo at the Pampa switch.

The sounds coming from outside the hopper car seemed routine, but the train was parked much longer than it had been in Clovis. Several times, the women felt the thud of cars being unhitched and hitched, as the train occasionally moved a few yards back and forth. Naomi had slept through the night, but she looked tired. Naomi had dark shadows of coal dust on her cheeks and clothes. Raquel could only imagine what she looked like.

After a couple of hours, Raquel heard the familiar shouts of men preparing to move the big train east. Raquel wanted to look out and see the rail yard at Amarillo, but instead stayed in the car and let the coughing Naomi lean against her. The train seemed to run smoother than it had last night, and Raquel thought it must be caused by the flat west Texas terrain. The sun was now high enough in the sky to shine over the lip of the hopper car and the two women moved to soak up the warmth of the sun after a long, chilly night in the open.

It took a little less than two hours for the train to make its next stop in Pampa, Texas. Raquel knew nothing of the town, other than it was a place where the train would switch. Raquel could not even be sure this stop was Pampa, but she was eager to get Naomi off the train. One thing Raquel knew was that they were now on their own. Hank Tilley had told them how to catch the train to Pampa, but they would have to find a way to continue. They had two cents and no contacts in the foreign west Texas town.

Raquel cautiously peeked over the edge of the hopper car to see a small but busy city that reminded her in some ways of their old home in Taft. The smell of petroleum hung in the air, and the wide-open spaces featured a few trees planted in the town. Two sets of tracks laid perfectly flat and parallel running next to a long white building with a terra cotta roof in the distance.

Seeing no one around, Raquel whispered to Naomi, "Let's go."

Naomi struggled to stand up in the uneven bottom of the hopper car, and Raquel had to assist her. Naomi tried to climb the interior steps with some dignity in her dirty dress, but Raquel finally pushed her gently to speed her ascent. Naomi groaned as she swung her leg unglamorously over the side of the car and slowly climbed down to reach the ground. Raquel quickly looked one more time to make sure they had not been seen and slid quickly down the steps to the ground.

"What now?" Naomi asked.

Raquel scanned the unfamiliar area and replied, "Let's get out of here."

Raquel took Naomi by the arm and moved her away from the train where they could have more deniability should they be confronted by one of the rail yard security men. The train they exited was long. Another short train was next to it. Looking down the rails, Raquel could see the switch house and two tracks dividing—one angled north and the other heading east.

"We'll want to head that way," Raquel said, pointing down the tracks heading east.

"How do we do that?" Naomi said.

"I don't know yet," Raquel frowned. "Let's hang out around the station and listen to see if we can pick up any information."

Naomi nodded and the two women walked slowly toward the white framed building a few hundred yards away.

"Looks like a nice town," Naomi said.

Raquel looked around at the small city with brick streets and said, "Yeah."

"Looks like an oil town," Naomi said. "Eli would have felt at home here."

As they continued to walk, a man wearing overalls and carrying a wrench stepped quickly toward them. Raquel instinctively looked away and tried to avoid any confrontation with the man.

"Good mornin', ladies," the man greeted with a tip of his cap, as he continued walking down the line.

"The people are certainly friendlier in Texas," Naomi quipped.

The two women continued walking and Naomi asked, "What's your plan?"

Raquel took a few steps and said, "I'm out of ideas. How about you?"

"I'm not crazy about riding any further in an open car," Naomi said. "I guess I'd do about anything to get home, though."

"Maybe I can find some work," Raquel said. "A bus ticket from here couldn't be that much. Maybe in a couple of days we could make enough. I could check at some restaurants to see if they need any work. At least we could eat."

Naomi sighed, "Are you getting tired of taking care of me?"

"Of course not," Raquel said. "I just thought I might be able to find some work."

"You're right," Naomi replied. "I'm too old and too tired for anyone to get much use out of me."

Before Raquel could reply, she stopped in her tracks. Naomi did not have to ask what was wrong, as Ned Farrell hopped out of a boxcar on the train they had been riding. Without saying a word, Raquel led Naomi toward the train and the only possible place where they could hide themselves. In a second, Raquel darted between two of the railcars and shoved Naomi out of sight.

"Did he see us?" Naomi asked.

"I don't think so," Raquel replied nervously.

Raquel carefully peeked underneath the railcar they were hiding behind and said, "I don't think he saw us, but he's still there."

"What's he doing here?" a panicked Naomi whimpered.

"I don't know," Raquel said. "And I don't want to find out."

Raquel stepped to the other side of the railcars to see that there was no one watching between the two trains that were idle next to each other.

"Let's get out from between these cars before we get killed," Raquel commanded.

Raquel jumped over the greasy coupling holding the two railcars together and turned to help Naomi. Her mother-in-law, however, had ducked underneath the coupling with much more agility than Raquel thought possible. Naomi tried to straighten herself, but Raquel motioned her to move to the area between the two trains. Raquel bent down again to get a look underneath the train for the legs of Ned Farrell before searching the front and back of the train for an escape. She did not find an egress, but noticed a half-empty boxcar on the other train with the door cracked open.

"We can hide in here," Raquel whispered, as she pointed at the open door.

Naomi nodded and the two women stepped quickly to the boxcar. Raquel looked inside to see it was empty except for the crates of freight, and she helped boost Naomi inside. Raquel stepped a few feet down the line to make sure that Ned Farrell had not seen them, before hopping into the boxcar to join Naomi. Raquel shoved several boxes to the side to make an area toward the rear of the boxcar where they could be out of view.

"Do you think he followed us?" Naomi asked.

"I don't know how," Raquel reasoned. "Hank was the only person to know we jumped that train. We weren't in town long enough for him to find out. I don't know what he's doing here."

"He must've been on that same train coming out of Albuquerque to get here so fast," Naomi whispered.

"He must have," Raquel agreed. "We'll stay here for a while. We'll be safe. I'll go check in a few minutes to see if he leaves."

"He'll still be in town," Naomi said. "We can't very well go looking for help with him running around town."

Before Raquel could agree with Naomi's logic, the door to the boxcar slammed shut leaving them in darkness.

"Is it him?" Naomi whispered urgently.

"Can't be," Raquel said. "I had my eye on him only a minute ago, and there's no way he could have gotten between the trains that fast."

A more muffled sound of another door slamming shut was heard from the boxcar next to them.

"The train's leaving!" Raquel whispered, as she recognized the sounds of the train's preparation.

Faint beams of sunlight dimly illuminated the wooden boxcar enough for Raquel to see the fear in her mother-in-laws eyes. If they were going to get off the train, it would have to be now.

"Where's this train heading?" Naomi asked.

"I don't know," Raquel answered. "I think I saw the engine pointed east."

"East would be good," Naomi said.

"I think we should see where it takes us," Raquel said. "We don't know anyone here, but we know Ned Farrell's out there."

Naomi nodded. In a few minutes the train heaved forward roughly, causing several boxes to shift uneasily. After a couple of more swaying movements forward, the train steadily and quickly gained momentum. Raquel hurriedly got to her feet and stumbled to the door to find a crack of daylight where she could see outside.

"Ned Farrell's behind us," Raquel reported. "He's making no move to get on this train."

Raquel continued to look out the small seam in the boxcar to see the upcoming switch. In a few moments, she rejoined Naomi in their newfound nest and settled next to her mother-in-law."

"Well?" Naomi asked.

Raquel grimaced, "I can't be sure. It was hard to see—but I think the train took the northern fork."

"Where will it take us?" Naomi sighed.

Raquel thought for a second and shrugged, "Somewhere."

CHAPTER 48

The train accelerated quickly as it sped out of Pampa, Texas. The boxcar had crates and boxes strapped to the walls. Naomi wheezed and coughed hoarsely before leaning against a crate that looked secure.

Naomi slid ungracefully to the floor and said, "I'm tired."

Raquel knelt down to touch her forehead and said, "You feel warm."

"It's hot in here," Naomi sighed.

Raquel walked to the large sliding door and gave it a shove. It rocked slightly before shifting back to its closed position. With a violent grunt, Raquel pushed the door with all her weight and moved it open. Warm fresh air rushed into the boxcar, and the sound of the clanking wheels on the rails was almost deafening. Raquel looked at Naomi, who had her eyes closed and seemed to be resting on the floor. The crates in the boxcar were large and concealed the merchandise being shipped. She explored the labels on the boxes and let Naomi try to nap. It had been a hard few days. The train ride from Albuquerque had been exhausting to Raquel, and she could only imagine how Naomi must feel.

As Raquel sorted through the contents of the boxcar, she stopped to look at a large crate sitting toward the middle of the car. She shoved a box to the side and leaned down to try to read the address. After finding the label, she stood up and smiled faintly.

"What is it?" Naomi asked.

"I thought you were sleeping," Raquel said.

"Just resting my eyes," Naomi replied.

"I don't know exactly where this train is going, but I think I know where this boxcar is going to stop," Raquel said.

"Where?" Naomi asked, as she sat up straighter.

"Higgins, Texas," Raquel said.

"The place where Mr. Tilley was from?" Naomi smiled.

Raquel nodded, "This box is addressed to the 'Hoover and Johnson Store' in Higgins, Texas. Didn't Hank say Higgins was close to Oklahoma?"

Naomi spoke with more energy and replied, "He said it was right on the border. In fact, didn't he talk about a little restaurant there?"

"Yes," Raquel said.

"What was it called?" Naomi asked.

Raquel thought for a second and replied, "West of the Border! The restaurant was called 'West of the Border' because he said it was right on the border."

"I remember," Naomi said. "He said they had the best chicken-fried steak in the world."

"Sounds delicious," Raquel smiled. "I don't know about you, but I'm starving."

"I'm hungry, too," Naomi said with a frown. "But I don't think we can buy a cup of coffee for two cents, much less a steak."

Raquel stepped to her mother-in-law and gave her an enthusiastic hug and said, "Where there's a will, there's a way. I'd scrub floors for a week for a good meal."

The two women spent the rest of their ride imagining and talking about the meal they could not afford. The train made quick stops in Panhandle and Canadian before pulling to a side rail in the small town of Higgins. Raquel had remembered Hank telling her to jump off the trains before they got into town and came to a stop, but she knew Naomi was not up to exiting a moving train. As soon as the train jerked to a stop, Raquel pushed Naomi to the door. She looked out the partially open door and after seeing no one, leaped to the rocky ground.

"Come on," Raquel coaxed, as Naomi clumsily tried to climb down.

Before Naomi's foot could hit the ground, a gruff man's voice yelled, "What'r ya'll doing?"

Raquel wanted to walk away, but Naomi was still having trouble, so she helped her mother-in-law.

The short, bow-legged man walked quickly to the women and said, "Did ya'll get off that train?"

Raquel nodded.

The man walked by them and looked into the boxcar and said, "I checked it. How'd you get on?"

"The door was open and we climbed in," Raquel said.

"Where?" the man asked.

"Pampa," Raquel said.

The man muttered some cursing under his breath and said, "I thought I checked the whole train."

He then looked at the two women and said in an almost apologetic voice, "I can't let you back on. This is a short run train. The supervisor will have my hide if he found out. You gals need to scat."

"You're not arresting us?" Raquel asked.

"I'm no rail detective," the man explained, as he looked around nervously. "I'm just the brake man. I don't want trouble, so git."

Raquel nodded and pulled Naomi with her toward the small town. The man watched them leave and then carefully inspected the boxcar they had left before shutting the door. Higgins was a small town with wide paved streets that ran parallel to the railroad tracks. A hotel was located adjacent to the tracks. Like the rest of the landscape, it looked brown and rugged, unlike the flat farmlands around Amarillo. The town had a lazy and relaxed feel. The few people they passed on the walk from the railroad tracks were friendly. All Raquel could think about, however, was how hard it would be to find transportation out of town. They would need to catch the train back to Pampa to get back on track to Sayre. She wondered how many trains stopped in Higgins, and was concerned that they would not be able to sneak back on easily in such wide-open country.

"Look there!" Naomi excitedly whispered, as she pointed to a small brick building on the corner.

A hand-painted sign stood inconspicuously in front of the building saying, "West of the Line Café."

"That's the restaurant Mr. Tilley told us about!" Naomi exclaimed.

It was about three o'clock in the afternoon. The early June heat was stifling and few people were on the streets.

"Let's go in," Raquel said. "Maybe they have some work."

A bell attached to the front door rang, and the two women stepped timidly inside. The place was clean but cluttered. It had a row of six stools at the counter and four tables to the side. A tall man with dark hair had his back to the door and appeared to be cooking in the small kitchen at an open grill.

Raquel and Naomi looked around, but they seemed to be alone except for the man who ignored them from the kitchen. Raquel took a step inside when a woman wearing a white dress appeared from the back. The woman's face showed deep wrinkles around her eyes from squinting in the west Texas sun, but she looked very spry and energetic for her age. She had a half-finished cigarette in her mouth and studied a stack of lunch tickets as she walked. The woman was thin and wiry with a no-nonsense demeanor to her gait. Raquel guessed her to be in her sixties, but could not tell for sure.

The woman looked up and noticed the two women. She said in a rough and gravelly voice, "I can't serve you now."

"Oh," a surprised Raquel sighed in a soft voice.

Raquel did not think they looked so destitute, but she imagined that the woman could tell they had been riding the rails.

The woman looked at the two women a moment and explained, "We're not serving supper yet, and we're cleanin' the grill."

Before Raquel could ask if the woman might have some work, the man from the back yelled with a strong twang to his voice, "Miss T, do I have to break this whole grill down this afternoon? It don't look so dirty to me as to need it."

The woman shouted back in an even more stern voice than she had used with the two women and said, "Clean it top to bottom, Chief! I ain't runnin' no greasy spoon here!"

"Okay, Miss T," the man replied.

The woman walked past Raquel and Naomi to open the cash register at the front of the diner to put the tickets under the cash drawer.

"Excuse me, ma'am," Raquel interrupted. "We didn't come to eat."

"Why'd you come to a restaurant then?" the woman asked bluntly.

Raquel took a half a step back and said, "I was looking for some cleaning work. I've cleaned a diner before and can make it shine."

The woman looked around and said, "You callin' my place dirty?"

"No ma'am," Raquel quickly assured. "It's just—it's just what I do, and I heard you say you need that grill cleaned."

"I got Chief back there doin' it," the woman stated factually. "I don't have any openings right now."

"Yes, ma'am," Raquel said. "It's just that we haven't eaten since yesterday, and I thought maybe I could do some work for some food."

The woman stopped working in her cash register and looked sternly at the young woman before saying, "My place serves a good meal at a fair price, and we're a cash business. Go get your money, and you can have a good meal."

"Yes, ma'am," Raquel replied softly. "Do you know anyone in town that might have some work?"

"No," the woman said flatly. "What do I look like, the WPA?"

"No, ma'am," Raquel said.

"Now, listen," barked the woman. "I'm sure you got as sad a story as anyone else, but a girl like you shouldn't be panhandling. I ain't goin' to cause no trouble for you, but if the law catches you bein' a nuisance, you'll be run out of town. You got soot on your face and coal dust on your britches. You're a disgrace."

"We're not panhandlers," Naomi said in a trembling tone of voice. "We were headed for home and ran into some trouble. This is my daughter-in-law, and she just asked if you had any work. You don't have any right to talk to her like that."

"Like what?" the woman challenged.

The emotional Naomi said, "Like we're some kind of trash."

"I didn't say anything," the woman declared. "I just tried to give you a little guidance."

"It's okay," Raquel whispered. "Let's go."

Naomi looked like she wanted to say more, but with Raquel tugging her arm toward the exit, she remained silent.

When they got to the door, Raquel stopped to say, "You have a nice place here. I wish I did have the cash. A friend of ours told us this was the best chicken-fried steak in Texas."

The woman continued to work in her cash drawer and asked, "Who'd that be?"

Raquel said in a humble and defeated tone, "No one you'd know."

The woman stopped working and looked sternly at Raquel and said, "Missy, I've counted every dime spent in this diner and met nearly every customer that'd come from four states for thirty years. Who was it?"

Convinced that she would prove the woman wrong, Naomi proudly stated, "Mr. Hank Tilley."

The woman dropped a roll of quarters on the ground and stared at Naomi with her nostrils flaring and her hands shaking.

"What did you say?" the woman asked.

Naomi looked nervously at the woman and repeated timidly, "Hank Tilley."

"Chief!" the woman shouted. "Get out here."

Raquel reached out to pull Naomi closer to the door and prepared to make a run for the street when the woman said in her harsh voice, but with a softer tone, "Sit down."

Naomi looked at Raquel, and the woman stepped from behind the counter to pull out a couple of chairs and said, "Please, have a seat."

Raquel nodded to Naomi indicating that she thought it would be okay, and they cautiously took a seat at one of the tables.

"You've seen Hank?" the woman asked.

"Yes," Naomi said.

By that time the tall man from the back came out front wiping his hands on a white towel. The man had dark hair, but pale skin and did not look like an Indian man to Naomi.

"Chief, these ladies have seen Hank," the woman said, as she took a seat at the table.

The tall man nodded and returned to his work in the back.

"You know Mr. Tilley?" Naomi asked.

"Hank's my son," nodded the woman.

"You're Mrs. Tilley?" Naomi said.

"Everyone calls me Miss T, but my married name is Mrs. Tilley," the woman explained. "Tell me about my boy. Is he all right?"

"Yes," Naomi said.

"Where'd you see him?" the woman asked. "I hadn't seen him in years. He must be near fifty by now."

"We saw him in Albuquerque two nights ago," Naomi said.

"We've been traveling with him for about a week," Raquel added.

The woman looked confused and Raquel explained, "We ran into some trouble awhile back, and Hank's been helping us to get back home."

"Where's home?" Mrs. Tilley asked.

"Oklahoma," Naomi answered.

"Good lord, you're almost there," Mrs. Tilley smiled broadly, showing her tobacco-stained teeth.

Mrs. Tilley pointed out the window and said, "You can see it from here. Ain't more than 500 yards east of that front door."

Raquel could not resist looking across the tracks at the barren field to see what she had been traveling to for over a week.

"Chief!" the woman shouted. "Fire up that grill and cook these ladies a steak."

"We don't open for supper for another hour," the man complained.

"We're always open," the woman scolded. "Now do what I said."

The tall man shrugged his shoulders and sauntered back to the kitchen.

After the man had left, Naomi leaned over and whispered, "Why do you call him Chief? He doesn't look a bit Indian."

"He ain't a bit of anything, but lazy," the woman whispered back. "Everyone calls him Chief, cause he's a big talker and thinks he's always right. He can cook like he made a deal with the devil, though. He's a good worker, if I stay on him. Tell me more about my boy."

For the next hour, Raquel and Naomi told their stories about Hank and how he had helped them. The woman seemed hungry for any detail, and they had the opportunity to tell her about most of their misadventures the past week. Raquel even told Mrs. Tilley about their first meeting with Hank in California, and explained how impressed she had been that he had not held a grudge. She also told his mother how he was helping Harry out on the road. Mrs. Tilley explained that Hank had left Higgins to live in Lubbock and work in a stockyard. She had known that he had gotten into trouble with the law, but she did not know many of the details. She had hoped he would come see her someday, since she lived so close to the border, but suspected that Hank did not want his mother to see the way he now lived. The tall man brought Raquel and Naomi two large chicken-fried steaks with mashed potatoes and green beans. Mrs. Tilley continued to pepper the women with questions as they ate.

"Where in Oklahoma is home?" Mrs. Tilley asked, as the women finished the apple pie that had been brought to them after their meal.

"Sayre," Naomi said. "My husband left me a place outside of town."

"Sayre?" the woman said, as she looked at the ceiling to think. "I've been there."

"It's south of here," Naomi explained.

"Chief!" Mrs. Tilley yelled. "Bring me that Oklahoma road map from the back."

In a moment, the man walked lazily to the dining room and tossed a road map on the table before returning to his kitchen.

Mrs. Tilley studied the map for a moment before pointing and asking, "There?"

Naomi nodded.

Mrs. Tilley looked at the map a moment longer as she calculated the mileage and said, "It's not more than two hours from here."

"Chief!" Mrs. Tilley yelled again.

The tall man ambled back to stand in front of his employer and said impatiently, "What?"

"Leave that stove be," Mrs. Tilley said. "You're driving these ladies home tonight."

Naomi looked quickly at Raquel before saying to Mrs. Tilley, "I can't expect you to do that for us."

"Of course you can," Mrs. Tilley bluntly replied. "You have no money, and the train won't stop here for a couple of days. I could buy you a bus ticket, but that'd take at least another day. You gals have had the devil of it, and if Hank was determined to get you home, I'll finish the job. Go fetch the truck, Chief."

The tall man nodded, before dropping his apron on the chair by the kitchen and walking out the door.

"I can't repay you for a couple of weeks," Naomi said.

Mrs. Tilley shook her head and said, "You brought me word about my boy and let me know he's okay for now. That's good enough for me. Let me be generous. It don't happen that much."

In ten minutes, Chief returned with a truck. Naomi and Raquel crawled into the cab with the man and headed east across the border into Oklahoma. In less than two hours, the truck pulled through the small town of Sayre, Oklahoma. It was nearly seven o'clock and the streets were empty except for a few children playing in the last lingering beams of the summer evening.

"There's the Belvedere store," Naomi pointed, as they drove slowly past a dry goods store in a corner building.

The store, like the rest of the main street, was closed. They passed the Beckham County Courthouse, and Naomi pointed to a dirt road leading south out of town. They were barely out of town when Naomi excitedly pointed to the silhouette of a house nearly two miles away.

"That's our place!" Naomi said, with a big smile on her tired face.

The flat rolling hills waved in the wind with the golden wheat nearing harvest time. As they approached the house, the rows of wheat stopped at a broken-down barbed wire fence that transformed into a field of brown matted grasses. The truck stopped at a rickety gate that had a drift of dirt covering the lower half of it.

"Thank you," Naomi said to the man, as they stepped from the truck after the two hour drive. "I'm sorry I don't have anything to offer you."

"You sure you'll be okay here?" the man asked, as he looked at the rundown house.

Naomi nodded, and the man shrugged before turning the truck around to head back to Higgins. Naomi stood shoulder to shoulder with Raquel and looked at the house standing a hundred yards off the dirt road.

"Looks like the house needs some work," Naomi said.

Raquel looked at the tattered house that had dirt piled up past the window sill on the south side. The house did not appear to have any paint on it and the grayish boards looked weathered and worn. Even from the road, Raquel could tell that the wood roof had several places that sagged and had at least one hole in it.

"Looks like it needs a lot of work," Raquel said.

Naomi looked at the house for a moment and then walked to the gate to try to open it. The drifted dirt blocked any attempt to swing the gate open in either direction. Raquel studied the landscape for a second and then walked up the piled up dirt and easily stepped over the fence.

"Let me help you," Raquel offered, as Naomi followed her.

Raquel held her hands over her eyes to shield them from the late afternoon sun and to see the surrounding countryside better. The barren pastures and fields around the dilapidated house declined slightly toward the bank of a small river with barely a trickle of water in it. On the other side of the river, the land was flatter and the wheat was tall and ripe for harvest. In the distance, Raquel could see a large two-story house.

"Whose place is that?" Raquel asked, as she pointed at the large white house that had a windmill and small pond nearby.

Naomi squinted and then frowned, "That must be Beau Lobaugh's place. He's a cousin of Eli's."

"Looks like he's doing well," Raquel said, as she continued to look at the large house in the distance.

"I've heard he has," Naomi replied.

"Maybe we could ask him for some help," Raquel suggested.

"No," Naomi said. "He's a rascal and he—he won't be so happy to see me back—especially with Eli and the boys gone."

"Why not?" Raquel asked.

Naomi looked perturbed by the question and she quickly said, "Don't you mind. Let's see what work this house will need."

As they got closer, the wreckage of the house appeared more apparent. Besides the lack of paint and the sagging roof, one side of the three-sided porch had completely collapsed. The front door leaned against its broken hinges, and more dirt filled the doorway. Naomi looked at the house in shocked disbelief. Raquel left Naomi staring at the ruined house and walked around the house on the north. Raquel's heart sank, as she turned the corner to see much of the back wall of the house had collapsed, exposing the interior walls to more blown dirt. When Raquel returned to the front of the house, a stunned Naomi had tears running down her face.

"What have I done," Naomi moaned pitifully. "We can't stay here."

The sun was setting behind a brilliant reddish-orange horizon over the barren brown land, as Raquel said softly, "We'll have to—at least for tonight."

PART III

CHAPTER 49

"I can't believe it," Naomi cried. "I knew the place would need some work, but nothing like this."

Raquel put her arm around her mother-in-law and stared at the rundown house. The sun was setting, and it would be dark in less than an hour. It was at least two miles back to Sayre, and they would be hard pressed to make it by nightfall. A warm, humid breeze stirred up puffs of dust and all the vegetation except a scrawny elm tree in front of the house appeared dried and dead.

"Let's look inside and see if we can clean a place to sleep," Raquel suggested.

Naomi nodded pathetically and followed Raquel to the front door, which leaned against its hinges.

"Let me look," Raquel said, as she motioned Naomi to stay on the porch.

Raquel stepped through the doorway into a vacant front room with nearly two inches of dirt covering a wood floor, as well as much of the plaster from the ceiling. A stone fireplace, with a mantel hanging precariously above it, had the remnants of a tumbleweed lodged in its opening. Raquel moved through the house and did not find a habitable room. When she opened the door to a back bedroom, Raquel saw the setting sun and felt the warm breeze from outside through a window that had fallen out, exposing the room to the elements.

Raquel stepped carefully through the missing window onto a sand drift that had blown up against the house. The yard with scraggly, knee-high grass had a small wood building about twenty steps away from the back door. Raquel shoved the door open to discover an outhouse, which seemed to be in much better repair than the house.

Further away from the house stood a broken-down chicken coop and a large barn, which seemed to be in better condition than the other buildings. Raquel opened the wide door to the barn and smelled hay, which was stacked neatly to one side. A few well-used tools were hanging on the back wall. Another wider door opened to a fenced area and into an animal pen inside the barn. In the corner of the barn, Raquel saw a single cot and a simple wood bench.

Raquel walked back to the distraught Naomi and said, "We can sleep in the barn tonight, and at least the outhouse is usable."

"The barn?" Naomi replied.

Raquel said, "It's in better shape than the house, and there's a cot inside. Where's the well?"

Naomi pointed to an iron pump by the side of the house and said, "There's a pump outside and one in the kitchen. It used to be the best well in Beckham County, but I don't know. I've been gone so long…I never expected this."

Raquel nodded in resignation and led Naomi to the cot in the barn. Naomi's coughing from the previous night had been suppressed for most of the day, but now she hacked violently in the warm evening air. Raquel was relieved to find the outside pump for the well worked. She went back to the house and found that the pump in the kitchen would not prime. She did find a couple of beat-up pots and some empty cans that she could use to take water to the coughing Naomi. Raquel ripped down some torn and raggedy curtains that she shook out for blankets. In the barn, she found some empty burlap feed bags, a large bucket, a wood barrel, and a kerosene lamp. Outside the barn, a wooden trough was situated near a small round stone indention that Raquel thought must have been for shoeing horses years ago.

Raquel made Naomi as comfortable as she could in the cot, before building a small fire in the stone pit in front of the barn. She drank the cool, sweet well water. She then boiled some water to clean the pots she had found in the house. Naomi fell asleep in the cot a little after dark, before she could fuss more about the condition of the home.

The fire danced in the night sky, and Raquel was content for a few moments to poke at the flame with a long stick. After the water boiled, Raquel decided to wash the dirty clothes she had been wearing the past week. She poured the boiling water into the bucket and scrubbed her trousers and shirt.

As Raquel looked into the dark and lonely night, she decided it would be a good time to treat herself to a bath. She went quietly back into the barn and retrieved one of the burlap feed sacks. She tore three holes in the sack to make herself a rough canvas skirt and put the rest of her clothes in the hot water to clean. Raquel then took the large bucket and carried water for the next thirty minutes to fill the trough next to the fire. After hanging her clothes to dry and adding some hot water to the trough, she slipped out of the burlap dress and into a warm bath under the starry sky.

Raquel immersed her head under the water for as long as she could hold her breath and felt the anxious tensions of the past few days fade away for a few seconds. When she lifted her head above the water, she felt clean and renewed. The warm, muggy air felt good on her wet skin. With her hair cut short, the night nipped at her wet neck. She stayed in the bath until the skin on her fingers started to wrinkle. The clean water invigorated her, and she playfully considered sleeping in the refreshing water for the night.

As Raquel wondered what the prudish Naomi would think if she caught her daughter-in-law naked in the outdoors, a sound in the night suddenly made her heart jump. She did not know what was in the darkness, but her instincts caused her to become motionless in the water as she listened for signs of danger. She thought about calling out into the night, but decided she was in much too compromising a position if someone were lurking in the dark. When she heard nothing but the silence of the night, Raquel slowly reached over the trough of water for the burlap sack. She slowly and silently stood up and could feel the night air on her naked skin for an instant before she quickly pulled the rough burlap sack over her shoulders.

Raquel stepped silently toward the door to the barn, as the fire she had built earlier had faded to a few glowing embers. She had about regained her sense of calmness, when she heard another sound much closer than before. Raquel lunged for the door of the barn, as she could clearly hear heavy steps coming behind her. The ruckus of Raquel's hasty entrance into the barn startled Naomi, as she grunted and wheezed from her snoring.

"What is it?" Naomi groggily asked, as Raquel trimmed the kerosene lamp and searched for some type of weapon before settling on a rusty pitchfork leaning against the wall. "Where are your clothes?"

"Someone's out there," Raquel replied curtly.

"Who?" Naomi asked, as she got to her feet and looked closely at Raquel's ragtag outfit.

"I don't know," Raquel answered. "I was washing clothes and heard footsteps, but I didn't get a look at them."

A loud bang from outside caused Naomi to squeal, and Raquel tried to look out of a small hole in the wall of the barn to get a look at the intruder. Raquel got a glimpse of a dark image moving close to the barn, but she could not see a face.

"Where are you going?" Naomi asked, as Raquel put her hand on the door of the barn to push it open.

"I'm going to see who it is," Raquel said.

Before Naomi could protest, Raquel disappeared into the night carrying the lantern and leaving her mother-in-law in the dark. Naomi moved to the door of the barn and watched Raquel peer into the dark night. Raquel moved toward the house as Naomi watched anxiously. Naomi could not see Raquel as she moved away from the barn, but she could track her daughter-in-law's movement by the motion of the lamp. As Raquel approached the house, the light disappeared into the darkness and Naomi gasped. Naomi quickly moved through the dark barn grabbing anything she might be able to use to protect herself. Naomi rushed out the barn door and stopped suddenly, as a smiling Raquel returned with a cow trailing behind her.

"Look what I found!" Raquel beamed.

"It was a cow making all that fuss?" Naomi sighed.

Raquel nodded, "It's a cow, and she needs milking. We'll have milk for breakfast in the morning."

Naomi nervously looked around and asked, "Anyone else out there?"

Raquel looked around, "Not a soul but us and this cow. There is that house on the other side of the river. You think it's their cow?"

Naomi looked across the river to the faint light far away and said, "We'll worry about that later. Let's get this cow in the barn. We'll need her for milk until we can get to town and make some arrangements."

Raquel agreed, and she led the obedient cow to the holding pen in the back of the barn.

When Raquel returned, Naomi looked at the girl's short burlap skirt and said, "That's quite a wardrobe you've found."

Raquel looked down at her odd dress before saying, "I washed my clothes and decided to take a bath. I needed something to wear."

"You took a bath?" Naomi asked excitedly.

"Yes," Raquel smiled. "It felt wonderful. There's still some water if you want me to heat it up again."

Naomi looked into the darkness for a second before frowning.

"No," Naomi said. "I'm getting some sleep. Maybe I'll feel better in the morning. Where are you going to sleep?"

"I made a pallet on the hay and put some of the curtains from the house on it," Raquel explained. "I'll be fine."

Naomi did not protest and returned to her cot quickly, to cough and snore her way into an uneasy sleep. Raquel did not think she would be able to sleep, wearing the burlap sack and lying on the uneven straw, but soon she dozed off in the corner of the barn, unsure of what the next day might bring.

CHAPTER 50

Raquel woke early the next morning. She felt rested, although the burlap night shirt, the straw bed, and Naomi's frequent coughing made for less than ideal sleeping conditions. Naomi still slept restlessly on the cot. Raquel pulled the makeshift blanket over her mother-in-law's shoulder and stepped quietly outside to find her clean clothes dry enough to wear. Raquel quickly dressed and found the cow she had tied in the pen the previous night. The cow grazed on a few pieces of brown grass. She gently patted the animal and noticed the letters "B L" branded on the cow's hind quarters.

Raquel had only milked a few times, but the cow seemed agreeable to her touch and in a few minutes she had produced a bucket full of milk. Raquel tasted the milk. It was warm and sweet. She stretched her back in satisfaction about her morning labor. The sun had risen above the eastern horizon, and she felt the warmth of the morning sun on her face. The morning was peaceful and comfortably cool, but Raquel could tell the sun would bring a warm early June afternoon. She looked across the river at the large house in the distance. Raquel was thinking about how alone this country seemed when a noise coming from near the river caught her attention. The unexpected noise was not as frightening as the sound in the dark had been the night before. Raquel put her bucket of milk safely by the barn and then walked toward the river to investigate.

Raquel only made it a few steps from the tied up cow, when a man on horseback emerged from the tall grass by the river's bank. The man's eyes had a stern, penetrating expression, and his skin was tanned and weathered. His head was covered by a large hat, but his straight brown hair was longer than normal and came down across his forehead. Even on horseback, Raquel could tell he had broad shoulders and narrow hips. He looked to be in his late thirties.

"Hello," Raquel greeted timidly.

The man did not seem to hear her, although Raquel was sure he had seen her.

"Is this your cow?" she yelled.

The man looked past her and seemed to be studying the broken-down place. Without saying a word or acknowledging Raquel, he swiftly turned his horse and galloped across the river. Raquel walked quickly to the bank of the river, which was almost two hundred yards away, and stopped short of the shallow waters. The man was nearly out of sight, but he stopped and turned his horse to look back at her. She waved to get the man's attention, but he nudged his horse and trotted away toward the big house in the distance.

Raquel walked slowly back to the barn and was relieved that the man had not claimed the cow. She did not know where the cow belonged, but she knew there was enough grass to feed it and that the cow would at least give them good milk for a few days.

As Raquel approached the barn, Naomi asked in a hoarse tone of voice, "Where'd you get off to this morning?"

"Is your throat sore?" Raquel smiled. "You sound a little stopped up."

"It's my sinuses," Naomi complained. "I had forgotten how much I liked the air in California—compared to this humid, pollen-filled country."

"I milked the cow, and there's fresh milk for breakfast," Raquel said, while pointing at the bucket.

Naomi took a large drink of the warm milk and said, "Thank you, dear. I was starving."

"A man rode up this morning," Raquel shared, as she took a sip of her milk.

"What!" Naomi exclaimed.

Raquel pointed toward the river and said, "He rode up just past the river bank. I hollered at him to see if the cow belonged to him, but he rode off."

"What did he look like?" Naomi quizzed.

Raquel thought and said, "Medium build, brown hair—kind of long hair. He was a stern-looking man, but he was pretty far away. He rode across the river and toward the big house."

Naomi bit her lip, "Sounds like it might've been Beau."

"The cow has a 'B L' brand on it," Raquel said. "I called to the man to see if he was looking for the cow, but he rode off."

"He'll be back," Naomi said with a hint of dread to her voice.

"Are you going to tell me?" Raquel asked.

"Tell you what?" Naomi sighed.

Raquel looked at her mother-in-law for a second and said, "This man is some kind of relative of yours, but you seem to want to avoid him like the plague."

"There's history there," Naomi said. "Let's just leave it at that."

Raquel did not push her mother-in-law for more details and took the cups of milk to clean them.

"What do you think we should do?" Naomi asked in an anxious tone of voice.

Raquel looked at the worn-out house and shrugged, "There's a shovel and some other tools in the barn. I thought I'd get a start on cleaning up the house. With a little work, it'll be more comfortable than this barn—especially when winter comes."

Naomi frowned, "We can't stay here, Raquel. This place is a wreck. Let's go to town and I'll see if we can stay with Beulah for a few days—at least until we come up with a plan. It looks like Beau Lobaugh's been using this place for a pasture, maybe he'll want to buy at a decent price."

Raquel looked around and said with a sly grin, "I don't know. I might rather camp out here in the barn than stay with Beulah. She doesn't think much of me, if I remember."

"Beulah is family," Naomi said. "I know she can be a little opinionated—but you probably think that about me sometimes."

Raquel smirked playfully, "Yes, ma'am."

CHAPTER 51

The walk from the Butler place into Sayre was a little over two miles north and one mile west to the main part of the town. A narrow dirt road ran to the river before a one-lane bridge crossed to the south. Raquel and Naomi, however, did not travel by the road, but walked diagonally across the fields north of the North Fork Red River, saving almost half a mile on the flat terrain. The shortcut would have been an inconvenience in wet weather, but it looked like it had not rained in months.

When they reached the highway heading into town, the domed tower of the Beckham County Courthouse dominated the town, and could be seen for miles in the wide-open country. They walked by the courthouse and down the busy Main Street. Cars were parked bumper-to-bumper in front of stores and in the middle of the street. Naomi explained that it was near wheat harvest time. Farm families filled the streets, and Raquel could sense excitement in the air as children played, women shopped, and old men whittled in front of a coffee shop. Several stores and a couple of banks lined the street. Naomi pointed out the Sayre Dry Goods Store that Arnold Belvedere managed. The store had a fresh coat of paint and many customers going in and out. Naomi explained that Beulah was a Sutton and that Naomi's mother had also been a Sutton. One of the bankers, Frank Sutton, was a distant cousin and the son of a prominent banker from nearby Elk City. Naomi explained that Frank Sutton had bought the Sayre Dry Goods Store after it had gone into default, and he had hired Arnold to run it.

When they came to Sixth Street, Naomi walked north across the railroad tracks and into a neighborhood of houses with large yards. At the northwest corner of Sixth Street and Locust Avenue, Naomi pointed at a large two-story house that looked like it was several years old.

"That's Beulah's house," Naomi said, as she stood and looked at it for a moment.

"It's nice," Raquel replied politely.

"It needs a coat of paint," Naomi noted.

Raquel tried to keep from smirking, thinking of the ramshackle house that awaited Naomi southeast of town.

"Arnold never was too handy with a tool," Naomi explained.

Naomi hesitated for a moment and sighed, "I guess we better see if Beulah's home."

Naomi walked slowly to the door and knocked timidly. In a moment, they heard movement inside before Beulah opened the door.

"Naomi!" the plump woman greeted. "I was wondering when you would get to town."

"We made it," Naomi smiled.

Beulah's smile vanished when she saw Raquel standing behind Naomi wearing her trousers and short hair.

"I see you brought the maid," Beulah curtly said.

Naomi maintained her even tone, "You remember my daughter-in-law?"

"Yes," Beulah replied. "What happened to her hair—lice?"

"Of course not!" Naomi blushed. "It's a funny story, really. We've had the devil of it getting out here. I suppose you know all about it from my telegram."

"Oh, yes," Beulah smiled. "I'm so sorry. I was in Oklahoma City and didn't get the message until yesterday. Sounded like you were—having a time of it."

"You could say that," Naomi said. "I'm sorry about your twenty dollars. I don't know when I'll be able to pay you back."

"I didn't wire any money," Beulah said.

"What?" Naomi asked. "I sent you a message saying I needed your help."

"Well," Beulah reasoned. "The message was several days old, and I didn't have any other messages. I assumed you had made arrangements. Besides—you know what they say—you don't keep good friends by loaning them money."

Naomi strained to smile at Beulah's attempt at being witty, while thinking how desperately she had depended on that money only a few days earlier.

"Are you going to invite them in, or let all the flies come inside," a man shouted from the back of the house.

Arnold Belvedere had come home for lunch and was growing impatient with his wife's chatter.

Beulah looked at Raquel carefully before surveying the neighborhood.

"Come in," Beulah huffed reluctantly.

Beulah held the door open. Raquel noticed Beulah watching the street nervously, while trying to make sure none of her neighbors saw the short-haired girl enter the home.

"Hey, Naomi," Arnold greeted pleasantly, as he walked over to give her a hug. "You've lost some weight since last time I saw you."

"Yes," Naomi replied proudly. "I've been watching what I eat."

"Well, sit down and have some lunch," Arnold said.

Beulah did not echo the invitation, but she did not protest either. In a few minutes, Raquel and Naomi enjoyed their first meal at a kitchen table in several weeks. Beulah kept asking questions about Naomi's trip, and Naomi supplied vague answers that Raquel knew bordered on fabrications about the circumstances of their plight. Beulah was careful to exclude Naomi's daughter-in-law from the conversation, but she looked suspiciously at Raquel several times.

"It's good to see you," Arnold warmly smiled. "It's good to see you home. When did you get in?"

"Yesterday afternoon," Naomi said.

"Yesterday?" Arnold questioned. "Why are you just now getting here? You didn't go out to your house, did you?"

"Well, yes," Naomi said.

"Oh," Arnold groaned. "Last time I saw it, the thing looked like it needed some work."

"It was in shambles," Naomi admitted. "We found a cot and managed for the night."

"That explains your appearance," Beulah said. "I thought it looked like you've been camping."

"Yes," Naomi smiled. "It was a difficult night."

"Maybe you need to stay here for a few days," Arnold suggested.

"Thank you, Arnold," Naomi smiled. "That's sweet of you."

"Now, Arnold," Beulah interrupted. "You know I've been planning renovations upstairs."

"But, dear," Arnold replied. "You're always planning some remodeling, and we usually don't get around to the half of it."

"I've got specific plans for the upstairs," Beulah defended.

When Arnold tried to argue the point further, Beulah interrupted him and looked at Naomi to say, "We've got one extra bedroom, but the girl—I might be able to make a place in the garage to accommodate her, but there's no room in the house."

"We can share a room," Naomi said, with a serious frown on her face.

Beulah tilted her head back defiantly and with a sigh said, "There's not room for the girl here."

Arnold looked like he would say something, but before he had the chance, Naomi used the tone of voice Raquel remembered from her first days of living with the Butlers saying in a flat, emotionless pitch, "That's kind of you, Beulah, but we've got a lot of work to do on the old place before I can sell it. We'll waste a lot of time if I have to walk back and forth."

"Naomi—" Arnold began to protest.

"It's fine, Arnold," Naomi assured. "Everything will be fine."

Arnold Belvedere nodded sympathetically, "I've got to get back to the store."

Beulah stared at Naomi, and spoke to her husband, "I'll see you at supper."

When Arnold picked up his straw hat and left, Naomi said to Beulah, "This girl has brought me home and sacrificed more than you'll ever know to do it. She's all the family I have left that I care for, and she's more family than you've ever been. I know you Beulah, and I knew you could be a petty and proud woman, but I'm ashamed of you."

Raquel felt incredibly uncomfortable at the conversation but proud of Naomi's declaration about her feelings.

"Arnold's gone, and I'll speak bluntly now," Beulah said. "I won't have this girl in my house—unless I need some floors scrubbed. I don't know what happened to you in California, but the Naomi I knew would have never let her own flesh and blood marry a girl like that."

Naomi took a step toward Beulah with a stern scowl to assert, "I know how you are, and I'm warning you to let this girl be, and don't be spreading any lies about her in town. I won't tolerate it!"

"What are you going to do?" Beulah huffed. "Have that rogue cousin of Eli's buy me out?" Beulah stared at Naomi to smile wickedly before saying, "Oh, I forgot. Beau Lobaugh might not be too happy to see you back empty handed like you've come. I forgot what a compassionate neighbor you have—just across the river."

Naomi clenched her jaw and said to Raquel, "Let's go, dear. We need to get back."

Naomi walked away from Beulah Belvedere's kitchen and Raquel followed close behind. Raquel got a glimpse of the smug look on Beulah's face, and she could sense Naomi's seething. Raquel breathed a sigh of relief when they were back on the quiet street under the hot sun.

"Of all the gall of that woman!" Naomi whispered harshly.

"It's okay," Raquel replied calmly.

Naomi was about to explain how it was not okay, when Arnold Belvedere stepped from behind the neighbor's hedge to say in a whispered tone, "I'm so sorry, Naomi. You can't stay in that old house until it's been worked on. Let me talk to Beulah and get her to apologize. You know she don't think straight when she gets stubborn. You took us in when we were at our wits' end in California, and I can't feel good about turning you out."

Naomi looked back at the house and took a deep breath to say, "It's fine Arnold. I don't want to be where I'm not wanted. Me and Beulah together is a fight fixin' to happen—I guess it's because we tend to be so much alike sometimes."

"I still don't feel right," Arnold said.

"We'll be fine," Naomi tried to assure, although Raquel was sure her mother-in-law was not so confident.

Arnold looked back at the house to make sure his wife was not spying on him and said in a low tone of voice, "I tell you what. Come down to the store and pick out some things you need to get your place fixed up right."

Before Naomi could protest, Arnold Belvedere said, "You have an open line of credit with me. I know Eli's place has plenty of potential. Come to the store with me, and I'll drive you out and deliver it myself."

Naomi looked back at the house and then turned to the quiet man and said, "Thank you, Arnold. That would be helpful—and decent of you."

CHAPTER 52

Naomi's attitude improved remarkably when Arnold Belvedere led her to his store and opened an account in her name. There were so many things she needed for the house that she hardly knew where to start.

With a big smile, Naomi said to her daughter-in-law, "The first thing we're going to do is get you out of those clothes and into a pretty dress." Naomi looked at her own feet and frowned, "The second thing is some decent shoes to replace these stupid-looking boots I've been wearing."

Raquel quickly found a blue dress with a yellow sash.

"Try it on!" Naomi encouraged.

Raquel slipped into the fitting room and found the dress fit perfectly.

"What do you think?" Raquel asked, as she slowly spun around to give Naomi a full look.

"I think you can make anything look good," Naomi smiled. "Let's have Arnold burn those old clothes of yours."

"No," Raquel protested. "They're comfortable, and I'll need them for work. In fact, I need to find a pair of overalls. We've got a lot of work to do—a lot of dirty work."

Naomi fussed, but ultimately agreed to let Raquel keep the work clothes. They were able to find new cookware, some kerosene lamps with fuel, a few tools, and two new cots to use until they could repair a bedroom in the house. Naomi also bought a kerosene camp stove to use until her kitchen was repaired.

Arnold was tallying the bill when a deep voice from behind them said, "Naomi?"

Raquel and Naomi turned around to see a rugged-looking man with a tanned face and chiseled features standing behind them. Raquel immediately recognized him as the man she had seen crossing the river earlier that morning.

"Beau," Naomi replied timidly.

"Thought someone was at the old place," the man stated flatly.

"Yes," Naomi stammered.

"It's been a long time," Beau Lobaugh said.

Naomi nodded.

Beau Lobaugh looked at Raquel carefully, as if studying her in her new blue dress when Naomi said, "This is Raquel."

"I saw you this morning?" Beau asked with a quizzical look in his eyes.

Raquel apprehensively replied, "Yes, sir."

"No one calls me sir, unless he's in the army," Beau said with a vague hint of a smile. "I thought you were a boy this morning."

"No, si—no," Raquel blushed.

"I can see that now," Beau said. "Very plainly."

"Raquel's my daughter-in-law," Naomi said in an uneasy tone. "Chili's wife."

"How's Eli?" Beau asked.

Naomi shook her head nervously and said, "Eli passed away last year. He had a stroke."

"I hadn't heard," Beau said. "I'm sorry."

"Thank you," Naomi muttered without making eye-contact.

Beau Lobaugh shifted nervously and asked, "How's Maylon?"

Naomi fought back tears and said, "Maylon and Chili were killed in a car accident a few months ago. They were together. I'm sorry—"

Beau Lobaugh's rigid and confident countenance seemed to transform to uncertainty as he interrupted Naomi and said quietly, "I hadn't heard."

Naomi stood uneasily in front of the man for a moment before Beau Lobaugh said abruptly, "I'm sorry for your loss."

Beau Lobaugh started to leave, but he stopped to say to Raquel, "I'm sorry for your loss, too."

The man looked like he would say more before he walked quietly out the store. Raquel stepped to the window and watched the man give instructions to several men, who looked to be in his employ. Beau Lobaugh looked back at the store one more time, like he might return, before driving away.

Naomi joined Raquel at the window and nervously said, "We better head back."

Raquel nodded. She wanted to ask Naomi about the man and the unspoken tension between the two, but she was ready to get home and start work on their house. Arnold pulled up in a small truck with the Sayre Dry Goods Store stenciled on the door.

They loaded the truck and were about to climb into the cab when a man's voice said playfully, "What are we doing, Arnold—packing up the store!"

Raquel turned around to see a tall, handsome man walking briskly toward them. He wore a well-fitting suit and polished shoes. The man had sandy hair that framed a smooth face and kind eyes. His business-like appearance stood out from the many other men in town who dressed in more utilitarian attire.

"Hey, Frankie," Arnold greeted, as he tugged on the rope to check the load one last time.

"Looks like quite a sale," the man said cheerfully.

"You remember, Naomi Butler, Frankie?" Arnold asked.

"Only the name," the man replied.

"I remember you, Frankie Sutton," Naomi smiled. "You used to bounce on Grandma Sutton's knee like a little ragdoll."

"Please call me Frank," the man smiled. "Nobody but family and the old church ladies call me Frankie."

"We are related, kinda," Naomi said. "Your mother and my mother were cousins."

"That'd make us second cousins or something," Frank smiled. "Well, you're still too young to call me Frankie, Naomi."

"It's good to see you again, Frank," Naomi said.

Naomi noticed that Raquel had caught the young man's attention.

"This is Raquel, Frank—Raquel Butler," Naomi quickly introduced.

"Another cousin?" Frank asked, as he nodded to Raquel.

Naomi answered, "Oh, no. Raquel is my daughter-in-law from California. I don't know if you've heard, but I lost both of my sons in a car accident a few months ago. Raquel's a widow."

Frank's carefree smile vanished, and he said solemnly, "No, Naomi. That's news to me—I didn't know. I remember hearing something about your husband, but I had no idea. I'm so sorry."

"Thank you, Frank," Naomi said.

Frank Sutton turned to Raquel to say, "And I'm so sorry for your loss. It seemed incredibly cruel for one so young to have lost a loved one. I am truly sorry."

"Thank you," Raquel said, as she looked into the man's soft eyes.

"Naomi and Raquel are moving back to Beckham County," Arnold explained.

"Good," Frank smiled. "We certainly need good people in this community—especially ones as pretty as these two. I'm guessing you'll both be attending the Independence Day picnic in a few weeks. The wheat harvest should be in by then."

"We hadn't heard," Naomi said.

"Oh, it's a big deal," Frank said. "It looks like it might be a decent harvest—at least in some fields by the river, but it will be a good time had by all."

"We'll certainly try to make it," Naomi said.

"I better get these ladies home with their things," Arnold suggested. "Naomi's moving into the old Butler home place. Going to fix it up and sell it."

"I know the place," Frank smiled. "In fact, I handled the paper work when Eli paid off the mortgage. Of course, your neighbor's a little less than friendly."

"Beau?" Naomi asked rhetorically.

Frank nodded, "The man's got a gift for investment, but he's lacking in social skills, if you ask me. The place might bring a fair price with a little work, but things are tough around here for a lot of people."

"We hope to do a lot of work," Naomi said.

Frank smiled, "If you get it ready to sell, let me know. I don't have much use for pasture land, but I wouldn't mind keeping Beau LoBaugh off both sides of the river."

"We'll see," Naomi replied. "Like I said, we have a lot of work and a lot of decisions to make the next few months."

Frank looked at his watch and said, "If I didn't have this darn meeting at the bank, I'd take you ladies home myself."

"I can manage," Arnold assured.

Frank looked at Raquel and said, "Maybe I could stop by sometime and visit—look over the old place. Folks around here will be pretty busy with harvest the next few weeks, so I'll have some time."

"That would be lovely," Naomi said in almost a flirty tone.

Frank Sutton tipped his hat to the ladies and strolled down the street and toward the bank. Arnold drove Naomi and Raquel home with their purchases. Raquel could see a remarkable improvement in Naomi's demeanor from the morning. Naomi thanked Arnold again after all the things had been stored in the barn. Arnold apologized again for his wife and drove back into town.

"This is exciting!" Naomi said after Arnold had left.

"There's still a lot of work to do," Raquel cautioned, thinking Naomi was talking about the new tools they had for their home.

"Not that," Naomi replied.

Naomi seemed frustrated that Raquel did not understand her meaning. "Frank Sutton was paying you a lot of attention at the store, dear. He's rich and single—and he couldn't take his eyes off you."

"He was just being nice," Raquel said.

"Yes, he was!" Naomi blurted out. "We've got to get you to that picnic. I know I'm a cranky old woman, but I could die a happy, cranky old woman if I can find you a good man."

"I have you," Raquel smiled.

"I know," Naomi retorted. "And I'm going to help you get a man!"

CHAPTER 53

After Raquel and Naomi put their purchases away, the two women worked through the afternoon to clean the barn and make it more livable. As dusk approached and the women had finished their supper of warm buttermilk, Raquel could tell her mother-in-law's optimism after meeting Frank Sutton was fading with the sunlight.

"It was nice of Mr. Belvedere to help us get these things," Raquel said. "It will go a long way in making this place into a home."

Naomi huffed, "Too bad Arnold doesn't sell groceries in his store. We have pots and pans—we have shoes and clothes, but we can't live on that old cow's milk forever. Besides, when Beau Lobaugh finds out we're hiding it, he's likely to have the sheriff on us."

"Mr. Lobaugh seemed reasonable to me," Raquel said. "And we're not hiding the cow—exactly. We just found a good place for her inside the barn—to keep her out of the sun."

Naomi grunted, "That still doesn't put bread or meat on our table."

Raquel moved next to her mother-in-law, put her arm around her shoulder to say, "You worry—a lot."

"I have a lot to worry about," Naomi defended.

Raquel suppressed a laugh and replied, "Why don't you let me worry about some things? The harvest is starting soon, and there'll be plenty of work."

Naomi would have liked to complain more, but Raquel smiled and walked to the house before dark to make plans for its cleaning. For the next two days, Raquel worked feverishly on the old house. She started by shoveling and then sweeping out the front room. Once she could see the floor, Raquel worked on cleaning the fireplace and chimney. Plaster still hung precariously from the walls and ceiling, but Raquel made the front room of the house habitable. After moving their cots and personal things from the barn into the house, Raquel attacked the ruined kitchen to see if she could make it usable.

"How do you do it?" Naomi asked, as Raquel bent under the cast iron stove to scrub the ragged floor.

"Do what?" Raquel replied, without looking up.

Naomi did not answer immediately. Raquel stood up to stretch her back and face her mother-in-law.

Naomi looked carefully at her daughter-in-law and declared, "Nothing gets you down."

"What do you mean?" Raquel smiled.

Naomi looked at her a moment before saying, "We lose our money, and you don't panic. We have to stow away on trains to make it east, and you manage to do it and get me home too. Beulah Belvedere insults you, and you brush it off. I—I kill a man in New Mexico—"

Naomi's forehead wrinkled as she painfully remembered their last night in Albuquerque, and then she continued, "We go through all of that and end up here—with a wrecked house, no food, no money, no prospects, and yet—and yet you cheerfully go about your business of making this house—livable."

"I don't know," Raquel said. "I guess I try to look for some blessings."

"Like what?" Naomi bluntly asked.

"I have you," Raquel smiled. "We have this house. It's not much now, but—I've seen worse."

"Have a seat," Naomi said, as she patted the wooden bench next to her.

Raquel put down the rag she had been using to scrub under the stove and joined her mother-in-law.

"What was it like?" Naomi asked in a concerned tone.

"What do you mean?" Raquel replied with a quizzical look.

Naomi sighed, "When you came to live with us—at the very first—you were running away. You were running away from home. Was it really that bad?"

Raquel frowned and nodded, "To me it was."

"I've seen the marks on your back," Naomi said softly. "Did he hurt you?"

Raquel flinched slightly and said, "Yes, but—I could put up with the beatings, and I could put up with being poor. This isn't the first time for me to be hungry, Naomi. Our house—this place would seem like a palace compared to the shack I lived in. Our house was nothing but boards and old highway signs to keep the sun off us, but I could live with that too. I learned that you can live with a lot—put up with a lot when you have to. I had to leave when—"

Raquel stopped talking and had decided to not say more until Naomi said, "What, Raquel? What was it? I really want to know. I really want to understand."

Raquel thought for a moment, smiled sadly, and said, "My mother loved me. I was her illegitimate child and it took me a long time to learn what that meant, but she loved me. I didn't understand at the time how much she suffered. She was cast out when I became inconvenient to the man that was my father. She married a man that never let her forget her past. My stepfather was a cruel man. He tormented my mother, but she endured. Once my mother died, I knew his meanness would be directed at me."

Naomi cradled the young woman into her arms, as Raquel cried softly, "I wasn't wanted by anyone, and I needed to get away from him. You had a family that you wanted and loved—I wanted that too."

"And you found Chili," Naomi sighed.

Raquel nodded, "But I found all of you. You made me feel like a part of your family. That's why I came with you. That's why we'll make this our home."

Naomi sat up and said, "We will. Things will be fine for us as soon as we get over the hump a bit."

Raquel nodded and wiped her eyes.

"I need to go to town today," Naomi said. "You want to walk with me?"

"If you can manage on your own, I'd just as soon stay here and work," smiled Raquel.

Naomi looked at her a moment and then said, "I can take care of things in town today but—but you'll have to come to town sometime. You can't let people like Beulah Belvedere run you away."

"I know," Raquel said. "I'd really like to stay for today though. I'll go with you to the Independence Day picnic. I promise."

Naomi nodded and patted Raquel on the cheek. After Naomi left for town, Raquel continued working on cleaning the kitchen. She worked until late in the morning before tossing the rag on the counter and looking at her labors. The kitchen was not close to being usable, but she was satisfied that she had made some progress. Raquel was tired of fighting the old house and decided to take a walk and explore some of the farm.

Raquel could see the remnants of fields that had once been plowed, but now they stood vacant with dried grass and drifts of sand. She meandered past the barn and found herself walking through tall grass and scattered trees along the bank of the North Fork Red River. She broke through the vegetation guarding the river's bank, and stepped onto the sandy river bed.

The shallow North Fork Red River had more bank than water as a result of the severe drought. The fine, pinkish-white sand glared in the sun. Raquel pulled off her boots, rolled up her pant legs, and waded into the cool ankle high water. She bent down to splash water on her face before shielding her eyes from the bright reflection. Raquel scanned the length of the river in both directions, as it curved slightly in the open terrain. She wondered if there were deeper pools to swim in further down, but all she could see was a thin ribbon of shallow water framed by the sandy river banks, tall prairie grass, and an occasional cottonwood tree. Raquel closed her eyes to feel the warm sun on her face, the cool wet sand on her feet, and to listen to the peaceful trickle of the river.

"You went back to britches," a man's voice said from behind the tall grass on the other side of the river.

Raquel felt her heart jump, as she was startled by the interruption. She stood motionless in the water, as Beau Lobaugh guided his horse lazily across the stream to the white sand on the other side. He effortlessly dismounted the dark horse and stepped toward Raquel.

"Last time I saw you, you were wearing a dress," Beau Lobaugh explained, as he looked at the young woman.

Raquel glanced down at her trousers, shirt, and bare feet before answering, "I've been working on the house."

Beau Lobaugh glanced over his shoulder toward the old house and said, "Needs a lot of work."

"Yes," Raquel said.

Raquel stood uncomfortably in the shallow river, as Beau Lobaugh studied her. He was not a particularly tall or menacing presence, but something about him intimidated her. He had broad shoulders, but he was only a couple of inches taller than Raquel. His eyes were sharp and piercing, as he seemed to be reading her. His face was smooth, except for a small scar above his left eye, but his overall appearance seemed stern and intolerant. The silence lasted only seconds, but to Raquel it felt like an hour.

"Naomi around?" Beau Lobaugh finally asked, as he stepped closer toward her.

Raquel unconsciously took a step backward away from the man and said, "No. She went to town."

"Left you alone?" Beau asked with a raised eyebrow.

"I'm a big girl," Raquel said in a tone of voice that tried to indicate that she was not defenseless.

Beau looked like he would almost smile as he asked, "How old are you?"

Raquel hesitated for a moment and answered, "Twenty-two."

Beau Lobaugh thought for a moment and then nodded.

He did not say anything after her answer, but continued to stand at the edge of the water, which made Raquel uneasy for some reason.

"How old are you?" Raquel clumsily asked, as she could think of no more pertinent conversation.

Raquel blushed at asking such a personal question, but Beau finally smiled slightly and said, "A bit older than you—"

Raquel did not think he would say more, but then Beau continued, "I'll be forty in the winter."

Raquel nodded nervously.

"When will Naomi be back?" Beau asked.

"I don't know," Raquel replied.

Beau Lobaugh moved closer to her and was now standing in the water with his boots. Raquel instinctively took a step back, but her back foot did not touch anything and seemed to go down indefinitely until she awkwardly plunged into a hole in the shallow river. The sudden fall surprised her, and she swallowed water as her head completely submerged under the slow-moving waters. The next thing Raquel sensed were strong hands clutching her by the shoulders to stand her up in waist high water.

"Are you okay?" Beau Lobaugh urgently asked, as he stood next to Raquel in the river to help her keep her balance.

Raquel coughed in convulsions from swallowing the water as she tried to nod. Before she could answer, Beau Lobaugh effortlessly picked her up and carried her the few yards to the edge of the river before putting her down on the sandy bank.

He lifted her arms above her head and said, "Try to cough it all out."

Raquel did not have a choice, as she gasped and coughed to catch her breath for a few seconds.

Beau Lobaugh seemed to sense that she would be okay when he asked again in an almost playful voice, "You sure you're goin' to be okay?"

"Yes," nodded Raquel.

Beau stepped back from the girl and said, "You got to be careful in this river. It's not too deep or too fast, but when the floods come through, it leaves plenty of holes. When the weather's not so dry, you can also find quicksand in those holes that can get you in trouble if you don't watch out."

"Okay," Raquel responded to the mild scolding.

Beau Lobaugh took off his wet hat and brushed his hair away from his face.

"You don't think much of me, for some reason," he finally said, as Raquel sat on the sandy bank in her wet clothes on the warm day.

"I—I don't know that I have an opinion about you, Mr. Lobaugh," Raquel replied.

"Oh, yes you do," Beau said with a sly grin. "Don't kid a kidder, and I can tell—you've heard stories—probably from Naomi."

"No, really," Raquel lied. "I don't know much about you."

Beau Lobaugh looked at her suspiciously with a slight smirk and said, "That's interesting, because I've heard quite a bit about you already."

Raquel quickly rose to her feet trying to brush the wet sand off of her and said hotly, "What have you heard?"

Beau Lobaugh walked away from her for a second with a sigh, before circling around to say, "I know you come from California. Don't think you're Indian—you don't quite have the temperament, but that complexion lets me think you're some Mexican. Don't hear no accent, so I think you were born in California, but your parents—maybe not."

"That's not anything," Raquel huffed. "Any fool could see that."

Beau Lobaugh smiled and continued, "Since you don't deny my description so far, I'm figuring I'm mostly right. What I'm wondering, though, is the rest of the story. I heard enough in town to know you're the widow of Chili."

"Naomi told you that," Raquel said.

"I'm betting you knew Maylon, too?" Beau suggested.

Raquel nodded nervously.

"I know things must have gone bad wrong for Naomi to come back here," Beau said.

"Why do you say that?" Raquel asked.

Beau looked up at the sky before saying, "It was Naomi's idea to go to California—talked Eli into it. I never thought she liked this place much, so if she's back, I'm figuring things weren't so good in California. If you followed her here, I'm guessing things weren't so good with you, either."

Beau stopped talking for a moment and watched her before saying, "I'm usually better at this. I can usually read people as easy as most people read a book, but I'm—I'll have to admit, you're more of a puzzle than I would have thought. Something don't add up, but I can't guess what that might be. I do know that you and Naomi had a hard way of it getting here. For that, I don't have to listen to the gossips and busybodies in town."

"What do the gossips and busybodies in town say about me?" Raquel asked nervously.

Beau smiled and replied, "Like I said, I don't listen much to the folks in town."

Raquel did not reply, but she could only imagine the stories Beulah Belvedere had been spreading about her. She believed Beau when he said he did not listen to people in town, and in some way she found that fact comforting.

"Is that your place on the other side of the river?" Raquel asked, as she pointed toward the big house in the distance.

Beau Lobaugh looked across the river and nodded.

"Looks like your wheat's ready to harvest," Raquel noted.

"Later this week," Beau confirmed.

"Need some help?" Raquel asked, thinking it would be convenient to wade across the river to work.

Beau looked at the girl and said, "You're serious."

"Yes, sir," replied Raquel.

Beau frowned, "I told you that no one but army privates call me sir."

Raquel asked apologetically, "Are you in the army?"

"I was," Beau admitted. "Retired after twenty years."

"Naomi said you were in the Great War?" Raquel said.

Beau smiled and replied, "I thought Naomi might've said some things about me."

Raquel blushed at his accusation, and Beau continued, "I'm betting she hasn't told you everything, though."

"No," Raquel said, as she stepped closer to the man. "But I am a good worker, and I've harvested before."

"Wheat?" Beau asked.

Raquel looked down to shake her head, "I can learn."

Beau hesitated before saying, "I use a combine to harvest the wheat and I already have a crew."

"Does everyone around here use a combine?" Raquel asked.

"No," Beau said. "Most still harvest by hand. They get all their friends and neighbors together to cut the wheat and gather them in bundles. They dry it, and then they take it to the threshing machine. It's hot, dusty, hard work."

"I've done hard work before," Raquel assured. "Is anyone hiring?"

"No one hires reapers around here," Beau claimed. "Like I said, they get their neighbors to do the work, and then they go help someone else."

"Oh," Raquel said in a deflated tone.

Beau looked over the river at his golden fields and said, "Come to my place tomorrow. I got a full crew to run the combines, but I'll find something for you to do."

Raquel looked unsure but asked, "What time?"

"We start at dawn," Beau said, as he stepped to his horse. "Come a little after that."

Beau was about to mount his horse when he stopped to say, "You're keeping a cow of mine?"

Raquel's heart stopped as she looked away nervously and stammered, "We—I—I found a cow and put it in the barn a few nights ago."

"I know," Beau stated factually. "I tracked it to the barn your first night here—and I saw you."

Raquel blushed, and she apprehensively asked, "You saw me?"

"Taking a bath in the trough?" he said in an even tone of voice.

Raquel could not respond, but she could feel her cheeks flush in embarrassment.

"Don't worry," Beau assured calmly. "I didn't see nothing but that burlap sack."

"You knew we had the cow?" Raquel confessed.

Beau nodded, "Old Bertha wanders over here all the time, and I come fetch her. I've spent more than a few nights camped in that old barn."

"Thought it looked like someone had been there," Raquel sighed.

Reaching into his pocket, Beau said, "I appreciate you looking out for the old girl—"

Raquel looked up in surprise, thinking Beau Lobaugh was talking about Naomi, but then he said, "Bertha the cow—she can be a handful and needs milking regular. Is twenty dollars a fair price for your effort?"

Raquel was flabbergasted as she said, "I—it hasn't been a problem and we've—we've been using the milk, if that's okay with you."

"Cow needs to be milked," Beau shrugged. "Take the money—please."

Raquel slowly reached out her hand and took the money.

Beau Lobaugh looked at the grateful girl for a moment before smoothly mounting his horse. The horse took a couple of steps before Beau pulled on the reins to steady her.

Beau looked down at Raquel and said, "I *have* heard things about you in town, but not from that windbag Beulah Belvedere.

Folks in town are talking about Naomi coming back, and they're saying you've taken care of her."

"We take care of each other," replied Raquel.

"I owe Naomi, so I appreciate your help," Beau said.

"Mr. Lobaugh, I've got the impression Naomi's been avoiding you," Raquel said, as she looked up at the man on the horse.

The horse jumped slightly, and Beau had to pull the reigns to get her to settle.

After he steadied the horse, Beau said, "Me and Naomi got history, but she's kin. That means something, I guess. I'll see you tomorrow morning?"

"I'll be there," Raquel smiled.

Beau looked at the girl a moment and said, "I got work for you to do, so don't go to any of the other fields around. Tell Naomi I'll be by to see her."

Beau Lobaugh tilted his head slightly before nudging his horse across the river. Raquel watched until he was nearly out of sight and then began her short walk back to the beat-up house. Her clothes were nearly dry, and her conversation with Beau Lobaugh had given her enough hope to continue preparing the old house to be a home.

CHAPTER 54

Raquel labored cleaning the stuffy and dusty house through the afternoon, trying to get the kitchen usable. As she scrubbed and cleaned, she could not stop thinking about her conversation with Beau Lobaugh and speculating about the conflict between him and Naomi. Beau did not appear to hold any animosity toward Naomi, but her mother-in-law seemed suspicious and even fearful of the man. Neither of them had been willing to share their past history with her.

A rattling noise caught Raquel's attention. As she looked out the window of the front room, a gray car bounced down the rutted, dirt road. She did not recognize the car, but as it got closer, she saw Naomi smiling in the front seat. As the car slowed down in front of the drive, Naomi's smile changed to a worried frown. She jumped out of the car almost before it stopped rolling. She turned to say something to Frank Sutton before walking quickly to the house.

"Change!" Naomi ordered in a loud whisper, as Raquel watched Frank Sutton walking leisurely behind her mother-in-law.

Before Raquel could respond, Naomi pleaded, "Get out of those trousers and into that pretty dress! We have company!"

Raquel started to dart for the front door, but before she could, Frank Sutton said, "Looks like you've been hard at it, Raquel."

Raquel stopped and said, "We're trying to get the house in shape." In an apologetic tone she added, "I'm wearing my work clothes today."

Frank Sutton looked around the place and said pleasantly, "It looks like you're making fine progress."

"Raquel's been a savior to me," Naomi nervously added. "She's quite a homemaker."

Frank smiled, "I've heard stories all afternoon about you, Raquel. Naomi's told the whole town about how much help you've been."

"Frank offered to give me a ride home," Naomi explained. "I was telling him how much you were looking forward to the picnic on the Fourth of July."

Raquel blushed, "Maybe I'll be a little more presentable then."

"There's nothing wrong with wearing work clothes to work," Frank said in an upbeat tone.

"Raquel's a tireless worker," Naomi assured. "I'm so sorry, Frankie, but we don't quite have everything in place or I'd have you stay for dinner."

"Oh, no," Frank said. "That'll be fine. I didn't come to impose."

Frank Sutton looked around the windswept and ragtag farm before asking, "I was wondering if maybe I could get a tour of the farm? I haven't been here in years. How many acres to you have, Naomi?"

"One hundred and sixty," Naomi said. "Raquel, you already have on comfortable clothes. Maybe you could show Frankie around?"

Raquel shifted uncomfortably but muttered, "Sure."

"Great," Frank Sutton grinned.

Naomi smiled enthusiastically and made up an excuse to go into the house and leave Raquel with Frank.

After Naomi left, Raquel said, "There's not much to see. The fields are nearly eroded away. You can see the barn and water well from here. I'd like to fix the chicken coup and get a few chickens."

"I'm actually fairly familiar with the place," Frank said in a whisper. "I used to hunt up and down this river and bother Eli when I was a kid."

"Oh," Raquel said with a puzzled look.

Frank walked toward the barn and motioned Raquel to join him.

As they walked, Frank Sutton admitted, "I came to see you. I wanted to make sure you were coming to the picnic on the Fourth of July."

"Really?" Raquel said. "I'm sure I'm going—I don't think Naomi would have it any other way."

Frank Sutton sighed and grinned, "What I'm trying to say is—I've been looking for an opportunity to see you again."

"To see me?" Raquel questioned.

"Of course," Frank said, as they walked by the barn with the cow tied up in the back. "We don't get that many pretty girls coming to a town like this. In fact, we've had considerable more people move out than have moved in."

"Oh," Raquel shyly replied.

Frank Sutton was tall and filled with confidence, as he walked down the trail leading through the tall grass and to the river. Raquel followed and listened to Frank talk about the river and the land surrounding it.

When they got to the sandy banks of the river, Frank stopped and said, "This old sandy soil will grow most anything, if you have water. That's why this land by the river's about the only property worth having."

"You think Naomi can get a good price for this place?"Raquel asked.

Frank shrugged, "I don't know. The market's terrible for sellers."

Pointing to the wheat fields across the river, Raquel said, "They're growing wheat up to my waist over there."

Frank looked at the field and declared, "Yeah, I tried to buy that place a couple of years ago, but Beau Lobaugh beat me to it."

Frank walked slowly on the sandy bank of the river until he came to the spot where Raquel had met Beau Lobaugh earlier.

"Looks like Mr. Lobaugh's been here today," Frank observed.

"Yes," Raquel said. "He came looking for his cow, I think."

"The one tied up behind your barn, with the 'B L' brand on it?" Frank asked slyly.

"We're keeping it for Mr. Lobaugh," Raquel explained.

"Really?" Frank replied. "Doesn't sound much like Beau Lobaugh to let anyone take advantage of his property."

"We're just keeping the cow for a little while," Raquel said. "What do you know about him? I've only met him a couple of times, but Naomi avoids him like a bill collector."

Frank laughed out loud, "I don't imagine Naomi's the only one."

"What do you mean?"

Frank shrugged, "I shouldn't really say, I guess. I mean—I don't really know the man well. He's not really from around here."

"I thought he had always lived across the river," Raquel said.

Frank shook his head, "He had a place south of here near Hobart, I think. He was some kind of war hero or something. Got a commission teaching artillery at Fort Sill in Lawton. Don't know what kind of officer he was, but I know he had a reputation as a shrewd rancher—some have said ruthless and worse. All I know is that he came up here after the depression got going and bought up some fine farm land. Brought in some big equipment and drilled down to the aquifer to irrigate. That's why his fields are yielding better than anyone else's around here. That's not why the farmers in Beckham County don't like him, though."

"People don't like Mr. Lobaugh?" Raquel asked.

"Not a bit," Frank replied. "Like I said, I don't know the man well. He keeps to himself, which is fine with most folks, but he's bought tractors and combines to harvest the fields. Most people think that's putting farm hands out of work. I don't know—I guess change is hard even when it's inevitable."

Raquel looked across the river at the waving, golden fields of wheat and wondered what she had gotten herself into by agreeing to cross the river to work. She had certainly witnessed that Beau Lobaugh was not affable like Frank. She knew Naomi had deep suspicions about the man, but Beau Lobaugh had given her twenty dollars. She knew that money would buy groceries, and even Naomi had to be happy about that.

Frank Sutton stepped closer to Raquel to admit, "I really didn't coax you down here to talk about Beau Lobaugh."

Raquel looked at Frank Sutton's pleasant face and said with a diminutive smile, "Why did you have me show you around a part of the country that you obviously know so much better than me?"

"Like I said," Frank gleamed. "I wanted to talk to you—without Naomi around. I want to make sure that you're at the picnic on the Fourth. There's a dance after the fireworks."

Raquel blushed slightly and said, "I'm not much of a dancer, but I'll be looking forward to seeing you at the picnic, Mr. Sutton."

"We do put on a shindig, that's for sure," Frank grinned. "Don't worry about dancing." Frank stepped closer, to Raquel and said, "Just put your hand in mine and—put your head on my shoulder and I'll lead you through it."

Raquel could not keep from looking at the handsome man's eyes and blushed, "I'll have to give that I try, I guess."

"Great," Frank said, as he continued to hold her hand.

Raquel gently pulled her hand away and said, "I better go check on Naomi, Mr. Sutton. She's probably wondered where I've gotten off to."

Frank looked at his watch and frowned, "Yeah, I better walk you back to the house. I've got to get back to town and get some work done at the bank. I've abandoned my duties this afternoon and need to catch up."

Raquel nodded, and Frank added, "But at least I played hooky for a good cause."

"What was that?" Raquel asked innocently.

"To come see you," Frank said.

The two walked slowly up the sandy bank and back to the paint-bare house. Naomi waited anxiously for them, although she tried to give the appearance of tidying up the porch. Raquel could tell, however, that Naomi was in an especially good mood to see Frank walking so close to her. Frank said good-bye to the two Butler women and drove away slowly, while Raquel and Naomi waved.

"Well!" Naomi screeched excitedly, as soon as the car was out of sight.

"Well, what?" Raquel replied coyly.

"What did Frankie have to say on your walk?" Naomi prodded.

"Not much," Raquel said. "We walked to the river and looked over the place."

Raquel could feel Naomi's excitement deflate until she added, "He told me that he wanted to make sure I came to the picnic, and—he asked me if I'd dance with him after the fireworks."

"He did!" Naomi squealed.

Raquel nodded.

"I knew he liked you!" Naomi exclaimed. "I ran into him in town and he steered the conversation to you almost immediately. He acted like he was interested to talk to me about my trip and experience in California, but he kept asking little questions about you."

"I think he likes me," Raquel said.

Naomi looked at Raquel, "The question is, do you like him?"

Raquel thought about the question and turned her head saying, "I don't know."

Naomi moved in front of her to ask frantically, "What do you mean, 'you don't know?'"

Raquel hesitated awkwardly, "It's not been that long since Chili passed—and so much has happened that it—it seems so long ago in some ways. I don't know what to think."

Naomi asked, "Don't you think he's handsome?"

"He's a very attractive man," Raquel admitted. "Tall, very pleasant and easy to listen to."

"Of course he is," Naomi said. "He is also a man of some means. His family owns the bank, and he has a nice house in town that needs a woman's touch."

Naomi stopped talking to look at the introspective Raquel for a second before saying, "I know things have been hard. I know losing Chili has been a fresh scar for both of us, but I know that Frankie is a decent man and that he could support you well. I can't tell you what to do—or feel, but I'll ask you to keep your options open and think with your head, as much as your heart."

Raquel nodded.

Naomi said, "Now, we'll have to get that pretty blue dress trimmed with some ribbon for the picnic. I wish we could do something with your short hair, but—it doesn't seem to bother Frankie, so maybe we can just put a ribbon in it, too."

"You don't have to make a fuss," Raquel said.

"That's where you're wrong," Naomi corrected. "The Fourth of July picnic is a big deal for the young folks. You've got to be as pretty as a peach."

"What about you?" Raquel teased. "Don't you have to look pretty?"

"Phew!" Naomi gasped. "I'm an old woman at a party like that. I'll be better equipped to coach you about how to get a man instead of hoping for the impossible."

"You're not that old, Naomi," Raquel stated.

"I'm not that young, either," Naomi said. "I got some ribbon at the dry goods store, but I didn't have the courage to ask the grocer for credit, when I don't know when I can pay. I'm afraid you're going to look thin and frail with nothing but cow's milk for our meals. I really don't know what we're going to do for money."

"Beau Lobaugh came by today—to see you," Raquel remembered.

The color went out of Naomi's cheeks as she said in a softer tone, "Beau Lobaugh was here?"

"Down by the river," explained Raquel.

"What did he want?" Naomi asked.

"He—" Raquel hesitated nervously before saying, "said I could come work for him."

"He wants you to work for him?" Naomi moaned. "Doing what?"

"Gleaning wheat, I suppose," Raquel said. She reached into her pocket and handed Naomi the twenty dollars Mr. Lobaugh had given her before confessing, "He gave me this money. He said it was for taking care of his cow."

Naomi shook her head, "Beau Lobaugh knows we have his cow, and he gave you twenty dollars?"

Raquel nodded, as Naomi took the money from her.

"It might be like thanking the devil for this twenty dollars," Naomi said, "but we can have some groceries tomorrow."

"You don't mind me working for him?" Raquel asked.

Naomi looked at her for a moment and then said, "God knows we could use the money. It's just—I don't want you to get into any trouble over there."

"It's just across the river," Raquel said. "I can walk there in twenty to thirty minutes."

"That's not what I mean," Naomi said. "Beau Lobaugh might put on a show about being nice, but his history don't give folks a lot of confidence about his virtue. Be careful over there."

"Why don't you like him?" Raquel asked. "I'll admit, he seems to be a smug and pretentious man, but he is Eli's family."

"Never you mind why I tread carefully with Beau Lobaugh," Naomi said. "You just be careful yourself."

CHAPTER 55

Raquel woke early the next morning. The house she and Naomi had worked so hard to rehabilitate the past week was starting to become more livable. The kitchen was not ready, but they had been living on cow's milk and did not need a stove for that. Beau Lobaugh had given them cash to buy groceries, and Raquel knew when she returned in the afternoon that Naomi would cook supper on the portable stove they had bought at the dry goods store. Raquel pulled on her trousers and headed out the door at dawn to work in the fields for Beau Lobaugh.

The morning was peaceful, but Raquel was anxious as she walked toward the river and Beau Lobaugh's house. She pulled off her boots and waded across the shallow stream to the other side. The water was cool in the morning air and the sandy river bed massaged her feet as she stepped across. The big house could be seen from her side of the river, but it was hidden from view on the other side until she walked through the tall grass and brush that grew along the river's bank. As soon as she broke through the vegetation guarding the river, she could see the big two-story house sitting on a slight rise in the distance. Although the house was in view, it was still more than a mile away. The terrain was flat and treeless, making any structure within miles visible.

Close to the river, Raquel walked through ripened wheat fields that came up above her waist. The wheat had a sweet, earthy smell. After a few hundred yards, Raquel looked back to see the smaller house where she and Naomi had been living. The barn was in plain view, as well as the old cow tied in the back pen. In the distance, Raquel could see the domed tower of the Beckham County Courthouse in Sayre that dominated the small town's landscape. Naomi was not in sight as Raquel continued her long walk to work.

After marching through endless wheat fields, Raquel came upon a dirt road angling toward the house. As she approached the fine house, she saw two huge barns and several other outbuildings including a bunkhouse that looked well used. The place was neat, but did not have much in the way of decoration. Everything in the yard looked utilitarian and orderly. Raquel stopped and took a deep breath when she saw Beau Lobaugh with five men in front of the larger barn. He stood straight with his shoulders pulled back, with an air of confidence to him. He pointed forcefully as he gave instructions to the men, who watched him carefully. Beau had not seen Raquel, and she thought for a brief moment about heading back to the house.

Before Raquel could make up her mind whether to go or stay, one of the men standing in front of Beau Lobaugh spotted her. He did not call out or even look too long, as he listened to his boss's directions. Beau Lobaugh, however, noticed the distraction immediately. Raquel was too far away to hear what was said, but Beau stepped closer to the man to talk face-to-face with him. The man timidly pointed to Raquel, and Beau Lobaugh spun around to glare at her. Beau seemed to be studying her for a moment, before he waved for her to join the group. He did not wait to see if she would comply, but instead he turned back around to give more instructions to his workers. Raquel walked slowly toward the men, and her heart pounded with anxiety.

As she approached the group, Raquel could see two of the men were close to Beau Lobaugh's age and the others were younger. One boy looked to be no more than fifteen and he had been the one that noticed Raquel's arrival. Beau Lobaugh barked orders like a sergeant in the army. Raquel could discern from the instructions that the crew would be running two combines that day—a small five-foot Allis-Chalmers combine and a large Baldwin twelve-foot combine. Each combine would have one man driving the tractor and another operating the machinery. The younger boy was given the job of hauling water and running errands for the workers. Beau asked if the men had questions, and they all shook their heads to indicate they understood their instructions.

Beau Lobaugh said to the men, "We'll start cutting as soon as the dew dries. Looks like it'll be a hot one, so we won't wait long. These machines will do the work, if you don't force 'em. Keep the speed steady and slow. We should be able to cut eighty acres today if we keep the machines running."

Raquel felt ignored and unsure of her role until Beau Lobaugh turned to her and announced, "This girl's goin' to be helpin' around the house for a few days. I don't want any of you boys getting rowdy around her today—especially you, Elmer. I mean it boys—watch your language around the lady or you'll be answering to me. Do I make myself clear?"

The men nodded and grunted their agreement. Beau Lobaugh had a forceful and stern demeanor. None of the men moved their heads to look at the girl. Beau dismissed his crew to the barns to start rolling out the equipment before he turned to Raquel.

"You made it," he said, without any indication of whether he was disappointed or pleased she had come to work.

"Yes," Raquel answered nervously.

"I wasn't sure you were coming," he said, as he watched the girl closely.

"I'm sorry to be late," Raquel apologized. "The house didn't look that far away from the other side of the river."

"Distance can be deceiving if you aren't used to the short-grass country," Beau said.

"Mr. Lobaugh," Raquel said timidly. "I heard you give directions to everyone—but me. Are you sure you need my help this morning?"

"You want to work?" he asked bluntly.

"Yes," Raquel said. "I can work."

Beau nodded, "I see you wore your field clothes, but I was wondering if you can cook?"

"A little," Raquel replied.

"Good," Beau said. "I've got some meat in the smokehouse and vegetables from the garden. I usually cook a stew for the boys myself, but I've got a new combine that I'd better keep an eye on.

If it's all the same to you, I could use your help in the house more than in the field."

"That will be fine," Raquel said. "Thank you."

"You can thank me at the end of the day," Beau smiled. "This crew can be a handful, and don't be too surprised if you get an insult or two—even after I warned them."

"I can take care of myself," Raquel assured.

Beau looked at her a second before saying, "I believe you probably can. The house is open. Can you find your way around okay?"

Raquel nodded, and Beau Lobaugh left her as he headed to the barns where the men were working to pull the combines out for work. Raquel walked slowly to the house not knowing what to expect. She had not exaggerated when she told Mr. Lobaugh she could cook "a little." Naomi had done almost all of the cooking the past two years, and Raquel had only helped her. Still, she thought to herself, work is work, and if cooking was what was needed, cooking is what she would do.

Beau Lobaugh's house was freshly painted and had a wide porch facing the town of Sayre, which could be seen in the far distance. The house was plain white with a gray wood porch. Like the rest of the place, the exterior of the house had little decoration but looked neat and tidy. Raquel opened the oak door and stepped into a nicely furnished front room that had a large sofa and two chairs on either side of a stone fireplace. Raquel could see the kitchen through the front room, and she went there immediately to take inventory of what she had with which to prepare a meal.

The kitchen had a counter stretching from either side of a porcelain sink. Raquel was surprised to see the house had running water. There was also an ice box in the corner that was stocked with fresh milk, eggs, jellies, and other food items. Raquel stepped outside the back door and found the smokehouse, which had hams and various cuts of beef stored inside. Further from the house, Raquel could hear the squawk of chickens in a henhouse. Raquel spotted a ham that had already been smoked and decided that would be the safest meat to serve. On the other side of the henhouse, Raquel saw a large garden where she found some green beans to snap and some radishes ready to cut up.

Raquel labored through the morning to prepare a meal of smoked ham, green beans, sliced radishes, biscuits, and gravy. She decided about mid-morning that the ham would have to be served cold, as she struggled to get her biscuits to rise. After the third batch baked as flat as a cracker, she looked outside to see the men were heading in from the field expecting their lunch. Raquel put the meal on the table that included cold ham, lumpy gravy, flat and slightly burned biscuits, and near-tasteless green beans. The radishes, which she sliced and put on a glass tray, were the only thing that resembled a delicacy. The men did not seem to mind, as they quickly ate their lunch and prepared to head back to the combines. In about fifteen minutes, Beau Lobaugh stepped through the back door, and the men all exited quietly back to their work.

"What's for lunch?" Beau asked, when he and Raquel were alone.

"Mr. Lobaugh, I'm so sorry," Raquel said, trying not to cry. "When I said I could cook a little, I didn't know how little I could cook for so many. I've burnt the biscuits, ruined the green beans, and have somehow caused the gravy to lump up into small balls of flour."

"It can't be that bad," Beau said, as he sat down at the table.

"I'm afraid it is," Raquel whimpered.

"If a man works hard enough and is hungry enough, I've found food is food," Beau proclaimed.

He dished himself a plate and took a bite of one of the flat biscuits. He was not able to bite through at first, but he managed to refrain from looking disappointed. He ate the rest of the food on his plate, while Raquel watched nervously.

"I'm so sorry," Raquel said again. "Naomi does almost all of the cooking, and I've only helped her. I don't expect you to pay me and if you want to send me home now I'll understand."

"It really wasn't that bad," Beau said, while shaking his head. "I remember Naomi's cooking from years ago, and you can't expect to compare your cooking to hers until you have some practice."

"It was awful," Raquel said.

"It was edible," Beau assured. "I've kept these boys hooked up all day, and they'd eat a coyote half-cooked and not complain. You'll do better tomorrow."

"You want me to come back?" Raquel asked with a raised eyebrow.

"Sure," Beau said. "This place has needed a housekeeper for a long time—and—you could use some more practice cooking."

"Thank you," Raquel said. "I'll clean the dishes and get to cleaning the house."

"There'll be time for that," Beau Lobaugh said, in an almost forceful voice, before realizing it sounded like he was giving orders. "Have a seat and tell me about California."

Raquel hesitated a moment before following his instructions. She sat nervously at the end of the table, looking at the intimidating man.

"What do you want to know?" Raquel asked.

Beau shrugged, "What's the land like?"

"It's kinda like here," Raquel said. "In our valley, the fields are wide open and planted in all kinds of vegetables. Some of the year the fields are green and lush, but for a lot of the year it's more brown and open like here. We could see the mountains from our home in Taft."

"How'd you wind up with Chili?" Beau asked.

Raquel smiled slightly, as she remembered her first encounter with the Butler boys in the fields of California.

"We were picking cotton," Raquel began. "The boys had not picked before—"

"You mean Maylon and Chili," Beau said. "Maylon was with Chili then?"

Raquel nodded, "Yes. Maylon's the one that invited me to the house. Some men tried to make things hard on me and the boys helped me. Maylon did not like being called an Okie and got into a little shoving match."

"What was Maylon like?" Beau asked. "I mean compared to Chili."

Raquel smiled, "Maylon was always the serious one. Always calculating—sometimes worrying about everything, but always dependable. He was married to my friend Orpha, and they had a little house.

"Maylon was married?" Beau interjected.

Raquel nodded.

"Any children?" Beau asked.

Raquel shook her head and said, "No, but they wanted to have kids. Maylon was doing good in the oil field near Taft. Chili and I were trying to find our own place, but Chili ran into trouble. With Maylon and Chili, if one was in trouble the other was in it with them."

"So they were close?" Beau asked.

Raquel nodded and continued talking about her experiences with the Butler family in California. Raquel answered random questions Beau Lobaugh had about the Butler family, the boys, and even Orpha. He did not cross-examine her about her past, and she was relieved about that.

"The boys were going to the coast to pick fruit," Raquel said sadly, as she told the part of the story about the accident. "The fog came into the valley, and they didn't see the truck. The highway patrol said they died instantly and didn't suffer."

Raquel winced at the memory of the two boys dying on the highway and said, "I don't know if the patrolman just told us that to make us feel better or not, but I always like to think that he was telling me the truth."

"I'm sorry for your loss," Beau said respectfully.

He looked like he would have liked to have asked more questions, but he rose slowly from the kitchen table and put on his hat. Beau Lobaugh seemed tired and solemn as he walked out the door. Raquel had turned to start cleaning the kitchen, when he stopped in the doorway.

"I'll be back later, and I'll drive you home," he said in a somber, lifeless voice.

Raquel nodded, and Beau Lobaugh walked back to his fields.

CHAPTER 56

Beau Lobaugh returned to manage his workers, and Raquel started cleaning the kitchen. The house was orderly, but Raquel could tell it had been awhile since the kitchen had been thoroughly cleaned. After two hours, she had the kitchen scrubbed and polished. Raquel looked across the fields and watched the two machines cutting neat rows through the waves of wheat. The men were far away, and Raquel could see Beau Lobaugh directing the operation from his truck.

Raquel returned to her work and quickly straightened the front room and dusted the furniture. The front room was void of any decoration except for a large panoramic photograph of hundreds of soldiers lined up in front of a barrack. There was some writing on the picture indicating the group was part of the 36th Division of the American Expeditionary Force in France. After finishing the front room, Raquel moved to an adjacent room filled with books, newspapers, and farm journals. The book room, like the rest of the house, was neat and did not take much effort or time for her to clean.

Raquel timidly approached Beau Lobaugh's bedroom, which was also downstairs. The room had a bed with massive wooden posts, a table by the bed, and a single dresser. The room also had a leather chair in the corner and another small table with an oil lamp on it. Books were stacked neatly by the chair. The patina of the leather chair indicated that Beau Lobaugh spent many hours reading in that corner of the room. The bed was already made, and everything was in order, so it only took a few minutes to dust and sweep the room.

The padded leather chair looked inviting to Raquel, who had spent most of her day on her feet. She gently lowered herself into the comfortable chair. Raquel closed her eyes and breathed deeply, enjoying her afternoon break in the plush chair. When she opened her eyes after a few seconds, she noticed the pictures sitting on the dresser facing the chair.

Raquel now took more interest in the five pictures on the dresser, thinking they might give some insight into her employer. She got up from the comfortable chair to look closer at the small collage of photographs. The first picture was of a younger Beau Lobaugh in his military uniform. Raquel was not familiar with the insignia, but by the ribbons and medals on his lapel, she could tell Beau Lobaugh had been an officer of some rank.

Another picture showed Beau Lobaugh with a group of men in uniform standing casually under a French sign. Raquel assumed the photograph was from the war. Unlike the more formal photograph in the front room, this picture looked like a group of friends. The men looked young and cheerful, and she spotted Beau Lobaugh smiling broadly with his arm around another soldier and a bottle of wine in his hand. The picture of a young Beau Lobaugh looking carefree and friendly with his comrades fascinated Raquel. This image of him contradicted the demeanor others had used to describe the man and the impression she had formed herself. Raquel remembered Naomi talking about the rambunctious and even wild-living Beau Lobaugh, but this was the first time she could imagine that aspect of his life. The Beau Lobaugh she knew was hard, stern, and in complete control of everything around him.

A third picture was smaller and of poorer quality. The image showed a much younger Beau Lobaugh with his mischievous smirk standing by a beautiful dark-skinned woman with long black hair. The woman looked pleasant, but she did not smile. The corners of the photo were worn and stained. Sitting next to that picture was another photograph of Beau with another woman and a young child. Beau was older and in civilian clothing. The woman was beautiful with long, light colored hair and a pleasant smile with matching dimples on her fine cheeks. Raquel was sure no woman was living in the house with Beau Lobaugh now, and she had not heard anyone talk about children. A date of 1922 was penciled in the corner of the photograph, and Raquel calculated that the little girl in the picture would have to be sixteen or seventeen years old by now. She had looked around the house enough to know that it had been a long time since any woman or girl had touched this house.

The fifth photograph caused Raquel to gasp slightly, as she picked up the picture to look at it closely. Raquel recognized the people in it, but the photograph of Eli and Naomi Butler showed them much younger than she had ever seen. Eli was thin and had an underdeveloped mustache. Naomi's smooth face showed a hint of a smile. She held a dark-haired baby in her arms, which partially hid the fact that she was expecting another child. Raquel picked up the picture and held it, realizing it was a picture of Eli, Naomi, and Maylon when he was a baby. She gently touched the part of the picture showing Naomi's belly and thought of Chili, who would soon join that happy family. Raquel sighed heavily and fought back tears, as she looked at the young couple so full of hope. Even Naomi had a look of calm optimism, contrasting to the bitter pragmatism she had been reduced to the past months.

Raquel put down the picture gently and wiped her eyes. She did not know why Beau Lobaugh kept a photograph of the Butler family, when he and Naomi seemed so distant. The photographs painted only a partial picture of Beau Lobaugh's past, and they left Raquel with few insights, but more questions. The afternoon sun began creating beams of light through the western windows, and Raquel decided to combat her sorrowful memories of Chili by starting the job of cleaning the upstairs rooms.

The wide oak stairway was completely bare with no pictures or decoration on the plain white walls. At the top of the stairs, Raquel noticed the hallway was dark, although hours of sunlight remained in the day. Each door on the vacant hallway was closed. The sound of Raquel's steps echoed against the bare walls and wood floor. Raquel opened the first door to find a completely empty room, except for an excessive amount of dust on the wood floor. She moved to the next room, and it too was vacant, except for a trunk pushed into the corner. The next rooms were even more puzzling as they were not only empty, but were unfinished with bare stud walls exposed. Each of the upstairs rooms had thick dust on the floor, but several also had sawdust and looked like they had been abandoned in the middle of construction. It looked to Raquel as if the interruption to the building had happened many years ago.

Raquel returned to the room with the solitary trunk in it and slowly stepped to the dusty piece of luggage. She bent down and tried to open it, but it seemed to be locked. She stepped away and was going to return downstairs, when she noticed two latches on the side of the trunk. With a simple click, the trunk lid released, and Raquel opened it.

A jumbled and disorganized mess of papers, photographs, and household items occupied the trunk. The disheveled contents looked as if they had been thrown in without any hint of planning. The messy trunk contrasted with every other aspect of the house that showed all the signs of organization, simplicity, and order. A copy of the Hobart Daily Chief newspaper dated from the 1920s sat on top of the pile of papers. Raquel glanced at the headline about a fire near Babbs Switch and sifted through the other contents of the trunk. Before she had an opportunity to explore further, she was startled by the sound of the front door opening downstairs. As quickly and quietly as she could, she closed the trunk and stepped lightly to the stairs. Halfway down, she could see Beau Lobaugh staring at her.

"What are you doing up there?" he asked firmly, as he continued to watch her.

"Cleaning," Raquel said, as she looked down at her feet and walked down the stairs.

"There's nothing up there," Beau explained.

Raquel nodded, "I finished cleaning down here—I didn't know the upstairs was vacant."

Beau looked around the front room and said, "It's never been opened; I don't need it. I can tell you did a good job down here. I don't make much of a mess, but I don't spend much time cleaning either."

"Do you need me to fix supper?" Raquel nervously asked.

"No," Beau said. "I'll send the boys home before dark, and they'll have supper at home. The small combine's down, and I had to come to the barn for a tool. I'd hoped to take you home by now, but I didn't expect to have a piece of equipment breakdown. If you want to wait a couple of hours, I'll drive you home."

"I can walk," Raquel quickly replied.

Beau Lobaugh nodded and started to leave before stopping to say, "Do you want to work tomorrow?"

Raquel did not expect the question, but she answered, "Do you need my help?"

Beau looked around the sparsely furnished room and said, "This place needs a woman's touch, and I have a hard time getting anyone to come out from town. If you're interested in work, I can use you around the house. You don't need to come quite so early, but in time to fix lunch would be fine."

Raquel nodded, "Thank you, Mr. Lobaugh. I'll try to do better tomorrow about lunch."

Beau Lobaugh did not know how to answer without criticizing the noon meal, so he awkwardly nodded and walked out the door leaving Raquel alone in the big house. Raquel waited until he had loaded his tools and headed to the broken-down combine, before she walked quickly through the cut fields and toward home. In a half an hour, she crossed the river and headed to the house. She wanted to tell Naomi she had found work close by, and she was anxious to get a quick cooking lesson from her mother-in-law before the next day's lunch.

CHAPTER 57

"You've got to change clothes!" Naomi shouted excitedly, as Raquel walked to the house from the river after her day working for Beau Lobaugh.

Naomi had been cooking on the portable stove, as she walked hurriedly to meet her daughter-in-law.

"It smells good," Raquel smiled, as she got a whiff of the sizzling meat. "What are you cooking?"

"Pork chops," Naomi said, "but that's not important."

Until her ill-fated lunch at Beau Lobaugh's, Raquel had eaten little but the milk from the old cow she had captured. She had difficulty imagining anything could be more urgent than their first real meal since coming to Sayre.

"Frank Sutton's coming to see you," Naomi squealed, as she followed Raquel onto the porch. "Get out of those trousers and into that pretty dress. He's likely to be here any minute."

"Frank's coming here?" Raquel said.

Naomi nodded enthusiastically, as she stepped behind her small stove to check the progress of dinner.

"I'm guessing you have something to do with his visit?" Raquel smiled.

Naomi sighed, "I saw him in town, when I went to buy groceries. You were all he could talk about, and I indicated that maybe you would need a ride to the picnic in a few weeks. I might have said that if he would ask, you would go with him. You don't mind, do you?"

The normally shy Raquel blushed and said, "It might be nice to have someone take me."

"Then hurry!" Naomi eagerly implored. "Let's get you into that dress—and oh my, I wish we could do something with your hair. I'll never forgive myself for letting that man talk me into cutting it off."

"It's easy to take care of," Raquel teased.

Naomi suddenly stopped and said, "I thought you were working in the wheat fields today? You don't look the least bit dirty."

"I worked in Mr. Lobaugh's house," Raquel said, as she went inside to change clothes.

"What do you mean?" Naomi shouted from the front porch.

"He said he had plenty of workers for the combine, but he needed help in the house," Raquel explained. After a hesitation she added, "He had me cook lunch."

Naomi replied in a dubious tone, "You cooked?"

"Not very well," Raquel frowned. "The biscuits wouldn't rise, and the green beans tasted flat. I cut up a smoked ham Mr. Lobaugh had already smoked, or I would have ruined that."

"Cooking's all in the spices," Naomi said. "You've got to have leaven for the flour or you'll make crackers."

"Cheese and crackers would have been better," Raquel said. She hesitated for a moment before asking, "What happened to Mr. Lobaugh's family?"

Naomi's face went flush, and she stammered before saying unemotionally, "We need to get you ready."

Raquel did not push Naomi for details, although she sensed her mother-in-law knew something about Beau Lobaugh's history she did not want to share. Raquel continued dressing, and Naomi silently returned to her pork chops. After Raquel changed clothes, she went to the porch to help the suddenly quiet Naomi with supper. Raquel tried to engage Naomi in conversation while avoiding the topic of Beau Lobaugh's family connection. Naomi was distant and appeared fatigued until she heard the sound of a vehicle rattling down the dirt road toward the Butler house, which caused her to smile more energetically.

"Frankie's here," Naomi said.

Dusk threatened to overcome the day, but they could clearly see a vehicle turning into the driveway. Naomi's smiling face turned to a worried frown, as she saw a farm truck driven by Beau Lobaugh heading up the drive instead of Frank Sutton's gray sedan.

"It's Mr. Lobaugh," Raquel said, when it became obvious Naomi would not acknowledge the man.

Naomi did not speak, as Beau Lobaugh drove slowly to the front of the house looking at the two women with a serious and formidable glare.

Beau stepped out of the truck and struggled with the broken-down gate, while Naomi stood trapped on the porch unable to make eye contact with the man.

"Hello, Mr. Lobaugh," Raquel greeted. "What brings you our way?"

Beau walked to the porch and said, "I didn't get a chance to pay you before you left and—I felt a little guilty that you had to walk home, that—combine really put us behind today."

"That's okay," Raquel smiled. "I like to walk."

An uncomfortable silence followed until Beau Lobaugh said, "Hello, Naomi."

Raquel was not sure Naomi would answer, but her mother-in-law finally said, "Hello, Beau. It's been a long time."

"Yeah," Beau replied, "a long time."

Naomi did not respond, causing an awkward pause.

"I didn't know you were coming back," Beau said, "or I'd have tried to fix things up a little bit. You could stay at my place, if you want. I've got plenty of room."

Naomi finally lifted her head revealing tear-filled eyes, as she looked at Beau Lobaugh and said, "I'm so sorry—sorry for everything."

Beau looked at her for a moment and then clumsily said, "You don't need to be—I mean you don't need to be sorry for me. I—I appreciated what you and Eli did. I—I probably didn't understand everything, but I was young. I said some things back then that shouldn't have been said, and for that—I'm sorry, too."

Naomi nodded, "It was a hard time, and I thought I was doing the best thing."

"Sounds like he was—a fine boy, Naomi," Beau said. "Raquel told me some about him today."

Raquel looked at the two, but did not understand what Beau Lobaugh was trying to say.

"He was a good boy," Naomi cried. "He was fine in every way, but—things went so badly."

Beau Lobaugh nodded, as Raquel looked puzzled.

Naomi turned to Raquel and sniffled, "Maylon was Beau's son. Eli and I adopted him when he was just a baby, and I—I never really thought about him being anything but mine. We had Chili a few months later."

"Maylon was your son?" Raquel asked the man standing in front of her.

Beau Lobaugh nodded.

"That's why you were asking all those questions about us back in California," Raquel said, almost to herself.

Beau looked at Naomi and said, "I tried to let him go. I knew he was your responsibility. I messed that up. I'm sorry I said what I did when you and Eli moved away."

"I understood," Naomi said, "but you were—out of control, and I thought it would be for the best."

"You were right," Beau admitted. "I'm sorry you didn't let me know you were coming home. I'm sorry you didn't let me know so I could help out with things."

"You were Eli's kin, not mine," Naomi reasoned.

"You took care of my boy when I couldn't," Beau said. "We're all family, Naomi."

"I didn't take care of him!" Naomi sobbed. "He's gone, and I'm so sorry."

Beau Lobaugh stepped to Naomi and gently put his arm around the woman to say, "Life is filled with death, Naomi. We're all headed to the same place, just at different times. It wasn't your fault."

Naomi bawled, "But it seems like it."

Beau let her cry for a few minutes until she started to regain her composure and then he said, "I came to give you this check. I've been running cattle on this property since I bought the river place. This'll help you get the place fixed up, and I'll be glad to rent the pasture for a monthly fee—if you're not using it."

Naomi took the check from his hand and looked at it.

"This is two hundred dollars," Naomi gasped.

"I can make it more if you think that's not fair," Beau said.

"That's more than fair—Beau," Naomi said, as she wiped her eyes. "Thank you."

"No need to thank me," Beau said. "I'm sorry things went the way they did."

Beau looked at Raquel, "You still want to cook for us tomorrow?"

"Are you that brave?" Raquel smirked.

"I like this girl," Beau smiled while looking at Naomi.

Naomi said, "Me too."

Beau turned to Raquel, "It wasn't that bad, and the old place needs a woman's touch."

"I'd like to," Raquel nodded.

Beau looked at Raquel and appeared that he might say more, but headlights from the dirt road indicated a car approaching.

"Looks like you got company," Beau observed.

Naomi looked at the car and said, "It's Frank Sutton. He said he might stop by."

"Frankie Sutton?" Beau asked.

Naomi nodded.

Beau frowned, "I wonder what he's got on his mind."

Raquel blushed and Beau continued, "I better get back to the house. Frankie's family wasn't too happy about me snagging that piece of property by the river. He'll be more—relaxed if I'm not around."

Beau nodded to the two women and walked to his truck.

Before Beau got into his truck, he stopped and said to Raquel, "You look nice in that dress. I don't have any field work for you, so you can wear it at the house—if you want."

"I will," Raquel affirmed.

Beau looked like he suddenly remembered something. "I got one more thing for you."

Beau went to the back of his truck and picked up a burlap bag and slung it effortlessly on his shoulder.

"We had a bag of wheat left," Beau explained. "I know Eli has an old millstone in the barn, and I thought you might want to make some bread with it."

"We will," Naomi smiled.

"You ladies want me to pick you up for church Sunday morning?" Beau asked.

"You're a churchgoer now, Beau Lobaugh?" Naomi asked.

Beau laughed slightly at her suspicious tone and said, "Since I moved to Sayre, yeah."

Naomi looked at her daughter-in-law and asked, "What do you think, Raquel?"

"Your church is my church," Raquel shrugged.

"It's not my church," Naomi grinned. "It belongs to the Lord."

Raquel nodded and laughed, "Church couldn't do us any harm."

"It helped me to get right with the Lord," Beau said. "Ask Naomi when I'm gone. It was a long trip back for me."

"That would be good of you, Beau," Naomi said. "I don't know many people from the old days, and it would be nice to go to church with you."

Beau walked back to his truck, but before he got in he said to Raquel, "Do I need to pick you up in the morning?"

"No," Raquel said. "It's not that far to walk, and it's cool in the mornings."

Beau smiled and nodded before he climbed into the truck and drove away, passing Frank Sutton on the way out.

"That was interesting," sighed Naomi.

"Why didn't you tell me about Maylon?" Raquel asked.

"It's complicated," Naomi said, dodging the question.

Naomi stepped to Raquel and gently pinched her cheeks to make them rosy as she said, "Frank's here."

Frank Sutton got out of his car and said with a puzzled look, "Was that Beau Lobaugh?"

"Yes," Raquel confirmed.

"What was he doing here?" Frank asked. "Is there any trouble?"

Before Raquel could answer, Naomi said, "He had some business about the place that he needed to straighten out."

"He's not giving you problems about this place, is he?" Frank Sutton asked.

"No," Naomi assured.

Frank looked at the truck churning up a cloud of dust on its way back to the house on the other side of the river.

Naomi said, "We haven't had supper yet. I think the pork chops are about dried out, but would you like one?"

"I had a big supper with Aunt Beulah," Frank said.

Naomi looked nervously at him and asked, "Did she know you were coming here?"

"I don't think so," Frank said. He then looked at Raquel and asked, "Would you like to take a walk? The moon'll be out soon, and the river's something to see with a full moon."

Raquel looked at Naomi, and her mother-in-law said, "Go ahead. I can heat your dinner up later."

"Are you sure?" Raquel asked.

"Of course," Naomi replied.

Raquel nodded and let Frank walk her the short distance to the river, which sparkled in the moonlight while fireflies floated in the dark skies. Frank Sutton was polite and clever. Raquel looked across the empty countryside and could see a single flickering light from Beau Lobaugh's house.

"What do you know of Mr. Lobaugh's family?" Raquel asked Frank, as they stood by the river bank.

Frank seemed slightly surprised by the question, but he answered, "Not much really. I know his family had a big ranch south of Hobart. I heard he got in trouble and had to join the army before the war. When his father died, he inherited a small fortune in land and cattle. For some reason, he moved this way and started buying land along the river. He was Eli's cousin. Why don't you ask Naomi?"

"It's not important," Raquel said, trying to change the conversation. "I was just curious."

Frank Sutton smiled, "I was wondering if you would let me take you to the picnic, on the Fourth?"

Raquel grinned, "I'm going. I told you yesterday."

Frank stepped closer, "You don't understand. I'm asking if you would like to go with me—as my date?"

"Yes," Raquel beamed.

CHAPTER 58

Frank Sutton walked Raquel back to the house a little before ten o'clock, but after visiting with the overly friendly Naomi on the front porch, it was closer to eleven when his car vanished into the darkness. A tired Raquel sat down for her late supper of a cold pork chop. Naomi was in a cheerful mood. She was as excited as Raquel at the invitation to the Fourth of July picnic.

"Your pork chops are better cold than my lunch was hot," Raquel frowned. "Can you help me come up with something to cook for lunch tomorrow?"

"Sure," Naomi smiled. "I'll write down some simple recipes to get you started, but I don't imagine you'll need many."

"Why not?" Raquel asked.

Naomi said, "It looks like Frank Sutton's paying plenty of attention to you. He's well off, and if you married him, you'd be able to hire a cook yourself."

"Aren't you getting a little ahead of things?" Raquel smirked. "I hardly know Frank, and he's just taking me to a picnic."

"I didn't know Eli two weeks before I knew he would ask me to marry him," Naomi boasted. "Of course, it took him about two years to find the nerve."

Raquel laughed, "Eli's cousin sure came through for us today."

Naomi said, "He's rich. He should be able to help us out around here. He was a rascal when he was younger, but I'll have to retract some of the things I said about him. He did get us out of a pickle, and I'll have to bake him a cake for that."

"He seems to be a formidable man," Raquel noted, "but there's a sadness to him as well."

"You can't dance with the devil and not get burned," Naomi shrugged. "Sometimes you reap what you sow."

"What do you mean?" Raquel asked.

Naomi shook her head, "Never you mind. He's paying us rent to use this place, and that money will help us get through until we can sell at a good price and get to town—maybe with you a husband."

Raquel smiled sadly and nodded slightly.

Naomi noticed and she stepped closer to her daughter-in-law and said, "You're a young woman, child. It's okay to dream of happiness again. I'm old, and it's easy for me to be bitter. I'm not sure I'd want another man if I could even get one. I don't have much to give you, but advice—and I want you to be happy. My Chili would've wanted that, too."

Raquel nodded and tried to smile.

Naomi said in a less compassionate tone of voice, "I'm tired now that I've had a decent meal, and I'm going to take the day's good fortune and sleep in my cot."

Raquel smiled, "Good night, Naomi. I'm going to wash up, and I'll be there in a few minutes."

Naomi nodded and the two women went to sleep with full stomachs for the first time in several days. Although Raquel had not been home to help, the house was even starting to look livable, and they hoped to have a bedroom ready to live in by the weekend. The kitchen still needed work, but Raquel was more concerned at managing the kitchen at Beau Lobaugh's house the next day. Plenty of food to eat and money in their pockets meant a good night's sleep for the night.

CHAPTER 59

Raquel slept later than she had in weeks the next morning. She quickly put on her dress and nearly sprinted through the fields toward Beau Lobaugh's house, fearful that he would scold her for being late. When she arrived, the men were already steering the combines through the field, and the house was vacant. Armed with several recipes that Naomi had scribbled down the night before, Raquel rounded up her supplies for the noontime meal without instructions from the head of the house.

At noon, the men filed in from the field to sit at the dinner table. Although not up to Naomi's standards, the food was much improved from the first day. The biscuits were still flat, but Raquel could tell the men were more enthusiastic about the meal than when they took their seats. The men did not say much to her. She would learn later that Beau Lobaugh had threatened them daily to be polite and to not bother the woman of the house.

Raquel quickly cleaned up and was about to dust the rest of the house and perhaps explore the trunk upstairs when she was startled by Beau Lobaugh, who was standing at the kitchen door watching her.

"Sorry," he said, when Raquel suppressed a startled squeal.

"It's fine," Raquel assured. "I just wasn't expecting anyone."

"I wanted to tell you that I enjoyed lunch," Beau said, as he stepped into the kitchen.

Raquel laughed insincerely, "It was adequate, I guess."

Beau stood in the kitchen for a second before saying, "You want to know, don't you? I could see it in your eyes last night."

Raquel put down her dishrag and took a seat at the table. Her attentive look said that she was interested, if Beau wanted to share his story.

Beau nodded, "I was young and head strong. Barely sixteen years old and had all the answers on the back of a horse with the wind in my hair. My dad had tried to rein me in, but I was stubborn and impetuous. I ran into this Cheyenne woman—she was not more than a girl. She was a half-breed, but lived on the reservation. I'd bring her gifts, and we—there's not a polite way to say this, but she got to be with child. My daddy had a fit, but I thought I was in love and married her. We got a place just north of Sayre—away from my dad back in Hobart. She died giving birth to Maylon."

"I'm sorry," Raquel said. "Was that her picture I saw in your room?"

Beau nodded without much emotion and said, "I couldn't very well take care of a child. My older cousin Eli had been married a few years and didn't have any children, so they took Maylon to raise. That was fine by me, I still had my wild oats to sow. Eli moved his family into the place where you and Naomi are now, and I moved back south to the ranch near Hobart. Things didn't go much better with my dad. Every mistake I'd make, he'd throw up the trouble I got into with 'that Indian girl.' I took to drinking more than I should and shot up the town one night. Fortunately no one got hurt, but my dad shipped me out to a military school back east before the sheriff could cause a fuss. That was about the start of the war in Europe. By 1915, I was eighteen and tired of military school. I hopped a ship to Europe and found a place in the French Army. By the time Pershing showed up, I had seen it all. I joined the American Army and was a seasoned soldier by then. Ended up the war as an officer in the 36th Division made up of Oklahoma and Texas boys mostly.

"War ended, and I made my way back in a couple of years and got stationed at Fort Sill in Lawton, not far from home in Hobart. By then Dad and me made some peace, and I'd grown up some. Met a real nice girl from Kentucky, whose daddy was a general. I loved her, and my dad loved her, too. Before we were married, I went to Eli and Naomi's place to see my boy. Naomi had Chili a few months after adopting Maylon, and they were a family. Maylon was five years old by then. I wasn't his father any more—just a stranger come to visit. I didn't take that too well and had some words with Naomi. Of course, I know she was right, now. It'd done no good for me to try to raise him after the fine job Naomi and Eli had done with him. I don't know if Naomi and Eli thought I'd try to make a fuss—history would've said that I would have. Next I know, they up and moved to California—so Eli could work in the oil fields out there. I always figured it was Naomi's idea, but I don't know. I thought about going out after them, but I was getting married and had my life here."

"The woman in the picture," Raquel asked, "was that your wife?"

Beau nodded, "That was my Ellen."

"And the little girl?"

Beau fought to control his emotions and he nodded his head, "That was my Mary."

Raquel was about to ask about his family, when one of the men burst into the kitchen and said, "We got a problem with that little combine again."

Beau Lobaugh's face flashed red, and Raquel believed that he would erupt in anger, but he said calmly, "Get to my truck and I'll see to it."

Beau turned to Raquel and said, "It hasn't rained a bucket full in two years, but there's clouds in the west, and if I don't get this wheat harvested before it rains I'll lose what's left in the field."

Raquel nodded and Beau Lobaugh went with the man. Raquel watched him climb into the truck and race into the fields to inspect the combine. She looked into the western sky and saw towering thunderheads billowing on the horizon. Things looked dry as a bone, but Raquel knew Beau Lobaugh was right. If it stormed before he got his crop in, he'd lose what was left in the field.

Raquel worked through the afternoon cleaning the house, but she did not feel she was earning her pay. Beau lived in the house alone, and after the first day, it took little time to maintain it. As the afternoon progressed, the skies continued to darken in the west. Thunder rumbled faintly at first and then grew louder and more ominous. Raquel looked at the fields and could tell most of the wheat had been harvested. Beau Lobaugh waved frantically for the smaller of the two combines and the truck holding the wheat to head to the barn. A single row of wheat was left in the field, and the larger combine toiled diligently in front of the impending storm.

The air was muggy, and the dark sky had a strange greenish tint, as Raquel was mesmerized by the hurried rush of men and machines. The first drops of rain were inconspicuous and splattered harmlessly on the dry dusty yard. A flash of lightning and a loud crash of thunder, which shook the house, caused Raquel to duck and retreat inside from the porch. She looked out the window to see Beau Lobaugh pointing for the large combine to head to safety, and he pulled a tarp over his half-full truck. The men scurried to push the equipment inside as the sporadic drops of rain became steadier. By the time Beau arrived to put the truck in the barn, the lightning flashed and the thunder crashed in a chaotic mess of a storm.

Raquel was alone in the house and watched apprehensively. She worried about Naomi in the rickety old house across the river and wondered how leaky the old roof might be. A tremendous crash of thunder shook the house, and heavy rain suddenly intensified into sheets of blowing water sweeping the countryside. Through the deluge, Raquel saw the door of the barn open slightly, and a man rushed across the rain swept yard sprinting toward the house. When he stepped on the porch and removed his hat, Raquel realized that it was Beau Lobaugh.

"Are you okay?" he asked loudly, talking over the pouring rain.

Raquel nodded, "I'm fine. Did you get your wheat in?"

"Most of it," Beau answered, as he looked over the fields, which were shrouded in rain.

"I guess it doesn't rain like this much?" Raquel asked.

Beau laughed, "Actually it does. The problem with this country is that the water seems to come all at one time. Lately, it hadn't come at all."

Beau continued to study the swirling clouds and the empty fields.

"Are we safe?" asked Raquel.

"I think so," Beau replied. "Looks like more thunder and lightning than winds but—"

Beau sighed heavily and then said, "It might be a good idea to get in the cellar."

"What about Naomi?" Raquel asked.

Beau thought for a second and replied, "It'd take twenty minutes to drive there in this mess. This thing'll be over by then. She'll be fine in the house, if she didn't head to the cellar. Have you cleaned it yet?"

"No," Raquel worriedly acknowledged.

"She'll be fine," Beau tried to assure. "I need to get you in my cellar, though. It won't do Naomi any good if you get blown away."

Raquel nodded and followed Beau to the edge of the porch. He stopped for a second and grabbed her arm firmly as they raced to the cellar that was about twenty yards from the back of the house.

With one motion, Beau lifted the heavy door and shouted to Raquel, "Get in!"

Raquel obeyed his directive and she was followed immediately by Beau as the heavy door slammed shut. With water dripping from her short hair, Raquel froze on the step, standing in total darkness surrounded by a dank musty smell. In a second, Beau struck a match and pushed past Raquel to find an old oil lamp. After trimming the lamp, Raquel found herself standing in a small underground room with empty shelves and cobwebs hanging ominously from the ceiling.

"We'd probably be okay upstairs, but better safe than sorry," Beau said, as he leaned against the wall a few feet away from the stairs where Raquel still stood.

Raquel nodded an instant before she heard a loud bang on the cellar door followed by a rapid succession of thuds.

Raquel looked anxiously up at the door and a frowning Beau said, "It's hail. This will be bad."

"But your wheat's in the barn," Raquel said.

Beau nodded, "I got my wheat in, but most folks around here were planning on harvesting next week—by hand. Their fields will be beat to a pulp in this."

Raquel listened to the devilish banging on the door and could hear the wind whistling outside. It sounded as if some evil demon threatened them from above.

"I hope Naomi's okay," Raquel said.

"We'll check on her as soon as this passes," Beau promised. "She'll be fine."

Beau looked at the young woman and said, "Sorry your dress got wet."

Raquel looked down and brushed at her dress while sighing, "It'll be okay."

"You looked nice today," Beau said awkwardly.

Raquel nervously nodded, "Thank you."

The two stood in the dimly lit cellar for a moment in uncomfortable silence until Raquel asked, "Your wheat—it will bring a good price?"

Beau shrugged, "Nothing brings a good price these days, but I probably won't lose money. This storm coming when it did might bump the price a few cents."

"Lucky for you," Raquel said.

"I don't believe in luck," Beau Lobaugh stated flatly.

"What do you believe in, Mr. Lobaugh?" Raquel asked.

Without hesitation, Beau said, "Myself."

Raquel nodded at the quick and affirmative answer but did not respond.

After a few seconds, Beau said in a more conciliatory tone of voice, "I guess—that's why some—most around here—call me arrogant."

Raquel struggled to hide a smirking smile caused by Beau Lobaugh's clumsy confession.

Beau looked at Raquel before grinning and saying, "I see you've heard that description—probably more colorfully stated."

Raquel laughed softly, "Yes."

Beau leaned back and asked, "What do people around here say about me? You're new to the area, but surely you've formed an opinion."

"They think you're arrogant, of course," Raquel said, repeating Beau's earlier admission. Raquel thought for a moment and said in a serious tone, "They say you're a hard man—very demanding. Successful but—I get the feeling people are—afraid of you. I think it's the strong tone of voice you use—almost all the time."

Beau frowned, "I don't mean to be so—mean. I learned to be stern and forceful in the army. It always worked for me. I guess it makes me seem like—"

"A bit of a bully," Raquel said without thinking.

"A bully?" Beau replied.

Raquel blushed in the dim light and said softly, "Sorry."

Beau thought about her analogy and asked, "Is that what you think of me?"

Raquel was caught off guard by the question and did not speak for a moment before replying, "I think you're different than people think—lonely, maybe. I—"

"Go ahead," Beau encouraged. "I'm beyond being insulted by now."

Raquel bit her lip nervously before saying, "I'm wondering how you've managed to do so well when so many others are struggling."

"Luck," Beau said quickly.

"You said you didn't believe in luck," Raquel said.

"I know," Beau smiled, "but it's been a long time since anyone's challenged me on that point."

"So you won't tell me the secret of your luck?" Raquel asked.

Beau thought for a minute and replied, "I like to think my luck has come from preparation and careful analysis. I try to look ahead and be ready for the worst. It served me well in the army and in business. My father was a successful rancher, and he had the gift, too. He could see the war coming and knew the demand for cattle would come. But my father's insight didn't always work with his family, so he didn't mind pushing his only son toward the conflict he would profit from."

"You survived," Raquel said.

Beau agreed, "That I did, and the army made me grow up. By the time I got home to show my dad and start my own family, he was sick. When he died, he left me the ranch and a nice nest egg to start life. I've done well since then, and when this depression hit, I had the money to buy things cheap."

"Like this farm?" quizzed Raquel.

"Yeah," Beau shrugged.

"Why did you—move here?" Raquel asked.

Beau replied, "It's good land. I used to come here and visit Eli. He was a lot older than me, but when I was little he was my hero. He'd take me hunting and fishing." Beau thought for a moment and continued, "Truth is, I needed a change and wanted to be somewhere different."

"Why?" Raquel asked.

Beau's strained smile indicated that he did not want to answer the question, and he instead asked, "How about you? What events have brought you to the short-grass country?"

Raquel frowned and replied, "A lot of things in my past, I guess. It seems like the past is hard to get away from."

Beau looked embarrassed at asking the question and consoled, "I think we learn from the past—no matter how painful—and live for today. That might be good advice for you."

Raquel smiled, "I'll consider it."

Beau looked up at the door and said, "Sounds like the hail's stopped. Let's get out of here and see the damage."

Beau Lobaugh gently pushed by Raquel on the stairway leading out of the cellar and opened the heavy door. Warm fresh air rushed in, and Raquel was glad to be out of the musty cellar. Drops of rain still fell, but the sky was clearing in the west and the dark clouds had moved off to the east. Beau did not say anything to her as he walked to the barns to check the damage. Pieces of ice the size of eggs littered the ground, and Raquel saw a few tree branches down, but she could not see any damage to the house. She returned to the porch and turned around to watch Beau Lobaugh point and give orders to his men. Raquel wondered if she would ever learn the secrets that brought him to this place.

CHAPTER 60

After the storm, Raquel returned to the house to finish her work while Beau Lobaugh assessed the damage to his farm.

In a few minutes, Beau walked into the kitchen, soaking wet and with a serious scowl on his face, "Ready to check on Naomi?"

Raquel nodded and followed him to the truck.

"Is your wheat okay?" Raquel asked.

"Yeah," Beau replied with a sigh, as he helped her into the truck for the short drive home. "We got most of it. Good thing too. What's left in the field is beat down and useless."

Raquel wanted to continue her inquiry about Beau's family, but before she had the chance he said, "I see Frankie Sutton's been coming around regular."

"Yes," Raquel admitted.

Beau looked at her a second before smiling to say, "You don't get it do you?"

"Get what?" Raquel replied with a puzzled frown.

"He likes you."

"Maybe."

"The question is—do you like him?" Beau responded.

Raquel grimaced, "Maybe. I don't know him well—yet."

"That won't take long," Beau Lobaugh scoffed.

"What do you mean by that?"

"Nothing."

Raquel turned in her seat to look at the man and said, "You don't think much of Frank."

"I didn't say that," Beau defended. "I think he's a nice young man, but he's just—"

"Just what?"

Beau Lobaugh sighed, "I just think he's going to do what his momma and daddy want him to do."

"What's wrong with that?"

"Nothing."

Beau Lobaugh turned into the drive at the Butler's house and seemed relieved to say, "We're here."

Raquel was not comfortable discussing her relationship with Frank Sutton any further, and she quickly exited the truck and headed to find Naomi. Beau Lobaugh followed and took the initiative to shout out for Naomi.

"What are you yelling for?" Naomi asked, as she stepped from the back of the house.

"We were worried about you," Raquel explained.

"Did you weather the storm?" Beau asked.

"I've seen worse," Naomi frowned. "This old roof leaks like a sieve, and I've been trying to salvage our things from the rain."

Raquel walked past Naomi to look in the front room that had several puddles of water between the buckets that her mother-in-law had tried to put under the leaks.

"We had hail the size of persimmons at my place," Beau said, as he looked at the leaking house.

"It beat down here pretty good, too," Naomi said. "How's the river?"

"Up some," Beau said, "but it'd take a lot more rain to get it out of her banks."

Beau inspected the house for a moment before he reached into his pocket and said to Raquel, "Here's your pay for the week. Why don't you spend a couple of days here and help Naomi straighten things up. I can manage at my place. When I get the wheat put up, I'll see if I can't get a couple of the boys to come over here with shingles and patch that roof."

Naomi's face twisted slightly as she said, "Thank you, Beau. That'd be a help for sure."

"Thank you, Mr. Lobaugh," Raquel said. "I'll come back Monday and clean for you?"

Beau nodded and smiled, "That would be good, but I'll see both of you Sunday."

He tipped his hat and walked through the muddy yard to his truck. He hesitated a moment like he might say more, but instead waved and left.

"What's gotten into Beau Lobaugh?" Naomi sighed, as she watched him drive away. "He's turned into a regular good Samaritan."

"I think he's different than people say," Raquel said.

Naomi looked at her daughter-in-law before looking back at the truck heading away from her house.

"Maybe," Naomi said with a slight grin.

CHAPTER 61

Raquel and Naomi settled into their new home, as the hot summer days got longer. Beau Lobaugh sent two of his men to fix their roof. Naomi's initial reservations about Eli's relative based on her experiences with him when he was younger began to soften as she more often turned to him for advice. Beau was nearly forty, but it took time for Naomi to see him as more than the reckless teenager she had known.

Naomi talked of selling the place and moving to town, but Beau convinced her that the depressed marketplace would not bring a decent price. He offered to pay rent for Naomi's pasture to give her some income for living expenses, and the women slowly made improvements to their new home. Raquel arranged to work at Beau Lobaugh's house to cook for him and his small group of workers. She kept his house, which was easy work, and most days she came home after lunch to help Naomi, who shared cooking tips with her each night. They soon rehabilitated the kitchen and two bedrooms. For the first time in over a year, Raquel had a room to call her own, and she enjoyed getting further away from Naomi's chronic snoring. Raquel also put on her work clothes and cleaned out their muddy and decrepit cellar. She had been close enough to a tornado to believe the effort would be a good use of her time.

Frank Sutton became another part of Raquel and Naomi's routine. The always well-dressed and well-mannered banker came several times each week. Naomi would cook dinner some nights and usually he would take Raquel for an evening walk. Naomi pretended to go to bed early, but she was almost always awake to question Raquel when Frank left. Naomi held a keen interest in the budding relationship and seemed anxious that Frank had not mentioned the Fourth of July picnic in several days. Raquel enjoyed Frank's polite company, but she too wondered why he always came to their place and never seemed interested in going to town.

A week before the Fourth of July picnic, Raquel waited patiently for Frank to come for his evening conversation with the women and his walk with Raquel. When he did not show up, Raquel was mildly concerned, but Naomi was almost frantic with apprehension.

"Where could he be?" Naomi fumed, as she paced quickly across the shaky front porch.

"Maybe some late business came up," Raquel speculated.

"At this hour?" Naomi said. "It doesn't take five minutes to drive out here. He's been here nearly every night for two weeks, whether I wanted him here or not, and then tonight he leaves us wondering what's happened."

"Frank has his own life," Raquel said. "He made no promise that he would be here tonight."

"Didn't you expect him?" Naomi asked, insinuating that maybe Raquel had gleaned some information from their talk the night before.

"Yes, but he didn't say for sure he would be here."

Naomi sighed heavily to indicate her displeasure at this development.

"It's not a big deal," Raquel said, trying to pacify her mother-in-law. "Something came up tonight, and he couldn't come. It's getting late, and I'm going to bed."

Naomi looked at the dark skies and checked her clock while refraining from saying more. She was annoyed with Frank Sutton, but she was equally frustrated with her daughter-in-law's calm response. Raquel stepped to Naomi and kissed her forehead before going to her bedroom. Naomi stood on the porch for a few minutes looking into the dark countryside. She stepped around the corner of the house to see the lights glowing from the small town of Sayre. When there was no indication of a car coming up the road, she finally retired for the evening with suspicions rattling in her head.

Beau Lobaugh began picking Raquel up for work after the storm caused the river to rise. Raquel heard Beau's truck rattling across the one-lane river bridge, the night after Frank Sutton failed to show up, and she was out the door after saying good-bye to Naomi.

"You cut your hair," Raquel noticed, as she climbed into the truck.

Beau touched his freshly cut hair and said, "Yeah, I thought I better have shorter hair than my cook."

Raquel laughed, as she said, "Hopefully, mine will grow back, but I like your hair cut short."

"Thanks," Beau smiled.

"It makes you look—younger."

"I need all the help I can get," Beau sighed.

Raquel looked forward to her morning rides with Beau Lobaugh, and she liked the way he let her tease him. Raquel believed she was one of the few people that would take that liberty, but Beau seemed to enjoy their morning talks.

Beau had been guarded about his comments after insulting Raquel with his opinions about Frank Sutton, but he noticed something was different when he asked, "Late night?"

"What?" Raquel responded, as the truck bounced along the dirt road.

"You look tired," Beau explained.

Raquel shook her head, "No, I'm fine."

Beau did not press the short answer but nodded his head and drove across the river toward his house.

"I guess you'll be going to the Fourth of July picnic next week?" Beau said in a cheerful tone, trying to change the conversation.

Raquel's face twisted uncomfortably as she said, "What do you mean by that?"

Her response took Beau Lobaugh by surprise for a second before he stammered, "Nothing—just making conversation."

He glanced over at Raquel and asked, "Is everything all right?"

Raquel nodded, embarrassed by her curt reply and she said, "Yes. I had too much time with Naomi last night."

Beau grinned, "I've had some of those nights myself."

"Are you going to the picnic?"

"Not likely," Beau laughed insincerely, as he stopped the truck between the house and the barn.

"You don't like picnics?"

"I like picnics, but I'm not big on socials."

Raquel nodded, "Me either, but Naomi says it's the 'can't miss' event in Sayre."

"Naomi would know," Beau shrugged. "You leaving after lunch, today?"

Raquel nodded.

"Want a ride?" Beau asked.

"I can walk."

"It'll be hot by noon today," Beau said. "You better let me drive you."

Raquel agreed and went to work on the house. She cooked lunch for the men, and after she finished cleaning the kitchen, Beau was waiting to drive her home. As Beau pulled up to the Butler house, Raquel saw Naomi sitting on the porch wearing her new dress.

"What's going on?" Raquel asked, as she stepped out of the truck.

"Hi, Beau," Naomi greeted, before answering Raquel's question.

"Hello, Naomi," Beau said, as he sat leaning against the steering wheel of his truck.

"I thought we'd go to the Belvedere's store today," Naomi said.

"Today?" Raquel asked.

"It's too hot to work on the house, and we'll beat the Saturday rush," Naomi explained.

"Would you like a ride to town?" Beau Lobaugh asked.

Naomi smiled, "That would be fine, but you don't have to wait on us. I've got a lot of shopping to do, and I'm sure Arnold or someone can give us a lift back."

Beau agreed, and Naomi pushed Raquel into the middle seat for the short drive into Sayre. Beau Lobaugh asked again if the two women needed a ride back, but Naomi insisted they would be fine. The two women waved as Beau drove away, and they headed into the Sayre Dry Goods Store. The afternoon sun beat down on the cement sidewalk. The store was stuffy and warm, but a large fan hanging from the ceiling circulated air, and the inside of the store felt relatively comfortable compared to the hot sun outside.

"It's going to be blistering hot on the way home," Raquel said.

"Not in a car," Naomi replied. "I thought it would be a good day to run into Frank Sutton. He'll be glad to drive us home this evening."

Before Raquel could reply, she stopped where she was standing and looked at two women talking loudly to a salesman at the cash register. Raquel immediately recognized Beulah Belvedere talking to a woman who was a few inches shorter, several inches wider, and appeared to be a few years older. Raquel tried to get Naomi's attention to leave the store, but to her horror, Naomi walked nonchalantly toward the women.

"I'll be, it's Naomi Butler," the woman who was standing by Beulah greeted.

Raquel stayed by the front door, several yards back from Naomi, when her mother-in-law said, "Hello, Constance. What are you doing in town?"

"Came to visit my sister," Constance declared, in a tone of voice that sounded so much like her sister Beulah that it sent chills down Raquel's spine. "I heard you were back in town, and I was so surprised. Beulah was telling me about your tragedy. I'm so sorry for you."

"Thank you," Naomi said. "It's been a very bitter time, but it's been good to be home."

"Naomi's moved back to the home place," Beulah informed.

"I didn't know that old place was still standing," Constance quipped.

"It barely is," Beulah said.

"It needs some work," Naomi admitted. "I've been seeing a lot of your boy Frankie in town."

"So I've heard," Constance said, shaking her head. "I don't know what his father and I are going to do with that boy. He needs to settle down, but he's still a young man I guess. I heard you had a stray dog follow you home."

"What do you mean?" Naomi squinted.

"Oh, you know what I mean," Constance exhaled in an exaggerated sigh. "Beulah told me that little Mexican girl followed you back from California."

"That young woman's my daughter-in-law," declared Naomi.

"Naomi, I'm sorry for your loss, but Eli and your boys are gone," Constance huffed. "That little Mexican girl is just taking advantage of your good nature."

"That's not true," Naomi defended. "If anything, I've been the burden to her. Your son Frankie seems to appreciate her pleasantness."

Constance looked at her sister with a slight nod and said, "That's really why I'm in town. I've been hearing some disturbing rumors about my boy and that girl you brought back."

"What kind of rumors?" Naomi hotly asked. "I've chaperoned every meeting the two have had, and Frankie has been a gentleman in every way."

"Of course Frankie's been a gentleman," Constance stated flatly, "because he is a gentleman. That's why I've sent him back to Elk City for a time to work more closely with his father. We've sent a man to manage the family's affairs and the bank until he can return."

"Frankie's left town?" Naomi asked.

"It was inconvenient," Constance said, "but it had to be done. I couldn't stand to see him get trapped like your poor son did."

"What do you mean by that?" Naomi angrily asked.

Constance bounced her head like a drunken peacock as she said, "I know your son Chili got in trouble with that girl and ended up having to marry her. That's how these people are, and they'll do anything to get ahead."

"Chili was in no trouble," Naomi said, shaking her head. "He loved Raquel."

"You couldn't possibly have approved?" Constance said. "Your poor dear departed mother would turn over in her grave if she knew her blood line was being polluted by some half-breed Mexican girl."

"You take that back!" Naomi demanded.

Beulah Belvedere tried to intervene by saying, "Our mothers were sisters, and we know how proper the Hancock family was. You'll have to admit, Naomi, that your mother would not have approved, if she had been alive."

"That's a ridiculous point," Naomi declared. "My mother never met the girl."

"Naomi, you don't have to get emotional," Constance said. "I don't know what things must have been like for you, and I'm not here to judge. I'm just not about to let my Frankie get involved with someone that would damage him and his family. You're our cousin, and you should understand. I've sent Frankie away, and he'll come to his senses."

Constance stopped to look at Raquel, who tried to stay out of sight of the women, before she said, "I've heard the girl is very pretty, and Frankie's got a soft spot for pretty girls. Frankie has a young lady that he's been promised to for many years back in Elk City. He'll come back to his senses, when he's away from some bad influences in this town."

"My daughter-in-law is no 'bad influence,'" Naomi replied hotly.

Raquel tried to maintain some composure as she stepped to her mother-in-law to say, "Naomi, let's go home now."

"Wait!" Naomi pleaded. "Constance, you've offended this girl in every way. I suspect Beulah has poisoned your opinion of her, but I demand you apologize to my daughter!"

"Daughter-in-law," Constance corrected.

"Raquel is as much a daughter to me as my own flesh and blood," Naomi said.

Constance replied smugly, "We know that's not a strong tie in the Butler family."

"What!" Naomi exclaimed.

"Oh, don't pretend to be so shocked," Constance glared. "The whole town knew that little dark-haired baby was Beau Lobaugh's bastard."

"Apologize!" Naomi shouted, which commanded the attention of the few people in the store that afternoon.

Constance Sutton took a deep breath and waddled to Raquel to say, "Stay away from my son! He's engaged—to a decent girl. You can flash those bright eyes at him and pout with those lips, but know that it's been explained to Frankie that he will be disinherited, if he continues to abandon his good senses and flaunt his attentions on you."

Raquel stumbled toward the door and exited the store. The hot outdoor air stung her tear-filled eyes, but all she wanted was to get far away from the women.

"Constance Sutton!" Naomi screamed. "You are a mean, spiteful woman!"

"I'm just protecting my family name," Constance haughtily declared. "Just like you should have done."

"That girl represents the only family I care about!" Naomi proclaimed. "I'm not a Sutton or a Belvedere, and I'm certainly not a Hancock any longer. I'm a Butler—and so is she."

Before Constance could say more, Naomi stormed out of the store to find her daughter-in-law. Raquel was already halfway to the courthouse and headed toward home. Naomi walked as fast as her sore knees would allow, but she was not making up ground. Suddenly Beau Lobaugh's truck sped by her before sliding to a stop.

"Get in," Beau said.

Naomi complied without asking why Beau was still in town. He put the truck in gear and rolled next to Raquel who was about a half a block ahead.

"Need a ride?" Beau asked.

Raquel wiped tears from her eyes and shook her head while continuing to walk.

"You better get her," Beau said to Naomi. "It must be close to a hundred out there in the sun."

"Do you know what happened?" Naomi asked.

"I can imagine," Beau said.

Naomi nodded and stepped out of the truck to catch her daughter-in-law. Raquel continued to walk, but she moved listlessly now, and Naomi easily caught up to her.

"I'm sorry you had to hear those things," Naomi said.

Raquel did not respond.

"Beau's giving us a ride," Naomi explained.

Raquel looked at the truck to see Beau Lobaugh sitting behind the wheel. He stared down the road leading out of town without making eye contact—trying to ignore the two women's conversation. Raquel let Naomi lead her to the truck. Beau slowly pulled onto the road, and the three drove silently for the short trip to the Butler home. Beau kept his eyes on the road, Naomi watched her daughter-in-law, and Raquel stared out the passenger side window at the dry brown grass withering in the blazing sun. When the truck came to a stop, Raquel got out quickly followed by Naomi.

Beau Lobaugh jumped out of the truck and said, "Raquel."

Raquel stopped to look at the man as he continued, "I've been thinking about what you said this morning."

"What was that?" Raquel asked lethargically.

"I was thinking I might want to go to the picnic on the Fourth," Beau explained. "I was wondering if maybe I could drive the two of you there."

Raquel thought for a moment and sighed, "I don't think I'll be going to the picnic, but thank you for the ride."

Raquel walked toward the house, when Beau said, "You can't let other people dictate your life. You can't hide from them and think they'll go away."

Raquel nodded and walked slowly into the house. Beau Lobaugh watched her and then returned to his truck.

As Beau climbed into the truck, Naomi stepped to the driver's side and said, "Thank you, Beau."

"It wasn't anything," Beau said. "I had some errands to do in town and saw her walking in the heat."

Naomi looked at the man for a minute and said, "Do you know what happened?"

Beau said, "I saw Constance Sutton in the store. I can guess."

Naomi looked away a second before asking, "Did I do the right thing bringing her back here?"

"I'd like to know what happened to cause her to follow you?"

"What do you mean?"

Beau shook his head, "It doesn't make any sense that a girl like that would travel all this way unless she's running away from something—or had nothing left to stay for."

"She's had a hard life, I'm afraid," Naomi said. "She is a dear, though, and I hate how she was treated today."

Beau looked at the house where Raquel had gone to hide and said, "She's special."

Naomi looked at him and asked, "You like her, don't you Beau?"

Beau did not answer for a second and then said, "She's a likable girl if that's what you mean."

"That's not what I mean and you know it," Naomi stated flatly.

"She's got her eye on Frankie," Beau sighed. "I can't blame her. He's more her age, and he's an affable guy. Unless he's more of a fool than I think, he'll come to his senses."

Naomi thought for a second and said, "Thank you again, Beau, and—don't make any plans for the Fourth of July."

"Why?"

Naomi smiled, "Because you'll be taking the two of us to a picnic that day."

CHAPTER 62

Raquel tried to forget her encounter with Constance Sutton and Beulah Belvedere from the day before. Frank Sutton had been friendly to her, but he had not promised her more. Raquel was not even sure about her own feelings about Frank. Still, she had enjoyed his company, and it hurt to think his mother would think her so unworthy. Naomi attempted to be extra cheerful the next morning. Raquel appreciated the effort, but she looked forward to walking to Beau Lobaugh's house alone that morning. The river had returned to a trickle again as the severe drought continued with a vengeance.

The house looked lonely to her as she walked toward it. There did not seem to be anyone around at first, but then she noticed a few men working down by the barn, including Elmer. Raquel walked into the empty house and started putting the kitchen in order for the day. The gentle sound of the creaking kitchen door caused her to frown, as she knew she would have to face Beau Lobaugh and apologize for her sulking behavior from the previous afternoon. She turned around and was startled to face Elmer standing in the doorway of the kitchen.

"Excuse me, ma'am," Elmer said, as he looked down at his shoes.

"You startled me," Raquel gasped.

"I'm sorry," Elmer apologized. "The captain told me to come see you when you got here."

"Where's Mr. Lobaugh?" Raquel asked.

Elmer looked around the vacant house and said, "He told me to tell you that he had some business come up in Oklahoma City and would be gone a few days. Captain said you could cook for us if you wanted or head home if you'd rather."

Raquel nodded, "Since I'm here, I'll fix your lunch, then head back."

"Captain said I's to drive you," Elmer explained. "I was supposed to pick you up this morning, but with the captain gone, I overslept a mite."

"I can manage," Raquel smiled. "Did Mr. Lobaugh say when he'd be back?"

Elmer shook his head, "Not much telling—could be a couple of days or maybe longer."

"Is everything okay?" Raquel quizzed.

"Oh, yeah," Elmer assured. "The captain goes for business all the time. Something just come up. It's pretty standard around here."

He tipped his soiled straw hat and started to leave when Raquel said, "Elmer?"

"Yes, ma'am," he replied, as he turned to face her.

"Mr. Lobaugh—he treats you different. Why?"

Elmer shifted his weight and replied, "I don't know what you mean."

Raquel stared at him a moment in an attempt to force him to say more before observing, "He talks to you different than the other workers. He talks to you more—it's almost like he's taking care of you sometimes."

"I pull my weight," Elmer defended.

"I know," Raquel quickly assured. "But you know what I'm talking about."

Elmer shuffled for a moment like he might dart out the door, but then he said, "I knew the captain from the war. We took an artillery shell right before the end. I ended up on top of the captain and took some of the shell in the back of my head. I's laid up in that hospital for a long time. Came back home and struggled to adjust—had some bad times. The captain stayed with me though. Made the army take care of me for a while and then hired me to work his farms. I'm just fine now, but I think the captain thinks he still has to coddle me sometimes."

"Mr. Lobaugh has another farm?" Raquel asked.

Elmer nodded, "He's got a big spread down south of Hobart. He sold part of the place before the depression, but he's kept his old home place and rents some of it out. He's got some property back close to Oklahoma City, but I don't know much about that business."

Raquel could tell Elmer was antsy to return to the barn, but she could not resist the chance to investigate her employer.

"Why'd he warn you to stay away from me that first day?" Raquel asked. "He almost threatened you."

Elmer smiled shyly, "The captain's teasing me's all ma'am. I'm shy as a coyote around women—unless I've been drinking. Then I've been known to say things ought not to be said, and—I've been in a few brawls the captain's had to bail me out of. The captain's made it clear to us boys that you's a lady and we're to treat you as such. That's why you get so much respect from us boys at first."

"I see," Raquel smiled awkwardly.

Elmer quickly added, "Of course, we all could tell you were a fine lady from the start. We're pretty ornery sometimes, but I'll make sure the boys behave while the captain's away, if'n that's what's worrin' you."

"I don't worry about things here," Raquel assured. She hesitated for a second before asking, "What happened to Mr. Lobaugh's family?"

Elmer's lazy disposition suddenly turned grave, as he said, "The captain don't talk about it, and he don't tolerate no one else talkin' about it either."

"But you know?" Raquel pressed.

"Not much," Elmer said, "and I'm not one to speculate."

Raquel nodded to indicate that she would not inquire further.

Elmer started to leave before stopping to say, "The captain's a good man—in his own way. People think he's hard or—they think a lot of things about the captain, I suppose—but they don't know what's in the man. They don't know what I saw when he took responsibility for his men. He's a hard man—they're right about that, but he's a fair man."

Elmer opened the screen door and said, "It's been good for you to be here, Miss Raquel. The cookin's improving, but it's been good for the captain—and I can appreciate that."

Raquel wanted to ask more, but Elmer quickly exited the house and walked hurriedly across the yard to the barn. Raquel watched him for a moment and saw him glance back at the house before he disappeared into the barn. Raquel cooked lunch for the workers, and they ate in uncomfortable decorum in front of her. She had heard the men enough when they knew she was not listening to know how difficult it must have been for them to watch their language, but after her conversation with Elmer, she had a new appreciation for their good manners. Elmer offered to drive her home after she had cleaned the kitchen, and he almost insisted. Raquel assured him that she would rather walk, and said good-bye to him as he smiled shyly at her.

The fields were bare after the harvest, and the wind was hot on her walk back. Heat shimmered off the flat fields and a dirt devil, an evil looking tornado-shape spiral of wind that was common on a hot day, boiled up and nearly covered her with dust before veering off to the empty reddish-brown fields. Raquel took her shoes off to wade across the shallow river. She stood in the slow-flowing stream for a few minutes to enjoy the refreshing water on her toes. After splashing some water on her hot cheeks and the back of her neck, she felt the tips of her hair, which had grown to cover most of her ears. As she walked from the river to the house, she was thinking about how long it would take for her hair to grow shoulder-length again, when she stopped to look at the house. Frank Sutton's gray car was parked in front, and Raquel watched Frank talk to a frowning Naomi. Raquel took a deep breath and walked slowly to the house.

"Hello, Frank," she greeted, as the handsome man watched her approach.

Frank did not talk until she stepped on the porch, and he said in a grim voice, "I heard what my mother said in front of you yesterday, and Naomi has confirmed it. I can't start to say how sorry I am, but I can assure you that my mother was out of line."

"She probably didn't mean anything by it," Raquel nervously noted.

"My mother meant it," Frank bluntly asserted. "She doesn't understand that I'm a grown man that can and will make his own decisions. I had a word with her this morning when I got wind of the gossip that Aunt Beulah was bragging about saving me from myself. I confronted mother and plan to do the same with Aunt Beulah when I leave here. I can only hope that you can somehow forgive me."

Raquel turned away from Frank a moment and looked across the wide-open countryside before turning back to declare, "You can't control what others say—what they think. You have nothing to apologize for—especially to me."

"I may not be able to control my mother's mouth, but I can certainly apologize—and scold her for being callous and unkind," Frank said.

"I appreciate that, Frank," Raquel sighed, "but that won't change your mother."

Frank glanced at Naomi, who was sitting on the porch listening, when he said, "Could we take a walk?"

"It's hot, and I'm tired," Raquel sighed.

Naomi rose from her seat and said, "I've got to draw some water to put on my plants before this sun bakes them. You two can talk on the porch."

"I've been foolish these past weeks," Frank said, after Naomi had left. "I confess that I've been worried about my mother. I haven't taken you to town or been upfront with you for fear she would find out and cause a scene like she did yesterday. Now that she's revealed herself to be an old biddy, I'm glad she knows. I have become attached to you these past weeks. You have an inner charm that you don't realize. You have captivated my thoughts the past weeks. Now that Mother knows, and I've told her that she can't run my life any more, I want the whole town to know you're my girl."

"I'm not anyone's girl," Raquel sighed.

Frank grabbed her by the shoulders and tilted his head to ask, "Can you tell me you don't like me—even a little?"

Raquel stepped away from his gentle grip and walked a few feet before turning to say, "I do like you, Frank, but I'm not in a good place right now to know how I feel about things. I'm in this strange town after a long trip, and I'm—I'm a different class of people than you're used to. I know how you look at me, and I know how that makes me feel."

"How?" Frank interrupted.

"It makes me feel special," Raquel admitted. "You're a nice man, and I enjoy you, but—I know how your mother talked about me yesterday. I know she's not the only one that has or will look at me like that again. We come from different places, Frank, and I don't want you to have to choose between me or your life."

"I'd choose you," Frank declared.

Raquel smiled with tight nervous lips and nodded in resignation.

"You're not convinced," Frank moaned.

"I'm not saying I don't believe you," Raquel corrected, "I just don't know how I feel."

Frank walked close to her again and hesitated for a moment before saying, "Will you still go to the picnic with me? Give me a chance to make some amends."

Raquel looked at Frank's kind eyes and reassuring smile and said, "I promised you I would go."

"Great!" Frank beamed. "I'll pick you up Thursday, and we'll have a day of it."

"That'll be fine," Raquel nodded. "But—I think Mr. Lobaugh was going to take Naomi and me."

"He won't mind a bit," Frank assured. "Everyone goes to the picnic, and we'll see him there."

"Okay," Raquel replied with an unsure smile.

Frank looked at his watch and said, "I need to get back to town. I've got to give Aunt Beulah a piece of my mind."

"Don't do that," Raquel pleaded. "It won't do anyone any good—especially not me."

Frank stepped close to Raquel and surprised her with a kiss on her cheek before he said, "You are too forgiving, but I'll respect your wishes."

Frank bounced off the front porch and stepped quickly to his car before speeding off toward town.

"Well," Naomi asked. "What's going on?"

"You heard every word," Raquel stated with a smirk.

"Uh!" Naomi grunted in protest. "I can't help it if Frankie talks loud, and—I didn't hear *every* word."

Raquel grinned at her mother-in-law, "Frank's taking me to the picnic Thursday."

Naomi stepped closer to Raquel and put her arm around her to say, "I know what's happened. I'm curious about how you feel about it."

Raquel replied, "I honestly don't know."

CHAPTER 63

The Fourth of July was boiling hot. The isolated hailstorm that had ruined the wheat harvest for so many area farmers had been the only trace of rain for months. Remnants of the sand drifts from the massive dust storms from the spring were still visible on some of the poorer pieces of land. Raquel and Naomi continued improving their house while devising ways to beat the stifling summer heat.

Frank picked Raquel up a little bit before noon on the Fourth of July to take her to the community picnic, as he had promised. His mother had returned to Elk City. Raquel sensed relief in his outlook, as Frank seemed more relaxed and sure of himself, like she had noticed on their first meetings.

"Want to go, Naomi?" Frank politely invited as he stood on the porch.

Naomi shook her head, "It's too hot for me. I'll see plenty of fireworks from my porch. Besides, Beau said he might come by."

"Do you think he'll mind?" Raquel asked timidly. "I mean—mind that we left him."

"I've never known Beau to get too ruffled about missing social engagements," Naomi replied with a forced smile.

"He'll be fine," Frank added.

Frank guided Raquel to the car, and they drove the short distance into town. Sayre buzzed with activity, as people from all over Beckham County came to celebrate. After a brief ceremony for the veterans of the Great War and several speeches from local politicians, the crowd settled into a lazy flow of activity. Various churches offered fried chicken and baked pies as fundraisers, although most people brought their own treats. A band played, accented with firecrackers that young boys had managed to acquire for their own entertainment. Later in the afternoon a few of the brave young men, including Frank, stripped down to their undershirts for an impromptu baseball game. Raquel watched from the stands wishing Naomi had accompanied her. The warm day kept most close to the shade, and Raquel sat alone watching the game. Although she felt somewhat awkward sitting by herself, Raquel was relieved knowing it was unlikely that Beulah Belvedere would be out on such a hot day.

Naomi spent most of her afternoon napping restlessly in a rocking chair on the shaded porch while trying to keep cool with a damp rag and hand-fan from the local funeral home. She had almost dozed off for another catnap when the rumbling rattle of an approaching vehicle caused her to sit up in her chair. She quickly recognized the familiar farm truck of Beau Lobaugh. He drove quickly down the dirt road with some sense of urgency, as he almost slid to a stop in front of the house.

"I made it!" Beau said, as he stepped out of the truck.

"Where have you been?" Naomi asked, as she looked past her own long shadow cast by the afternoon sun.

"Been to Oklahoma City for some business and went on over to Chandler to see an old army buddy of mine," Beau explained. "He asked me to go with him to Shawnee. They dedicated a new courthouse, and Governor Marland stopped by to give a speech. I didn't get back until an hour ago."

"Was Governor Marland's wife there?" Naomi asked.

"No," Beau grinned, "but I wish she had been. She's a mite prettier than the governor."

"A mite younger too," Naomi noted.

"Ya'll ready for the picnic?" Beau smiled, as he looked into the house for Raquel.

Naomi frowned, "We didn't think you were going to make it back. Your men said they didn't know either—and said sometimes you'd be gone for a while on your trips. Raquel's gone to the picnic with—Frank Sutton."

Beau Lobaugh did not show any emotion as he asked, "She went with Frank Sutton? I thought she was pretty upset with him a few days ago."

"I don't think Raquel has it in her to be upset," Naomi said. "Frank came by the next day to apologize and invited her to go."

Beau nodded, "I see. I—I guess that's a good thing."

"I don't know anymore," Naomi muttered.

Beau Lobaugh watched Naomi carefully and waited for her to say more.

Naomi finally huffed, "I thought Frankie would be good to Raquel—and good for Raquel, but now—"

"Has he done anything to her?" Beau asked pointedly.

"Frankie's not the problem," Naomi assured. "I think he really cares for her, but his mother and Beulah Belvedere—I don't see how they can keep from poisoning him against her, even if he might propose marriage."

"They're that serious?" Beau said with a slight sigh.

Beau looked away from Naomi and back toward his land on the other side of the river.

Naomi watched him for a moment and then asked, "What's going on, Beau Lobaugh?"

"What?" Beau turned around and responded. "Nothing's going on."

Naomi moved closer and said, "I've known you since before you had whiskers on your chin, and I knew you to be selfish and wild. Suddenly, I come back and you're giving away cows, paying rent on land you don't have any use for, and giving a cooking job to a girl that can barely scramble an egg."

"A man can change," Beau defended.

"That he can," Naomi agreed, "but I'm sensing something more. Do you have feelings for the girl?"

"You ought to know better than that, Naomi," an aggravated Beau muttered. "I needed someone for the house, and she's—she's a good influence on the men. I haven't had half the fights, and they're as polite as schoolboys in Sunday school when she's around."

"I see," Naomi said, while continuing to study the man. "What did happen to you, Beau?"

"What do you mean?" a frustrated Beau replied.

"What changed you?" Naomi clarified. "You still have that irritating veneer of self-importance, but you're not the boy I remember."

"I thought that would be a good thing in your mind," Beau huffed.

Naomi nodded and watched him for moment before saying, "Maylon was a fine young man. I'm starting to see where he got some of it."

"A man's more a product of his environment than his ancestry," Beau said. "Maylon was your boy, Naomi. You raised him. You and me haven't always seen eye to eye, but I always knew you would be a good mother. I never questioned your motives."

"I never questioned yours either, Beau," Naomi said. "That, I'm sure, you never knew."

Naomi watched the uneasy Beau for a moment and asked in a timid tone, "Are you ever going to let it go, Beau?"

"What?" he answered with a puzzled, tormented look.

"Ellen and little Mary," Naomi said softly. "It wasn't your fault."

Beau stood silently for a moment before groaning, "I know—I know in my mind that's true. In my heart I'm never so sure—but a heavy heart don't do nothing to bring 'em back."

Naomi nodded and sighed, "I'm having problems letting go, too. I lost Eli and the boys—I think I'd have gone crazy without Raquel stepping in to fill the void."

Beau's face twisted uncomfortably, as he said, "She's special—to you she's special. I can tell."

Naomi looked at him carefully and replied, "She is."

Naomi studied the man standing in front of her for a moment and said in a less serious tone, "Why don't you take an old woman to a picnic? Who knows—some 'do-si-dos' and 'swing your partner' might do us some good."

Beau smiled, "I've had a long day. I don't think I'd be great company."

"Why don't you let Raquel be the judge of that, Beau Lobaugh?" Naomi scolded.

"Naw," Beau sighed. "Frankie's a good sort in his own way. Besides, what interest would she have in an old codger like me?"

"You aren't that old," Naomi said, as she studied the man, "and Raquel's not that young. Why don't you let her decide what she's interested in?"

Beau grinned mischievously, "Not tonight. I got some business I still need to attend to in Oklahoma City. I'll let Frankie entertain her tonight."

"You're not driving back tonight?" Naomi replied.

Beau looked at the setting sun and said, "I'll head out early tomorrow morning. I better turn in. I'll be seeing you, Naomi."

Naomi watched Beau Lobaugh walk away slowly. He looked back toward town for a moment before getting in his truck to drive back to his lonely house across the river.

CHAPTER 64

Twilight still had a hint of indigo when the first of the rockets shot into the sky to the cheers of the crowd that had gathered for the Fourth of July celebration in Sayre. Frank Sutton stood closely to Raquel, and by the time the last climactic blast of fireworks exploded in the sky, the night was dark. The crowd applauded enthusiastically and began to disperse, as the older people and those with small children headed to their homes.

A string of lights now gleamed in the night sky in front of the courthouse. A wood platform that had been used earlier for games was transformed into a dance floor for couples wanting to socialize a little longer on the warm summer night.

"Let's go," Frank smiled, as he took Raquel by the hand and led her to where a fiddle player tuned his strings, while the caller tried to organize the gathering group.

Raquel had enjoyed her day, and now that the older citizens of the town were heading home, she felt confident that she would not have to confront Beulah Belvedere or Constance Sutton for the evening. Frank seemed to know almost everyone, as he greeted people with a pleasant smile and usually with some clever quip. A tall man in bib overalls caught Raquel's attention, and she let go of Frank's hand for a moment and walked toward the man.

"Elmer?" Raquel greeted.

Elmer turned around to see Raquel walking toward him and said, "Good evenin' Miss Raquel. Are you coming to the dance?"

Raquel looked back at Frank Sutton, who was engaged in conversation with a young couple and said to Elmer, "Yes."

"Been a full day, ain't it?" Elmer said.

Raquel smiled, "It has. Has Mr. Lobaugh made it back?"

"No," Elmer said. "I wouldn't worry none. The captain's likely to be gone several days when the harvesting and planting ain't in full swing."

"I know," Raquel stammered. "I was just wondering if I needed to come clean tomorrow."

"I ain't seen him," Elmer shrugged.

"Elmer!" a healthy-sized woman yelled from near the dance floor. "They're about to start!"

Elmer blushed, "Excuse me, Miss Raquel. Nadine's ready to get to the dancin'—and—I promised to be her partner."

Elmer took a flask out of his overall's pocket and quickly took a swig.

"It ain't real liquor," Elmer blushed. "Just a little something me and the boys distilled from some corn."

Elmer hesitated a second and added, "You won't tell the captain you seen me here, will you?"

"Your secret's safe with me," Raquel smiled, as Elmer sauntered off to meet his partner.

"They're about to start!" Frank shouted from the edge of the dance floor.

Raquel nodded and walked to meet him. Frank still talked to the young couple as Raquel nervously approached.

"Raquel, I'd like you to meet Dale and Denise Baker," Frank smiled. "Denise and I graduated together in Elk City."

"Good to meet you," Raquel replied.

The couple smiled and returned her greeting.

"Dale's a lawyer here in Sayre," Frank explained. "He started his practice last year."

"Sayre's a little smaller than Elk City," Denise explained cheerfully, "but we've been able to keep entertained."

"I bet you have," Frank teased, as he gently nudged a grinning Dale.

"Let's go couples!" a loud man commanded from the wood platform, as partners joined hands in a circle.

"We've missed the first dance," Frank said, as he reached out and put his arm around Raquel.

"That's okay," Raquel smiled. "I'd rather just watch."

"You square dance don't you?" Denise asked.

Raquel shook her head.

"You should try it," Denise said. "It's fun—it's not like real dancing, if you're Baptist or something."

"I wouldn't know how," Raquel replied.

"Just watch and see how they follow the caller's directions," Denise coached.

Raquel nodded politely and Frank said, "Dale, let's see if we can find some refreshments for these ladies. We've missed this first go-round."

"Sure," Dale said, and the two men left Raquel and Denise at the side of the dance floor to watch the couples start their dance.

"Allemande left!" the caller shouted, as the fiddle player started his tune.

Raquel watched as the people standing in the square faced each other to grasp hands and slowly turned to the left.

"Now allemande right!" the caller commanded.

The partners repeated the simple move to their right.

Raquel watched carefully as the caller then shouted, "Swing your partner right, then left, and do-si-do."

This command set off a flurry of motion that Raquel did not understand, although she was fascinated by the coordinated orchestration of the group following the caller's instructions.

"It's not as hard as it looks," Denise smiled. "Once you know the calls, you just follow directions."

"I think I'll just watch tonight," Raquel said.

"You're a lucky girl," Denise said pleasantly.

Raquel turned from watching the dancers to focus her attention on Denise.

"Frank's a really nice guy," Denise continued.

"You've known him for a while then?" Raquel asked.

"Ever since grammar school," Denise replied. "Frankie used to tease me in school and put frogs and lizards in my desk."

"I have a hard time seeing Frank doing that," Raquel said.

"He was just a boy," Denise said. "He was ornery like all little boys are, I suppose. But his mother kept on him, and he never got out of line much."

"I met his mother," Raquel frowned.

"She's a pill," Denise said. "Half the women in Elk City are scared of her."

"I can see why," Raquel admitted.

"It didn't hurt Frankie, though," Denise said. "He was always the most popular boy in school. All the girls wanted him to be their boy."

"Including you?" Raquel asked.

"Oh, no," Denise said. "We knew each other too well and—"

Denise caught herself saying too much, but Raquel stood silently waiting for her to finish.

Denise sighed and continued, "Frankie always had a girl."

"Really," Raquel said, as she turned back to watch the dancers shuffle across the floor to the chaotic chants of the caller.

"Frankie had a girl, but that was in school," Denise confessed. "Mary Wareham was always the prettiest girl in school, and well, Frankie was always the most handsome. I guess it made sense they would be a couple. Frankie's mother was friends with Mrs. Wareham, and they were—engaged until last year."

"Engaged?" Raquel said, as she turned to face the woman.

Denise blushed, "I'm sorry, I thought you knew."

"Oh, no," Raquel stammered. "That's fine—I'm new to town and—don't really know much about what goes on around here."

"I don't know the details," Denise said softly, almost in a whisper, "but Frankie moved over here to manage his father's bank. Mary went away for a while, but she's back in Elk City now, I hear. You don't have to worry, that's all behind Frankie now."

"Here we go," Frank smiled, as he approached carrying two drinks followed by Dale. "Don't worry, I've already tasted it, and there's nothing but pure punch in it."

"Thank you," Raquel said, as she took the drink.

"What have you girls been gossiping about?" Dale asked, as he handed his wife her drink.

Denise blushed, but Raquel said, "Denise has been coaching me on how a square dance works."

"Are you ready to give it a try?" Frank said in a playful tone.

"I don't think so," Raquel said, shaking her head. "I wouldn't know a do-si-do from a sashay."

"You can't learn if you don't try," Frank prodded.

"Some other night," Raquel said.

Frank shrugged and turned to Denise to ask, "How about you?" Frank then looked at Dale and said, "You don't mind if I guide your wife around the dance floor, do you?"

Dale laughed, "That'd keep me from embarrassing myself."

"What do you say, partner?" Frank asked. "Want to give it a whirl?"

Denise smiled and took Frank's outstretched hand to accept, saying, "If you can keep up."

Dale and Raquel stood leaning against a wood rail as the new couples lined up for the next dance, while several of the couples that had been dancing retired to the sidelines. Raquel smiled to see Elmer being dragged by the larger Nadine to the square. The fiddle player started a lively tune, and the caller barked out his first instructions, as the dancers started to move. Raquel almost laughed to see how effortlessly the gawky Elmer glided around the dance floor with the more plodding Nadine at his side. Denise smiled playfully as Frank guided her smoothly through the calls. Raquel could not contain a giggle, when Nadine turned the wrong way and caused Elmer and Frank to temporarily become partners.

"Frank seems to be a great guy," Dale said, as he watched his wife on the dance floor.

"How long have you two been married?" Raquel asked.

Dale gleamed, "We'll have our second anniversary this December. How long have you and Frank been a couple?"

"Oh," Raquel said hastily. "I don't think you could call us a couple. We've only known each other a few weeks. I just moved to town."

"Really?" Dale smiled. "The way you two look, I'd thought you'd been together awhile. Where'd you move from?"

"California," Raquel replied, "close to Bakersfield."

"I've never been there," Dale confessed. "Is it nice?"

Raquel thought for a moment and said, "I guess."

"What brought you out here?" Dale asked.

"I came with my mother-in-law," Raquel said. "She has a place close to town near the river."

"You're married?" Dale asked with a raised eyebrow.

Raquel frowned and said softly, "I'm widowed. My husband was killed in a car accident back in California. That's the real reason we're here."

"I'm sorry," Dale apologized. "I'm sorry for your loss, and I'm sorry for being so nosey."

"You couldn't have known," Raquel said. "It's fine."

Dale awkwardly tried to keep the conversation going and said, "You must live close to Mr. Lobaugh."

Raquel turned to look at the young attorney and asked, "You know Mr. Lobaugh?"

"Yes," Dale said. "He's a client."

"Is Mr. Lobaugh in any trouble?" Raquel asked.

"I can't talk about a client or their business," Dale informed.

Raquel looked at the young lawyer for a second, but she did not press the point.

Dale smiled slyly, and after looking around to see that they were alone, he whispered, "Mr. Lobaugh's not in any kind of trouble."

"That's good to know," Raquel said. "I work for him, and I'd hate to see him in jail."

Dale laughed, "Not all law is about keeping people out of jail."

Raquel looked at him a moment and said, "What kind of law do you do, Mr. Baker?"

"In a town this size, all kinds," Dale explained. "I prefer contracts, but a young lawyer can't be too picky."

"What if someone killed someone accidently?" Raquel asked.

"Are we talking hypothetically, or do you need to confess," Dale playfully teased.

"Oh, I'm just always interested in those detective stories and all," Raquel explained.

"Well," Dale said, as he thought. "It depends on a lot of factors. If it was truly an accident, a person is held harmless. Of course, if the person was negligent, that could change things. Manslaughter's a possibility."

"Is manslaughter bad?" Raquel asked.

"Can be," Dale said. "We're just talking hypothetically still?"

"Of course," Raquel said. "What about self-defense?"

Dale frowned, "Self-defense can be used as a defense, but it's not as common as you find in the novels. It can be hard to prove. The main thing is you'd want to show there was no prior intent to do harm—no premeditation. That moves it to a homicide, and that's when they'll strap a fellow into the chair."

Raquel thought for a moment and then asked, "I heard that if something happens in one state it doesn't carry over to another."

"A crime is usually a crime," Dale said. "Especially when it's a capital crime—but the law usually has enough to worry about in their own jurisdiction, and they don't spend much time on other people's problems, unless there's a threat."

"I see," Raquel said, as she thought.

"The law's complicated, and like I said, the devil's in the details," Dale smirked.

The dancers still sashayed around the floor, as Raquel turned back to watch them.

"Speaking of your neighbor," Dale interjected, "isn't that Mr. Lobaugh over there?"

Dale motioned to a dark spot across the dance floor where Beau Lobaugh stood alone watching the dancers. Raquel made immediate eye-contact with him, and Beau seemed surprised to be detected. He turned to leave, as Raquel excused herself and headed after him. By the time she made it to the other side, he had vanished into the night. She walked away from the lighted dance floor and toward an area where cars were parked. Beau Lobaugh drove away in his truck before she could catch him. Raquel looked into the night wondering why he had left so abruptly.

Raquel turned to walk back to the dance, when a voice in the darkness said, "Hello, darling."

Raquel was startled by the voice, but she froze in terror, as Ned Farrell stepped out of the shadows to face her.

"What are you doing here?" she asked nervously.

"I didn't come for the party," Ned said, as he spit on the ground and walked closer to her.

"Leave me alone," Raquel warned.

"I'm not goin' to hurt you," the man calmly assured. "I just came for a little reward."

"What reward?" Raquel asked.

"There's a reward for the murderer of Jack Fisk," Ned smiled evilly.

"That was no murder," Raquel defended.

Ned was unfazed as he said, "There's a dead man with a knife in his back in Albuquerque's all I know. A witness said he saw a woman stick it into him while her accomplice was robbing him."

"That's a lie," Raquel sneered.

Ned laughed, "Problem is, the police only got one witness. The others ran with their tails between their legs—not very becoming, and it don't look too good for the ones that ran. The going rate for reward money for a murder is a thousand dollars. It'd cause me a lot of trouble to have to drag the law into this. I'll be the first to admit that Jack's persona was not too noble. I'd just as soon get the money from the woman with the ranch south of town—the woman that put that knife in my friend's back—than get it from the police in Albuquerque. You ladies pay me my thousand dollars, and I'll be on my way out of town and out of your life."

"We don't have that kind of money," Raquel pleaded.

Ned Farrell's nostrils flared angrily and he said, "You've got land. You've got to have something. Besides, I've been watching you with your rich banker friend tonight. You've got a spell cast on him for sure, but he don't seem like the kind of man that would want a felon for a girlfriend."

"Raquel?" Frank Sutton shouted from near the dance floor.

Raquel waved nervously and turned to Ned Farrell to say, "I've got to go."

When she started to walk away, Ned roughly grabbed her arm and said, "You tell that old woman to get my money in three days, or she'll be fryin' in the electric chair in New Mexico."

"Is that man bothering you?" Frank asked urgently, as he walked quickly toward them.

Ned watched the approaching man and said, "Three days," before slipping back into the darkness.

"Are you okay?" Frank asked, as he stepped up to Raquel.

"I'm fine," Raquel said.

"Who was that man?" Frank asked.

Raquel looked into the dark shadows and said, "No one. Could you take me home now, Frank? I'm tired."

"Sure," Frank said, as he looked to see if the man were lurking near.

Frank took Raquel by the arm and walked her to the car. The fiddler still played in the background, and she could hear the caller shouting his instructions to the jubilant dancers in the distance, but the sounds seemed surreal to her. She talked to Frank on the short drive back to her house, but she could not remember what they said. Raquel abruptly said goodnight to her escort and walked quickly to the dark house. She opened the door, and Frank drove away. Raquel sighed deeply and sniffled slightly, as she stepped into the dark front room.

CHAPTER 65

Naomi slept peacefully in the next room, until Raquel urgently shook her shoulder to awaken her.

"What—what is it?" Naomi asked from her sleepy stupor.

"We have problems," Raquel worriedly informed.

"We always have problems," Naomi muttered, as she sat up in the bed. "What's broke this time?"

"I saw Ned Farrell in town," Raquel stated.

"What?" a suddenly alert Naomi whimpered.

"In town, not half an hour ago," Raquel confirmed.

"What's he doing here?" a flustered Naomi asked, as she searched for her clothes, while Raquel trimmed the oil lamp.

"He wants one thousand dollars," Raquel informed. "He says that's the reward for us, and he'd forget the whole thing if we pay him."

"A thousand dollars!" Naomi exclaimed. "It might as well be a million."

"Frank introduced me to a friend of his that's a lawyer," Raquel said. "Maybe we should talk to him."

"No," Naomi pleaded. "Frank can't know—no one in town can know."

"What are we going to do?" Raquel asked worriedly.

Naomi thought for a moment and said, "First, we're not doing anything. You're not involved. It was me. It's my problem."

"It's your problem because you were protecting me," Raquel cried.

"Don't worry about that," Naomi reasoned. "I'm an old woman—there's no sense ruining your life."

"Beau would help," Raquel said. "He's back in town."

"How'd you know?" Naomi asked.

"I saw him tonight," Raquel explained. "He was at the square dance."

"The square dance?" Naomi said with a raised eyebrow.

Raquel nodded.

"Beau could help," Naomi said softly, almost as if she were talking to herself. "He's not connected to the town, and he's—discreet."

"I know he'll help," Raquel said. "He'll know what to do."

The women tried to sleep that night, but Raquel found herself acutely aware of any sound from outside the house. She barred the door, but went to look out the window several times during the night. At first light she was prepared to walk to Beau Lobaugh's house. Naomi had wanted to go with her, but she took a little longer to get ready, and she walked much slower than Raquel. It was almost eight o'clock before they were on the porch of Beau's house.

Raquel walked in without knocking, since most mornings Beau was already giving instructions to his men and left the house open for her.

"Mr. Lobaugh," Raquel greeted, as she stepped into the empty house.

"Beau!" Naomi shouted with more urgency.

"He's not here," Raquel said. "He'll be in the barn."

Raquel went out the back kitchen door and walked quickly to the barn while Naomi trailed behind.

Raquel did not see Beau immediately, but nearly ran over Elmer on her way into the barn.

"Where's Mr. Lobaugh?" Raquel asked the sleepy-looking Elmer.

Elmer rubbed his eyes and said, "The captain left before sun-up. Had business in Oklahoma City I think."

"When did he leave?" Naomi demanded.

Elmer scratched behind his ear and said, "Sun-up, I said—an hour—an hour and a half ago. He wanted me to go with him, but I wasn't in any shape to drive that far. He's halfway there by now."

"When will he be back?" Raquel asked in a calmer voice than Naomi used.

"I don't know, Miss Raquel," Elmer said. "A day or two maybe—maybe more."

Raquel looked at Naomi and could see the anxiety in her eyes at the delay.

"It'll be okay," Raquel tried to assure.

Elmer looked at the two women and said, "Is everything okay with you ladies?"

"Yes," Raquel lied.

"Would you like a ride back to the house?" Elmer offered. "There's only me and one other guy here today so there's no need for you to cook."

"Didn't Mr. Lobaugh take the truck?" Raquel asked.

"He took the old Ford and left his good truck here," Elmer explained. "He won't mind."

"Thank you," Raquel said.

The women rode with Elmer back to the house without saying a word. Elmer looked at Raquel a couple of times and sensed something was amiss, but he did not bother her with questions.

"What are we going to do now?" Naomi fussed, when Elmer pulled out of the drive.

Raquel thought for a moment and replied, "Ned Farrell said he'd give us three days. That should give us enough time for Beau to get back."

Naomi nodded nervously, "Maybe."

The two women tried to busy themselves with repairs to the house, but the distraction of Ned Farrell being near and the oppressive heat kept them from accomplishing much. By the time the afternoon sun began to get lower in the sky, the air was still stifling hot, as Naomi prepared a simple meal of tomatoes and okra. Raquel helped Naomi clean up, when the sound of a car coming down the road caused both to stop what they were doing and to listen anxiously.

Raquel stepped to the window to look out and said, "It's Frank."

"Thank goodness," Naomi sighed. "Don't tell him anything."

Raquel agreed and went to the porch to meet Frank.

"Hello, Frank," she greeted, as he stepped out the door.

Frank nodded, but looked grim and serious.

"Is everything okay?" Raquel asked, as he walked slowly to the door.

"Is Naomi around?" he asked.

"She's inside," Raquel replied nervously. "Do I need to get her?"

"No," Frank said meekly. "I wanted to talk to you—alone."

"We can talk here," Raquel said, as she looked around to see that Naomi was not in the front room.

Frank took her gently by the arm and moved her away from the house and toward the well a few yards away.

"What's wrong, Frank?" Raquel asked, although she thought she knew the answer.

Frank walked around the well for a moment as if searching for what to say.

"Last night," he began.

"Listen," Raquel interrupted. "I can explain. I didn't want you to get involved, but it's really not Naomi's fault."

"Of course not," Frank said with a puzzled expression. "It's not Naomi's fault in the least—it's—it's all my fault."

"I'm confused," Raquel admitted. "Didn't you want to talk about what happened last night?"

"Of course," Frank said with a hint of impatience in his voice. "I talked to Denise this morning, and she told me about your conversation."

"Yes," Raquel said, trying to remember the details.

"She told you about Mary," Frank prompted.

"Your old girl friend?"

"Yes."

Raquel watched Frank nervously pace around for a few moments. He wanted to say something, but the naturally calm and poised Frank seemed timid and uneasy.

"She's not your *old* girlfriend, is she Frank?" Raquel deduced.

"No," Frank fretted.

"Denise told me she was nice."

"I feel terrible," Frank said. "We had a fight, and she went away to school for a while. I thought I had gotten over her, but—when I went to Elk City last week, she was back in town."

"You don't need to feel badly."

"I haven't been honest with you," Frank said. "I've spent all my time out here this summer, and I probably sent some signals that—could be misread. And my mother—"

Raquel walked around to where she could see Frank's face and said softly, "It's okay, Frank."

"It's not okay," Frank frowned. "I really do like you, but I've—I've known Mary since I was a kid. You'll think it's my mother. That's why I tried to forget Mary. Last night, I tried to start new with you, but—I realized I was trying to prove my mother wrong more than I was trying to forget Mary."

"Frank," Raquel said uneasily. "You don't understand. It's *really* okay. I—I don't feel that way about you either."

A bewildered Frank looked at her a moment before saying, "Really?"

"I like you," Raquel said. "I like you a lot, Frank, but—a lot of things have happened in my life lately. You've been wonderfully kind to me."

Frank looked baffled and stammered, "But Naomi told me—"

"Naomi thinks she has to take care of me," Raquel explained. "But it's okay—I like the fact that she wants to take care of me. I'm a big girl, but Naomi likes to mother—and I don't mind. I do like you, Frank. Can we still be friends?"

Frank nodded, "I'd like that. I'd like that a lot."

Raquel stepped to Frank and gave him a hug, and she could feel his sense of relief in the relaxed way he held her.

"Will you be moving back to Elk City?" Raquel asked.

Frank shook his head, "Not if Mary will marry me and move here."

He stepped away from Raquel and grinned, "Would you want to live in the same town with my mother?"

Raquel laughed out loud at Frank's disrespectful comment about his pretentious mother.

"Raquel!" Naomi shouted from the porch. "A car's coming!"

Raquel ran to the house followed by a confused Frank. A black car raced down the dirt road stirring a massive cloud of dust in its wake.

"Do you recognize the car?" Naomi nervously asked.

"No," Raquel answered.

"I do," Frank sighed. "It's my father."

The car continued up the road before turning wildly into the drive.

"Let me handle this," Frank said.

Before Frank could get off the porch and approach the car, the passenger door swung open as Constance Sutton barreled angrily out of the car.

"I told you he would be here!" Constance charged, as a slightly overweight and balding man stepped out of the driver's side door.

The stern and distinguished-looking man had an authoritative manner, and he looked displeased as he followed his wife.

"I told you he would be with that girl!" Constance continued.

Naomi stepped in front of Frank and said, "Hello, Richard—Constance. Welcome to my home."

"Don't play innocent, Naomi Butler," Constance Sutton quipped.

Before his wife could say more, Richard Sutton took control of the conversation and said, "Hello, Naomi. I need to talk to my son."

Naomi did not challenge the commanding man, but nodded her approval.

Constance said in her cackling voice, "I told you—"

"Shut up, Constance!" Richard Sutton roared. "I'll handle this now."

Richard Sutton sneered at his wife and took a second to look at Raquel before saying, "Let me spell this out for you, Frankie. You have an important choice to make. You can quit seeing this girl and enjoy your job and your life, or you can run off and do what your heart tells you and get a job digging ditches. You'll have no part in my enterprises, if you run off with this girl. With your skill set and this economy, you might do well to live in a place like this."

Richard Sutton looked at the rundown farmhouse with some contempt and waited for his son's response.

"This girl will be the ruin of you!" Constance cried harshly.

"Be quiet mother!" Frank curtly demanded.

Constance was surprised at her son's assertiveness, but she did not challenge him.

Frank looked at his father and said, "If you think I manage your affairs poorly, I'd expect you to fire me, Father. But I'm a grown man, and you cannot run my life anymore. I'm prepared to make it on my own."

Richard Sutton's neck turned red, and he started to respond to his son when Raquel stepped in to say, "This isn't necessary, Mr. Sutton. Frank and I—"

Frank interrupted Raquel and said, "Raquel was just telling me that she was breaking up with me, when you two stormed in."

"What!" Naomi and Constance shrieked in unison.

Richard Sutton looked at the young woman and then examined his son.

"That's right," Frank said. "Your paranoia about my life was a wasted effort. We're not a couple."

Richard shifted nervously before saying awkwardly, "Let's go Constance."

"I think you owe Raquel an apology, Mother," Frank said.

Constance hesitated long enough for Frank to say, "Apologize, Mother."

"Constance, what did you do?" Richard said angrily.

"Nothing," Constance said.

"Mother!" Frank warned.

Constance said in a timid tone, "I may have said some things."

Richard looked disapprovingly at his wife and turned to Raquel to say, "Young lady, I'm sure my wife has insulted you in every way, but you'll have to excuse her condescension and poor manners—mine, too."

Raquel looked at the Frank's parents with quiet dignity and nodded her acceptance.

"Constance, we have a long drive back to Elk City," Richard Sutton said. "Say you're sorry and get in the car."

Constance's face twisted bitterly, but she muttered, "I'm sorry," before returning to the car.

Richard Sutton walked to his car and turned to say, "Good evening, ladies—Frankie, we'll see you Sunday for lunch?"

"Yes, Dad," Frank said.

The Suttons drove away with nearly as much haste, as when they arrived.

"Sorry about that," Frank said when his parents had left.

"You broke up with Frankie?" Naomi said with a wrinkled forehead.

Raquel looked at Frank and said, "It was mutual. We were never really together."

"We're still friends," Frank offered.

Naomi looked at the two young people and said, "It's good to have friends, and you've been a good one to us Frank. Thank you."

Frank nodded, "I guess, I need to be going."

"Frank," Raquel said, as he started to walk away.

"Yes," he smiled.

"Could I ask a favor?"

"Anything."

"Could you set up a meeting with your friend Dale?"

"Yes," Frank said. "Is everything okay?"

"Yes," Raquel said with superficial confidence. "Naomi just has some questions about the deed to this place."

Frank looked at Naomi and then back to Raquel and said, "I'll set up a meeting for Monday."

"Thank you, Frank," Raquel smiled.

Frank drove off in his gray car. Raquel had mixed feelings about his exit. She had enjoyed Frank's company during her first weeks in her new home, but Naomi had always been more excited about their relationship than she had been. Still, Raquel knew she would miss their walks by the river in the cool of the evenings.

Naomi watched her daughter-in-law as Frank drove away and said, "Are you okay?"

"Yes."

"You want to talk about it?"

"I'm fine," Raquel said. "It just wasn't right—for me or Frank."

Naomi did not press for more details.

"Frank's setting up a meeting with your lawyer friend for Monday," Naomi said. "You said Ned would be here Sunday?"

Raquel watched the final puff of dust disappear from the tail end of Frank's car and said, "Let's hope Beau's back by then."

Naomi listened to Raquel's confident tone, but she wondered if Beau Lobaugh could or would help.

CHAPTER 66

Raquel woke before dawn the next morning. She had not rested well, thinking of Ned Farrell's threats. Naomi slept in the next room as Raquel slipped on her clothes. She stepped outside and felt the warm, pleasant pre-dawn breeze flow across her neck. A thin crescent moon faintly glowed on the stark landscape. She decided to pump some cool water from the well to splash on her face. As she looked across the river, she could barely make out the outline of Beau Lobaugh's house in the distance. The dark house looked lonely and hopeless. Raquel remembered how fearful she had been of the man only a few weeks earlier, but now she believed he might be their only hope.

Raquel took a deep breath after rinsing her face and walked slowly back to her bed, to wait the few hours until morning. When she awoke, the sun was already beaming through the eastern window, and she was surprised how late it had gotten in the morning. She rubbed her tired eyes and found Naomi sitting on the porch, enjoying the cool of the morning, but watching the road coming from town cautiously.

"Good morning," Raquel said. "I overslept."

"I thought you needed your rest, so I tried to be quiet and let you sleep this morning," Naomi said.

"Any sign of Beau?"

"No."

"How long have you been up?"

"A little before dawn and a little after you came back to bed last night," Naomi replied.

"Sorry, I woke you," Raquel apologized.

"You didn't," Naomi claimed. "I didn't sleep much last night."

"Me either, until morning," Raquel said.

Raquel stretched and yawned before asking, "Will you be okay here by yourself for a while?"

"Yes," Naomi said. "Where are you going?"

"I thought I'd walk to Beau's this morning," Raquel explained.

"It's Saturday, and Beau's not back," Naomi frowned.

"I know," Raquel said, "but Elmer might have heard something, and—I might ask him to come check on us tomorrow, if Beau doesn't make it home."

"Okay," Naomi said. "I'll be fine."

Raquel kissed her mother-in-law on the cheek and walked quickly to the river. The shallow stream had dried to nearly a trickle in the hot weather, and she easily jumped the narrow expanse without getting her shoes wet. The fields were bare dirt, and the men had just started tilling for the next planting. Raquel walked steadily toward the house, until she was about a quarter of a mile away. When she saw Beau Lobaugh's old truck parked beside the house, Raquel sprinted with all her might across the dusty field toward the house.

As she burst through the front gate to the yard, she yelled, "Beau!"

The house looked quiet and empty, so she decided to head to the barn. She was out of breath and sweat glistened off her forehead as she frantically searched for signs of Beau Lobaugh.

"Raquel?" Beau greeted from behind her.

Raquel stopped immediately and turned to face him standing on the porch wearing his trousers and an undershirt.

"You're here!" Raquel cried, as she ran to him and grabbed his arm firmly.

"Of course I am," Beau calmly replied. "What are you doing here on a Saturday?"

Raquel breathed heavily as she struggled to say, "We need your help, Beau. Something terrible has happened."

Beau Lobaugh's demeanor immediately changed as he asked in a commanding voice, "What's happened?"

Raquel tried to talk, but her emotions overwhelmed her as she broke down in tears.

Beau let her cry into his shoulder for a moment before saying, "Sit down and catch your breath. I'll get some water."

In a moment, he returned with a glass of water, which he handed Raquel.

As he pulled on a shirt to button he asked, "Tell me what all this fuss is about."

"We've had trouble," Raquel said vaguely.

Beau straightened up and asked, "What kind of trouble? Is Naomi hurt or sick? Are you okay?"

"Naomi's fine," Raquel said. "We had trouble with a man in town."

Beau looked sternly at her and said, "I would have thought Frank Sutton would have been better help. He knows this town better than me, and he's obviously taken an interest in you."

"Frank's—Frank's just a friend of mine," Raquel explained. "This isn't something he could help with. It's something that happened in New Mexico—on our trip here. Could you please come and help, Mr. Lobaugh?"

"Let's go," he said in a non-emotional tone.

Beau Lobaugh had not known Raquel Butler long, but he had never seen her like she was in his truck on the way to Naomi's house. She had always been pleasant and shy, but had never seemed as anxious as she did this morning.

"About the other night at the picnic," Beau said. "I didn't mean—I mean—I don't know why I was even there. If there's anything I've done to offend Frank—or you—I'll try to—make things right."

"Frank and I had a talk yesterday," Raquel said. "He's got a girl in Elk City, and I'm fine with that. Frank and I are just friends. But when I saw you that night—I went after you—to see where you might have gone. That's when I ran into that despicable man."

"What man?" Beau asked.

"Ned Farrell," Raquel said with a worried look on her face.

Beau Lobaugh stopped the truck in the middle of the field and asked bluntly, "Who's Ned Farrell?" Before Raquel could answer, Beau said, "I think it's time you told me everything."

Raquel took a deep breath before starting, "When Chili and Maylon died, we didn't have any money except the little Orpha made at the drugstore. I had made some money in the past cleaning clothes, but when Chili got blacklisted, that included me. We scraped by as best we could. Naomi had never had to worry much about money, but I—I knew how much worse things could get. In the end, we sold everything, and all we had left was this place. We pulled our money together for a bus trip out here. Orpha had some family, so she stayed behind. I had no one, but Naomi, so I came with her."

Raquel sighed and continued, "We met a man on the bus. Naomi bragged and exaggerated about this place to him. He turned out to be a swindler. He tricked us out of all our money. We tried to hitch a ride as far as Gallup, New Mexico, but ran into the man again. In the end, we were reduced to living off the charity of a group of hobos who taught us how to beg for food and hop rides on the train."

Beau Lobaugh looked intently at Raquel's pained and worried face without judgment.

She continued, "Naomi wasn't cut out for that kind of life, but she managed. We cut my hair off short so I'd look more like a boy. They thought that might make things simpler."

Beau smiled for the first time that morning, which caused the anxious Raquel to ask curtly, "What's so funny?"

"Nothing," Beau replied, as his smile quickly disappeared. "It just explains a lot about your hair—I've always wondered."

Raquel ignored the reference to her hair and continued, "With some help, we finally caught a ride and got to Albuquerque, where Naomi and I got arrested for vagrancy and spent the night in jail."

Beau Lobaugh could not contain his smile anymore as he asked in an impish tone, "Naomi Butler spent a night in jail—for vagrancy?"

"Please don't tell anyone, Beau," Raquel pleaded. "That's not what our trouble's about—and it would kill Naomi to find out anyone knew."

Beau nodded, "Not a word. I promise."

"Anyway," Raquel continued, "Naomi finally decided to wire for some money from her 'friend' Beulah Belvedere for bus fare. The problem is Beulah never wired the money. We were headed to the women's shelter for the night when—"

Raquel stopped talking and looked pathetically at Beau Lobaugh while trying to work up the courage to tell the rest of the story.

Finally she said in a soft and detached voice, "On the way to the shelter, we ran into the swindler again. A man named Jack Fisk. By that time, we had nothing else he wanted—besides me. He tried to pull me into the alley to—"

Raquel cried softly and could not speak for a moment.

Beau handed her a handkerchief and asked, in a gentle tone, "Are you all right? Did he—did he hurt you?"

The tearful Raquel shook her head, "I fought him. He was strong though and was pushing me to the alley, when Naomi stabbed him in the back with a knife."

Raquel could not continue, as she leaned over and buried her head in Beau Lobaugh's stiff shoulder.

"There, there," Beau tried to console. "It was self-defense. Any judge would see it that way. The important thing is that Naomi protected you."

"I know," Raquel sobbed, "and now she's willing to go to the electric chair in New Mexico for me."

"That won't happen," Beau tried to assure. "It was self-defense."

"It was," Raquel wept, "but Jack Fisk had a partner who saw us—Ned Farrell. He claimed Naomi had murdered his friend in cold blood and that I was robbing him. He was the only witness besides me. He said it would be my word against his. Naomi and I had been arrested the night before. We panicked and decided to run—decided to get across the state line as fast as we could. That's how we got here with nothing, and then this house was wrecked. If you hadn't taken care of us in your own way—and don't think I don't know that you've been taking care of us—we would have been ruined."

"It was clearly self defense," Beau said. "No law's going to come into Oklahoma for a couple of women involved in an incident in New Mexico."

"Last night—last night when you saw me," Raquel said. "I met some friends of Frank's—an attorney. I asked him some questions, and he said we could be convicted if the law in New Mexico knew we were here. I found out Frank has a girl back in Elk City, and then I saw you."

"I'm sorry about Frank," Beau apologized.

"Don't be," Raquel interrupted. "I'm happy for Frank. I didn't have feelings for him—not real feelings. But when I saw you—What *were* you doing there, Beau?"

Beau Lobaugh looked stunned by the question and stammered for an answer before finally saying, "I—I thought I'd see what was going on at the dance—thought I'd check and see if you were okay."

Raquel smiled slightly, "I went to say hello, but you were gone. That's when I ran into Ned Farrell."

"Last night!" Beau said with a renewed sense of urgency. "Here in Sayre?"

Raquel nodded, "He followed us here, because he said there was a reward for us back in New Mexico for a thousand dollars. He said if we would pay, he'd forget about it. We don't have a thousand dollars, and you're the only one we know that might have that kind of money—that'd show an inclination to help us."

Beau started the truck as it coughed to life and said firmly, "He's blackmailing you, and blackmailers are dangerous. We need to get to Naomi right now!"

CHAPTER 67

Beau Lobaugh drove wildly on the short trip from the field to Naomi's house. Raquel for some reason felt better after confessing their story to him. Raquel looked over at the determined man and believed he would know what to do. Naomi watched nervously from the porch, as Beau slid to a stop in front.

"Beau we're in a terrible mess," Naomi babbled in a frenzy of worried chatter.

"Raquel's told me," Beau said, as he walked toward her. "Has he been here?"

"No," Naomi said.

"Let's get inside," Beau suggested.

"Did she tell you everything?" a nervous Naomi asked.

Beau looked at Raquel and diplomatically said, "Enough to know you're being blackmailed."

"So you'll help us?" Naomi asked hopefully.

"Yes," Beau said.

"You'll give us the money to pay him?" Naomi gleefully said.

"No," Beau replied, shaking his head.

Naomi looked confused as Beau explained, "If you pay a blackmailer, he'll keep coming back again and again. Every time you pay, it makes you look guilty and gives him more control. We'll get to an attorney Monday morning."

"Frank's already agreed to set up a meeting," Raquel interjected.

Beau looked at Raquel, "Then your friend Frank Sutton's not as stupid or useless as I imagined. The next thing we've got to do is to move the both of you to my house. I have plenty of room and should have insisted on it from your first day here."

A frightened Naomi nodded her head in agreement.

"I'm going into town and alert the sheriff to watch out for this character," Beau said. "You two pack up some things, and I'll be back for you. I'll stop by the house and have Elmer come down here until I get back."

Beau Lobaugh drove off with an efficient sense of urgency, as the women quickly prepared for the short trip to Beau's house. It did not take Raquel long to pack her few possessions. She went out to the porch to enjoy the breeze, as the morning was already starting to make the house stuffy. Raquel felt at ease for the first time since meeting Ned Farrell in Sayre and knew Beau had the means and the temperament to handle the situation. Raquel's sense of safety evaporated immediately when she spotted a lone man walking slowly toward the house.

"Lock the doors!" Raquel shouted to Naomi, as she ran into the house. "Someone's coming."

"Oh, my!" Naomi panicked, as she bolted the doors.

Raquel quickly went to the window to watch the man's progress. Naomi nudged her to make room at the window, and the two women watched the man together. It took Raquel a moment to recognize the lazy, long-legged gate.

"That's not Ned Farrell," Naomi said in almost a whisper.

Naomi went to the door without saying more and stepped to the porch to get a better look at the approaching man. Raquel quickly joined her and strained to see the man's face.

In a more animated voice, a suddenly energized Naomi repeated, "That's not Ned Farrell at all!"

Raquel said in disbelief, "It's Hank!"

"Yes it is!" Naomi said, as she walked quickly to greet the long-legged Hank Tilley.

Raquel followed Naomi, but she had a hard time matching the older woman's pace.

"Mr. Tilley!" Naomi cried out.

Hank Tilley heard the greeting and raised his arm to wave.

Naomi turned to Raquel and beamed, "It's Mr. Tilley!"

Naomi stopped at the front gate and waited for Hank Tilley to approach before asking with a big smile, "What on earth are you doing here, Mr. Tilley?"

Hank walked up to the two women and tipped his hat. He was clean shaven, which they had never seen, and he appeared to have a fresh suit of clothes.

"Hello," Hank greeted with a smile.

"Mr. Tilley," Naomi said cheerfully. "I don't know if I've ever been more surprised than now to see someone. What are you doing here and in the heat of the day?"

"I came to bring you some money," Hank Tilley explained.

"Money?" Naomi replied.

"You were having some money wired to you in Albuquerque when you took off," Hank explained. "I used a little of it to buy a new suit of clothes, but I've got the rest for you."

Hank Tilley reached into his pocket and handed Naomi some money. Naomi took the money and stared at it for a moment.

"You came all this way to return some money?" Naomi quizzed.

"I didn't bring all of it," Hank smiled. "I remember you saying you might need a hand at your place and thought maybe I could work off the balance—you know—try my hand at some honest work."

Naomi looked at Raquel and smiled before saying to Hank, "You didn't bring any of my money, Mr. Tilley."

"Oh, no, you're wrong," Hank Tilley corrected. "There's nearly thirteen dollars there."

"Mr. Tilley," Naomi stated factually. "That money was never wired to Albuquerque so I don't see how you could have picked it up to bring it here."

Hank Tilley shifted his feet nervously at being caught in his lie. He looked sheepishly at Naomi Butler, expecting to see the disapproving and scolding look he remembered so well from their previous time together.

"It's good to see you," Raquel said, as she stepped to the man and gently hugged him.

"It's very good to see you, Mr. Tilley," Naomi added. "Why don't you get out of the sun and tell us why you're really here?"

Hank nodded his head and followed Naomi to the porch, while Raquel went to get the man a cool drink of water from the well.

"Mr. Tilley, if I didn't know better, I'd think maybe you've been doing some honest work," Naomi said. "Clean clothes, clean shaven. Doesn't look to me like that would be a good appearance if your purpose is to talk people into a charity meal."

"No, ma'am," Hank Tilley confessed. "Truth is I wanted to make sure you ladies made it home, and it does me good to see you here and doing so well."

"We're here, but I don't know about doing well," Naomi sighed.

"What do you mean?" Hank said with a frown. "This place looks like it's got all kinds of potential."

"It's not the place, Mr. Tilley," Naomi said. "It's the past. You can't run from your past."

"You can't run from it, but you can change from it," Hank Tilley replied.

Naomi smiled faintly, "Ned Farrell's here in Sayre, and he's blackmailing us."

"What for?" Hank asked.

"What for?" Naomi said with a hint of impatience in her voice. "He's blackmailing me for killing Smiling Jack."

Hank Tilley sat back and studied Naomi carefully with a perplexed expression on his face before saying, "That's right. You wouldn't know that. You wouldn't know that at all."

"Know what, Mr. Tilley?" Naomi asked.

Hank Tilley smiled strangely, "Smilin' Jack—Jack Fisk—ain't dead. He might have a nice scar on his back, but he's as alive as you and me."

"What?" Naomi said trembling.

"That's right!" Hank said. "You skedaddled—so you wouldn't know—but Ned Farrell'd know. Jack Fisk spent two nights in the hospital and had twenty-two stitches, but he's fine. Ned Farrell's just trying to scam you."

"Raquel!" Naomi cried. "Raquel get here quick!"

Raquel came rushing around the corner of the house and asked, "What is it?"

"Tell her, Mr. Tilley," Naomi sobbed happily. "Tell her!"

"Tell me what?" Raquel asked.

Hank Tilley sat up straight and proudly delivered the good news, "Jack Fisk is alive and well. Naomi didn't hardly hurt him back in New Mexico. That little weasel Ned Farrell is just trying to fleece you again."

"Isn't that wonderful news," Naomi cried.

"Yes," Raquel beamed.

The unplanned celebration was interrupted by the sound of tires spraying gravel, as Beau Lobaugh and Elmer leaped out of the truck and rushed Hank Tilley.

"Is this him?" Beau Lobaugh shouted, as he firmly grasped the taller Hank Tilley by the collar.

"Stop it!" Naomi pleaded.

Hank Tilley was caught off guard, but quickly regained his wits to break free of Beau Lobaugh's grip and land a punch to his jaw.

"Stop it!" Naomi screamed again. "This isn't the man!"

Raquel moved quickly to grab Beau's arm, as Elmer prepared to enter the melee.

"This isn't Ned," Raquel said softly to Beau, as she held his arm tightly.

She could feel him pulling at her grip, and she knew that she could not physically hold him, yet he seemed to be in her control as long as she held on to his arm.

"It's okay, Elmer," Raquel said in a calm voice to cause Elmer to stand his ground. "This is our friend, Mr. Tilley. He has been a great friend and helped us on our trip here."

Beau Lobaugh relaxed his tense muscles somewhat and motioned for Elmer to stay back.

"Mr. Tilley has brought some wonderful news," Raquel explained. "The man Naomi stabbed—he's alive! They stitched him up, and he's alive! Ned Farrell can't blackmail us now."

The men all took a step back and relaxed as Beau said, "That is good news, but the man that attacked you is out there somewhere, and his accomplice is here in town. He's still a dangerous man."

"He's right," Hank Tilley said. "Ned and Smilin' Jack are a dangerous pair."

"I'm going into town to get the sheriff," Beau Lobaugh said. Turning to Raquel he asked, "Will you be all right?"

Raquel said, "Yes, Beau."

"I'll go with you," Hank Tilley offered.

Beau Lobaugh seemed unsure until Hank said, "I know what he looks like."

"Get in," Beau nodded, as he headed to the truck. "Elmer you stay here."

In a moment, Beau and Hank sped into town.

CHAPTER 68

Raquel and Naomi watched the dust cloud from Beau Lobaugh's truck disappear, as he sped into town with Hank Tilley in the passenger seat.

"Is Bertha behind the barn?" Elmer interrupted, as he stood behind the two women.

It took Raquel a moment to realize Elmer was asking about Beau's cow they had been keeping.

Raquel replied, "Yes."

Elmer nodded, as he hitched his overalls and walked in his awkward gait to the barn. When Raquel turned around, she noticed Naomi staring down the empty road. Naomi's earlier anxiety seemed to have been replaced by a contented excitement.

"It was good to see Mr. Tilley," Raquel said.

"Yes," Naomi smiled. "Can you imagine he traveled all this way to give us thirteen dollars? Very impractical."

Raquel smirked at her mother-in-law's attempt to downplay the arrival of Hank Tilley, as she said, "Mr. Tilley didn't travel across two states—"

Raquel stopped herself and said, "Hank won't go through Texas, so he must have traveled through Colorado and Kansas to get here. A man doesn't travel that far for money—it must be something else."

"Psst!" Naomi exploded. "I'd never let a man like that near you."

"He didn't come for me," Raquel stated. "He came for you."

"What!" Naomi exclaimed. "No one would come for an old woman like me."

"You need to learn to take your own advice," Raquel scolded playfully.

"What on earth are you talking about?" Naomi huffed.

"You're always preaching to me about believing in myself," Raquel explained. "You need to do the same thing. You're not that old, and he likes you. Why else would anyone put up with you?"

Naomi stared at her daughter-in-law, as her lips twisted nervously, and her forehead wrinkled in concentrated thought.

"Besides that," Raquel continued, "you like him, too."

"Nonsense," Naomi protested. "You don't know what you're talking about! What interest would I have in a vagabond and a felon?"

"You thought you were a felon, too," Raquel observed. "And we lived the vagabond life as well."

Naomi tightened her lips, as her neck and cheeks blushed.

Raquel grinned at her frustrated mother-in-law, but knew she had better not tease her further.

The agitated Naomi said, "I've wasted enough time in this hot sun, and I've got work to do!"

The flustered Naomi marched defiantly into the house, slamming the screen door behind her. Raquel smiled playfully at her mother-in-law's childish tantrum before walking slowly toward the barn.

"Are you missing her?" Raquel asked, as she watched Elmer gently hold Bertha's neck with one hand while stroking the long nose of the animal with the other.

"Naw," Elmer said. "I miss her fresh milk, but not having to milk her every day."

"What have you been doing for milk?" Raquel asked.

"The captain drives into town a couple of times a week for milk and ice," Elmer said.

"I'm surprised Mr. Lobaugh was willing to give up his cow then," Raquel said.

"The captain would surprise you in many ways."

"How?" Raquel asked, as she patted the cow along beside Elmer.

"Oh, no," Elmer replied, while shaking his head. "I won't get into any gossip about the captain. It ain't my business."

For the next hour, Raquel visited with Elmer and tried to steer the conversation toward Beau Lobaugh and particularly his past. Elmer was friendly and even more talkative than he had been, but he repeated the phrase "ain't my business" a half dozen times. By the time Raquel had given up on her failed interrogation, the afternoon was hot, and she invited Elmer to the porch where they might catch a breeze to relieve them from the heat. In another half hour, Beau's truck bounced back toward the Butler house.

By that time, Naomi had joined Raquel and Elmer on the porch to await the news about Ned Farrell. Beau Lobaugh climbed out of the truck slowly, followed by Hank.

"Well?" an impatient Naomi asked. "Did you find him?"

"Yeah," Beau said. "It wasn't hard to find a stranger in a town this size. The sheriff's got him locked up for tonight. I had him make some phone calls in New Mexico, and found the guy had a whole slew of warrants in a dozen different places. They'll be shipping him back to New Mexico next week."

"Any sign of Smiling Jack?" Naomi asked, looking at Hank Tilley.

"Naw," Hank said. "Ned thought he'd cash in on this scam himself without having to split it with Smilin' Jack."

"Thank goodness," Naomi said.

Beau moved next to Hank before suddenly grabbing him by the arm and saying to Elmer, "Now, let's get this fellow to the train station and out of town."

Elmer quickly moved to help Beau contain the man, while Naomi frantically screamed, "Let him go!"

Raquel and Naomi had watched Hank fight in the past and did not want a scuffle in their front yard. Hank struggled slightly, but he did not create a more hostile situation.

"This man put you and Raquel in danger!" Beau said, as he continued to hold Hank in check. "I won't let him bother you further."

"Mr. Tilley didn't put us in danger," Naomi said strongly. "He took care of us. I don't know what would have happened to us without his help."

Beau looked confused, as Raquel added, "It's true. Mr. Tilley saved us—he saved me."

Beau let go and motioned for Elmer to step back.

"You want him here?" Beau said.

"Yes," Naomi cried, as she walked quickly to step between the men.

"I won't stay where I'm not wanted," Hank Tilley said, as Naomi moved close to him.

"Won't you stay for a while—maybe longer, Mr. Tilley?" Naomi asked.

"I was hoping to find some work around here," Hank said. "But I don't want to be a bother."

"I need plenty of help to fix up this place," Naomi said.

"Wait a minute," Beau interjected, as he tried to understand Naomi's hospitable attitude toward the drifter.

Naomi looked innocently at Beau waiting for him to finish his thought. Beau looked at Raquel for some guidance and then back at the stranger, Hank Tilley.

"Now, just wait a minute," Beau repeated. After another hesitation he continued, "It's not right—it's not going to look right for a man to stay here with two women. I'm renting that field, Naomi—and been paying you for it."

"Uh-huh," Naomi groaned.

Beau seemed to be thinking his way through a problem as he said, "I'd like to rehabilitate that field, and I could always use a good man. If Mr. Tilley would like to come work for me, I guess that I could give him some time to work on this old house."

"What do you say, Mr. Tilley?" Naomi asked. "Wouldn't you like some steady work for a change?"

Hank Tilley looked around nervously and replied, "I'd like to try."

"I've got room in my bunkhouse across the river," Beau said. "You can stay there if you like."

"Thank you, Mr. Lobaugh," Hank said humbly. "Thank you for the chance. I won't disappoint."

"Don't thank me too much," Beau Lobaugh growled. "People tell me I'm not the easiest person to work for. Let's go Elmer."

"He's got that right," Elmer said, as Beau started walking back to his truck.

Beau grimaced, as he stared at the slow-moving Elmer, before climbing back into the truck.

Beau leaned out the window and said to Hank Tilley, "Come up to the house before sunset, and I'll get you stowed away in the bunkhouse. No drinkin' and no cursin' when the women folks are around."

"That didn't used to be a problem," Elmer fussed, loud enough for his boss to hear.

"I'll be there before the sun goes down," Hank confirmed.

Beau nodded, as he and Elmer drove away from the house.

After they left, Hank said, "I don't know if I made a good deal or not. Mr. Lobaugh seems like a hard man."

"That's just his way," Naomi explained.

"Mr. Lobaugh will surprise you," Raquel added. "He's a good man—a fair man."

"It'll be good to have a bed for a while," Hank said.

"Where have you been, Mr. Tilley?" Naomi asked.

Hank replied, "After you two ladies left, I decided I needed to get straight with the law. I crossed the line into Texas and decided to do my time. Come to find out, they have a statute of limitations, and I couldn't find no law that seemed to care about a fight in a speakeasy from ten years ago. Harry decided to hop a train to Iowa—to try to find his people. I didn't have much interest in ridin' to Iowa, so I worked my way back to Higgins. Got there and found out you two had been through and made it to this place. I wondered if I should come down or not to visit, but—it'd been awhile since anyone had criticized me proper, so I figured I needed to come see you, Mrs. Butler."

"Oh, you," Naomi fussed.

"You did tell me I had a place at your table if I ever came close, so I decided to show up," Hank said.

"We're glad you did," Raquel smiled.

"Oh, Mr. Tilley," Naomi said, almost crying. "I can't believe how good it is to see you. I'm going to cook you a feast before you head up to Beau Lobaugh's."

"Naomi doesn't think much of Mr. Lobaugh's cook," Raquel teased. "That's me."

Naomi shook her head in resignation and excused herself to begin dinner. The trio had a relaxing meal at the table and talked fondly of their adventures that had seemed so dire not so long ago. They laughed and reminisced. Naomi even cried a couple of times for no apparent reason, but it was obvious that she was glad to see Hank Tilley again and to have the opportunity to show him her genuine gratitude. Before sundown, Raquel walked Hank to the bunkhouse. Beau Lobaugh questioned her one more time about the man, but he seemed satisfied that he posed no threat to her or Naomi. Beau drove Raquel home a little after dark. The day that had been so foreboding earlier had ended up being their happiest day since returning to the farm in Oklahoma.

CHAPTER 69

The summer of 1935 had been the driest, hottest, and most miserable anyone around Sayre could remember. Temperatures soared well above 100 degrees almost every day in July and August. The nights offered little relief, and irritating dust storms sometimes paralyzed any effort to work the land. Still, people survived. Some migrated west down Route 66, but many others made the best out of the harsh conditions.

Hank Tilley turned out to be a good hand for Beau Lobaugh. There was little use in trying to prepare the dry fields around Naomi's house, but he helped Beau and his crew drill a new water well that might support irrigation in the spring. Hank spent more time at Naomi's house than in the fields during the hot summer. Hank proved to be handy with tools, had a good eye for angles, and knew how to measure, which made him a better than average, although novice, carpenter.

By late August, Raquel's hair had grown out enough to almost touch her shoulders. Naomi took her to town and treated the two of them to a trip to the beauty shop and a new dress. Naomi said that they might be poor, but there was no reason for them not to get their hair fixed. After getting their hair done, the two women stepped into the Rexall Drugstore. Raquel stopped by the cosmetics counter and stood staring at the choices.

"Finding anything?" Naomi asked, as Raquel looked at some products listlessly.

"Huh?" Raquel replied.

"Make-up," Naomi said. "That shade would be good with your complexion."

"Oh," Raquel sighed. "I wasn't thinking about the shade."

Naomi could tell something was amiss as she asked, "What's on your mind?"

Raquel smiled, "I was just thinking about Orpha. She used to coach me on what make-up to wear."

Naomi put her arm around Raquel and sighed, "I miss her, too."

"Do you think she's all right?" Raquel asked.

"Of course," Naomi said. "Orpha's a bright girl and she's got family. I'm sure she's fine."

Raquel nodded and smiled, convinced Naomi was right about Orpha. It had been less than a year since they had left her behind, but it seemed longer to Raquel. The women completed their trip to town, that included much more shopping than buying, but if felt good to be away from the farm for a day.

Beau started letting Hank drive the old farm truck to Naomi's house for work, and he had taught Raquel to drive the truck back, so that she would not have to walk in the extreme heat. Hank may not have accomplished much in regenerating the fields around Naomi's house that summer, but he had revitalized the woman's attitude. Their increasingly overt flirting caused Raquel to spend more time at Beau Lobaugh's house, and she became friends with Elmer, his chief helper.

August 1935 saw national news that shocked the small town of Sayre almost as much as the hated dust storms. Oklahomans Will Rogers and Wiley Post were killed in a plane crash in Alaska.

Frank Sutton became engaged to Mary Wareham that August. Raquel was happy for him, but Naomi still fussed about Frank being a momma's boy and his fiancé having no spirit. Raquel had met the girl, and the couple seemed very happy.

By early September, the blazing-hot days continued, although the longer evenings brought some relief from the heat. Beau Lobaugh went on one of his business trips, and had taken his old truck. Without the truck, Raquel had to walk across the river to get to Beau's house, but by that time of year, the river bed was dry as a bone, and Raquel had more of a chance of getting dust on her shoes than mud.

As Raquel approached the Lobaugh house, she sensed something different this morning. The men that lived in the bunkhouse, including Elmer, stood out front polishing and admiring a pale-green Buick parked there. The car had a long hood with a sloping chrome grill and headlights. The teardrop-shaped fenders led to an elegantly curved rear end. Raquel had always been impressed with Eli Butler's Ford, but it had been black and simple compared to this machine. The men did not notice Raquel as she approached. Their full attention focused on the new car.

"What's that?" Raquel asked, as she walked up behind the men.

"The captain's new car," Elmer boasted. "Got it from Oklahoma City."

"Is Mr. Lobaugh back?" Raquel asked.

Beau had been gone most of the week and had seemed to be busier with business outside of the farm as the summer days slowly shortened toward fall.

"Got back last night," Elmer said, as he split his attention between talking to Raquel and admiring the new car. "You just missed Hank. He took the old truck to your place a few minutes ago."

"What do you think?" the voice of Beau Lobaugh boomed from behind her.

"She's a beaut, captain," Elmer whistled.

"I wasn't talking to you," Beau scolded his employee. "You've been polishing that thing since last night."

"Think I might take her for a spin?" Elmer asked.

Beau seemed somewhat frustrated with Elmer, as he huffed, "Maybe if you can stay out of trouble and get that well across the river done, I'll let you take it to town."

Elmer smiled and went back to examining the shiny paint job on the new car.

"What do you think, Raquel?" Beau asked in a kinder tone, as he stepped closer to her.

"It's nice," Raquel smiled. "I don't know anything about cars, but I love the color, and it's so shiny."

"I've got a lot of help polishing it," Beau said sarcastically, as he pushed Elmer out of the way to stand near Raquel. "What's on your plate today?"

Raquel thought, "Not much. I'll cook lunch and clean a little. You haven't been home, so there's not much to do."

"How'd you like to take a trip?" Beau asked apprehensively.

"Where to?" Raquel asked, as she used her hand to shield her eyes from the morning sun.

"I've got a meeting at Fort Sill," Beau explained. "Shouldn't take long at all. Thought you could do some shopping for me at the commissary. I got a piece of land near Hobart I can check on too. We'll be back by dark."

"Sure," Raquel said. "Are we taking your new car?"

"If I can get Elmer off it, we will," smiled Beau.

Beau stopped by Naomi's house so that Raquel could tell her that she would be late. Naomi seemed nervous to have Raquel take such a long car trip, but she appeared equally as excited for Raquel to have a day away from work. Beau headed the car south, and Raquel reclined in the plush cloth seats. The car smelled new, and she caught herself rubbing the soft fabric on the seat.

They drove south through the flat and barren farm land around Sayre. By the time they reached the tiny town of Willow, Raquel could see pinkish granite mountains on the southern horizon, with a seemingly endless flat plain in front of them. Beau then drove through the slightly larger town of Granite, which was named after a protruding granite mountain. They drove east toward the larger town of Hobart, which had a railroad junction for the Rock Island line. As they drove past the station, Raquel caught herself analyzing how easy it would have been to catch a freight train in the unguarded yard. They stopped for breakfast in Hobart. Raquel was surprised by how many people knew Beau there. She learned later that he had gone to high school in Hobart and that his father had a large holding of land south of town.

After breakfast, they continued driving south. Raquel couldn't believe that the land seemed even flatter and more desolate than the property around Sayre. The immense flat valley was flanked by two short mountain ranges to the east and to the west that were barely visible in the hazy distance. Beau told her that the mountains to the west were the Quartz Mountains and to the east, the Wichita Mountain range. Beau became more sullen and less talkative driving through this lonely valley. He pointed out the borders to his property, but he did not seem eager to explain much more than that to Raquel. At one point, he became so distracted near a small village called Babbs that he let the wheels of his new car drift onto the loose sand beside the road, which caused Raquel to squeal in fright. Beau apologized and seemed to snap out of his malaise.

Near Roosevelt, Beau pointed out a sagging mountain to the west, appropriately called Saddle Mountain. He told Raquel that near the mountain there was a place off the road called Cutthroat Gap where a peaceful band of Kiowa Indians had been attacked by an Osage war party almost a hundred years earlier. Nearly a hundred and thirty Kiowas had been killed in the massacre, mainly women and children. They had been beheaded with their heads put in pots for the hunting party to find on their return. Raquel was suspicious of the story, but Beau swore the tale was true. He claimed that the few people venturing to the sight said the cries of the slain could still be heard in the dead of night.

Raquel did not have any interest in finding out if the stories about cries in the night were true, and she was glad when they turned west toward Lawton. The road headed into the rugged Wichita Mountains, where the flat, straight road transformed to a gentle winding mountain road surrounded by short pin oaks and jagged outcrops of dark rock. Beau pointed to a road leading to a place called Medicine Park that he said Raquel would enjoy. In a little less than half an hour, their two-hour drive had brought them to the gates of Fort Sill.

"We're here," Beau informed, as an army private saluted and motioned for him to continue through the gates.

"Do you always get this type of respect?" Raquel asked, as they drove by the young man in uniform.

"I was stationed here for a long time," Beau explained. "I taught in the artillery school."

Raquel looked out the window of the Buick to see several gray stone buildings and other wooden structures. To the west, tents were arranged in orderly rows. They passed a small church building, which Beau Lobaugh identified as the chapel, and then he parked in front of a long limestone building with a porch stretching over the entire front of the structure.

Beau turned to her and said, "That's the commissary. Here's a list of things you can get for me."

"I don't have any money," Raquel said.

"That's okay," Beau smiled. "Tell them it's for Captain Lobaugh, and I'll settle up with them later."

Raquel nodded and took the list from his hand.

"I've got a meeting, but it shouldn't last long," Beau explained. "Have one of the soldiers put the things in the trunk. If you have time, there's a museum they opened in the old guard house next door. I'll meet you there, and we'll have some lunch."

"Okay," Raquel said, before Beau walked quickly across the campus to another building that looked like it had a more military purpose.

Raquel walked timidly into the commissary and felt strongly that she did not belong. She was the only woman in sight, but when the sergeant discovered she was shopping for Captain Lobaugh, he immediately assigned a young private to assist her.

After filling Beau's list, Raquel walked to the old guardhouse, which had recently been converted into a museum for the army base. The building was nearly square, with steps leading up to the main level. The museum had old pictures and plaques describing some of the history of the fort. Raquel learned that Geronimo had been a captive and later lived at the fort. He was buried in the Indian cemetery at Fort Sill, and there was a small granite pyramid marking his grave.

As Raquel strolled through the exhibits, a plaque and some pictures caught her attention. The picture showed a young Beau

Lobaugh with a group of men in front of a large cannon. She leaned closer to get a better look at his picture. He looked determined, focused, and in charge—much like she had experienced him at the farm. The plaque said he was awarded the Silver Star for gallantry in action, and the Distinguished Service Medal for his role in developing Counter-battery fire techniques during the war.

"Are you bored to tears, yet?" Beau asked, as he walked up behind her.

"That's you?" Raquel asked, although she knew the answer.

Beau leaned over to look at the picture and said, "A skinnier me. Speaking of which, are you ready for some lunch?"

"That sounds good," Raquel smiled.

"We'll be meeting a friend of mine that I ran into," Beau said. "Do you mind?"

"No—but if you'd like to eat lunch with him alone, I'll understand."

"Nonsense," Beau replied. "I'd like for you to meet him."

Beau walked Raquel down the avenue to the Officer's Club where they met a tall, slender man that looked to be in his mid-thirties wearing a business suit.

"Raquel, I'd like to introduce you to Jonathan Kendall," Beau said. "Or as we called him, Lazarus."

Jonathan Kendall reached out his hand and said, "It's good to meet you, Miss—"

Raquel blushed and awkwardly replied, "Raquel will be fine."

Jonathan smiled pleasantly, "It's good to finally meet you Raquel. Beau has told me so much about you."

"Has he?" Raquel said with a puzzled expression.

Beau quickly interrupted, "Let's find a table and catch up on things."

Jonathan Kendall seemed to sense Beau's anxiety and said, "Good, I'm starving."

Raquel took her seat and asked, "Why do they call you Lazarus, Mr. Kendall?"

"Silly army talk is all," Jonathan replied.

Beau straightened up in his chair and said, "Jonathan led a forward group one night to find German artillery positions. He knew some of the code talkers—some Choctaw soldiers—that relayed messages for the forward observers. They ran into a fight, and we at headquarters heard he had been killed in action. A big mess up and the command sent telegrams and everything back home. The war ended a couple of weeks later, and Jonathan, it seems, had been hiding out in a German hospital."

"That must have been terrifying for your family," Raquel sighed.

"Yes," Jonathan said, "but I guess almost everything about war is terrifying. Unfortunately, people forget how terrible war is, and we seem to repeat our mistakes again and again."

"Do you think we'll have another war, Mr. Kendall?" Raquel asked.

"I hope not," Jonathan said grimly. "Captain Lobaugh's not so optimistic."

"You think there'll be a war?" Raquel asked, turning to Beau.

Beau shook his head, "I know we're woefully unprepared. That's what my meeting was about—to look at updating some training manuals for the field artillery school."

"Would they send you to war?" Raquel asked seriously.

Jonathan laughed at the idea, "They'd have to have two soldiers pulling a cart to get me into the field."

Jonathan stopped talking suddenly and then said to Beau, "But you—they wouldn't send an old guy like you into the field, but they sure might bring you here as a training officer."

"Let's hope it never comes to that," Beau Lobaugh said. "Let's eat."

The three had sandwiches, and Raquel spent her lunch listening to the two former soldiers talk about their time in the war and old comrades they had known. Raquel learned Jonathan was a bachelor, but he had once been engaged. He was as vague about his circumstances as Beau Lobaugh was about his past, however.

After an hour, the two men had exhausted their old stories about friends living and gone. Beau gave his friend a firm handshake before Jonathan Kendall headed back to his home in Chandler, Oklahoma.

The Officer's Club had been warm, but large fans circulated the air to make it as comfortable as possible. As Raquel walked into the early September afternoon, the humid heat felt like a furnace.

"It's a hot one," Beau stated the obvious.

"You'll have to drive fast," Raquel quipped.

Beau smirked, "Are you that anxious to get home?"

"Not that," Raquel said quickly. "I meant the car going fast will feel good with the windows down."

"How about we get cooled off?" Beau suggested.

"Okay," Raquel replied in an unsure tone.

"I know a place," Beau smiled, as he walked around to open her door.

Beau Lobaugh exited the army base and headed the Buick north on a two lane road that skirted the fence around the military base. Beau turned off the highway onto a winding road that headed into the Wichita Mountains and to a small village in a narrow valley.

"What is this place?" Raquel asked, as she looked at cobblestone buildings overlooking a stream with two dams, which created two small lakes next to the town.

"Medicine Park," Beau replied, while he searched for a place to park.

"It's pretty," Raquel said, as she observed a series of paths leading to the lakes and stream.

"I used to spend a lot of time here," Beau said, "in my wilder days."

Medicine Park had been built as a resort for tourists years earlier. It thrived during prohibition, because several speakeasies were able to operate with near immunity in the isolated enclave. The small community was situated near the main entrance to the Wichita National Forest and Game Preserve. A large building with a sign that said Apache Inn advertised a dance hall. A poster said that Bob Wills and the Texas Playboys would be playing there that weekend. There were several restaurants, a couple of hotels, and a bathhouse in the quaint village.

"I thought we might take a swim before driving back," Beau suggested.

Raquel hesitated before saying, "I don't have any swimming clothes."

"They rent them at the bathhouse," Beau explained.

Raquel smiled strangely and did not reply.

"You can swim, can't you?" Beau asked.

"Not exactly," Raquel said. "I can wade, but I've never been in water above my knees."

"I thought everyone in California swam in the Pacific Ocean," Beau teased.

"Not in my part of California."

"Do you want to learn?" Beau asked. "I'm a strong swimmer and could teach you."

As her forehead glistened from the hot afternoon sun, Raquel smiled nervously, "I might just wade."

"Suit yourself," Beau said. "Let's go get some swimming suits."

Raquel agreed. In thirty minutes she met Beau at the head of a short trail leading to the lake. Beau had rented a dark pair of swim trunks with a mismatched horizontal stripe tank top.

"Ready?" he asked.

Raquel nodded. Beau walked to the edge of the water and waded out a few feet before diving into the water head first.

"The water's great!" Beau smiled. "A little warm, but refreshing."

Raquel looked around the swimming area and watched a few other people playing in the water. Beau had told her the place was packed on the weekends, but she was glad the area was less crowded this day. She stepped timidly into the water and waded to her knees before stopping to splash water on her hot shoulders.

Beau swam a few feet away and occasionally dove under the water for a few seconds before surfacing.

"Want to try it?" Beau asked, as he encouraged her to come further into the water.

Raquel looked at the wide expanse of water and said, "Okay."

Beau moved into the more shallow water and took her by the hand. She moved deeper and held his hand tighter with each step as the water slowly came up to her shoulders.

"Don't worry," Beau said gently. "I got you."

Raquel nodded. There was something reassuring in his tone of voice.

"We're going to try to float," Beau said. "I'm going to put my arm behind your back to hold you up, but I want you to lean back until your feet don't touch. If you slip, don't panic. I'll be right here, and your feet will touch if you get in trouble."

Although Raquel tried to follow his instructions, relaxing around him was not easy. Beau gently helped her lean back into the water. When Raquel's feet left the safety of the lake bed, she tensed up and instinctively began to flay her arms in the water.

"I've got you," Beau calmly assured. "Just relax."

Raquel took a deep breath and could feel Beau's firm and sure hands on her back. She nervously exhaled her air, causing Beau to hold her more tightly. After a few seconds she relaxed and felt herself floating, although Beau still had a tight hold on her.

"You're getting it," Beau encouraged. "Now kick your feet."

Raquel obeyed and water splashed high and came down on her face.

"Good!" Beau said. "Now I'm going to slowly let go and let you float on your own, but stay relaxed."

As Beau released his grip, Raquel panicked, her head dipped under the water for an instant. Beau quickly grabbed her, and helped Raquel balance on her feet.

"Are you okay?" he said in a worried tone.

"I'm fine," Raquel assured with a smile. "I just slipped. Let's try again."

She repeated the procedure and was able to lay flat in the water with Beau's arm underneath her. He slowly removed his arm until she was floating on her own. She kicked gently and moved slowly toward the shore.

After a few seconds, Raquel lowered her feet to the bottom and screamed with glee, "I did it!"

Beau laughed, "You picked that up faster than anyone I've taught before."

Raquel splashed excitedly in the water and asked for more tips. Beau patiently showed her how to perform different strokes. He stayed close to steady her and made sure she was safe.

"That was fun," Raquel gleamed, after nearly an hour of swimming.

"It will certainly cool us down for the drive home," Beau said. "Are you ready to go?"

"Yes," Raquel said, "Will we make it by dark?"

"Sure," Beau replied, as he looked at the sun in relation to the mountain ridges to the west. "It's not much more than a two-hour drive from here, but we better get dressed and on the road."

By the time Raquel changed into her dry clothes Beau leaned against his new Buick. He looked relaxed and comfortable as he stood waiting for her. Beau made a move to open the car door for her, but Raquel stepped around the door to stand next to him. Raquel looked around the placid village and the cool pools of water before taking a deep breath.

Raquel said, "I like this place. It's a good retreat from the heat."

"You should see it in the spring when there's been some rain," Beau said. "The water flows over the lower dams, and you can hear the waterfalls echo in the valley."

"I'd like to see that," Raquel smiled.

"Maybe we can come back sometime," Beau said.

Raquel looked at the man for a moment and said, "You didn't have to go to all this trouble, you know."

"It was no trouble," Beau said. "I had the meeting at the fort, and it was nice to have the company for the ride down here."

"That's not what I mean," Raquel frankly stated.

"What do you mean?" Beau asked with a puzzled expression.

Raquel looked around the peaceful village for a second before saying, "You didn't have to try so hard to impress me today."

"I—I didn't try to—" Beau stammered.

Raquel put her finger on his lips to silence him and said, "I'm talking about the ride in the new car, the trip through Hobart to see all your property—I'll have to admit that seeing the soldiers salute you was impressive, but I thought the tribute to you in the museum was a little over the top."

Beau listened silently without defending himself.

Raquel stepped closer to him and whispered, "This place was a nice touch, too, but I have a couple of secrets for you—I was impressed already."

Beau smirked nervously, "Impressed by what?"

"You," Raquel said, as she smiled affectionately at him.

Beau seemed to be in a trance as he looked into Raquel's eyes. He reached up and gently touched her soft brown cheek. He leaned in like he might kiss her before stepping away.

"I'm sorry," Beau said nervously. "I was out of line."

Raquel reached out and grabbed his hand to pull him close to her.

She rested her other hand on his shoulder and said in a sincere and earnest tone, "I'm not a little girl, Beau. I'm a twenty-three year old widow. You're not going to hurt me, I've been kissed before."

Beau searched desperately for something to say when Raquel leaned in and kissed him.

After the kiss, Raquel still held onto his hand and said, "I've been wanting to do that most of the summer."

"Really?" Beau gasped. "I've wanted to kiss you for longer than that, but I didn't think it would be right."

"It felt right to me," Raquel said.

"You said you had a couple of secrets," Beau said slyly.

Raquel thought for a moment and answered with a mischievous grin, "Maybe."

"What was the other secret?" a confused Beau asked.

Raquel leaned close to whisper in his ear, "I've been able to swim since I was six years old."

CHAPTER 70

Raquel was not sure if she had ever been truly happy before, as she leaned on Beau's shoulder as he drove through the winding roads of the Wichita Mountains. Raquel was sure she had never felt as content as she was at that moment.

"Here I thought I was a great teacher," Beau huffed playfully, as he drove with one arm around Raquel. "I was thinking to myself, this girl was afraid of the water an hour ago, and now she's swimming like a fish."

"You were a good teacher," Raquel said. "I was just a better student."

"I'm glad we made this trip today," Beau said.

"Me too," Raquel sighed, as she nuzzled even deeper into his shoulder.

"How will we tell Naomi?" Beau asked with a worried frown on his face.

"Tell her what?" Raquel asked innocently.

"You know," Beau replied, "about us being a couple."

"Are we?"

"If you'll have me."

"I'll have you."

Beau thought for a second and said in a more serious voice, "Really, Raquel. Naomi doesn't think that highly of me—what will she say?"

Raquel shrugged, "Don't worry about Naomi. Who do you think told me to pretend that I couldn't swim?"

"She didn't?" Beau gasped.

"No she didn't," Raquel affirmed. "But she would have if she'd known you would take me swimming."

Beau laughed and seemed to be in a happy and carefree mood, as they drove on the desolate road out of the mountains. Beau's cheery demeanor changed, however, as they passed Saddleback

Mountain and drove into the flat plains south of Hobart. Raquel had been content to rest her head on his shoulder, but she noticed him getting quieter and could feel the tenseness in his shoulder.

"What is it, Beau?" she asked, as she sat up to get a better look at him.

Beau's forehead was wrinkled in concentration and his lips were clenched tightly. His eyes were on the road, but he had a weary faraway look. Raquel had noticed the same thing when they passed the area earlier.

"Nothing," he said dispassionately.

Raquel continued to study him and knew that he was not telling her the truth.

"Is it me?" she asked, anxiously. "Have I been too forward with you?"

"No," Beau said immediately. "It has nothing to do with you. It's just—"

Beau stopped himself from saying more, but Raquel could see the pained look in his face and knew that something was not right.

"You need to tell me," Raquel coaxed. "If you really do care for me, you can't keep secrets."

Beau nodded slightly, but he kept driving without responding. Suddenly he slowed down and veered off the highway onto a dirt road. Raquel was alarmed because he had nearly driven off the road earlier in the day. This time, however, he was in control of the vehicle, although Raquel could tell something was troubling him. Beau stopped the car about a quarter of a mile off the highway in front of a rectangle pile of stones that had once been a foundation.

Raquel was confused as she looked around the desolate, flat country. It was late in the afternoon, but there were still a couple of hours of sunlight left as Beau opened the door without talking and walked listlessly to an old foundation. Raquel watched him stand alone in the great plain for a moment, staring at the vast emptiness, before she quietly got out of the car and stood by him.

"Are you okay?" Raquel asked in a soft tone.

Beau nodded as he reached down to hold her hand. He did not speak at first but looked at the distant mountains and the faint outline of buildings that were barely visible from the nearby town of Hobart.

"What happened here?" Raquel finally asked.

Beau fought with his emotions, but Raquel sensed he wanted to answer.

"There was a school here—my daughter's school," Beau began. "It was her first year. She was only six. I worked at Fort Sill in those days—a few years after the war—as an instructor. We lived in a house on the old home place about a mile from here."

He pointed in the distance, but Raquel could not see where the house had been.

"We were happy," Beau continued. "I'd been—I'd been a handful as a kid. Had that tryst with Maylon's mother and got sent to military school—then to the war in Europe. I grew up some and was more of a man when I got back. Mary was the daughter of one of the officers at Fort Sill. She was beautiful and smart—she could see right through me, and I needed that. We had Ellen after our first year.

"Ellen was in first grade, and the school had a big program planned on Christmas Eve. I'd got caught up in a project at the fort and was running late. Ellen was supposed to sing in it. They had painted the school the week before. It was cold that winter, and the windows had been bolted shut to prevent vandals from breaking in. A fire started near the Christmas tree—"

Beau took a deep breath, and Raquel was not sure he would continue. Beau stared out across the flat countryside, and Raquel stood by him.

Beau fought back tears and stoically stated, "The one-room school house was packed. The doors opened in, and—the whole place went up in flames. Thirty-seven people died that night. Some of them made it out, but they had drained the radiators in the cars to keep them from freezing in the cold. In the confusion, most of the cars trying to rescue survivors overheated on the way back to

Hobart. My Ellen didn't make it out of the schoolhouse—they said she was in Mary's arms, but I don't know."

Beau could not continue but bowed his head and rubbed his forehead while Raquel patted his back and gently massaged his neck.

"I'm so sorry," Raquel finally said in a soft voice.

"It was a long time ago," Beau moaned, as he raised his head and wiped his eyes. "I couldn't bring myself to live here anymore. I had a lot of skeletons in the closet from my younger days in Hobart. I had bought the place near Sayre and had planned to move them there for a fresh start. I was building that house for Mary and Ellen. We planned to move in the spring. I—I never got around to finishing the house. I couldn't see the point."

"That must have been painful," Raquel softly replied.

"It still is," Beau admitted with a forced smile.

Raquel looked at him a moment before timidly saying, "Someone told me once that we learn from the past—no matter how painful—and live for today. That someone was you."

"Some things are easier said than done," Beau lamented.

Raquel sighed, "I agree—but it's still good advice."

Beau walked slowly back to the car holding Raquel's hand. He stopped and looked around the empty landscape. He turned to face the sun and breathed in the warm dry air.

"I didn't know what I wanted in life for a long time," Beau explained. "My father lost patience with me—and nearly lost faith in me. When I met Mary, I understood more about my father's frustrations. I learned that I wanted a family. I wanted to take care of them and see their dreams and hopes. That fire took it all away from me. I still rationalized that I had Maylon somewhere far away and that would be good enough, but Maylon always belonged to Naomi. I know that now."

"It's not too late," Raquel whispered.

"What?" Beau replied.

"For a family," Raquel explained. "It's not too late for you to have a family."

Beau turned to look at the young woman standing in front of him. He had admired her quiet self-confidence since her first days in Sayre.

"Raquel?" Beau said slowly and surely.

"Yes," she replied quickly.

"I have no right to think you might have these kinds of feelings, but I've lived enough to know life's too precious to waste," Beau reasoned. "There are many things I can't offer you, and my faults are countless. I can promise that I will protect you, take care of you, and provide for you."

Raquel looked at him carefully and thought for a moment before asking, "Can you love me?"

Beau smiled sincerely and replied, "I already love you, and I can promise that not only will I love you—I will cherish you."

Raquel nodded her head and hugged him tightly, "I know. I've hoped for a while, but now I know."

CHAPTER 71

It was nearly sundown, when Beau pulled his Buick in front of Naomi's house. Raquel had spent the hour drive from Hobart making plans for her future as Mrs. Beau Lobaugh. Beau had been smiling and playful during the drive from Hobart, but now he had become more sullen and serious.

"What's wrong?" Raquel asked.

"Naomi," Beau said. "She won't approve."

"She will," Raquel said confidently. "She'll be happy."

"I guess I better ask her permission," Beau nervously suggested. "You don't have any other family."

"Naomi's all the family that matters to me."

Beau nodded and slowly got out of the car to walk to the house. As soon as his door slammed, however, Hank Tilley bolted out of the house with his hair in a mess.

"Hank?" Beau said in a questioning tone. "What are you doing here this late?"

"Hello, Mr. Lobaugh," Hank waved. "Been working on a squeaky door in the back of the house. I didn't hear you pull up. How'd the car run? She's a beauty."

"The car did fine," Beau said. "Is Naomi around?"

"Sure," Hank said. "She's been helping with the tools and such. I put a coat of grease on that old door, and it's doing fine now."

As Raquel climbed out of the car to stand by Beau, Naomi came out of the house with her hair in a mess.

"You're back!" Naomi greeted nonchalantly. "Mr. Tilley was just leaving. He's been such a help around the house."

"I was just leaving," Hank repeated.

Raquel grinned as she looked at Naomi. Besides her hair being out of place, Naomi had a spot of grease on her cheek and a greasy hand print on the back of her dress.

"If that door gives you anymore trouble, Mrs. Butler, let me know," Hank said. "I better be getting back to the bunkhouse before it gets too dark."

"Thank you, Mr. Tilley," Naomi smiled, as she waved.

Raquel barely contained her laughter at the disheveled appearance of the prudish Naomi. Beau was so nervous he did not notice.

"Naomi," Beau said in a matter of fact tone.

"Yes," Naomi timidly replied, sure she had been found out.

"I need to talk to you," Beau informed. "I need to talk to you tonight, if you have a few minutes. Now this is going to be a shock to you, so I don't want you to overreact. Just listen and hear me out."

"What on earth are you babbling about, Beau Lobaugh?" Naomi tersely interrupted.

Beau was speechless, but Raquel blurted out, "Beau's asked me to marry him, and—I've said yes."

"Heaven's be!" Naomi squealed, as she moved quickly toward Raquel.

"Don't be mad, Naomi," Beau quickly added. "I've come to ask your permission, and I don't want you to think anything improper's been goin' on."

"Get out of my way, Beau," Naomi ordered. "I need to hug my daughter."

"You're not mad?" Beau asked.

"Of course not," Naomi replied. "I know that she's too good for you, but I could tell from the first that you two would be a good match. You're sour and serious. Raquel's just sweet."

Naomi reached out and hugged Raquel tightly and cried, "I'm so happy! I'm so happy for you!"

Naomi turned to a shaky Beau and said, "I'm happy for you too, Beau. You're getting a good woman here—far more precious than jewels, but I'm guessing you've figured that out by now."

"Yes, ma'am," Beau smiled.

"When's the date?" Naomi asked.

"I don't know exactly," Beau said. "I'll leave that up to Raquel. I'd rather it be sooner than later."

"We won't wait too long," Raquel smiled, "but let's enjoy our engagement."

"And you don't mind, Naomi?" Beau asked one more time.

"Nothing has made me this happy in a long time," Naomi assured.

CHAPTER 72

Autumn came, and Raquel had never felt so spoiled. She still went to see Beau regularly, but he refused to let her do any of the cleaning or other household chores. Raquel spent much of her time finishing the upstairs of the house, as she prepared to move in as his wife in the spring after the planting. Beau took any opportunity to see Raquel, and she enjoyed getting to know her future husband better. Although Beau's first impression to most people seemed cold and reserved, his long-time friends who occasionally visited held him in high regard. His friends were loyal, and Beau always took opportunity to point out Raquel's best qualities to them.

Thanksgiving Day was a bittersweet reminder for Raquel of her first holiday with Naomi, but she felt uplifted to see her mother-in-law eager to help her prepare the dinner that day. Most of Beau's workers headed home to be with family on the chilly Thanksgiving, but Elmer and Hank were happy to have dinner with Naomi, Raquel, and Beau. Naomi tried to let Raquel cook Thanksgiving dinner, but she gave careful directions through the morning and could not keep from taking over some tasks. When dinner was served, however, she gave her daughter-in-law all of the credit.

Christmas Day was a difficult time for Beau Lobaugh, and Raquel would learn that it would always be a melancholy day for her future husband. It had been Christmas Eve eleven years earlier when he had lost his young family. Raquel noticed the change in his demeanor a few days before Christmas. Beau had been relaxed and very attentive to his fiancé since their engagement, but during that week he seemed preoccupied and distant. It had been Raquel that suggested they take a Christmas Eve drive to the site of the fire.

Beau lavished many gifts on Raquel that Christmas, but the most special was a simple gold ring for their engagement. They also set a date of March 31st for their wedding. It would be a simple Tuesday night ceremony in Sayre. Beau offered to take his bride on a long honeymoon to anywhere she wanted to go, including a trip to California, if she wished. Raquel surprised him, by asking if they could stay in one of the cobblestone cottages in Medicine Park. Raquel explained the place was special to her and always would be.

After the brutally hot summer, Raquel promised not to complain about colder weather. Autumn and most of the winter had been a relief from the heat. As the late January wind blew cold across the treeless plains, however, she found herself thinking fondly about the long, hot days of summer. It had been during the summer she had fallen in love with Beau Lobaugh, and he had captivated almost all of her thoughts since then.

"What are you doing?" Beau yelled from his porch, as Raquel walked through the bare winter fields toward his house.

Beau quickly stepped into the house to grab a thick blanket before running out to greet her.

"It's freezing out here," Beau scolded, as he wrapped the wool blanket around her.

"It didn't feel that bad when I headed out," Raquel shivered.

"I was coming to see you," Beau said, as he guided her toward his warm house.

"I know," Raquel smiled, "but two days inside with Naomi was enough."

The weather had been cold the last week, and there had even been a dusting of snow. Raquel had not seen snow fall before and ran outside to try to catch flakes on her tongue. Beau had laughed at her, but as he admired her joy at the simple pleasure of seeing her first snow, he joined her. The early morning had been sunny, but by the time Raquel walked to Beau's house, the clouds had returned as the wind howled out of the north.

Beau smiled and opened the door to the house to let Raquel warm by the fire as he said, "I'm glad you came, but I feel bad you had to walk through the wind."

"It was to my back," Raquel said, as she rubbed her hands by the fire. "I thought I might find a ride back."

Beau walked up to his fiancé to hug her gently and said, "I'll give you a ride home, but I won't be in a hurry."

"A few more months and this will be home," Raquel smiled.

Beau frowned, "I wish we'd just tied the knot."

"I know," Raquel said, as she leaned her head into Beau's shoulder, "but I've enjoyed the courtship."

The two spent the day doing small jobs around the house and hanging some pictures in the bedroom upstairs, but mostly they talked and enjoyed their time together. As the winter afternoon waned, it started getting darker outside. A few pings of sleet caused Beau to take a look out the window at the changing weather.

He watched the skies for a moment and said, "Looks like some weather's coming in. It's starting to sleet."

Raquel stepped to the window to see the gray skies hanging low and said, "Think you might need to drive me home before it gets bad?"

Beau smiled, "It would be a shame if a blizzard snowed us in."

"I'm afraid Naomi would come looking for me," Raquel grinned. "She likes you, but that doesn't mean she trusts you."

Beau laughed and looked out the window again to say, "Hank's driving up the road now. He may have distracted Naomi already."

Raquel laughed, since Hank Tilley and Naomi had been an item for most of the autumn and winter, although her mother-in-law emphatically denied what was obvious to everyone. Hank parked the truck in front of the house and ran through the stinging sleet toward the shelter of the porch before Beau signaled him to come inside.

"Looks like it's getting bad," Beau said, as the sleet became heavier.

"You got that right," Hank said. "It's worse in town."

"How's Naomi today?" Beau asked, while sneaking eye-contact with Raquel.

"I didn't have no business at Mrs. Butler's," Hank claimed. "Besides, the roads are getting slick, and I didn't want to put your truck in the ditch."

"That's thoughtful of you," Beau said suspiciously.

Hank nodded nervously and handed Beau a stack of mail.

As Beau looked through the mail, he asked, "Anything happen in town today?"

"Not in Sayre," Hank shrugged, "but there was some big news out of Elk City."

Beau looked up as Hank continued, "The bank over there was robbed this afternoon."

"In Elk City?" Beau asked.

Hank nodded.

Beau continued reading his mail and said, "I thought the G-men had cleaned up all the bank robbers."

"These boys weren't no pros," Hank said. "They held up the bank, but the robbers didn't know how to get to the vault. They panicked and got away with less than five hundred dollars."

"Five hundred dollars is a lot of money to most folks," Beau observed.

"That it is," Hank agreed. "But those boys got their old car shot up so bad that they'll be caught by morning, they say. They shot up the place and hit one of the tellers."

"Is it bad?" Beau asked.

"Bad enough," Hank shrugged. "The highway patrol has the borders guarded and they can't get far in this weather."

Hank looked over at Raquel and asked, "How's Miss Raquel this evening?"

"Fine, Hank," Raquel smiled.

"How'd you get here?" Hank asked. "I didn't think Beau would get out until I brought the truck back."

"I walked," Raquel said.

"In this?" Hank frowned.

"It wasn't that bad when I left," Raquel said.

"You must have been here for a while," Hank grinned.

"Awhile," Raquel confessed.

"You want me to take you home?" Hank offered. "It's getting pretty bad out, and Mrs. Butler's probably getting worried."

"Thanks, Hank," Beau interrupted. "I was just fixing to drive Raquel home. I was going to take the Buick, but I'll take the truck now. It should be warm."

"I don't mind getting out," Hank offered.

Beau smiled, "That's okay. I'd like to check the roads out myself."

"They're bad," Hank assured.

"I'll be fine, Hank," Beau said. "Raquel, get your coat, and we'll get you back before dark."

Sleet rained down harder, as Beau headed the truck toward Naomi's house. Almost two inches covered the road, but Beau did not have difficulty finding traction on the dirt road.

"Sleet's better than ice," Beau said, as Raquel watched the sleet ping off the hood of the truck.

"Why's that?" Raquel asked.

"The ice around here comes fast and heavy sometimes," Beau explained. "It'll take down trees and make driving nearly impossible."

Beau looked at the darkening gray skies and said, "What we need is a good wet snow to put some moisture in the ground before spring."

"I'd like to see a big snow," Raquel said playfully.

"We'll see," Beau grinned. "I might have you and Naomi come stay with me tonight in case it gets worse."

"That'd be fine by me," Raquel replied.

Beau pulled the truck up the drive to Naomi's house, and he slowed down to let the vehicle creep through the sleet covered road. He saw something strange, but before he could say anything to Raquel, he saw an even stranger sight, as Naomi waved frantically from the porch without wearing a coat.

"What's that silly woman doing?" Beau said, as he peered out the partially frozen windshield.

"I have no idea," replied Raquel.

Beau stopped the truck and hopped out to yell, "What are you doing out in this cold?"

"Never you mind!" Naomi barked back. "What are you doing with that girl out so late?"

"It's not that late," Beau defended.

"What's the matter?" Raquel asked, as she stepped out of the truck.

"Nothing," Naomi nervously replied. "Why don't you just take her back home with you since it's so late, Beau? Go ahead and get out of here!"

Naomi glanced toward the barn, as a confused Beau stared at her. Raquel did not know what to think, but the cold wind was blowing and she headed toward the porch.

"I told you to leave!" Naomi cried, as Raquel started walking quickly toward her.

Beau sensed something was not right, as he headed back toward his truck.

"Nice try, old woman, but I think we all need to come inside for a while," a man shouted from the doorway.

Raquel looked up to see Ned Farrell standing with a pistol pointed at Naomi's head.

"You too!" Ned shouted at Beau. "Let's all get inside and get comfortable—and keep those hands where I can see 'em or someone's getting shot."

Raquel glanced at Beau, and he nodded for her to head into the house. She stepped by Ned Farrell, who had grabbed Naomi by the neck and now pointed his pistol at Beau Lobaugh. As Raquel stepped inside, a man grabbed her roughly and threw her onto the floor.

"Hello, sweetheart," Jack Fisk smiled, as he stood over her. "This is an unexpected surprise to see you here."

As Raquel tried to get up from the floor, Jack Fisk reached down and stood her up while holding her firmly by the collar.

"Leave her alone!" Beau ordered, as he stepped into the room with the pistol pointed at his head, followed by Ned Farrell dragging Naomi.

Ned slammed the door behind them and said, "Let's all be real careful right now."

Jack Fisk continued to hold Raquel, and he pulled her closer to him to defy Beau.

"I said take your hands off the girl!" Beau barked.

Ned Farrell pushed Beau from behind with his pistol before saying, "Knock it off, Jack."

Jack Fisk looked defiantly at his partner before embracing Raquel and forcing her to kiss him.

"Ouch!" Jack Fisk screamed, as he pushed Raquel to the ground and grabbed his lip. "She bit me!"

Ned Farrell stuck the gun into Beau's back, as Jack Fisk rushed toward Raquel and slapped her, knocking her back to the floor before cursing.

"If you hurt that girl again, you're a dead man," Beau stoically stated.

Ned Farrell moved the gun from Beau's back to the temple of his head and said, "That's bold talk for a man with a gun to his head."

Beau did not respond, but Ned Farrell pushed him further into the room and moved a safe distance away.

Jack Fisk roughly grabbed Raquel from the floor, but this time Ned Farrell yelled, "Leave the girl alone! We don't have time for your nonsense now."

Jack Fisk glared at his partner before releasing Raquel and smiling pleasantly, as if nothing out of the ordinary had happened.

"Tie the girl up," Ned ordered. "Let's all get comfortable and figure this thing out."

CHAPTER 73

Jack Fisk tied Raquel's hands tightly together and then put another rope between her wrists before throwing it over the rafter and pulling it until her arms were uncomfortably extended above her head. The tall man was rough and seemed to relish manhandling the girl while Beau and Naomi could only watch.

"How'd you get here?" Beau Lobaugh calmly questioned.

"It ain't that hard to escape from a New Mexico jail," Ned Farrell grinned, "especially when you got a partner on the outside."

"You boys are in a pickle," Beau said coolly, as he watched his fiancé being tied helplessly to the rafter.

"We got the guns," Jack Fisk mocked, as he pulled the rope a little tighter before securing it.

"You boys robbed that bank in Elk City," Beau continued.

"How did you hear about that?" Ned Farrell asked anxiously.

"News like that travels fast," Beau said, as the man continued to point the gun at him. "Heard a teller got killed."

"Who told you that?" Jack Fisk asked, as he left Raquel tied to the rafter and stepped toward Beau.

"Just what I heard," Beau said. "By the looks of those tracks going to the barn, you rolled here on the rim. You won't be outrunning many highway patrolmen in a shot-up car."

Ned Farrell glanced at his partner and motioned for him to start tying Beau's hands.

"Thing is," Beau said. "They'll have every road covered by now. I bet the FBI's on the case, too. But that's not the worst."

As Jack Fisk grabbed Beau's arm to start tying it, he said, "What's the worst?"

Beau shrugged slightly, "By the look of this weather, you boys have maybe two hours to cross the state line—four at the most. If this snow picks up, we could have five-foot drifts by morning with this wind howling like it is. It won't take 'em long to search all the buildings in this country."

Ned looked at his partner nervously, and then said, "That'll be bad for you folks, I'm afraid."

"It don't have to," Beau claimed.

"What do you mean?" Ned asked.

"Don't listen to him, Ned," Jack protested.

"No, you don't have to listen to me," Beau mocked. "But I might just be the only guy that can get you across the state line in this weather—without the law finding out."

By this time, Jack had Beau's hands securely tied, when Ned motioned him to stop. The wind howled outside the drafty house, as the storm seemed to intensify. Ned looked at Beau for a moment, as if trying to read his intent.

"I'm listening," Ned said, as he watched his prisoner carefully.

"I know a back road south of the river that goes through my place," Beau explained. "The road's not on the map, and even in this weather, a man could be in Texas in less than an hour."

Ned studied Beau Lobaugh a few seconds before saying to his partner, "Get the keys to that truck."

"What about the girl?" Jack asked.

"We'll take her with us," Ned said flatly. "We'll need a hostage."

Beau laughed and shook his head.

"What's so funny?" Ned hotly asked.

"You," Beau said. "You two have already messed up a bank robbery today, and if you take off across this country in this weather, they'll find you frozen by morning—especially if you take my old beat-up truck that has less than a quarter tank of gas in it. The only way you're going to make it, is if I take you."

Jack Fisk looked at Ned Farrell, before the shorter man stepped closer to Beau.

"Why would I trust you?" Ned quizzed. "You might just lead us to the highway patrol."

"You don't have a lot of choices," Beau said. "Back at my house, I've got a brand new Buick that will outrun anything the police can put on the road. It's got a full tank of gas and could make that drive easy. Besides, I got nearly a thousand dollars in cash in my safe. I'll give it to you to boot, if you'll let the ladies go."

"Can't do that," Ned said. "The women are my insurance policy."

"Fine by me," Beau shrugged. "Take one of them with us. You promise to let us go when we get to Shamrock, and I'll get you there."

The two men looked at each other before Jack Fisk said, "He may be right, Ned. We don't want to get snowed in this close to Elk City. They'll find us for sure."

Ned thought for a moment and said, "I'll take the old woman to his place and get the car."

"That won't work," Beau said. "I've got half a dozen men that live on the place. They're going to want to know where I am. You send me with the tall fellow and I'll be back in half an hour, and you'll be nearly clear."

Ned smiled, "I think I'll feel better if I go with you."

"No deal," Beau replied.

"No deal?" Ned smirked. "I didn't realize things were negotiable when we're holding all the guns."

"I'll do what you say, but I'm not leaving that man alone in this house with these women," Beau stated defiantly, as he nodded at Jack Fisk.

Ned smiled, "Jack, keep your gun on him. If he so much as twitches funny, you shoot him dead."

"Don't go Beau!" Raquel pleaded, as she tried to balance herself with the rope stretching her arms in the air.

"It'll be fine," Beau assured. "It's the only way. We need to help these fellows to get away from here."

"You better listen to him," Ned said, as he walked closer to her. He looked back at Beau Lobaugh and said, "You've got half an hour."

Beau nodded, and Jack Fisk pointed his pistol at his back to nudge him toward the door.

As Beau opened the door to the cold wind outside, Ned Farrell said, as he caressed Raquel's cheek, "And Mr. Lobaugh, if you try anything—let's just say, you won't want this girl back by the time I'm through with her."

CHAPTER 74

"What are you going to do with us?" Naomi demanded, as Ned Farrell kept his gun pointed at her.

The man looked blankly at her and said, "If he comes back with a car and some money, I'll tie you up and take the girl hostage to Texas. We get there, everyone goes free."

"I don't believe you!" Raquel said, as she stood awkwardly, with her hands pulled above her head and tied to the rafter in the ceiling.

Ned walked closer to her and said, "You don't have much choice. The question is—can I trust Mr. Lobaugh. He seems awful attached to you, so I'm hopeful."

Raquel twisted futilely trying to release herself, as Ned Farrell laughed evilly.

"Can't you cut her down?" Naomi asked. "She's getting tired standing like that."

"If her boyfriend comes through, she'll be comfortable soon enough," Ned said.

Ned walked to the window to look out at the dark night with the strange glow of the sleet on the ground.

"Your boy better hurry," Ned commented.

"He'll be here," Raquel said.

In a few minutes, Ned smiled, "I see headlights. Let's hope for your sake that your man has my money."

Raquel could see over Ned Farrell's shoulder out the window into the darkening night. Beau's Buick pulled up, and she could see Beau stepping cautiously out from behind the wheel, while the tall man followed him with the pistol in plain sight.

Ned Farrell turned back around and closed the curtains before saying, "They're alone. That's a good start. Let's just hope your boyfriend keeps playing it smart."

Ned Farrell motioned Naomi to move to the corner of the room. He moved closer to Raquel while keeping his pistol alertly in his hand. Raquel breathed easier, when she saw Beau Lobaugh step into the doorway holding a small bag.

Raquel could not take her eyes off Beau as he said, "Here's your money."

Beau tossed the bag toward Ned Farrell. When Ned reached for the bag, two gunshots roared and echoed through the house.

"Beau!" Raquel screamed.

As she looked up, Beau stood at the doorway with a pistol in his hand, while Ned Farrell lay motionless on the floor.

Beau quickly moved toward the frightened girl to make sure she was okay. Tears flowed down her eyes, as he took out a knife and cut the rope holding her arms in the air. Her arms felt like lead, as they fell around Beau's neck as she stumbled to get her balance.

"Mr. Tilley?" Naomi cried from the corner.

"Are you all right, Mrs. Butler?" Hank asked.

"Yes," Naomi nodded.

Hank moved to check on Ned Farrell and said, "He's dead."

"What happened?" Raquel cried. "I thought you had been shot."

"You're safe now," Beau assured. "I got the tall one to the house and was able to distract him and take his pistol. I wanted them to send him with me, because I knew he was close to the same build as Hank. We dressed Hank in his coat and clothes. That gave us the edge we needed to get the drop on the dangerous one."

"Where's that scoundrel, now?" Naomi asked.

Hank smiled, "We heard the ruckus from the bunkhouse, but by the time we got there, the boss was beating on Smilin' Jack pretty good. I got a few licks in myself! Jack's hogtied and the worse for his effort. Elmer and the other boys have him in the back of the truck headed to the sheriff's office."

Hank moved over to untie Raquel's hands, as Beau continued to hold her. When her hands became free, she threw them around

Beau and held him tightly. She felt something warm and wet. As she pulled back her arm, she saw a red blob covering her sleeve.

"You're hurt!" Raquel cried anxiously, as she stepped back to examine Beau.

He lifted up his shirt to show a wound on his side and said, "It just grazed me."

"You've been shot!" Raquel shrieked.

"It's nothing," Beau refuted. "Jack got a shot off when I grabbed him, but it was just a ricochet."

"Naomi get some bandages," Raquel ordered.

Beau tried to hug her again, but she demanded that he take a seat and let her doctor him. The wound turned out to be superficial, as Beau had claimed, but he enjoyed Raquel's caring hands, gently doctoring him.

"You both are staying with me tonight," Beau said. "The weather's getting worse and you both need a break from this house."

Naomi nodded her agreement, "You never meant to take them across the state line, did you Beau?"

Beau shrugged, "I was willing to do whatever to keep you safe. It seemed like separating them would give me the best chance. There is a road across the state line, but I doubt we could have made it—even in my Buick. No offense, Naomi, but my other plan was to get them to take you and me hostage and leave Raquel behind."

"No offense taken," Naomi said. "I'd like to have had a shot at Mr. Fisk myself."

Beau laughed and then let out a little yelp, as Raquel poured alcohol on the slight wound.

"You could have gotten yourself killed," Raquel fussed.

Beau took his scolding and winked at Hank with a grin before saying, "Yes, dear."

Raquel looked up at Beau and then apologized awkwardly, "But, thank you."

Beau pulled his shirt back over the bandaged wound and stood up to hold Raquel.

"Those men were inexperienced, but desperate," Beau explained. "I could tell by the way they handled their guns that they didn't know what they were doing. Desperate men do desperate things, and I'm afraid they might have killed us all to save their own necks. I couldn't take that chance. I knew if I could separate them, I could take them out. Ned was so comfortable with me having a gun in my back that he never considered I was a threat. As soon as I walked in and saw that he didn't have the gun on you, I knew what I had to do."

"What about me?" Naomi interrupted. "What if he had the gun pointed at me?"

Beau grinned slyly, "You're my future mother-in-law Naomi. I was willing to take that chance."

CHAPTER 75

Ned Farrell was dead. Jack Fisk was headed for a life sentence in the federal penitentiary for robbing the bank and killing a bank teller in the process. Watching Ned Farrell shot dead had not been pleasant, but Raquel did not mourn his passing, or the incarceration of Jack Fisk. Raquel's wedding was not until late March, but she and Naomi moved into Beau Lobaugh's big house for the rest of the winter.

Beau and Raquel were married in a simple service at the church building on 6th and Locust in Sayre by the local minister. Beau took Raquel for a honeymoon at the Skirvin Hotel in Oklahoma City for a couple of days before taking her for a weeklong getaway at a cobblestone cottage overlooking the lake at Medicine Park. When the couple returned from their trip, they offered to let Naomi stay with them, but it was spring, and she insisted that it was time to move back to her house.

Raquel believed that Naomi's move was motivated to give the couple some privacy. Within two weeks, however, Naomi surprised Raquel and shocked Beau by announcing that she was marrying Hank Tilley. She decided that a church wedding would be ridiculous at her age, so she was married by a judge in the Beckham County Courthouse.

The winter weather did little to break the persistent drought, and many questioned whether it was worth the trouble to plant. Beau Lobaugh, however, had faith things would get better, and they did. Hank Tilley was able to rehabilitate Naomi's field, but Naomi was not cut out to be on the farm. She sold her land to Beau for a good price and moved into town. Hank had demonstrated an aptitude with tools. With a little help from Beau, he set up a carpentry shop in town making cabinets and doing small repair jobs. He and Naomi made the drive to Higgins about once a month to visit Hank's family. Naomi always came back bragging about the chicken fried steak she got at the West of the Line Café.

The summer of 1936 was nearly as bad as the previous year. By August, most of the fields were bone dry, and each day temperatures soared over one hundred degrees. Beau had drilled several irrigation wells, and Raquel enjoyed watering her garden by the house. It had been a hot week and Naomi had come to visit and help snap green beans for canning. Raquel had told Naomi a few weeks earlier that she and Beau were expecting a child in January. She had never seen a man as happy as her husband at the news.

"How are you feeling?" Naomi asked.

Since the news of the baby, Naomi had become even more protective of Raquel. Naomi found an excuse to drive out from town nearly every day.

"I'm fine," Raquel assured. "How are you?"

"What do you mean?" Naomi asked. "I'm fine."

Raquel continued snapping her beans and quipped, "You're more of a newlywed than me. I thought you might need some advice."

"Oh, you," Naomi fussed, as Raquel smiled kindly.

"Seriously," Raquel said. "How are things with you and Hank?"

Naomi sighed, "It's not always easy. We're both stubborn and set in our ways. Each day brings a whole new level of frustrations, but—it's been fun. He needs me—and I need him. We need each other, and that's a good feeling. How about you and Beau?"

"It's perfect," Raquel smiled. "He's rarely cross with me and seems determined to find new ways to spoil me."

"You deserve to be spoiled after what you've been through," Naomi said. "Do you think we would do it again?"

"Do what again?" Raquel asked.

Naomi shook her head, "Make that ridiculous trip cross-country to get here."

"I would," Raquel smiled. "I'd make it a hundred times to be with Beau."

"Speak of the devil," Naomi said. "Here he comes."

Raquel looked off the front porch and could see Beau's car kicking up dust in the distance, coming from town. Raquel continued snapping beans, but kept her eyes on the approaching car. Naomi looked at her staring intently at Beau's Buick and smiled. Beau stopped the car and walked quickly to the porch to kiss Raquel.

"Anything exciting happening in town?" Raquel asked.

"Not much," Beau smiled, "but I've got some news."

"What?" Raquel sweetly asked.

"I've been invited to West Point to give a lecture on field artillery tactics," Beau smiled.

"I thought you're retired," Raquel frowned.

"I am," Beau said. "A friend of mine got me the invitation. You don't seem too excited."

"Of course I'm not excited," Raquel protested. "You'll be gone a week, probably longer. I'll miss you."

"No you won't," Beau stated.

"What do you mean?" Raquel asked.

"You're coming with me," Beau smiled. "I thought we could make a little trip out of it—see New York—Washington."

"You want me to come?" Raquel quizzed.

"Of course," Beau replied. "It won't be so easy for us to travel in a few months after the baby comes, and I thought it would be a good vacation."

Raquel smiled, "That sounds wonderful."

"No one takes me anywhere, but Higgins, Texas," Naomi muttered.

Raquel ignored Naomi and asked, "When do we go?"

"Two weeks."

"Will we drive?" Raquel asked.

"No," Beau smiled. "I got us tickets on a Pullman sleeper. We'll catch the train to Oklahoma City and catch the Pullman there. You have traveled by train before, haven't you?"

Raquel smiled slyly and looked at the grinning Naomi before saying, "I've been on a train a time or two—with Naomi."

"You've never traveled until you've ridden a Pullman," Beau said.

"I can believe that," Raquel replied with a smirk.

"Who's that?" Naomi asked, as she pointed at another car driving toward the house.

"Are you expecting someone?" Raquel asked Beau.

"No," Beau replied, as he strained to see if he recognized the visitor.

They watched the car drive slowly up the road, as if the driver was unsure of the destination, although the Lobaugh house was the only home for miles on the road. The car finally stopped, and a young man in his mid-twenties climbed from behind the wheel to look around. Raquel stood up to see better and noticed a passenger.

In a second, the passenger door swung open, and an exuberant Orpha screamed, "It's them, Bill!"

Raquel glanced briefly at Naomi who had her hand across her mouth in excitement before shrieking, "Orpha!"

Raquel hastily put down her green beans and ran to hug the bubbly Orpha.

"What on earth are you doing here?" Naomi screeched, as she walked quickly toward the young woman.

"We came to visit," Orpha replied, as she was being squeezed by the two women. "I've been so worried about you and couldn't wait to come."

"It's so good to see you, Orpha," Raquel gleamed. "We've got so much to tell you."

"I have some surprises, too," Orpha said. "Bill, get over here!"

The lanky man sulked over at Orpha's command.

"Bill, this is Naomi and Raquel," Orpha smiled.

The two women greeted the nervous man, and then Orpha announced, "Bill's my husband."

"Oh, my," Naomi gasped. She quickly regained her composure and said, "It's so good to meet you Mr.—"

"Parker," Bill said shyly.

"So good to meet you, Mr. Parker," Naomi greeted.

"Good to meet you," Bill smiled nervously.

"Sounds like I'm not the only one with big news," Orpha smiled. "We stopped in town to get directions to the place and to ask about you. I understand you're Mrs. Lobaugh now, Raquel."

"Yes," Raquel admitted.

Orpha leaned in and whispered, "According to everyone in town, you've made quite an impression."

"What do you mean?" Raquel asked.

"Look around," Orpha said. "You live in this big house, and as far as I can see have the only fields with even a hint of green."

"Beau's a good farmer," Raquel admitted.

"But is he a good kisser?" Orpha teased.

"Orpha!" Naomi protested. "You're being naughty!"

"I was just wondering," Orpha grinned. "Oh! I almost forgot why we came out here."

Orpha went back to the car and carefully unwrapped something from the rear seat. In a moment, Orpha walked back proudly carrying a baby.

Orpha smiled proudly and announced, "I've got something to show you. This is Marla."

Naomi wheezed unevenly and gasped to catch her breath, as she looked at the baby cradled in Orpha's arms.

"She's beautiful, Orpha," Naomi whispered, as she walked closer.

The normally high-spirited Orpha bit her lip and looked like she might cry, as she said, "She'll be one year old in December."

Naomi's eyes shifted from the baby to Orpha.

Tears poured down Orpha's face as she cried, "She's Maylon's."

Raquel looked at Naomi to see the older woman's face go pale for an instant before beaming with joy at the news. Raquel looked at her husband and smiled as tears welled up in her eyes. Beau had a stunned look, but he also had a faint smile.

"Can I hold her?" Naomi asked softly.

Orpha nodded and handed the baby to Naomi.

"She's precious," Naomi sighed, as she gently cradled the baby.

"She is to me," Orpha smiled, as she wiped her eyes.

"Beau," Raquel said to her husband. "I'm sure Bill's had a long day. Will you go get him something cool to drink and show him around the place?"

Beau was not going to disobey his wife, but she could tell he was puzzled.

"We need some time for girl talk," Raquel explained candidly.

"Oh—sure," Beau replied. "Bill, I think we have some sweet tea in the ice box. Let's get a glass, and I'll show you around."

Bill nodded, and followed Beau into the house.

"This is why I couldn't come with you," Orpha explained. "I wasn't a hundred percent sure then, but I thought I might be expecting."

"Why didn't you tell me?" Naomi asked.

"I wasn't sure, and I didn't want to ruin your trip," Orpha said.

Naomi looked at Raquel before saying, "It was good you stayed behind."

"A hard trip?" Orpha asked, having no idea about the problems the two had encountered.

Before Naomi could complain, Raquel said, "A hard trip, but a good trip. It brought us here."

"I can't get over how beautiful she is," Naomi sighed, as she continued to marvel at the child.

"I wanted to bring her sooner, but I waited until she was a little older for the trip," Orpha explained.

"And Bill," Naomi asked. "How long have you been married?"

"We got married a few months ago," Orpha answered. "I met Bill when I was as big as a boat, when he would come to the store.

He was always so sweet to me. After the baby came and I had to stop working, he would find excuses to come visit. My brothers were always rude to him, but he didn't seem to mind."

"I can tell he adores you," Raquel said. "He couldn't take his eyes off you."

"Bill's an engineer for the oil company," Orpha explained. "He's got folks over by Tulsa. We're heading there tomorrow. We're trying to have another child."

"Orpha, I swear, you'll say the most outlandish things!"Naomi scolded.

"What?" Orpha grinned impishly.

"We don't need to know the naughty details of your marriage," Naomi frowned.

"Beau and I are expecting in January," Raquel smiled.

"Oh, Raquel!" Orpha sighed. "I'm so happy for you. You'll be such a wonderful mother."

"How about you, Naomi?" Raquel teased.

"I'm happy for you too," a confused Naomi replied.

"No," Raquel said, as she smirked at Orpha. "Are you expecting too?"

Naomi huffed, "I'm too old for that kind of nonsense."

"What am I missing here?" Orpha asked with a puzzled expression.

"You don't know," Raquel said, almost to herself, before announcing, "Naomi's a newlywed too!"

Orpha, who was rarely at a loss for words, could do nothing but stare at Naomi for a moment while her mother-in-law blushed awkwardly.

"You remarried?" Orpha finally was able to ask. "Who's being naughty now?"

Naomi did not respond, but Raquel finally said, "You wouldn't believe how she carried on while she was courting Mr. Tilley. I nearly caught them in compromising situations more than one time. It was embarrassing."

Naomi took the teasing in silence as Orpha giggled loudly, remembering how strict Naomi had been with her boys.

"That's right," Naomi finally replied defiantly. "I'm starting a new life, as a fifty-year-old newlywed, and I'm not ashamed of it. That's what we do when life gets hard—we start over again."

"I'm happy for you, Mrs. Tilley," Orpha said pleasantly. "I'm happy for all of us."

The three women talked on the porch for the rest of the afternoon, while Beau patiently toured Bill Parker around the farm and away from the women's conversation. Orpha, Raquel, and Naomi laughed, cried, and remembered the circumstances that had brought them together and had nearly torn them apart.

"We made it through, girls," Naomi said, as the sun setting in the western sky painted a salmon ribbon of light against the turquoise remains of the blue sky. "We've seen the worst of times and survived."

"Thank you," Raquel said.

"What for?" Naomi asked.

"For loving us," replied Raquel. "You kept us together, Naomi. You chose to let me be a part of your family, and I thank you."

"Me, too," Orpha said, as she gently patted Naomi's shoulder. "I learned a lot from you. I'm not saying that the lessons were always pleasant, but I guess sometimes we learn the most through our adversity."

"I've learned too," Naomi said. "I was angry at everything for a while, and sometimes everyone. When Eli passed, I couldn't reconcile in my mind how bad things could happen to good people—people that were trying to make good decisions and the right choices. I felt anger and rage over that. I felt like God's wrath had singled me out. When I lost my boys, I think I nearly lost my mind. I felt that I had nothing—no parent should ever have to bury their child. Then I realized I had you girls, and I couldn't have asked for more. And now this child is like a blessing from God."

"Children are always a blessing," Orpha said, as she reached down and handed the baby to Naomi. "They give us hope for our old age and prove to us that life restores itself."

"What are you going to name your baby?" Orpha asked Raquel.

Raquel smiled, "If it's a girl, we're thinking of naming her Marilee—if it's a boy, Jesse."

"Those are nice names," Orpha said.

"Come here, girls," Naomi sighed, as she held the baby in her arms. "Give an old woman a hug before I start crying again."

Raquel and Orpha looked at each other before stepping to their mother-in-law to hug her and give her a kiss on each cheek.

"You girls mean the world to me," Naomi stated. "You've taught me more the past year than I learned in half a century when my life was easy. You showed me that it's not what happens to you that matters, but it's how you handle what happens."

Raquel smiled, "Beau always tells me you get out of life what you put into it."

Naomi looked at her daughter-in-law and said, "Beau Lobaugh's a smart man—he married you."

THE END

If you enjoyed

***Return from Wrath*,**

look for these other Bob Perry novels:

The Broken Statue

Mimosa Lane

Brothers of the Cross Timber

Guilt's Echo

Lydie's Ghost

The Nephilim Code

www.bobp.biz

Notes from the Author

Return from Wrath's plot was inspired by the Biblical *Book of Ruth*, which has long been one of my favorite stories. Ruth's words served as a theme to the story when she said to her mother-in-law, "Don't urge me to leave you or to turn back from you. Where you go, I will go, and where you stay, I will stay. Your people will be my people, and your God, will be my God. Where you die, I will die, and there I will be buried."

The *Book of Ruth* used about 2,500 words to tell the story, while *Return from Wrath* took over 139,000. Obviously, there are some enhancements to the original plot, but readers familiar with the *Book of Ruth* may notice some similarities. In both stories, Naomi's family comes from their home to a new land during a time of great famine. In the *Book of Ruth*, the family comes from Israel to the land of Moab. In *Return from Wrath*, the family migrates from Oklahoma, to California. Both stories focus on the return home. The name of Ruth, the Moabite, has been replaced by Raquel in *Return from Wrath*, who is a California girl with a Latino heritage. In the *Book of Ruth*, Naomi's husband is Elim'elech, while in *Return from Wrath*, it is shortened to Eli. The names of the sons have been adapted from Mahlon and Chil'ion, to Maylon and Chili. Ruth's sister-in-law is Orpah, while Raquel's sister-in-law is Orpha.

The *Book of Ruth* describes tragedy and love in the lives of ordinary people. The allure of the story comes from the loyalty between Ruth and Naomi. The Biblical book creates supreme suspense as the faithful Ruth relies on her mother-in-law Naomi to find happiness from the calamity of their family misfortune. In the end, Ruth finds Boaz, with help and advice from Naomi. I hope *Return from Wrath* captures some of the charm that readers have found in the *Book of Ruth* for thousands of years. For me, I enjoyed writing about the relationship and quirks between the two women in the 1930s setting.

Some may think of John Steinbeck's *Grapes of Wrath* when reading the title since the story is set in the same time frame and involves characters with "Okie" roots. Although there was no attempt to mimic Steinbeck's epic tale or the themes he presented over seventy years ago, I could not resist describing two details from the film version of *Grapes of Wrath.* First, the description of the family that Raquel and Naomi encountered at the diner in New Mexico, could have easily been the Joads on their way to the "promised land" of California. The second reference involves the Beckham County Courthouse. In the movie, the travelers go through Oklahoma City and pass what looks to be a state capitol building. At the time, the Oklahoma Capitol did not have a domed roof, so the courthouse in Beckham County was used in the film. The Beckham County Courthouse is located in the center of Sayre, Oklahoma.

Although *Return from Wrath* is fiction, there are a few historical facts mentioned in the story. Famous Oklahoman's Will Rogers and Wiley Post died in an airplane accident in 1935. It is hard for people of this generation to understand how popular and influential Will Rogers was at the time. Cutthroat Gap is also referenced in the story and was the actual site of a grisly massacre of Kiowa Indians from a rival tribe in 1833. It is thought that nearly 150 died in the attack. Another tragedy in western Oklahoma happened in a place called Babbs Switch, which is talked about in the story. On Christmas Eve of 1924, thirty six people, including many children, were tragically killed in a blaze caused by a candle illuminating the Christmas tree.

I hope you enjoyed following the journey of Raquel and Naomi with me in *Return from Wrath*, and I look forward to sharing another story with you sometime.